Also by Sam Ba

ISBN-13: 978-0692983003

ISBN-10: 0692983007

Please feel free to contact the author with suggestions and comments.

Email at: barone@sambarone.com

Or visit my website at: www.sambarone.com

Sentinel Star

by

Sam Barone

New International Space Station (NISS)
(formerly the ore freighter Lady Nostromo)

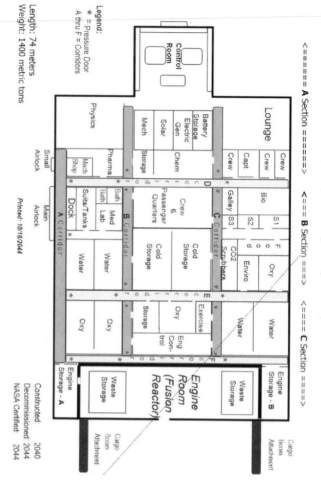

<============ **A** Section =======>   <=== **B** Section ===>   <===== **C** Section ====>

Control Room

Legend:
* = Pressure Door
A thru F = Corridors

Length: 74 meters
Weight: 1400 metric tons

Constructed: 2040
Decommissioned: 2044
NASA Certified: 2044

Printed: 10/18/2044

Lounge

Physics

Battery Storage | Electric Gen | Solar | Mech | Chem | Storage

Crew | Capt | Crew | Crew

Pharma

Mech Shop

Small Airlock

Suits/Tanks

Med Lab

Bath | Bath

Dock

Main Airlock

A Corridor

Crew & Passenger Quarters

B Corridor

Cold Storage

Cold Storage

Water | Water

Galley | S3 | S2 | S1

Bio

CO2 Scrubbers

C Corridor

Enviro | Oxy | F l o o d

Water | Water

D C o r r i d o r

Oxy | Oxy

Storage | Oxy | Eng Con-trol | Exercise

E C o r r i d o r

Water

F C o r r i d o r

Engine Storage - A

Engine Room (Fusion Reactor)

Waste Storage

Engine Storage - B

Waste Storage

Cargo Boom Attachment

Cargo Boom Attachment

Sentinel Star

Prolog

The planet Jupiter, named by the ancient Romans after their greatest god, ruled the night sky over their mighty Empire. In modern times this massive planet, a shimmering ball of gas, floats serenely in space, a benign eye observing the universe. By far the largest planet in our solar system, Jupiter traverses the heavens accompanied by four major moons, each large enough to be visible with the simplest telescope. To the casual beholder, Jupiter remains an object of tantalizing, ever-changing beauty with its banded atmosphere flows and picturesque storms.

But the human eye perceives only a narrow band of visible light. When examined under the cold gaze of precision instruments, Jupiter's dark side emerges – a frightening place of intense magnetic storms, gravity anomalies, and hellish radiation – a place where nightmares are born.

Despite the danger, humans had ventured into Jovian space and visited its closest moon, Io, to search for desperately needed rare earth elements. That first expedition discovered a treasure trove of mineral wealth. However Io churned with volcanic activity and particle radiation. From that initial mining mission, less than half the explorers survived the eight month expedition. Even so, the haul of rare metals the voyagers brought back to Earth orbit paid for the enterprise's total expenses five times over.

The governmental and corporate elites ruling Earth made the logical business decision. With Earth's resources growing ever scarcer, the riches of Io would be mined, no matter the cost in human life. Construction of larger and more powerful ships began. These utilized the latest advances in nanocrystalline alloys to create stronger, lighter, and better shielded hulls. Two years later, in 2039, the first of these vessels landed on the Jovian moon Io to establish a permanent base and begin digging. In less than eighteen months, miners established a second base to increase production. Soon new and advanced fusion-powered space freighters and transports arrived and departed Io every forty to sixty days, carrying the riches of

Jupiter's moon back to insatiable Earth.

Extreme danger remained ever present for Io's miners. The slightest fluctuation in Jupiter's gravity might result in the bases on Io being buried under a lake of erupting lava. Miners and base personnel lived knowing that horrific death could strike at any moment. How long the mining operation could continue to exist haunted every man and woman working on Io. Huddled beneath the surface, the miners wondered what other dark secrets Jupiter and its moons possessed beyond those of radiation bursts, lava flow, or volcanic eruption.

On September 17, 2052 (Day Zero), at 0345 Zulu time, Jupiter revealed a secret far more dangerous than mere radiation.

Chapter 1

On board the New International Space Station, orbiting 116,000 kilometers above Earth, September 17, 2052 . . .

Day Zero: 0345 Zulu

Jupiter writhed within its enlarged and flexing magnetosphere, its surface mottled with massive storms. Passing through one of its periodic, highly-active phases, the gas giant's over-stimulated internal processes roiled the thick atmosphere. The planet's mass and metallic hydrogen core generated enormous amounts of energy. By far the most powerful planet in the solar system, physicists had long theorized Jupiter subtly altered the space-time environment surrounding it.

Strong surges in radiation accompanied the whirlwinds. Recently the magnetic lines of force generated at the planet's poles had doubled in length, spilling far into space, and waxing and waning well above normal levels. Atmospheric turmoil, always fierce, also intensified.

Whatever the reason for Jupiter's instability, instruments aboard the New International Space Station (ISS) had aimed their electronic eyes toward Jupiter at the insistence of European Space Ventures, SA, headquartered in Geneva. Its largest and most profitable subsidiary, Jovian Exploration Company (JovCo), managed every aspect of the mines, miners, and ore transport on Jupiter's closest moon, Io. Ten days earlier, the directors of JovCo grew concerned that Jupiter's increased activity might cause interruptions in the flow of ores to Earth.

The powerful corporation urged NASA – managing the International Space Station with Alliance approval – to monitor the Jovian system for possible danger to JovCo's income flow. The Alliance consisted of the three major world powers, China, United States, and Russia. Together they had ruled Earth for the last seventeen years. Since all three depended on the rare earth minerals, the Alliance approved the request from JovCo, and NASA received new orders.

Astronomers remembered that forty-six years earlier Jupiter had acted up in this same manner. At that time no one took much interest in monitoring the intensified Jovian storms, because no nation had anything in orbit to scrutinize it properly. A handful of observatories studied the activity as best they could and noted several unusual readings. A few astronomers published papers that hardly anyone bothered to read.

This time, however, the Station's high-energy spectrometer pack – ultraviolet, infrared, X-ray, cosmic ray, gravity wave, and dark matter detectors – was focused on the gas giant, supplemented by the 1.5 meter optical telescope. Jupiter happened to be in fairly close proximity to Earth's own orbit, only 610,000,000 kilometers away. The instruments, controlled by a single computer, had already collected a host of data.

Eight days of surveillance had elapsed, and Jupiter showed no sign of settling down. Years, decades might pass without significant fluctuations in the readings. Even the JovCo scientists agreed that in a few more days they would have enough data to allay their main concern – that Jupiter's intensified activity might amplify volcanic eruptions on Io. The instrument pack would then be refocused to its original target, the star Epsilon Eridani.

As JovCo relaxed, Jupiter unleashed a surprise. Abruptly, just beyond the outermost orbit of the four big Jovian moons, something extraordinary occurred. Local space, already under stress from the immense planet's gravity, flexed and curved far beyond normal spatial conditions.

Invisible to the naked eye, gravity waves formed from a pinpoint opening in the fabric of space, bending and stretching in undulating patterns and emitting intense bursts of radiation. In seconds the waves stabilized, then spread fan-like to form a gravity well, its opening pointed toward the planet. During those few seconds, this new energy source emitted more EMG activity than Jupiter itself.

The Space Station's gravity wave detector, a modified interferometer, caught the first burst of high energy. At the same time the software controlling the instrument detected the anomaly. A few milliseconds passed while the computer digested this new data, consulted its pre-programmed logic, and arrived at its first conclusion. It assumed that the interferometer either had drifted off its target point or that Jupiter had moved.

To compensate, the chip refocused on this new, more powerful energy source. Another few ticks of the computer's clock confirmed that Jupiter still remained in its proper position. However this second energy source was spitting out radiation from a location where the program's code insisted none should exist.

This confusion activated another sub-routine which fired off a fresh series of programmed instructions. First, the instrument malfunction alarm activated, and a soft but insistent chime echoed in the ISS science lab. Then the software performed a memory dump to provide a check point for later debugging. Though the unknown engineer who had originally written the software never planned for this particular contingency, he or she had thoughtfully programmed the chip to continue functioning while resolving the anomaly. That kept the interferometer, the spectrometer and the other instruments recording.

As a secondary debugging aid, the meticulous programmer, in an effort to get as much data as possible to diagnose any malfunctions, directed the computer to focus every available instrument in the observation pack at the same source. Those included one infrared and the primary optical telescope, both maintained at a temperature of 50 Kelvin. Mounted on the outer hull and shaded from direct sunlight, the two instruments could track Jupiter almost as accurately as the spectrometer.

The forty-two year old 1.5 meter optical telescope, a hand-me-down gift from the Chinese lunar science base, took a lengthy fourteen seconds to reset, calculate a new target, and recalibrate its focus. Activated simultaneously with the telescope, a digital video recorder came to life and captured the most important visual record in the history of planet Earth.

Out beyond the Jovian moons and slightly above the plane of the planets, another spike of energy accompanied the creation of . . . something. Wormhole? Space Portal? Black Hole? Tear in the space-time fabric?

Whatever its name (wormhole was later deemed to best describe the anomaly), within two seconds an object emerged from that . . . wormhole, energy blazing from its own power source. Three seconds later, a second vessel appeared, followed by three more at the same three second intervals. The mini-flotilla immediately changed direction, angling away from the gas giant and heading toward the inner worlds of the solar system. Within thirty seconds of the last emergence, the five craft had established a classic V-formation.

Without the intervention of a single human, a series of instruments orbiting planet Earth had captured an unknown and theoretically impossible event near planet Jupiter, one about to change the world of mankind.

Flight Engineer Colonel Nikolai Kosloff had the duty shift in the science module. Of the five crewmen currently onboard the ISS, two were Russian. The International Space Station wasn't really a station, and everyone had long since dropped the 'New' from its abbreviation. It existed within the thick hull of an obsolete ore freighter, presented to the United States government and NASA by JovCo in return for five years of considerable tax credits. Parked in high earth orbit and stripped of its main drive and anything else useful to the Company, the hollow craft possessed plenty of room for scientists and their equipment to live and work in relative safety. Compared to the original ISS, stuck in a low earth orbit that limited its use, the new Station possessed far more utility for scientific observations.

Kosloff spent his days happily maintaining the Station's basic systems and instrument packs, a never-ending but satisfying task. He had just completed some overdue repairs to the air distribution equipment when he heard the soft chime of the science lab malfunction alarm.

Annoyed at whatever science experiment failure might delay his dinner, he floated through two of the vessel's compartments and into the primary science module, the Physics Lab. He hovered over the spectrometer and glanced at the monitor's read-out. The data displayed on the screen appeared unusual, but Kosloff wasn't a science specialist, so he didn't make any guesses.

A quick check of other monitors indicated that the instrument pack continued to function properly. He noticed the digital recorder and optical telescope had changed to active status and started recording, so he turned on the telescope's display screen. As always, the sheer power of the telescope impressed him. Originally designed for stellar observations, the powerful scope now captured a sharp picture of Jupiter less than 610,000,000 kilometers away. With no atmospheric distortion, Jupiter looked almost as close as Earth's Moon and showed just as much detail.

Right away Kosloff noticed that the big planet had moved off-center and was now barely visible in the lower right corner of the screen. So the instruments had drifted, he concluded. That must be the malfunction. Easy enough to correct. His hand went out to adjust the track-ball that controlled the instrument, to manually re-center its focus on Jupiter. But his hand stopped three centimeters away from the controller, and for a second, Kosloff thought his heart had stopped as well.

Barely visible on the screen flew five tiny red dots, arranged in a V-pattern. Kosloff knew he wasn't seeing the actual blips themselves. Even the 1.5 meter telescope wasn't powerful enough for that, not at 600,000,000 plus kilometers. He was seeing substantial energy signatures emanating from these blips, and the glow from those sources had lit a spectral trail behind them. That meant the objects themselves might be big, very big.

The blips showed visible movement, and the fact that the motion could be detected by his eye meant that they must be traveling extremely fast. As he stared, mouth agape, he realized the blips were curving slightly away from Jupiter's gravity embrace. With a shock, Kosloff grasped that these dots could not be any natural phenomena.

In another few seconds they would be off the screen. Kosloff spun the track-ball to center the alignment guide on the moving lines, then pressed the button that ordered the instruments to track this new anomaly.

The new instructions satisfied the computer chip that had previously noted the change in energy from the false Jupiter. But even as the instrument pack began to shift its focus, another energy burst occurred, one that later analysis would show to be forty percent larger than any of the five previous ones.

This new ship – already Kosloff was thinking of the energy trails in terms of ships – burst into existence. This one appeared to be traveling faster than the preceding vessels and taking a slightly different track. Its blood-red dot, significantly darker than the first five, indicated a larger, more energetic trail than the others. This sixth craft changed its heading to follow the first five vessels.

"Mother Russia protect us," Kosloff muttered, his heart pounding. Without taking his eyes off the monitor, he fumbled for his intercom, fastened as always to his shirt collar. It took three tries before he found the proper button. "Maks, wake up! Come to the science lab. Come at once. Bring everyone! Hurry!" Though English remained the primary language of the Station, Kosloff spoke in Russian without realizing it.

Before anyone could reply, Kosloff remembered his training. He flipped himself away from the monitor, crossing the chamber with the ease acquired by his five months in orbit. At the main console was a red alarm switch, designed to be activated only in an emergency, such as a power failure or air breach. The General Alarm triggered sensors and cameras throughout the ship that would record the crew's actions.

Kosloff slapped the alarm before he'd even stopped moving. He caught the console with one foot and pushed off back to the spectrometer pack. The resulting alarm, a pre-programmed computer alert, was loud enough to wake the entire space station's crew.

The telescope might be old but its lens remained powerful, easily capable of spotting the glowing energy trails. While the spaceships themselves – Kosloff continued thinking of them as ships – were too small to be picked up by the telescope at that distance, the instruments had no problem spotting the output from their power plants. They must have one hell of an engine source, he reasoned, and each one emitted impressive energy.

His second glance showed the larger vessel gaining on the first five. Their V-formation had disappeared, morphed into something else. The blips on the monitor glowed more intensely, and Kosloff guessed their power plants had kicked up with greater energy output. As he watched, they drifted apart, widening the distances between themselves. The larger vessel closed the gap, somewhat slower now, as the smaller ships sped up and reconfigured into a roughly circular configuration.

The entrance to the science module was briefly blocked as two Americans dove through the opening. Station Commander Susan York had been sending emails to grade school children when the alarm sounded. Just over forty years old, she had blond hair cropped close and carried a few extra pounds on her diminutive figure. Besides commanding the Station, she conducted deep space and solar research. She also backed up Kosloff as mission engineer.

Lieutenant Colonel William Welsh, science specialist, was right behind her. Tall, black-skinned with a long, thin face that matched his slender frame, he wore his hair in a buzz cut, the same style as when he flew real fighter planes and combat drones for the United States Air Force. Colonel Welsh specialized in orbital mechanics.

Both Americans had been in the adjacent module, referred to by the crew as the Lounge. When they saw Kosloff staring open-mouthed at the monitor, they oriented themselves to see what held his attention.

"What's happening, Nikolai?" Susan had taken command of the ISS almost three months ago, a civilian and the first woman to run the Station in nearly eight years. None of the current Station's crew had ever triggered or responded to a General Alarm. Her immediate thought had been a hull breach, but Kosloff wouldn't be watching a science monitor if that were the problem. She focused on the screen. The tiny colored dots were clearly visible now, back-lit against the round glow of Jupiter.

"The interferometer alarm went off," Kosloff mumbled. Then he realized he was speaking Russian and repeated himself in English. "When I went to check, I saw the … the … ships appear out of nowhere." The word 'ship' was out in the open now. "Then the larger vessel appeared and began to … chase the smaller ones." Kosloff didn't say anything further. He didn't have to.

"Oh my God," Susan heard herself say. "You think they're ships? A First Contact? Alien ships?"

On the monitor, the distance between the large ship and the smaller ones had almost disappeared. Susan stared in fascination, but it was Welsh who first understood the significance of what they were watching. He had begun his career as an Air Force pilot and had flown with the Blue Aces Fighter Squadron in the last Middle East war – conflict, he corrected himself. Wars had been outlawed twenty years ago, but Earth had many rogue nations, and some people never received the memo.

One of the smaller blips disappeared in a flash of red-orange that turned bright white before fading into nothingness. The other four blips reacted by changing course. Monitoring the visible light spectrum, the telescope couldn't show the energy bursts that had been directed at the five vessels nearly simultaneously. But the spectroscope continued functioning, and its records would later confirm what their eyes perceived. Some type of particle energy beams had emanated from the larger ship.

"It's a furball," Welsh said softly. His deep baritone voice lent even more emphasis to his assessment. "We're watching a dogfight. A space dogfight."

Maksim Mironov, or 'Maks' to everyone, entered the Physics lab. An astrophysicist, he had worked for the Russian space program, and therefore the Russian military, since he graduated from the Moscow Institute of Physics and Technology. In his early sixties, with distinguished white hair, he reminded everyone of a short Santa Claus. This was his first venture into space. Maks positioned himself over Kosloff's shoulder and studied the instruments.

The final crew member, Dr. Derrell Parrish, arrived breathing hard, but no one paid attention to the British payload and biology specialist jarred awake from sleep. A graduate of both Massachusetts Institute of Technology and Oxford University, at eighteen he was by far the youngest and most junior scientist aboard. "What's going on?" he asked. Nobody bothered to answer.

A child prodigy with an off-the-scale IQ, Derrell obtained his Masters from MIT at age sixteen, then returned to England to earn his doctorate at Oxford. NASA, always eager to accumulate good publicity, had invited him aboard ISS. The more senior NASA people, on and off the Station, considered him a lightweight, the latest iteration of press-worthy people selected for ISS missions.

Another red blip disappeared in a second flare-up of energy. "*Alpha's* gone, *Bravo* is gone," Colonel Welsh said, counting the kills as if he were back at Creech Air Force Base in Nevada manning a drone console. A third blip, one he named *Charlie*, glowed bright blue as it shifted course and speed so radically that it appeared damaged. The two remaining ships, *Delta* and *Echo* arched out further, turning away from each other in a scissor maneuver, and forcing the larger, blood-red blip – *Bogey One* – to choose its target. It selected *Delta* and began pursuing.

But instead of running, the *Delta* ship again changed course, curving back toward its companion vessel. Once *Bogey One* began pursuit of *Delta*, *Echo* also reversed course, and now followed *Bogey One* as it continued its chase. *Delta* maintained its curved path, and its new trajectory soon brought *Bogey One* directly in line with *Echo's* weapons. By this time all three ships had nearly reversed their original course away from Jupiter, and *Delta* led the way back to the planet.

The three ships, *Delta*, *Bogey One*, and *Echo*, formed a rough line, but this time *Bogey One* found itself in the second position and attacked from behind. Meanwhile *Charlie*, though apparently damaged, continued following an intercept course for *Bogey One*, already moving toward it.

"Can ships turn . . . maneuver like that?" Kosloff asked. "I thought they could only follow straight lines?"

"Not any ships we have." Welsh spoke softly, but everyone gathered around the monitor not only heard him but understood the significance.

Somehow *Delta* managed to turn on its axis, no doubt to decelerate faster while it returned fire on *Bogey One*. In a masterful display of coordination and timing, both smaller ships fired at *Bogey One* at the same time. But it was *Charlie*, the one damaged and left behind, that provided the killing blow, as it aligned itself at an angle to the others before firing its own energy weapon as *Bogey One* flashed by.

"A Thach Weave," Welsh muttered. "Never thought I'd see the day."

The first hint of trouble to the big attacking ship came with a sudden change in its course, then another, in an attempt to avoid *Charlie*. *Bogey One's* energy signature became a brighter red glow, then into another, more intense flash that changed the blip from red to yellow-orange. No doubt wounded, *Bogey One* tried to escape the three ships who continued focusing their weapons on it. But *Bogey One's* ability to return fire or maneuver had diminished. The three ships continued the attack, giving their former assailant no respite.

Welsh foresaw the ending. "Splash one bad guy." A few more seconds ticked by, while the ships kept changing angle and speed. Then came a burst of white light and *Bogey One* suddenly vanished in an explosion as furious as a mini-sun, as whatever space drive powering it exploded. The first known space battle in Earth's solar system had ended about thirty-five minutes earlier, the time it took for the light and other energies to reach Earth orbit.

"What's a Thach Weave?" Again it was Parrish who asked the

question. A moody and occasionally annoying young man, Derrell hadn't made any close friends during his stay on the Station. Even Susan's patience had worn thin, and the adults were looking forward to Derrell's scheduled return to Earth in two weeks.

Everyone turned toward Welsh. He shrugged. "It's *Thach Weave*. An aerial dogfight tactic. Old, but still sound. Invented during World War II by American naval pilots to fight the faster and more powerful Japanese Zero. First used in combat during the Battle of Midway. It's a technique that allows two weaker aircraft to fight a larger or more powerful enemy. The fighter that's being pursued becomes the bait. The bait leads the enemy plane in a curve back toward the second fighter, called the hook, who usually gets a clear shot."

His explanation didn't give them much insight, but no one really wanted to follow up. They were too busy trying to comprehend the incomprehensible – wormholes, alien ships, incredible energies, a brutal space battle – and wondering how much their lives had just changed.

*   *   *

Day Zero: 0446 Zulu

An hour later, the five crew members assembled in the Lounge. Looking grim, no one had much to say. Each had worked non-stop, as required by event protocols and their specific specialties. They had created a complete duplicate file of the telescopic record and watched it three times, searching for any new data.

Commander Susan York had spoken briefly with Kosloff, the senior Russian on the Station, and they had agreed not to notify NASA or their respective governments until after they analyzed all the data from the instrument pack. Complete analysis would take time, but the initial read-outs from the spectrometer and infra-red cameras confirmed the exchange of high energy beams of some unknown type. Lasers, particle beams, nothing fit the minimal data the instruments had detected.

Until they had more information, they must consider the beam weapons as a new type of energy. They had many questions, but few enough answers. After the final data review, they stared at each other in silence, everyone tense and nervous.

Maksim Mironov finished up on his tablet. "I've plotted their course," he said. "I can't find an energy signature from the third ship, the one that appeared to be damaged. It may have been left behind. Only two ships appear to have survived. They moved away from Jupiter and climbed above the planetary plane. The survivors are accelerating toward the inner planets. If I were a gambler, I would wager they are aiming toward Mars. At least the initial readings indicate that direction."

"How long will it take them to reach Mars orbit?" Since reviewing the recorded battle, Welsh had said little.

"Their speed . . . it varies," Maks answered cautiously, "and it is difficult to estimate. I'll be able to give you a better guess when I've got more data."

"How long before you can be certain?" Commander York asked. Her voice remained calm. "We need to know what we're dealing with."

"Commander, we are dealing with a First Contact situation. Kosloff adjusted his black glasses on his nose. "A First Contact that turns out to be a bloody space battle." Kosloff had learned his English in London.

Susan ignored the comment and kept her eyes fixed on Maks.

"In about ninety minutes," Maks said, "By then I should have enough data to plot a course and time line. But they may move faster or slower, or ..." He wet his lips.

"What is it?" Welsh's knuckles gleamed through his dark skin as he gripped his stick pen.

"They may change course and head toward Earth," Maks answered. "They will probably pick up radio and television signals from Earth and the Moon, if they haven't already. If they decide to come here directly, it's possible they could reach Earth in fifty or sixty hours."

Derrell Parrish spoke up. A bioengineer responsible for running the Station's numerous biological experiments, he hadn't contributed much to the prior discussions. "So, they're on their way to the inner planets. We can't get to Mars in less than two or three months with our fusion engines, and they'll do the trip in less than three days. I don't even want to think about that."

Derrell was the second youngest person to run a mission on the

Station. His research had already expanded the concepts of cell adaptation to unusual environments. Space genetics was something NASA wanted to learn more about. At least Dr. Parrish had some credentials. The NASA selection for the previous mission had been an acrobat, assigned to research new ways of moving and exercising in zero gravity.

Parrish shook his head. "Whatever they want, they're not exploring or wasting time on the gas giants. If they want to land somewhere, there's only three places in the solar system where you can stretch your legs and get something to eat: Mars, Earth, or the Moon."

The scientist might be young, but he asked good questions. "Mars is empty, the Moon is empty," Welsh answered, "so, that leaves . . . Earth. The Station will be their first stop. Maybe we should prep the escape module."

His serious tone silenced them. The escape module was a one-time, one-way vessel, recently enhanced to carry a maximum of ten people back to Earth in the event of an emergency. Station personnel were required to keep it in a fifteen minute ready state. The obvious thought remained unspoken. They could be back on Earth in four hours.

"Why would they threaten the Station?" Susan asked, brushing the idea of escape from her mind. "We haven't harmed them and we're unarmed."

"I don't know," Welsh answered. "All I know is that some bad-ass dudes just slugged it out, and one of them lost big-time. Who knows how many dead aliens are floating around in Jupiter's space? We don't even know who the good guys are, or whether they just won or lost."

"If any of them are good guys," Maks offered. "They seem to be carrying... how do you Americans say it . . . a lot of iron."

"And they know how to use it," Parrish finished the thought. "What are we going to tell NASA?"

Susan had thought about that. "Maks, let's prepare all the data we have for transmission to NASA. Kosloff can help you. Meanwhile, Colonel Welsh can prepare the module for a return trip, just in case."

"I will help prepare the data, but Maks will make two copies," Kosloff said firmly. "In addition to NASA, one set must be sent to

General Demidov in Star City. He will contact the necessary authorities in Moscow."

Star City, northeast of Moscow, was home to the Russian space program. "Is that necessary, Nikolai?" Susan asked. "We should wait to hear what NASA has to say first."

Before Maks or Kosloff could reply, Welsh cut in. "Susan, NASA will take a week to convince themselves the data is correct and that we're not hallucinating. This is too big for NASA." He turned to Maks. "On second thought, make three complete data sets, exactly the same. I'll transmit one to General Klegg in Washington. If he approves, then we transmit one to NASA."

Susan tightened her lips. "I should remind you that I'm in command here, and that this is a NASA operation. Our first duty is to inform NASA."

Welsh kept his voice soft and his tone gentle. "Susan, I'm an Air Force Officer, and I swore an oath to protect and defend the people of the United States." He nodded toward Maks and Nikolai. "Just as they did to their government." He reached over to touch her arm. "If you call NASA, the cat will be out of the bag, and both our governments will be furious. Why don't you wait until you hear what General Klegg recommends? This is too big for NASA, and anyway, they'll be out of the picture as soon as this news hits Earth. This Station will become a military operation within a few hours."

"A JOINT military operation," Kosloff said firmly.

"Jesus, I hope so, Nikolai. If we have to defend ourselves against these guys, we'll need everybody and everything we've got."

"You're assuming they'll be hostile," Susan argued. "If we keep on like this, we may provoke them into some action. NASA would know more about such things."

"We have to think in terms of capabilities, not intentions," Welsh said. Civilians seemed incapable of grasping that basic military concept. "These people… whatever they are… can take our three or four month journey from Earth to Mars and turn it into their weekend jaunt. Think about that kind of power. Those ships are big. Big enough for their engine signatures to be picked up optically by the telescope. And they've got particle beam weapons or lasers or something that can hit and kill a high-speed moving object in space. What does that tell you?"

Susan looked around the table, but no one met her eyes. The

situation had slipped out of her control and they knew it. But she hadn't risen to command a space mission by wilting under pressure.

"Then we prepare a single statement," she said. "Let's make sure that NASA and our governments get exactly the same information, to avoid confusion and panic. Can we agree on that, at least?"

Welsh looked at Kosloff, who nodded agreement. "A good idea, Commander," Welsh said. He thought it likely in a few hours he would be placed in command of the space station, at least temporarily, but there was nothing to be gained by talking about it. "The last thing we want is any disagreements between our governments because of what we say to them. Perhaps it would be better if we spoke with one voice."

Maks unhooked his leg from the table stanchion. "Yes, I agree. Then we'd better begin. The sooner we prepare the data packets, the sooner we can alert our governments."

The next ninety minutes went by quickly. For security reasons, Welsh shut down the computers and communications systems that provided contact with Earth. Not that he thought anyone would try to contact Earth, but he didn't want any incoming questions. No email, no phones, no radio communication. Private phones wouldn't work up here, since the communications satellites they linked to looked down, not sideways.

When Welsh finished securing the Station, the crew gathered for a second meeting. Everyone looked somber now that they'd had more time to think.

"The two surviving ships are still moving toward Mars," Maks began, his voice a little too loud, "and it appears that they have stopped accelerating. It took them a little less than four hours to reach their present speed. Remember, what our instruments show is what happened about thirty-five minutes ago, maybe less since they're on the move and heading toward the inner planets."

"Any idea of when they will reach Mars orbit?" Kosloff's accent seemed more pronounced.

"For a rough estimate, assuming they coast along at their current speed," Maks said, "I would say about fifty-two hours at most. Their acceleration seems to have leveled off, and if we assume they will require another three or four hours to decelerate, then . . ."

He hesitated. "They've been traveling . . . let's see, for nearly five hours now, so they could be in Mars orbit in forty-eight hours, give or take an hour."

"And you're still tracking them?"

"Not exactly. Once they stopped accelerating, their signature emissions and power levels dropped, so now we can't pick them out with the instruments. They're moving too fast for the telescope. But we did get their plot before they disappeared. We might be able to get them visually once they begin decelerating."

And that was the way to travel in space, Welsh thought. Crank up some honking big engines and just blast away. No orbital matching, no complicated trajectories, no gravity slings, no worries about fuel, no long coasting flights in zero gravity that wasted food and oxygen. Just glance out the viewport, pick your destination, then point and shoot, pure power going and coming. The only navigational equipment needed would be a good pair of binoculars.

"That's a sizeable percentage of the speed of light," Welsh commented. "They must have power to burn."

"It's 0.008 light speed," Maks offered. "We could do the same if we had engines capable of sustaining a one gravity acceleration for four hours."

These speeds were impossible, Welsh knew. Nothing could travel that fast. Even if you could move at that speed, contact with even a grain of dust might be dangerous, let alone a pebble sized meteor. The fact that it was actually happening said plenty about their visitors' level of technology.

"We don't have anything that could come even close to that, not for a single hour," Welsh said. Not even the big fusion engines that powered the ships traveling between Jupiter's moons and Earth. Instead Earth travelers relied on fusion plants that could achieve several gravities acceleration for a few minutes, and then coast the rest of the way.

An engine that could burn steadily for four hours, then do the same burn in reverse upon arrival remained the stuff of science fiction. There was no source of fuel, no fusion reactor on Earth that could manage that. Not with Earth's current technology. Not to mention fitting such a drive into a space ship, carrying enough fuel, or dealing with the resulting radiation.

"So that means some type of super fusion drive," Kosloff

offered, thinking along the same lines, "or maybe even anti-matter. Something that doesn't use much fuel."

"Whatever it is, they've got it, and it's powerful," Welsh said. "Maybe we should be asking a different question. Why are they going to Mars?"

"Perhaps they haven't picked up any Earth broadcasts yet," Susan York offered, commenting for the first time. "They're still pretty far out, and you'd have to search the radio and TV bands."

Welsh shook his head. "No, Susan, these are warships. Warships scan all the frequencies all the time, in every direction, looking for anything unusual or dangerous. By now they must know that Earth is broadcasting energies on multiple wavelengths, while Mars is almost totally silent. The three bases there don't put out much traffic. But the ships haven't changed course. I wonder why?"

No one had any good ideas about that. Interesting as Mars remained to everyone on Earth, it didn't have much in the way of useful resources. No surface water, no hydrogen in the atmosphere that could be mined for fuel, just lots of iron oxide, rocks and sand. It might one day be terraformed into a world habitable for human beings, but that day remained far in the future. Mars offered nothing in comparison to the treasure trove of minerals on Jupiter's moon, Io.

"Well, if they're so interested in Mars," Susan answered, "maybe that's all they want. Maybe they'll leave, I mean, go back to Jupiter, once they get whatever it is they're looking for."

"Or maybe they'll decide to visit Earth," Derrell Parish said. "If they do come here, we could be the next in line to entertain our guests. Us, or the lunar bases."

China had established two self-sustaining bases on the Moon, ostensibly for research, mining, and tourist operations. The United States and England shared another, smaller research station. European corporations operated two more refining bases to process ores shipped from the mines on Io.

"I would like to take a look at those engines, though," Kosloff said. "That would be an incredible breakthrough for us. If that abandoned ship is still out there . . ."

"All of this is already a breakthrough," Welsh said. "Just knowing this is possible, it changes everything."

No one said anything. Everyone could envision what this news would do to Earth rotating placidly below them. Their world was going to change overnight, and very little of the resulting change was likely to be good.

"Right now, we've got our own problems," Welsh said finally. "We have to track these guys. We need to confirm that Mars is their destination, then figure out what they're going to do when they get there."

"Do you think their arrival has anything to do with that freighter crew from Io? The ones who lost that ship, the *Lady Drake*, wasn't it?" Parrish asked.

Less than two months ago something strange had occurred on the Io to Luna run. JovCo management released a brief story about some unknown space madness overcoming the crew, but provided no details or explanation. Very few knew exactly what happened, and those who did weren't saying anything. But the ore freighter and its cargo had overshot the Moon and headed toward the sun. Only the freighter's escape craft had managed to make an emergency lunar rendezvous two days ago.

"Let's not waste any time on that," Susan said. "But why didn't our visitors notice our bases on Io?"

"I'd say because Io is on the opposite side of Jupiter right now," Maks said. "With Jupiter in the way, the mining bases probably weren't transmitting anything. Not to mention the background noise."

Jupiter's moon, Io, was the closest thing to a hell hole in the solar system. Constant volcanic eruptions, massive bursts of particle radiation, and intense magnetic storms caused by Jupiter's proximity, it remained a place no sane person wanted to visit. Except that it possessed seemingly unlimited resources of precious minerals in short supply on Earth.

Even so, the fatality rate for its workers remained high, and only the truly desperate signed up. The pay might be commensurate with the risks, but few enough wanted to take the chance. Volunteers for the Io mines remained scarce. Every individual employee insurance contract had to be drafted with care, negotiated down to the last detail.

Welsh nodded. "I agree. Let's forget about Io for now. I suggest we keep every instrument we've got on our visitors," Kosloff said. "Maybe we can eventually deduce something about their engines from their burn signatures. Maybe we can take a guess at their size as well. At least it will give us something to do while the brass down below make up their minds."

"We need to be asking NASA those questions," Susan said. "They're the ones that will have to make the decisions."

Welsh unhooked his feet and floated up from the table. "Susan, I think we've got a better chance of figuring out what these aliens are going to do than NASA. We're here, and we've got the data and all the instruments. By the time they collect the right people and reach any decisions, we'll have sifted through a mountain of data."

And that thought gave no one any comfort.

*   *   *

Day Zero: 0631 Zulu (01:31 a.m. – Washington, D.C.)

Thanks to the latest in quantum mechanics, secure communication transmissions and phone conversations could be conducted directly from the space Station. It required extra time to setup, but in less than an hour, Welsh switched on the communication device. He sat at the communications console with Commander York and Colonel Kosloff hovering nearby. Even with all the latest equipment, it still took five minutes to reach the duty officer, General Klegg's adjutant, a Major Mitchell.

"Yes, Colonel Welsh," Mitchell said. "What can I do for you?"

From his voice, Welsh guessed that Mitchell had been taking a nap somewhere, and didn't want to be bothered at this time of night, especially by the ISS, where nothing ever happened.

"I need to speak with General Klegg privately and on a secure line. Immediately. Inform him that Station Commander York, Colonel Kosloff, and I have important information for him."

"Colonel, it's almost 2 a.m. in Washington, D.C. The General went to bed almost four hours ago. Why don't you give me the message, and I'll relay it to him first thing in the morning. He's up at 5 a.m. every day."

"This is urgent and personal for General Klegg. Wake him up immediately, please."

"Colonel, I'm sorry, but I have to know more about what is so important that it can't wait a few hours. If you . . ."

"Fine, Major. If you won't wake him, I guess I'll just have to call the Russian government. It's morning over there. Make sure you explain to General Klegg why General Demidov received this information first, after Klegg reads about it in his *Washington Post* news feed this morning. Sorry to have disturbed your nap."

Welsh waited, knowing it took almost three seconds for the message to travel down to Earth and back up. It would have been better to have a video call, but that took even longer to establish and was less secure.

"Wait a minute, Welsh." Even from thirty-six thousand miles away they could hear the irritation in Major Mitchell's voice. Still, the man wasn't going to risk his ass in a career-ending situation. If the crisis turned out to be a false alarm, Colonel Welsh would take the blame. "I'll wake the General. Stand by."

"Roger that," Welsh answered.

"How long before he comes on the line?" Susan asked.

Lieutenant General Klegg was the Air Force Joint Chief of Staff. Just recently given his third star, Langdon Klegg had started out a fighter pilot, and had seen action in two Middle East conflicts. Intelligent, flexible, and with real command ability, he had proved to be one of the brighter stars in the US Military. Welsh had met him twice a few years back at briefings in Washington, though he doubted the man would remember. Through the chain of command, Klegg had the ultimate responsibility for the Station.

"Oh, probably ten, fifteen minutes," Welsh answered. "Mitchell will have to call him at home, wake him up, waste time telling him what we said. Then Klegg will want to get some coffee so he can think straight. We'll just wait on this circuit."

Either Klegg didn't need the coffee or he slept lightly. In six minutes the communicator blinked as the link transferred from Mitchell's Pentagon office to Klegg's residence.

"Klegg here. You're Major Welsh? I remember meeting you three years ago at some briefing." The voice sounded brisk, wide-awake. No stupid questions about why are you waking me in the middle of the night, or bullshit about this had better be important.

"It's Lieutenant Colonel now, General. I'm on the ISS. With me are Station Commander Susan York and Colonel Nikolai Kosloff. Please set your encryption to match mine," Welsh pressed a button on the phone that transmitted a temporary key, "and please make sure you're alone and can't be overheard."

Silence. Welsh felt his shoulder squeezed in sympathy, and glanced up to see Kosloff smiling. The shit was about to hit the fan. Whatever happened, there wasn't much they could do to him now, was there?

The silence lasted nearly fifteen seconds, before the encryption kicked in. The tiny green light on Welsh's communicator blinked several times, then stayed green. A secure, encrypted connection had been established between the two phones. Maybe the Chinese or Koreans could crack it in a week or two with a super computer, but maybe not.

"OK, Colonel," General Klegg's voice returned. "I'm alone and the phone is secure from this end. Major Mitchell is off the circuit."

"Copy that, General," Welsh answered, looking down once again to verify the encryption lock. "I'm putting you on the speaker now. General, we have a confirmed First Contact Situation."

The normal delay came and went, followed by another five seconds or so. "What type of First Contact, Colonel?"

No "are you sure," or "have you confirmed it?" Just a matter-of-fact follow up question.

"An instrument detection, General. The contact took place directly over the planet Jupiter, just above the planetary plane. We happened to be monitoring Jupiter because it is undergoing one of its more turbulent periods, and our instruments detected six spacecraft that appeared out of nowhere. The last vessel to arrive was considerably larger. It pursued and attacked the first five. It destroyed two of them for sure, and killed or severely damaged at least one other before it was destroyed. You understand that most of this information came from instrument readouts, and some optical sighting from our telescope."

That was enough, Welsh decided. He paused to let the General think it over, and took time to squeeze a drink from his water bottle.

"Go on, Colonel." Klegg's amplified voice sounded hollow in the command center.

Welsh swallowed quickly, then wiped his lips with his hand. "After the dogfight, the two surviving space craft of the six moved above the planetary plane and set course for the inner planets, probably Mars. We're tracking them as we speak." He paused a moment. "Sir, they're moving at a very high rate of speed. They could reach Mars orbit in forty-two to forty-eight hours. That indicates a continuously powered flight for four hours. Mars isn't that far away from Earth right now. If they can maintain that kind of speed, they could reach Earth orbit in another twenty-four hours. And General, these ships are big, big enough to detect at 600,000,000 kilometers. Larger than our ore freighters."

This time the pause lasted longer as Klegg digested the information. "You have records of all this activity?"

"Yes, Sir. The data is ready and I can transmit it to you right now, over this line."

"All right, do that. Then place the Station on total blackout. Nobody else is to transmit anything until further notice. No email, phone calls, radio transmissions, nothing. Nothing to the press or family members. Can you do that?"

"Yes, Sir, we'll do that. But first Colonel Kosloff will notify his superiors in Moscow. We've agreed to that, General. And Commander York insists on notifying the head of NASA."

There was some extraneous noise, probably fingers drumming on a desk, as Klegg mulled over that information. Welsh hadn't asked permission, which meant he would let Kosloff place the call no matter what Klegg ordered. In fact, Klegg had no authority over either of the two Russian crewmen. It didn't take him long to work out the reality of the situation. "Oh, dammit to hell, I suppose we've got to notify Russia. Damn. But not NASA! I'll notify NASA from here, in a couple of hours, as soon as I've established some security. Otherwise they'll have the story all over the net in five minutes. Do you understand that, Commander York?"

"General," Commander York leaned forward so that her words would be clear. "I work for NASA and I have a responsibility to them. This information is too important to hold back."

"We're not holding it back, Commander. I'll have NASA contact you as soon as I brief them. Meanwhile, no contact of any kind. I'm placing the Station under Air Force control, under a state of national emergency. Colonel Welsh, you will assume command of the Station from Susan. After Colonel Kosloff speaks with his superiors, you will shut down the space station."

"General Klegg," Susan answered, "I must protest this action. We're . . ."

"Protest all you want, Commander. In the event of a national emergency, the Station can be placed under military control, and I have just declared such an emergency. If you have any issues, I suggest you read your contract with NASA. You're subject to military authority as of now. Welsh can explain exactly what that means. In fact, Colonel Welsh, you'd better do that with all the other Station personnel. I'll call you back with new security codes just as soon as I've seen the data. Are you transmitting it?"

"Yes, General, it's on its way."

"Good. Keep tracking the bogies. Get Kosloff's call out of the way, then shut down the Station, and I mean tight. Colonel Kosloff, give my regards to General Demidov. We're going to need him. Meanwhile, I'm heading for the White House to brief the President. I'll get back to you later. Klegg out."

The line went dead.

"So, that didn't go too badly," Welsh offered, letting out a deep breath and lifting himself out of the chair.

"I think this is wrong," Susan said. "This Station is supposed to be a scientific outpost, not some military operation. I still think NASA has a right to know what is happening on their Station."

Welsh faced her, holding onto the edge of the console for support. "Susan, NASA will find out soon enough. A few hours delay isn't going to matter, since they won't have any say in how the Station is used."

"You notify the Air Force," Susan's voice sounded bitter, "Nikolai tells his superior, but I can't talk with the head of NASA."

"Susan, you are a good mission commander," Kosloff said. "But in this you are wrong. NASA would start a panic before your government and mine could prepare to respond. People could die."

Susan glared at him. "You think the military knows better than NASA? There isn't anything . . ."

"Commander, I want your word that you'll give General Klegg time to speak with the President," Welsh said. "If you try to communicate with NASA or anyone else, I'll have to put you in restraints. You'll be off the Station the next time a shuttle docks. Is that what you want?"

Welsh didn't wait for an answer. He floated off to the side while Kosloff occupied the chair, hooking his foot under the mount to anchor himself.

The call to Star City went through almost at once, maybe

because it was already morning there, and people were up and about. General Demidov, a pilot for many years until he developed problems with his eyesight, had just arrived at his office. Most Russians prefer to work late and sleep in, but Demidov, tall, fit, and just entering his sixty-sixth year, had become accustomed to western ways. He usually managed to get himself to his desk by 10 a.m.

Surprisingly, he took the call himself. Possibly his aide was busy making tea, and Demidov needed a few extra minutes to set up the encryption match. The commercial grade software the Russians utilized to communicate with the Station didn't provide as much security as the one the Americans relied on. But it worked and finally the connection light blinked green. Kosloff, now speaking Russian, related the same set of facts to his superior.

Welsh listened hard, to make certain he caught every word. His Russian language skills were adequate, but not good enough to be deemed fluent. Commander York, however, spoke excellent Russian, and she listened to make certain what Kosloff said was accurate. They both trusted Kosloff, but better safe than sorry.

Kosloff appeared just as concerned about making any mis-statements. He spoke slowly, relaying the same information in almost the same words. Welsh had no trouble understanding him. When Kosloff finished, however, the conversation took a different turn.

"You say you have notified the American military, but not NASA. Is that correct, Kosloff?"

"Yes, Sir. General Klegg wanted to review the material first. No doubt," Kosloff glanced at Welsh, "he wants to make sure NASA can maintain security."

Welsh smiled at that one. "Maintain security" was a Russian euphemism for keep your mouth shut or else. With NASA's reputation of being unable to keep anything quiet for more than three minutes, no doubt anyone there in the know would have a full-time FBI agent assigned.

"NASA is well known for its leaks." Demidov sighed. "We may have the same problem here, Kosloff. You're sure that what you saw on your monitor was a hostile action?"

"That's what it appeared to be, General," Kosloff answered.

"Sir, this is Lieutenant Colonel Welsh speaking. I've flown in combat, as you have. This was a military engagement."

"You have no idea where these ships came from? Or what . . . no, never mind."

"None, General," Kosloff answered, his hand tightening on the chair at the question.

"I will assemble a team," Demidov said, "if I can find enough people I can trust. We will review your data. You will be available when we need you?"

Kosloff looked at Welsh, who nodded. "Yes, General. I will call back shortly and give you a new access key. All the regular channels will be blocked, and no one else will be able to communicate with us for now. Officially, the ISS is experiencing communication difficulties."

"Yes, of course. Thank you very much, Colonel. And Commander York, Susan, I am sorry that such a thing has to happen on your command."

Susan leaned forward as she spoke. Demidov had taken a liking to Susan York when she trained in Star City. "Thank you, General. As always, you are most kind."

"Send the data," Demidov said, and broke the voice connection. The data link remained open, however, and Kosloff initiated the file transfer down to the planet. There was a lot of information, and even using all the bandwidth they had available, it would take almost ten minutes to transmit.

The situation for the Alliance appeared bleak, and it might be even worse for Russia. Demidov, tugging on his iron-gray mustache, felt certain that the biggest obstacle the Russians would face would be their own leader, President Garanin. Demidov knew the President of Russia would not grasp the military implications of the arrival of aliens. He would instead look for a political solution. Demidov would have to use care to make sure President Garanin accepted his advice.

With the call ended, Kosloff let himself float up off the chair. "OK, we've done it. Now what do we do?"

"Yes, Colonel." Susan couldn't keep a hint of bitterness from her voice. "What do we do now?"

Welsh looked at both of them. He hadn't wanted this assignment, but there was no way to avoid it, either. "First, Nikolai will make sure that nothing can be sent to Earth without our approval. Susan, I would like you to prepare for the NASA briefing.

They may take it better coming from you, and I'm sure they'll have questions. I'll be there to help out if I can, and inform them of the new security." Welsh knew that only he and Kosloff were real military. The other three were all civilian scientists. Even Maks was just a scientist wearing a uniform.

"Assuming I ever do get to brief them," Susan said. "What will you be doing?"

"Kosloff and I will set up the security keys so that only Star City and Washington can talk to us. Everyone else will find we're temporarily unavailable and experiencing communication difficulties. Then we all pitch in and help Maks analyze the data we're receiving."

"Won't they be able to do that better on Earth?" Susan questioned. "They could have a hundred scientists working on this in a few hours."

"Don't be so sure, Susan," Welsh said. "First they'll have to get people together. Then they'll need to find people who can be trusted to keep quiet."

"You can't keep this a secret, Welsh. You know that. It will be out in less than a day or two. Pretty soon anyone with a telescope is going to detect those two ships heading for Mars or coming at us."

"All the more reason for us to get ready," Welsh said. "We may be able to discover something before they do."

"You mean before all hell breaks loose," Susan said.

"That's what I mean," Welsh said. "That's exactly what's going to happen. All hell is going to break loose down there in a few days. We may be safer up here in the long run."

"If there is a long run," Kosloff said. He pushed himself away and floated toward the exit.

"Let's hope there is." Welsh met Kosloff's gaze. "Now, we'd better start praying for a lucky break, like maybe these aliens are just peaceful citizens of the galaxy coming to pay a social call."

"We'll need a way to communicate with them," Kosloff muttered.

"That we will," Welsh said. "That we will."

Chapter 2

Day 1: 00:52 (Central European Time, Paris, France)

Captain Joseph (Joe) J. Delano, USMC, rolled onto his back with a satisfied smile. He remained under the still-warm covers of the bed, trying not to wake the woman beside him. He was only partially successful. In a light sleep, Eugénie Fanette Giboz turned toward him, mumbling something he didn't catch as she snuggled closer. Adjusting the duvet, he slid his arm around her shoulder. Her blonde hair felt silky on his chest, and he could still smell the heady fragrance that had first attracted him. Leave it to a French woman to know all about perfume.

Delano had discovered earlier in the evening that Eugénie wasn't a natural blonde, but at this stage of their relationship, he felt magnanimous enough to overlook that minor defect. So far, everything else had turned out to be not only genuine but first class in every way. He had met her for the first time tonight, so there remained plenty of time to learn new and interesting details about Eugénie's personality.

He had seen her across the room at the American Embassy monthly cocktail party, a popular event for those privileged enough to receive an invitation. Delano had joined the Embassy staff only three weeks earlier, and this was his first social. Eugénie had arrived alone, looking aloof and very French, with that natural attitude of superiority so intimidating to American men and women. The wife of a senior trade councilor at the French Agricultural Ministry, Eugénie appeared to be about thirty years old, but now, seeing her in his arms, Joe guessed her closer to forty. He decided he could overlook that flaw, too.

Her husband had jaunted off to Brussels on business, and she had come to the Embassy social out of boredom, arriving fashionably late at 8 p.m. Now that Delano thought about it, her being married might be considered another defect. He couldn't be certain about that yet, since a married woman might have offsetting advantages.

Joe watched as a handful of men of various nationalities, ranks, and age made overtures to her, but Eugénie remained polite but indifferent. Even a dashing young American naval officer, in his dress whites, had been rebuffed. Joe's Marine uniform appeared dull by comparison. Still, he doubted she had come to the party intending to stand around and ignore everyone. As the hour grew late and passed 9 p.m., Joe decided he had nothing to lose. Three weeks in Paris and he hadn't had time for a date. He finished his drink and approached her.

"Enchanté, Madame," he said. "It appears you are not enjoying yourself. Perhaps I can be of some assistance?"

That earned him an interested look. Delano's perfect French held the subtle accent of the educated Parisian upper-class.

Up close her good looks impressed him even more. Of medium height, she had creamy porcelain skin and her thin face revealed fine bones and even white teeth. Thoughtful brown eyes studied him from beneath perfectly aligned eyebrows. A deep yellow gown bordering on saffron set off her golden hair.

"Your French is very good, Monsieur," she answered. "How long have you lived in Paris?"

"Only three weeks, Madame. I learned your wonderful language as a child in the United States." Delano had nearly said 'America,' but he had learned that lesson. Europeans didn't like the term as used by US citizens. It implied that the other countries in the Americas were unimportant. "My name is Joseph Delano, and I am the recently arrived senior translator at the Embassy. But please call me Joe."

She introduced herself, and that had given Delano another opening. "Eugénie. A lovely name. If I recall, it means 'noble.' Very appropriate."

Eugénie regarded him with more respect. Not only an American who spoke with a fluent and cultured Parisian accent, but one who knew the meaning of French names. Très intéressant!

"Oh, my. Quite impressive. My second name is 'Fanette.'" There was a hint of a challenge in her voice. "Do you also know what that means?"

"I might guess, Eugénie. Delano let his eyes drift down to the clingy gown that exposed a goodly amount of warm-looking flesh. A thick gold chain glinted against her skin. "Is there a prize if I guess right?"

"Perhaps." A hint of a smile crossed her carmine lips. "Although you American soldiers always seem to take so much for granted."

"I am a Marine Officer, Eugénie Fanette, not a soldier. My mother taught me that a good woman is like a special treasure I should always keep close. And Fanette, I believe, means 'crowned with laurels.' Am I correct?"

They left the party thirty minutes later, separately of course. Once again Delano's linguistic skills had captivated a girl. Some men needed flashy jewelry, piles of cash or great physiques. Sports jocks wasted a lot of time sweating. But Delano could whisper sweet nothings to almost any foreign girl in her native language. Even American women got a thrill when he murmured Italian or French endearments in their ear.

Twenty-eight years old, Delano had learned his second language – English – at the age of two. Until then, though born in Brooklyn, his parents had spoken only Italian with their son. By now he could proposition a girl in more than sixty languages and dialects.

Eugènie had mentioned that the Hotel Napoleon, near the Arch de Triomphe, was very old fashioned, with an intimate bar, big rooms and discreet help. Perhaps they might meet there for a drink? When Delano arrived, he found the entrance already locked for the night, and late returning guests were expected to have their own keys. The elderly desk clerk took his time answering the night bell, in no rush to open the door for an annoying young American in uniform.

Once again Delano's language skills won the contest, as the clerk deferred instinctively to Delano's cultivated French. He explained that he expected a very beautiful guest, and the clerk grudgingly admitted that he might have a room, though it would be expensive. Delano shrugged. It hadn't taken long to learn all about Parisian prices. The registration and credit card paperwork required ten minutes, and he had just picked up the large, old-fashioned key when Eugènie arrived.

She had changed clothes somewhere. The evening gown was gone. Now she dressed all in black, the favorite color of European women. Black jeans, pullover, and leather jacket, though she still wore the gold chain around her neck. The clerk had taken one look at her through the glass door and jumped to let her in. If he recognized her, he was far too tactful, too French, to show it. He led them toward the tiny bar, empty at this hour and just large enough to seat four.

The night clerk poured two small glasses of brandy for them before returning to the main desk, discreetly out of sight. After each took a small sip, Eugènie's hand rested on Delano's thigh. The room key sat temptingly on the bar between them. Numeró 308.

From then on, things had moved quickly. Eugènie took one more sip of her brandy before she stood, picked up the key, and guided him down the hall to the tiny elevator. By himself, Delano would never have found the room. It was on the fourth floor, American style, in the rear, with large, ornately carved double doors painted a cream color and trimmed with polished brass.

Delano hadn't heard a sound from the other rooms they passed. Once inside, she had tossed the key on the dresser and then her jacket. For a moment he stood there, gazing at her, admiring the gold hair falling over the black sweater. Both striking and tempting in the gown, now she appeared even more sensual. Her perfume wafted across the space between them.

Unbidden, a word came to his lips. Not English, not even French.

"Allettante."

"Ah, Italian as well. You think I am alluring? Or is it tempting?"

"Oh, yes. You are both."

She tilted her chin up, took a deep breath, and moved her shoulders back. Her breasts now strained against the dark fabric. "Do you like what you see?"

"You are very beautiful in black, Eugènie." The hoarseness in his voice made her smile. That, or perhaps the growing bulge in his trousers.

She crossed her arms and lifted the sweater over her head, shaking her hair loose as she pulled free from the garment. No bra under the pullover. Eugènie must have approved of his reaction. She flashed a big smile and toyed with a strand of hair, pulling it across her chin. "Are you going to keep me waiting?"

That had been the last sentence either of them spoke for some time. He reached her in two steps and she came into his arms, holding him tightly for a long moment before she began fumbling with his uniform buttons.

In bed she had been voracious, as if she hadn't made love in some time, which seemed impossible. But Delano didn't think much about it, because by then he had moved past the thinking stage. Her skin seemed hot to his touch, and it didn't take long before he had her shuddering through her first orgasm. Three minutes later, he was out of control himself, with her legs locked around his thighs and her nails digging at his back, holding him close long after he came.

The second time was better, slower, as if the first had been merely physical and urgent. Now they took their time, both wanting to draw it out as much as possible. Eugénie Fanette knew how to please a man, and probably a woman, just as she knew exactly what she wanted.

As Delano lay there, cradling her sleeping body, he already looked forward to taking her again. French married women often preferred single encounters, so he intended to enjoy himself as much as possible, just in case.

But he could afford to let her doze a little longer. Eugénie had mentioned that she needed to be home before 7 a.m. in the morning when the servants arrived. Delano glanced at his watch. Not quite 1 a.m. Yes, plenty of time for a memorable night. He closed his eyes in anticipation and breathed deeply.

A phone rang, making him start. Delano didn't recognize the odd ring tone and thought it must be Eugénie's. Then he remembered the emergency alert. The Embassy provided his phone, and before taking possession, he had agreed to keep it with him at all times and always answer the emergency signal.

"Damn," he muttered. He reached across Eugénie's body for the phone resting on the night stand.

"What is it?" Eugénie's voice sounded sleepy. "Must you answer it?"

Yes, I must. Damn. "Just for a moment. Go back to sleep."

Wondering what idiot wanted a translator in the middle of the night, Delano answered. "Who is this?"

"This is Ambassador Allitt, and I better be speaking to Captain Joseph Delano, goddamnit!"

Wide awake now, Delano sat up. The US Ambassador to France seldom spoke to anyone at the embassy outside his immediate staff. Since Delano's arrival, he had met the Ambassador exactly once, for about ten seconds, more than enough time for Delano to classify the man as an uptight bureaucrat. But the American Ambassador did not call junior Marine officers in the middle of the night without a very good reason. "This is Captain Delano."

"Your commanding officer couldn't be reached, so Washington called me," Ambassador Garland Allitt snarled. "I'll have his ass when I get a hold of him. Someone on the President's staff woke me up and ordered me to handle this personally. Ordered me!" He paused for breath. "You're to be at Le Bourget Airport in exactly . . . seventy-four minutes. No later. An aircraft will be waiting for you. Do you understand, Captain?"

"Yes, Ambassador, but what . . ."

"No questions, just get moving and don't be late."

The connection went dead before Delano could answer. He knew where his commanding officer was – sleeping with his mistress at her apartment in the Île Saint-Louis district, no doubt with his phone turned off. Delano had glimpsed the stunning woman a few days ago, and would have turned his phone off, too.

He glanced at his watch. Le Bourget was seven or so miles north of Paris, and at this time of night he could be there in fifteen minutes. He wanted to return to his apartment and pack a bag, but his rented studio was in the opposite direction, and he wouldn't have enough time. Not that he knew what to pack anyway.

Wide awake now, he picked up the hotel phone and ordered a cab or limo service to be waiting for him in twenty minutes. The night clerk protested, but Delano promised him some cash, and triple the fare for the car's driver. By the time the arrangements were completed, Eugénie had sat up and leaned against the headboard, the duvet crumpled around her waist.

"You have to leave?"

One look at her bare breasts made up his mind. *Fuck the Ambassador.* "Yes, I have to go. But I have a few minutes, if you . . ." He lifted his hands and let them fall.

"Americans. Always in a rush." Her smile softened the criticism. Eugénie tilted her head. "Well?"

He wasn't going to walk out on that, no matter what the asshole Ambassador wanted. "Viva la France," he muttered.

Sixty-six minutes later, Delano hopped out of the cab before it stopped moving. At this early hour of the morning only one entrance to Le Bourget airport remained in operation. As he passed through the security checkpoint manned by three gendarmes, he found the Ambassador waiting for him just inside the door. He wore a brown leather coat over what looked like pajamas.

"You cut it pretty fine, Delano." Allitt strode off, heading for the departure gates. Delano tried to answer, but the Ambassador kept moving and didn't reply. Three minutes later, they passed through another checkpoint and stepped onto the tarmac.

At first Delano didn't see a plane, but then he noticed an American Air Force jet fighter half concealed by the darkness, its dual engines whining annoyingly at idle. A slender man dressed in a flight suit leaned against the aircraft, a small duffle bag slung over his shoulder.

"Is he the one, Ambassador?"

"Yes, goddammit, he's Captain Delano, and he's all yours." Without another word or look, Ambassador Allitt turned and stalked away.

Another word jumped into Delano's mind – dummkopf! 'Idiot' always sounded better in German. Whatever questions Delano had would go unanswered. The pilot tossed the duffle bag at him. "Flight suit. Hurry up and put it on."

He managed to catch the bag. "Is there a bathroom where I can change?"

"You're standing on it. If you don't stop fucking around and get moving, I promise to make you puke your guts out before we reach cruising altitude."

In two minutes, with the pilot's help, Delano donned the suit. He climbed up a tiny ladder and wormed his way into the back seat. The pilot, Air Force Captain Demetrio Cabrera – Delano read the leather name patch on his flight suit – buckled his passenger in. Then he plugged in Delano's helmet. "Push this button if you have to talk, but don't waste my time. Otherwise, you make sure you don't touch nothing, not a fucking thing. Play with yourself if you get the urge."

"I've never flown in anything like this." Delano's apprehension rose, and Captain Cabrera wasn't helping.

"Ask me if I care."

Cabrera jumped down from the ladder, repositioned it for access to the pilot's seat, and climbed into the front cockpit. He kicked the ladder away and dropped the canopy. Belting himself in with two quick movements, Cabrera eased the throttle forward.

The jet swayed and bumped across the tarmac while Cabrera mumbled something to the control tower. The tower was still talking when he turned the plane onto the runway and hit the throttle. In ten seconds they were airborne.

Delano, his gloved hands clenched on his thighs, felt his heart racing. Fear and exhilaration competed over his stomach. The jet's incredible acceleration finally eased off and the plane steadied. When they reached what had to be cruising altitude, Delano gazed out the cockpit, fascinated by the night sky full of bright stars. Already the plane had climbed high enough to see the Milky Way.

After five minutes of stargazing, Delano saw the plane cross over the French shoreline, leaving only the blackness of the Atlantic beneath them. Since the pilot showed no interest in explaining anything, Delano pushed the com button. "Where are we going?"

Captain Cabrera's laughter rang in Delano's ears. "Where we're going is fucking nowhere. The middle of the Atlantic. And if the tanker isn't waiting for us, I will roll this fighter upside down and personally eject your ass before I have to ditch."

That was the first and last conversation for the next two hours, as the jet screamed through the air at thirty thousand feet, traveling at Mach Two, if Delano read the display right. But at 04:40 the aircraft reduced speed, its fuel tanks nearly dry, and made contact with a tanker dispatched out of Greenland.

Transfixed, Delano watched the mid-air refueling, scared to death that Cabrera would crash into the tail of the big flying fuel truck, blow both planes to bits, and scatter parts of Delano's body over the Atlantic. Or worse, the fragile fighter could break apart, spilling Delano out of the aircraft and into a fifteen thousand foot fall.

When the refueling ended, Cabrera throttled the jet back up to Mach Two, climbed to his previous altitude, and punched the com button. "None of my business, Marine, but do you mind telling me what the hell you did to make a three-star want to fuck you in the ass so bad?"

"Three-star!" Delano didn't like the idea of that much brass pulling him out of a warm bed in Paris. "Captain, I have no idea who wants me or why. I don't even know where we're going."

Cabrera laughed again, the sound hollow over the mic. "We are going to Andrews Air Force Base, where I understand you'll be met by MPs or FBI or some other security types who will probably enjoy taking close up snaps of your butt. I hope your underwear is clean."

"Who's the three-star?"

"Well, I'm not supposed to know," Cabrera said, "but after I got my orders from General Carpenter, he's the brass hat running Alconbury, I kinda stopped outside his office to tie my shoe, if you know what I mean. And I heard the name General Klegg."

Delano remembered that Alconbury was a US base in the UK. "Klegg? Never heard of him."

"He's a Joint Chief, you ignorant Marine. Air Force. Supposed to be a real hard ass."

That General Klegg. Of course he'd heard of him. "Damn!" Delano didn't know what else to say. His luck had taken a turn for the worse. Instead of warming himself with Eugenie's delightful body, he was shivering in the cold cabin at thirty thousand feet and trying to keep control of his stomach.

Captain Cabrera said nothing else for the rest of the flight, even after they landed at Andrews. Two minutes after the jet stopped rolling, Delano climbed into an unmarked car headed for the Pentagon. During the ride, the two Air Force SFs let him change back into his rumpled uniform. They searched his clothes first, though without telling him what they were looking for. Fortunately, no one checked his underwear.

*   *   *

Day Zero: 10:25 p.m. – Washington, D.C.

At the Pentagon, two Marine sergeants, both armed, took over from the SFs. The Marines escorted Delano to security for a quick identity check, got him a badge and entered an elevator for a quick lift to the third floor. Getting to General Klegg's office required a long walk down a wide hallway punctured by doors every few steps, most of them closed. Despite the lateness of the hour – Delano wasn't even sure what time it was – the third floor rooms close to Klegg's office buzzed with activity.

General Klegg, doing something on his computer, motioned to

the sergeants and they closed the door behind them, leaving Delano alone with the General. Delano had time to study Klegg, still pecking away at his computer. He appeared tall, with short-cropped white hair that made his face looked distinguished, despite a crooked nose. A thick upper body and muscular arms indicated plenty of time spent in a weight room or maybe a boxing ring. The eyes, when he turned away from the computer monitor, were cold and gray.

At first Delano thought they were alone, but then he noticed a third person in the room. A woman, stretched out on a leather sofa next to a coffee table. She stirred and he took a quick look. Her face seemed familiar, but Delano couldn't put a name to it. He took two steps in, shoved his cap under his left arm, came to attention, and saluted.

"Sir, Captain Joseph Delano, reporting as ordered." He wished his uniform didn't look as if he'd slept in it.

"Sit down, Captain." Klegg stared at his visitor for a long moment. "You're late, should have been here hours ago. I remember meeting you at some function a while back. You look like hell."

"Thank you, Sir." Delano sank cautiously into a chair, not at ease despite the casual greeting. "I never flew in a fighter before. No sleep, and my stomach still hasn't landed."

"Don't let yourself get too comfortable. You're leaving for Holloman Air Force Base as soon as I finish briefing you." He saw the blank look on Delano's face. "That's in New Mexico. From there you'll travel by chopper to Spaceport, also in New Mexico. A shuttle is being prepped there to lift you and a few others to the ISS."

Stunned, Delano couldn't react. "Sir, I don't understand . . ."

"I'm sure you don't, Captain. So I'll give you the bottom line. Your skill as a translator is required on the space station." He looked down at his notes. "I understand you have a PhD in Experimental Linguistics, with a minor in psychology, and another minor in Computer Sciences. Very impressive. Everyone says you're a whiz at picking up languages. 'Achieves fluency in as little as two days. Near eidetic memory.' Both parents deceased six years – airplane crash. Sorry about that, must have been tough. No brothers or sisters. Your last review indicates that you often have trouble following orders. 'Tends to improvise rather than follow orders.' Our G-1 computer spit out your name, along with four others. Those lucky bastards, while equally competent, are either too old or have medical conditions or family ties that prohibit them for going into space and risking their lives."

Klegg looked up. "That means you win the prize, since we have nobody else. You are young, healthy, and except for being a Marine, I have nothing against you. I tell you frankly I have not had a lot of luck working with Marines. Too thick and hard-headed, always wanting to shoot first and talk later. Honestly, you are not my first choice for this mission."

He shook his head. "But I haven't got anybody else. It will be a good experience for you, look great in your service record, if you come through this. The Commandant will be outside in an hour to explain your new situation and why you're needed to hold up the honor and tradition of the Marine Corps. Not that it matters to me, but he'll officially promote you to Major, paperwork to follow. Are you getting all this, son?"

"Well, Sir, I think so . . ."

"Glad to hear it, because here's the interesting part. Less than twenty-four hours ago, I received word that alien spacecraft had arrived off Jupiter. As we speak, two alien spaceships are approaching Mars, and our scientists say their next stop is likely to be Earth. That means the folks on the ISS may be the first to make contact with an extraterrestrial race, assuming the aliens don't just settle down over the White House and burn it into dust with their particle beam weapons. We've already seen a demonstration of those. Still with me?"

"Sir, I don't . . . don't think I can translate for an alien race. What if they don't speak anything recognizable? I need something to work with."

"Heard all this before, Major. Hell, we don't even know how they communicate. Maybe they wiggle their toes, if they have any, or use telepathy. But they're intelligent and smart enough to conduct a space battle, so they must communicate somehow. I'm sure you'll figure something out. You'd better."

Klegg held up his hand. "More about that later. In New Mexico you'll be joined by two other translators. One's from Russia, some hotshot on all the local and ancient languages. The other is from China, supposedly the master of every Chinese, Japanese, Korean dialect, whatever. With the three of you, we hope to establish some form of communication with our new alien friends."

"Sir, General Klegg, suppose I don't volunteer for this mission. I don't think you or even the Commandant can order me to . . ."

"Think again, son. This is a declared national emergency. You're going if I have to put you in cuffs and have you carried onto the shuttle. I'm not going to let the United States be the only Alliance power on the space station without an interpreter."

Alliance? How the hell did they get involved? Delano sat in stunned silence. All this was happening too fast.

"Captain Delano?"

The woman on the sofa had woken and now sat upright, brushing hair from her face. As soon as she spoke, Delano recognized her. Dr. Vivian Spencer, National Security Advisor to the President, had a very distinctive voice.

"This may sound trite, Captain," she said, "but your country really needs you. You'll soon learn what is at stake, and we want you to join the team. If you like, I can have President Clarke call and tell you how much you're needed."

Delano slumped back in the chair. The last person he wanted to hear from was the President. Overwhelmed, exhausted, and jet-lagged, Delano knew when to throw in the cards. Besides, Marine officers go where they're sent and follow orders without protesting. "That won't be necessary, Dr. Spencer. I'll do what I can. But thank you."

"Good, glad that's out of the way," Klegg said. "Because for now you're the senior American officer on this mission. Since you will be the one calling the shots, I will break all the rules and inform you of everything that's happened. The political ramifications may be as serious as the alien arrival. The more you know and understand what's at stake, the better you'll function up there. You will, of course, keep everything you hear to yourself. Understood?"

"Yes, Sir."

Klegg leaned back in his chair, a big smile on his face. Delano took that as a bad sign. When smiling superior officers revealed more than necessary about an operation, the unlucky junior officer usually ends up getting screwed.

"Sit back and relax, Captain." Klegg glanced at his watch. "It all started about twenty-four hours ago, just beyond Jupiter's moons. Instruments on the ISS detected the first signs of alien life. Less than three hours later, I received a call from the scientists at the Station. I'll pick up the story from there, so pay attention. We don't have time to waste."

Chapter 3

Day Zero: 02:09 a.m. – Washington, D.C.

After he ended the call to the Station, General Klegg put his head in his hands and thought about what this news meant. He wanted to believe it was all a mistake, but three level-headed, highly intelligent, and coolly objective trained scientists had just informed him that alien forces with unknown intentions had invaded the solar system. He stopped himself. Better not to think of this as an invasion. Their intentions might still be peaceful, though Klegg had trouble squaring that with the space battle.

All the same, when two sides fought, innocent bystanders often took the greatest casualties. These spacecraft had appeared out of nowhere and could move at speeds that Earth's engineers considered theoretical. If the intruders possessed weapons in proportion to their speed capability, their arrival presented a real danger.

Klegg recalled the lesson of Admiral Perry opening up Tokyo in 1854. Perry sailed into Tokyo harbor with his modern gunships, and the Japanese understood he had the fire-power to level the city to the ground. They'd swallowed their pride and signed the treaty that opened up the mysterious Land of the Rising Sun to the outside world. Japan's rulers had no choice. Klegg wondered if planet Earth now faced the same situation.

He reached over and pushed a button on his secure landline. His aide would be waiting at the office, no doubt curious since the call had lasted so long. Mitchell answered on the first ring.

"Major Mitchell, tell my staff to report to my office as soon as possible. No delays or excuses. And tell them to cancel any plans they might have for the next few days."

General Klegg's personal staff consisted of two lieutenants, two sergeants, and a corporal in addition to Major Mitchell. "Send a car with an armed driver to my house immediately." Klegg didn't want to drive or take a service, not with this running through his head. Besides, he could use the time to think. "And get General Crammer and Colonel Reyes in ASAP." Army General Crammer was G-1, head of personnel for the Joint Chiefs, while Reyes was Acting G-3, an operations man. "Have them meet me at my office in . . . four hours."

"Yes, Sir," Mitchell answered. "Are you coming in, Sir?"

"Not yet, Major. I have a stop to make first. Hurry up with that car."

He broke the connection, checked the download process, and found it almost complete. The data flowed directly to a thumb drive attached to the phone. Klegg removed the drive and plugged it into his computer.

Colonel Welsh had organized the data in an orderly fashion, with the four minutes of optical video of the battle first, followed by the same four minutes in infra-red. Klegg had worked with infra-red displays, and that file showed the battle with greater clarity. Welsh had it right, they were space ships, it was a battle, and the little guys won the fight. But sixty percent casualties, plus possible damage to the two survivors, didn't give the victors anything to boast about.

Klegg watched the action again, then began studying the data. The doorbell ringing interrupted his analysis. He moved down the hall, bumping into his half-asleep housekeeper. She wanted to know why he was up in the middle of the night. He told her to go back to bed, that he had to work. He opened the door to find a standard grey Air Force sedan waiting at the curb of his Alexandria, Virginia home. A young sergeant saluted, even though Klegg still wore his pajamas.

"Wait in the car, son. I'll be out in ten minutes."

It was closer to fifteen. Klegg washed his face, shaved, and put on his uniform. Then he used the private phone again, this time to dial a number that he had to look up on a card that he carried in his wallet at all times. The phone answered on the second ring. "White House. How may I help you?"

"This is General Langdon Klegg from the Joint Chiefs." He added his service number before she could ask. "Please wake the President. I need to speak to him."

"One minute, General."

Her voice sounded pleasant and unruffled, as if calls to wake the President in the middle of the night were routine. She would first run the voice analyzer to verify his identity, then check the emergency call list, to see if General Klegg had immediate access to the president. That relatively short list didn't take long to search. "I've sent someone to awaken the President, General Klegg."

Klegg didn't know exactly what the protocol was, but no doubt you didn't just ring the president's bedside phone. Some Secret Service agent was probably knocking on the bedroom door, while other agents verified Klegg's current location. He glanced at his watch. Nearly three minutes elapsed before the president's voice, hoarse and dry, sounded in his ear.

"What is it, General Klegg?"

"Mr. President, I need to brief you immediately on something urgent. I suggest you have your National Security Advisor with you." At this time of night, Klegg could get to the White House, less than nine miles away, in twenty minutes. He gave himself a cushion. "I'll be there in thirty minutes."

"This can't wait until morning? What's the problem?'

"This is an unsecured line, Mr. President. It's critical and immediate. Please send a car for Dr. Spencer."

Doctor Vivian Spencer had been National Security Advisor for only three months, replacing Anthony Krimmer who had died of a heart attack.

"Alright, Klegg. This better be important."

"It is, Sir. I'm on my way now. Thank you, Sir."

The line went dead. *What an idiot! No, Mr. President, I enjoy waking you up in the middle of the night, just to piss you off and ruin my career. Asshole.* Klegg glanced again at his watch. He had just enough time to brush his teeth and tell the housekeeper – his wife had died almost five years earlier – he didn't know when he'd be back. None of his three grown children happened to be visiting, which might be a good thing. He'd try to contact them in the morning. There might not be time later.

*   *   *

Day Zero: 03:12 a.m. – Washington, D.C

Klegg arrived at the White House four minutes late. An accident, complete with roadside flares, flashing red lights, and the highway police had slowed his driver. When they reached the first security checkpoint two blocks from the White House, two guards checked Klegg's identification while another three inspected the vehicle.

Satisfied, they directed the driver to the underground entrance to the complex.

Klegg didn't mind the delays, as they gave him more time to think. He'd started the military machine in motion. Glancing over notes he'd made during the drive, he thought about the coming meeting. His country might be in danger, and he doubted whether the President was up to the task. Nevertheless, before the country could react to an unforeseen threat, the political infrastructure had to be established. Threatened by a potential danger, the initial response usually proved the most critical.

President Mathew M. Clark had won the office two years ago with a big smile, good looks, wonderful sound bites, and a decent economy behind him. The Washington insiders called him the latest in a line of Bill Clinton clones − he never offended anyone, had something for everyone, and always checked the polls before making any decisions. Everyone called him a clever politician. No one claimed he was very intelligent.

Klegg pictured how this president, left to himself, would deal with the situation. On national TV he'd flash his reassuring smile and announce that he had empaneled a blue-ribbon committee, one that represented all political parties and with enough diversity to placate everyone. No doubt in a few months the committee would issue a twenty thousand word document giving everyone credit for something. Klegg shook his head. Not if he could help it. The fate of his country, perhaps even the world, might depend on what happened in the next few hours, maybe days.

Klegg's car reached the underground checkpoint to the White House, where military guards again halted the vehicle. He and the driver got out and stood there, as a second team of specialists searched the car. Only when they finished did two Secret Service agents start on General Klegg. They checked his ID, scanned his retinas, matched his fingerprints, and verified his voice. Then they searched him.

Satisfied that he didn't have any weapons, canisters of nerve gas, or poisoned needles, they escorted him into the lower entrance. An elevator lifted them to the second level and the agents escorted Klegg to the President's briefing room. That turned out to be a small conference room a few steps from the Oval Office.

Dr. Spencer arrived at nearly the same time, though she

obviously hadn't entered the White House in the same way as Klegg. Vivian Spencer, age thirty-seven, had found time to put on a matching skirt and sweater. Her hair looked a little rushed. She possessed the usual doctorate in political science and assorted other teaching credentials from Harvard. Her strengths, if any, lay in the soft sciences, not in national security. Rumors said that she provided the President with additional and very personal services beyond her current position.

Washington buzz considered her a lightweight for the job, but President Clark had wanted a woman to carry on the tradition established years ago by Condoleezza Rice. Even so, no one compared Spencer to Rice, at least not favorably. Klegg had spoken with her twice before, at Washington socials. She came across well enough. He felt certain he'd know more about her strengths and skills before the night was over.

The President arrived a few minutes later, dressed in a sweatshirt and jeans, and wearing slippers. He hadn't shaved and his hair needed combing. Medium height, he appeared even more paunchy around the waist than he did on TV. His plain face, enhanced by dark rimmed glasses, looked irritated. No sign of the trademark big smile and nodding head. He carried a bottle of mineral water.

A tray holding carafes of coffee and water rested on a side table, along with cookies in case anyone, especially the President, got hungry. Spencer headed straight for the coffee, and Klegg accepted her offer to pour him a cup, though the President declined. A Secret Service agent glanced around the room, then stepped outside. He would be on the other side of the door, ready to jump in at the President's signal or the first sound of trouble.

"This better be urgent, General." President Clark sounded annoyed. "I was sound asleep."

Klegg, busy loading the data on the thumb drive into the computer that controlled the projector, ignored the comment. "I'll show you the details while I'm explaining what's happened. It's a First Contact situation."

The President was slower on the uptake than his security advisor. "First Contact?" Vivian Spencer's voice rose. "What type of First Contact?"

"The astronauts aboard the International Space Station recorded this activity less than . . ." Klegg checked at his watch, "less than five hours ago. This same information is already on its way to Star City in Russia."

File folders appeared on the monitor. With a tap of his finger, Klegg opened one and projected its contents onto the viewing screen.

"Instruments monitoring Jupiter's internal activity captured these images of alien spacecraft. We have the data in infra-red and X-ray as well as optical." Klegg carefully stepped his way through the data. He took his time, since he had only seen it once before and didn't want to say anything that the recorded data didn't confirm.

Klegg kept talking while the images and data projected, wanting to get through the initial brief before his small audience recovered enough to begin their questions. But his presentation took less than ten minutes. Based on the data, he didn't have much to say.

"So, Mr. President, these two surviving spacecraft, having defeated a larger sized vessel, are now roaming our solar system. The attacking ship, by the way, felt strong and confident enough to pursue and assault five separate targets simultaneously. The smaller ships may have gotten lucky. Our best estimate at this time is that the survivors are heading toward the inner planets, probably Mars. Where they'll go after that is conjecture at this time. These spacecraft have enormously powerful engines. Their power plants are emitting enough energy to be tracked all the way from Jupiter to Mars. Colonel Welsh's rough estimate is that these vessels are physically large as well, possibly double the size of our biggest freighter. That would make them about a hundred to two hundred meters long, and weight upwards of nine thousand tons. That's larger than a missile cruiser. If they decide to visit Earth after Mars, they could arrive in sixty hours or so, if they can repeat their demonstrated rate of speed."

While letting that sink in, Klegg rose and poured himself another cup of coffee, this time adding fresh cream and a good spoonful of sugar. He needed all the energy he could get for the next few hours.

"You say the Russians are being notified?" Dr. Spencer sounded even more peevish than the President. "Who authorized that?"

Unfortunately for her, the first crisis on her watch had turned out to be a nightmare. They both knew, as Klegg did, that military protocol required that the Russians and the Chinese receive immediate notification of something like this under the terms of the

Alliance. The three major military powers had created the Alliance more than twenty years ago, to stop worldwide unrest and keep the planet from plunging into chaos. Each power had its own recognized sphere of influence, and any nation destabilizing the world order ended up on the wrong end of a ruthless and combined force. Despite many challenges and occasional differences, mutual self-interest held the agreement together. The idea that now the United States would withhold critical information from its joint partners was ridiculous on its face.

Klegg had a flash of insight. In the next few days, a lot of people would make fools of themselves as they tried to grasp what was happening. There would be many stupid questions, even from those supposedly smart enough to understand the implications. This First Contact would require a leap in comprehension that not everyone would achieve.

"Dr. Spencer," he answered gently, "I authorized the release. It *is* an International Space Station, the sighting was initially observed by a Russian Colonel, and the entire Station team agreed to distribute the data to their two governments simultaneously. Besides, there was no sense in issuing an order that wouldn't . . . couldn't be obeyed. The astronauts understand very well the significance of this information. That's why they spoke to me as a group, and that's why they'll do the same with the Russians."

"So these spaceships just appeared out near Jupiter? And now they're headed for Mars?" President Clark's voice had jumped an octave. "Why didn't they just go there first?" His mind rambled as well.

Klegg decided that he had been right to keep the first Presidential briefing small. Better to let the President make a fool of himself privately, instead of in front of a room full of people.

"Mr. President, I can't answer that one. Perhaps they couldn't travel directly to Mars orbit. Maybe they had to arrive near Jupiter for some reason we don't understand."

"They must have come from some place, didn't they?" Dr. Spencer asked. "I mean, they couldn't just appear out of nowhere. Maybe they came from some planet beyond Pluto? NASA keeps finding new dwarf planets all the time."

They were both still in denial. The only planets, dwarf or otherwise, beyond Pluto's orbit were frozen rocks. But Klegg knew better than to point that out. "I suppose they could have. However, after they appeared on our instruments, they moved at very high velocity up and above the planetary belt. If they were coming from within our solar system, they would probably have stayed within the planetary plane."

Klegg took another sip of coffee. He needed to be sympathetic but not condescending. "So I'm guessing they appeared somehow near Jupiter, and after the fight they decided to head for the inner planets. Mars would be the logical first stop, since its orbit is a bit closer to Jupiter right now. Both Mars and Earth are on the same side of the sun at this time."

"And you have no idea where they came from? Or what their intentions are?" The President's questions sounded like a challenge to Klegg's competency, almost as if Klegg had created this situation.

Klegg let that pass, too. No sense reminding them that the sighting occurred only hours ago. "No, Sir, not yet. But the scientists aboard the Station were very precise in their language. The instruments were monitoring Jupiter. One second there was just normal activity. Suddenly a strange energy source affected the instruments, then the ships appeared. Since they've arrived, we haven't had any problem tracking them."

"That doesn't mean they couldn't have come from some secret Chinese or Russian base where ..."

"Mr. President," Klegg interrupted, not wanting to waste more time on a discussion with no answers. "Even if they were Chinese or Russian, why would they fight each other? They didn't come from any planets in the solar system. I'm sure that Dr. Spencer will confirm that. They're not from Earth, because no nation has engines capable of such speed and maneuverability. Once we accept those premises, it doesn't really matter where they came from, does it? I think we should concentrate on what we're going to do if they come here next. We might be wasting valuable time trying to figure out their origins." He kept his voice soft, his tone reasonable.

If the President realized he was being handled, he didn't show it. Instead, he turned to his science advisor. "What do you think, Vivian? Is all this making sense?"

"Not completely. I'd like to study the data. There are people at NASA who can analyze this, see if it's real or not. But they are probably not the best people to respond to this situation."

The President looked at her. Klegg knew she had been considered a long-shot for the post, almost a political payoff. Or maybe she was just another mistress. But girl friend or not, Clark recognized a stall when he heard one.

"What about the UN?" The President continued to clutch at straws. "Didn't they implement some protocols for these situations?"

After getting kicked out of New York, the UN had become a half-empty gathering hall for second rate nations, with almost no political or military clout. None of the Alliance countries bothered to remain members.

"I've reviewed those First Contact protocols, Mr. President," Klegg said. "They consider only situations where we receive extraterrestrial signals from space. There's nothing about this type of encounter."

"OK, then, what do you think, General?"

Klegg decided Clark had run out of ideas. "Mr. President, Doctor Spencer is right. We have to analyze the data in great detail, and more data will be coming from the Space Station." He took a deep breath. "However I think you need to think about the national security issues first. We may not have much time. When this story breaks, and it will break soon, you'll want to go on the air and announce how you've prepared for this situation. I would recommend setting up a security team to control access to the data while we get the pieces in place. Once you give it to NASA, you might as well announce it to the press."

The President knew all about NASA's poor security. He looked at his now empty bottle of water and pushed it aside. "You've obviously thought about this longer than we have. What would those pieces be, General?"

"We want to put together a team of experts to back up the military. We'll have to work closely with the Russians, the Chinese, and NASA. Total security will be required at first, to prevent civil panic. We'll also have to get the military ready, in case these aliens are hostile. Basically, I believe it's essential to setup a 'Manhattan' type project to manage all aspects of this new situation."

"If these are aliens," Doctor Spencer offered, "why should we assume they came to attack Earth? Why should we jump to that conclusion?"

"These aliens have powerful weapons, Doctor. They've already used them inside our solar system. I certainly hope they are peaceful, because I don't think there's much we can do to stop them. A particle beam from space, with plenty of power behind it, could do a lot of damage."

Klegg paused to sip his coffee. "Whatever their intentions, we have to deal in capabilities. Maybe we can't even touch them. But it wouldn't hurt to line up as many satellite killer missiles as possible, and see if we can launch some small tactical nukes by aircraft from high altitude." He shrugged. "I haven't thought much about that yet. One thing I'm sure of, we can't keep this a secret for long. But if we can control the information for two or three days, we can have something in place if they come here. And before the media get it. After that, there may be panic in the streets, a massive exodus from the cities, a run on the banks, and the stock market will plummet. Worldwide chaos will follow."

The President looked grimmer now. "Who should head up this new project, General? Are you asking for it?"

All three knew the Chairman of the Joint Chiefs was about to retire. General Stimson had been nearly too old when he took the job. His five year term ended in three months. But many in the military, including Stimson, considered Klegg too young to be his replacement.

Klegg took his time before answering. "Mr. President, that's up to you. Perhaps Dr. Spencer can advise you." He had been waiting for an opening like that. "If you want me to do it, Mr. President, it's got to be done right. That means complete authority and full powers, up to and including martial law, if need be. The situation won't be pretty and it may get downright ugly."

The President turned back to his National Security Advisor. "What do you think, Vivian?"

This time she was ready. "Mr. President, whoever you appoint will have to work with NASA and should understand the science as much as possible. I think you want someone from the military. That will reassure the country. The Air Force has always collaborated with both NASA and the NSA. I don't think the Navy, the Marines, or the Army should take the lead."

General Klegg admired how smoothly Vivian passed the buck back to the President. She realized that her own career was now on the line. If the aliens turned out to be trouble, her neck might be on the chopping block. Regardless of what went on behind closed doors between the two of them, Klegg knew the President wouldn't hesitate to throw her under the bus.

Vivian Spencer looked up, not at the President, but at Klegg before she went on. "General Klegg has taken the right steps so far. He's brought it to our attention and sealed up the Station. He is the ranking Air Force member of the Chiefs. I think you should put General Klegg in charge. We don't have much time. Of course we can monitor and advise him."

Or replace him whenever we want. Neatly done, Klegg thought. She's not stupid, and realizes she's over her head. He had backed her earlier, and so now she returned the favor – the old Washington two-step.

But Klegg didn't intend to dance. "If I take this assignment, Mr. President, that means I call all the shots until we know what we're dealing with. My first order would be that you don't tell anyone, not your wife, not any of your advisors, not your best friend without my approval. If this leaks out before we're ready, it will precipitate a crisis, one you'll have to deal with."

The President didn't like it, but he knew all about leaks from the White House. He could already feel the press cameras in his face. For something like this, he had no one else to advise him. But he could always change his mind later if it came to that. If anything went wrong, Klegg could take the blame. "OK, General, you're it. I'll tell no one. What do we do next?"

Klegg had the list in his head. "First, can you call Director Summers at the FBI and tell him to report to my office. Right now. Tonight. We'll need the Bureau to implement security around the personnel we'll be bringing onboard. Second, I'll take Doctor Spencer back to the Pentagon. She can help me set up the staff and coordinate the requisite NSA resources. Third, I suggest you talk to China as soon as possible. They may not be aware of this situation and if so, it's important they learn about it from you. After you deliver the bad news, refer them to me or Doctor Spencer for more details and a copy of the data. Meanwhile, I'm sure General Demidov is getting his ducks lined up for a visit to the Russian Premier. You'll need to talk to them, too, when you finish with the Chinese leader. By then, I hope to have a plan ready that you can share with him. It's essential that both China and Russia understand the need for security, and how to handle the leaks that will inevitably begin in a few days." He stopped and took another breath. "I expect that Doctor Spencer or I can give you a full briefing later in the day, say around 1 p.m. if that's alright."

"OK, General. I'm not happy, but I don't seem to have a lot of choice in the matter. Let me know who I can bring to the briefing. If there's nothing else, I'm sure you want to be on your way." He stood. "God help us all." He nodded to Vivian and left the briefing room.

Klegg looked at Spencer. "Let's go, Doctor. We can take my car and talk on the way." He removed the portable drive from the computer, deleted the temporary file and shut the machine down, a process that automatically wiped the drive. The sequence would be repeated the next time the computer booted up.

As they left the White House, Klegg had a nerve-wracking thought. For the next few days, he would be one of the most powerful persons in the country. Still, it would only be for a few days, and he could manage that well enough. If the crisis worsened, he might be the one taking all the blame. But in his heart, he knew he was the best man for the job. He remembered the astronaut's prayer – *Dear God, please don't let me fuck up.*

By the time they reached Klegg's office, his staff had arrived. Since they had to know the truth, he stepped them through the material, to bring them up to speed. Doctor Spencer watched as attentively as she had the first time. At least nobody asked dumb questions. Military personnel understood the implications and the nuances.

Meanwhile Klegg revised his opinion of Dr. Spencer. She knew when to shut up, and listen. Her questions concerned specifics and her suggestions made sense. Maybe the President had lucked out in selecting her after all.

It was nearly 5:00 a.m. before Klegg called the Chairman of the Joint Chiefs, General Stimpson, waking him and inviting him to the 1:00 p.m. briefing. Stimpson demanded to know what was going on, but Klegg refused to tell him, citing Presidential orders. Klegg didn't trust even the Chairman to keep this quiet. When Stimpson found out, he would try to take charge, and Klegg wanted the FBI in place before that power struggle began.

As that conversation wrapped up, FBI Director Mark Summers arrived. He looked more like an investment banker than the nation's number one cop. Two of his senior aides accompanied him, which was just as well, as the top-tier FBI field agents had to know everything. Klegg finished briefing them at 6:15 a.m. He then called the Strategic Air Command at Offutt Air Force Base in Nebraska.

U.S. Space Command headquartered there, having been merged with the Strategic Command into an expanded STRATCOM. General Malcolm S. Brown happened to be an early riser, so despite the one hour time difference, Klegg knew General Brown would be awake. Another three-star, Brown and Klegg had worked together in the past. As commander of STRATCOM, General Brown had a secure phone at his home.

"Good morning, Mal, this is Klegg. I need your help."

"Hey, Lang, isn't this pretty early for you? I just got out of the shower. I thought you liked to sleep late."

"I haven't been to bed yet, Mal. I've just come from the White House. The President has created a special project and placed me in charge. I need you to start pulling it together as of now. Drop whatever else you're doing or turn it over to your deputy. I want everything that can launch a missile at a space-borne, high-orbit target ready to go. I want both nuclear warheads and regular HE. Ground and sea-based as well as air lofted. Everything you can get your hands on, and I don't care which branch of the service has what you need. Anybody tries to slow-boat you or hold anything back, tell them I'll have them relieved of duty within the hour. You've got about thirty hours to be fully operational. Start the ball rolling, then get down to Washington ASAP."

Silence for a moment. "Jeez, Lang, I assume you've got authority for this order?"

"Dr. Spencer is here with me. I'll put her on the line to verify what the President authorized. Then you can call the President direct to get his confirmation."

"I surely will, Lang. Do you want bomber command in on this, too?"

"No. No bombs, no submarines, no ground troops. Just missiles that can track orbital targets and anything that can launch them."

"What's going on in space? Are the Chinese doing something?"

"No, but thanks for reminding me. You may be coordinating

with the Russians and Chinese on this." He paused. "General Brown, I am formally ordering you to keep this information strictly to yourself. You tell no one, and I mean no one. It's a First Contact situation."

"Jeez! Are you sure? I mean . . ."

"I know what you mean, Malcolm. Cut the necessary orders to get everyone in motion. I want you at the Pentagon by 1:00 p.m. for a briefing. President Clark will be there. Figure you'll be in that meeting for about two or three hours. So you haven't got much time."

"Yes, Sir. I'm on my way. Does this project have a name?"

Damn. The first detail Klegg had forgotten, but probably not the last. "Not really. But I guess we'd better give it one." He didn't want to waste time getting a computer-generated moniker. Two non-related, never-used words were required. "Let's call it Operation Sentinel Star for now."

"Sentinel Star it is. Thanks, General Klegg. I'll see you later. Now if you don't mind, please let me speak to Doctor Spencer to confirm this."

With the military part of the operation underway, Klegg and Spencer tackled NASA. First they placed a call to the Space Station to discuss the cover story with Colonel Welsh. Klegg understood NASA and its bureaucratic ways, having dealt with them for years. As far as NASA knew, a communications problem had cropped up with the Station but everything was all right. By now the NASA communications team would be getting antsy about being out of contact. Klegg grabbed one of the FBI agents and ordered him to go get Ted McChesney, NASA's Administrator.

"Find him. No matter where he is or what he's doing, pick him up and have him here by 11:00 a.m."

McChesney wouldn't like the preemptory summons nor the way he received the news about his own station, but Klegg didn't care about his feelings. NASA would likely turn into a major stumbling block in this whole process. Klegg wanted to make sure McChesney knew where he stood in the pecking order, and that there would be no leaks, none, or a new person would immediately be appointed to head NASA.

By 9:00 a.m. a squad of twenty more FBI agents was in place. None knew exactly what was happening, but that didn't matter for their initial duties. Klegg's office had been secured, and some agents already had their assignments. Klegg and Spencer began drawing up The List (it immediately acquired capital letters even in conversation) of everyone who needed to know what was going on.

Anyone on The List who could not be completely trusted would have an FBI officer permanently assigned, who would stay with the individual at all times. This "bodyguard" would serve as an official reminder of what might happen if the information leaked out. No one was permitted to notify their significant other, let alone "suggest" family members take a vacation to the countryside.

The FBI also handled another mundane but necessary task. With their usual efficiency, they moved everyone else out of Klegg's wing of the Pentagon. About twenty offices would be freed up, including those of two generals, both furious at being evicted.

Klegg had discussed that part of the effort with the FBI Director. The move would be covered as a security issue, and the unwilling occupants would be relocated off the floor for a few days. Meanwhile, they were ordered to say and do nothing that might call attention to the fact that this relocation had occurred. Klegg wanted to make certain everyone understood the concept completely, and hearing it from the FBI Chief personally would reinforce the need for security.

Finally, Klegg leaned back in his chair, taking his first break. The wheels had started to turn and trusted staff members had begun analyzing the data. Now he just had to keep it in motion and hope for the best. If this visitation from space turned into a conflict, he knew the best organized side usually had the advantage. He intended to make sure the Alliance had prepared as much as possible.

He glanced at his watch: 10:15 a.m. The alien story might go public at any moment, but Klegg guessed he had a few days to get the country, and the Alliance, ready. The next forty-eight hours promised to be interesting. Once word leaked out, the shit would hit the fan. *Dear God, please don't let me fuck up.*

Chapter 4

Day Zero – 11:05 a.m. EST – The Pentagon

General Klegg had a small conference room adjacent to his office, convenient for informal gatherings. Carafes of water and a coffee wagon stood in one corner. By 11:05 a.m., a good sized crowd filled the chamber. Dr. Vivian Spencer, representing the President, sat next to Klegg at the head of the table. His aide, Major John Mitchell, sat at the opposite end, ready to follow up on any new developments. On either side of Mitchell sat two more of Klegg's aides, Lt. Foster, and Sergeant Navarro.

General Crammer (Army, G-1) and Colonel Reyes (Army, Acting G-3) sat side by side, facing Dr. Spencer. Around 7:00 a.m. both had received a quick briefing on the First Contact situation. Admiral Arthur Goodwin, Director of the NSA, took the chair next to his boss, Dr. Spencer. Director Summers of the FBI sat opposite Admiral Goodwin.

Dr. Ted McChesney, NASA's Director, was the last to arrive, looking dismal and clutching a Styrofoam cup in one hand. NASA's headquarters was right here in Washington, but McChesney had been lecturing in Chicago. The FBI had picked him up in mid speech and flown him to D.C. But whatever complaints he might have had died in silence, after one look at the somber faces in the room.

"Please sit down, Dr. McChesney," Klegg began without preamble. "We need to brief you on a First Contact situation monitored by the ISS about twelve hours ago." He gave the Head of NASA a few seconds to digest the words.

"First Contact . . . what do you mean . . ."

"This will go faster if you hold your questions, Dr. McChesney," Klegg interrupted. "We have a lot of ground to cover, and I'm holding a conference call with the Chinese and Russians at 12:00 noon. Also Dr. Spencer will brief the President, General Stimson, and General Brown at one p.m."

Klegg gave him the entire story, the call from the ISS, his transfer of command from Susan York to Lt. Colonel Welsh, the meeting with the President, and the President's calls to Moscow and Beijing. Major Mitchell projected the visual and infra-red sightings on the conference room monitor, then replayed it. Everyone else in the room had seen the data earlier, but each wanted a second or third look.

When Mitchell finished the projection, McChesney, a stunned look on his face, slumped back in his chair. "Why wasn't I told about this? This is NASA's responsibility. I should have been informed first, immediately."

"You weren't told, Dr. McChesney, because everyone, including the personnel on the ISS, knows that NASA cannot keep a secret." Klegg made it matter-of-fact, nothing personal. "You're only being brought in now because we need NASA's expertise to analyze the data more thoroughly, and because Director Summers has had time to establish security procedures."

"I resent that comment, General. NASA has a long history . . ."

"Resent whatever you like, McChesney, but as of this moment, you are under my authority, part of Operation Sentinel Star and subject to its security. You will tell no one what you have just heard and seen."

Klegg leaned forward and locked eyes with McChesney. "Let me make that very clear: no one. We are relying on you to identify the top three or four scientists who, for now, can best understand what this data means. We want their names, and the FBI will bring them here as soon as possible. Director Summers has an agent waiting outside, who will remain with you every minute of every day until this information is released to the public. If you attempt to inform anyone – and I mean anyone – you will be immediately fired from your position. If you do reveal any information, either by accident or design, you will be arrested and sent to prison. Do you understand me, Doctor?"

"You don't have the authority . . ."

"Dr. McChesney," Vivian Spencer broke in, "the President has given General Klegg full authority under the Emergency Powers Act. Speaking for President Clark, we expect this situation to become public in a few days, a week at most, so this isn't an undue hardship. Until then, by the President's directive, you will follow General Klegg's orders. If you can't do that, please say so now. You will be removed from NASA and held incommunicado until it no longer matters."

Klegg hid a smile as he leaned back in his chair. Spencer was learning fast. "Do you understand the consequences, Dr. McChesney? And spare me the protests and indignation. A simple yes or no will suffice."

McChesney glanced around the table but found no sympathy on anyone's face. He swallowed, perhaps choking on his pride. "Yes, I understand."

"Excellent, Doctor." Klegg could afford to be polite. "Now if you please, will you accompany Sergeant Navarro to Major Mitchell's office, where you can prepare a list of NASA specialists we want to bring in on Operation Sentinel Star. Please be certain they are the top experts in their fields, not friends or cronies. You and they will be making important decisions in the next few days, and we need the best advice possible. Also we must know what launch capability NASA has available ASAP. We have to get nine people up to the Station immediately, tomorrow if possible. After you finish with Sergeant Navarro, you'll be given an office here at the Pentagon, for yourself and your security agent. Thank you. Carry on, Sergeant."

"Yes, General." Sergeant Navarro rose. A few seconds passed before McChesney realized he'd been dismissed.

Klegg waited until the door closed behind them. "Good. At least we've taken care of NASA. Now, what have we got for the Chinese and Russians?"

"We've put together a preliminary plan," Colonel Reyes of G-3 said. His pencil-thin black mustache contrasted with his slick graying hair, making him appear younger than his sixty-odd years. "Our air defense forces are ramping up and should be in training mode within the next few hours. Supplies, missiles, support teams, and aircraft are being moved into optimum locations to launch warheads. If Colonel Welsh's estimates regarding the alien vessels are correct, we have two or three days to put our forces in position. Since we don't know what the aliens will do, we've worked with the Russians to defend as much of planet Earth as we can. But the Chinese resources will be needed."

"I'll cover that in the conference call," Klegg said. "What about the Station? Who are we sending up there?"

"We've searched through the personnel databases," General

Crammer, G-1, replied.

Trim and fit, Crammer had moved up the ranks through several combat assignments. He'd last commanded the 101st Airborne Division at Fort Campbell. For the last two years Crammer had developed and executed manpower plans for the Joint Chiefs. "The first and most critical people we want at the Station are linguists. If we can't communicate with these aliens, we're in deep trouble. My recommendation is that we send three linguists to the Station. One should be fluent in European-based dialects, one in Russian and Slavic, and one in Asian. If we have experts in those three language bases, we should have a good shot at communicating. Assuming they communicate via a spoken language, of course."

"Even if they don't," Klegg said, "these people are still experts in communication, and should be able to interact somehow with the aliens. What about all our language translation software? Can those applications help?"

"The people who know those programs best are the linguists," General Crammer said. "They will identify which platforms to utilize."

Klegg nodded. "Who do we have?"

"Our database produced half a dozen names and we're checking their suitability now," Crammer said. "We may have to exclude some for various factors. For example, those with health problems or anyone whose genes indicate a potential problem with zero gravity. Unless you want me to search the civilian language schools?"

"No, no civilians, not yet," Klegg said. "I definitely prefer a member of the military, if we can find one qualified."

"Good. Hopefully we'll dig up a few," General Crammer said. "Meanwhile, please ask the Chinese and Russians to assign their own linguist immediately. I'm also recommending an expert in both modern and obsolete communications."

Crammer referred to his notes. "We'll need highly secure links from the Station to the Pentagon and wherever else we want in on the dialogs. Also this expert might be able to tap into whatever communications technique the aliens use for their ship to ship. Fortunately, we have a young Sergeant working right here in Washington, D.C., at the NSA. Admiral Goodwin knows the man."

The Admiral in charge of the National Security Agency nodded agreement. "Steve Macey, Army Sergeant First Class, Electronics Command. He's young, but he's the best, General," Admiral Goodwin said. "A bit of a nerd, but he can hack into anything we've got. Hardware, software, communications, equipment, he knows it all. We were lucky to get him at NSA."

"OK, who else?"

"Colonel Reyes and I think that we may need some shooters on the Station," Crammer said. "After all, we'll be trying to extract information from these aliens. Who's to say that they won't want to just take over the Station and start learning all about us? There will be some highly technical personnel up there. I don't think we want them to fall under alien influence, physically or mentally."

At least not alive. Klegg drummed his fingers on the table while he thought about that. The G-1 was correct. Those people could not be allowed to be captured alive by the aliens. As a last resort, the Station might have to be destroyed. "Damn. That means weapons and explosives, plus the will and expertise to use them. I don't like it, but we have to protect the Station. How many additional staff are we talking about?"

Colonel Reyes checked his notes. "We also want a medical doctor. Don't forget, a lot of the specialists we want to send up there have never been in space before, let alone a zero gravity environment. And I'd like a navigator, someone who can track orbits, read star charts, and maybe figure out where the hell these aliens came from. Their celestial maps won't look anything like ours. One of our first priorities should be finding out their origins."

Reyes paused to sip some coffee. "Also, we would like someone skilled in cultural anthropology. We need to understand as much as possible about our visitors, and their behavior and physiology may tell us a lot. So in total, we think we need to send up nine people."

"How many can that Station support at one time? I know it's a big ship, but . . ."

"It's not that big, General Klegg," Reyes said. "With all the instruments and ongoing experiments up there, the maximum recommended crew is ten. Maybe twelve in a pinch. Ten is all the escape shuttle can carry in the event they have to bail. So our nine plus the five already in place, that's fourteen. The Station's air supply will be stretched. If something breaks down . . ."

"Can we relieve any of the present staff?" Klegg glanced at his own notes, examining the ISS roster.

"Commander Susan York's specialty is deep space research and solar activity," General Crammer said, "so it's not likely she'll be needed. We should pull her out. But the others include an astrophysicist, a flight engineer, and Colonel Welsh, who is the backup mission commander. All three are highly qualified and already accustomed to a zero gravity environment. We would need those fields of expertise anyway."

"What about the biologist, Parrish? Do we need him?" Klegg sounded doubtful. "He's just a kid, right?

"Yes, only eighteen, but he's very smart and he's there. We think a biologist might be useful in identifying what kind of planet these aliens are from," Crammer said, "you know, living conditions, food, water and atmosphere. Dr. Darrell Parrish is one of the best anybody's got, and he's a quick learner as well. If we can manage the numbers, Reyes and I recommend he stay. Otherwise he's the next to cut."

Klegg shrugged. "So what does the new T.O. look like?"

The Table of Organization was the official roster for the project. General Crammer passed out a sheet of paper to everyone.

Current ISS Staff:

Commander Susan York, NASA	- Original Mission Cmdr. (relieved)
Col. William Welsh, USAF	- Current Mission Cmdr. & Science Spc.
Col. Nikolai Kosloff, Russia	- Flight Engineer
Col. Maksim Mironov, Russia	- Astrophysicist
Darrell Parrish, NASA/UK	- Biologist

New Personnel:

Unknown, USA	- European Linguist
Unknown	- Asian Linguist
Alexi Stepanov, Russia	- Linguist
Sgt. Steve Macey, US Army	- Communications specialist
Demitri Petrov, Russia	- Cultural anthropologist
Sgt. Jack Stecker, USMC	- Weapons/explosive spec.
Unknown	- Weapons / explosive spec.
Unknown	- Medical officer

Unknown   -   Solar / Celestial navigator

"To summarize," Crammer said, "we recommend sending up nine people, and pulling out Susan York. That gives us thirteen in total. Conditions will be very tight, but workable. At least for the short term."

Klegg studied the roster. "Who is Alexi Stepanov?

"A professor at the Russian Language School in St. Petersburg," Crammer said. "One of the best in the world. He's had some flight training, but no space experience. We think the Russians would select him anyway."

"And Demitri Petrov?"

"Another Russian. World famous anthropologist. Specializes in socio-cultural studies, archeological research – he has supervised several worldwide digs around the globe and in Russia – and knows quite a bit about biology, too. Top expert in the field hands down, and he's done research for the Russian government before."

"OK, I'll ask General Demidov about them." Klegg studied the list again. "That leaves only one slot for the Chinese. They're not going to like that."

General Crammer nodded. "I agree. Maybe along with their linguist, they could provide the shooters?"

Klegg shook his head. "I don't want the only weapons on the Station in the hands of the Chinese. They can provide one shooter, plus their linguist. Maybe they could fill the medical or navigator slot."

"Not much selection in the military databases for space navigators," General Crammer observed. "Best ones for this sort of mission already work for JovCo, on the Moon to Io run."

"OK, then the Chinese can fill the medical slot." Klegg glanced around the table. "Good job putting this together, everyone. Now Dr. Spencer and I need to prepare for our conference with the Russians and Chinese." He picked up the roster and started to rise.

"One moment, General. I might have something for you." Admiral Goodwin, Director of the always secretive NSA, hadn't said much. In fact he'd been working his tablet for most of the meeting. "When Colonel Reyes mentioned JovCo, it reminded me of something I noticed yesterday. I've just contacted my office and requested a follow-up."

Admiral Goodwin took a few more moments to review his notes, then lifted his gaze. "There is something odd here, maybe just a coincidence. How many of you are aware of the ore freighter the *Lady Drake?*"

The name meant nothing to Klegg, and a glance around the table showed more blank stares.

Except for Major Mitchell. "I heard something about it, Admiral. Ore freighter on the Io run. Some space madness caused the crew to start murdering each other. During the fighting, someone accelerated the ship, burned all the fuel so there was nothing left for lunar braking. Two crew members escaped in the vessel's shuttle. The freighter was moving too fast when it reached the Moon, and JovCo had to send another shuttle loaded with nothing but fuel pellets to catch up with it. They managed the rendezvous, but it will be six to eight weeks before they and the *Lady Drake* limp back to the Moon."

"That's the official story," Admiral Goodwin agreed. "However we intercepted transmissions from the *Lady Drake's* shuttle before it reached lunar orbit, and they appeared a bit strange. The survivors onboard transmitted three highly encrypted messages directly to a law firm in New York. Very expensive use of bandwidth. That seemed odd, so our people checked JovCo's protocol. One of their strictest regulations requires that all communications from Io or ships in transit must be routed through the Company's Lunar Base for review and approval. No exceptions."

General Klegg checked his watch. "I'm not getting the connection, Admiral."

"Strictly as an exercise, some of my staff cracked the first message to the lawyer. It consisted of two files. One was a request for legal representation on behalf of the two survivors against JovCo. Apparently they had something on board, some artifact they found on Io. Accompanying the request was a video file. We haven't tried to examine the file attachment. It's quite large and decrypting video files is a tedious and resource intensive process."

Goodwin glanced at his notes. "The names of the two survivors who escaped on the shuttle are Med Tech Linda Grayson and Navigator Peter Tasco. He was third in command of the *Lady Drake*. The lawyer's name is Jerry Ullmann, of Rubio, Ullmann, and Lambert, based in New York. Very exclusive firm specializing in suing large corporations, class actions, that type of thing."

"That does seem odd," Dr. Spencer said. "If they wanted to hire a lawyer, why would they send him a long video file? And why couldn't they wait a few weeks until they reached Moon Base?"

"JovCo again." General Klegg had no love for the company. They had clashed with the Air Force before. "A slimy bunch of greedy bastards." He shook his head. "Probably no connection, but I don't like coincidences. These alien ships appeared near Jupiter, and the freighter was inbound from Io. Admiral, if you can decipher the messages the two sent, I would greatly appreciate it."

"Will do, General. I'll tell my people to crack them, and get the files to you as soon as possible. I'll make sure enough resources are assigned. Shouldn't take long."

That ended the meeting. Everyone left, except General Klegg and Dr. Vivian Spencer. They didn't have much time to prepare for the conference with the Chinese and Russians.

*   *   *

Day Zero: 12:05 p.m. – the Pentagon

The Pentagon had a secure communications facility in Sub-basement B. Constructed only six years earlier and completely sealed from the rest of the building, it offered the most secure communications within the Pentagon. However it lacked the usual comforts.

A more luxurious but similar facility existed in the White House, and a third at NSA headquarters. The State Department or Department of Defense possessed nothing to equal it. The communications staff had just completed the setup when General Klegg and Dr. Spencer arrived. They took their seats, facing the cameras and the large screen monitors. Only two screens were powered up, one connected via satellite to Beijing and the other to Star City, Moscow.

At noon, the links went active. A communications tech turned on the encryption devices, checked the readings, adjusted the microphones one last time, then left the room, closing the soundproof door behind him. As Klegg straightened his tie, the monitors started transmitting. The Chinese connection went live first.

"Good day to you, General Zeng," Klegg nodded his head just enough to show respect. "Have you seen the files our President sent to the General Secretary?"

General Zeng Weimin of the Chinese Air Force did not bother to hide his anger, or perhaps it was merely frustration. "Yes, I received them a little over an hour ago. We are still not certain that they are real. But you should have transmitted them as soon as you received them."

Zeng, looking much like the serious scholar he was, spoke fluent English, and Klegg had no problem understanding the man's irritation. The Chinese, with the largest population and strongest military forces on Earth, had received the data last. "General Zeng, as soon as I gave the information to my President, he initiated contact with your General Secretary within the hour. The delay was only a few hours, and we needed the time to implement security measures. We had no idea who should receive the files on your end. That's why I asked our President to call your General Secretary." That was as much of an apology as Klegg would give.

"The Russians received the data at the same time as you."

"Yes, because they obtained it from their scientists on the ISS. May I suggest, General Zeng, that we consider what our next steps should be. We have worked out an operation plan to send people to the ISS. That will likely be the first point of contact, should the aliens come to Earth."

The Russian monitor had come online, and Klegg saw General Demidov at his desk, the hint of a smile on his face.

"So you and Demidov have already worked out a plan," General Zeng said, "again without any input from us?"

Klegg reminded himself that people needed time to come to grips with this revelation. "That, General Zeng, is the purpose of this call. We are hoping for the full cooperation of your government. I believe, and General Demidov agrees, that the Alliance must work together to meet this crisis and time is short. Word will soon leak out, and then our governments will have to deal with that headache as well. Our National Security Director, Dr. Spencer, is here with me, and she can confirm that President Clark believes our governments should cooperate and stand united. But if you would rather make your own plans, that is your decision, of course."

"General Zeng," this time it was General Demidov who spoke, "I have just talked with our astrophysicist on the ISS Station. He and the others there are studying the data. The energy output from the alien weapons was high, powerful enough to do considerable damage to our population centers even from high orbit. I strongly urge you to work with us, to meet this situation with a unified front."

Before General Zeng could respond, the Chinese screen went dark.

On the Russian screen, General Demidov smiled and took a sip from a glass of tea. "I hope it was not something I said."

Before Klegg could reply, the Chinese screen resumed transmitting. He saw a second person taking the chair beside General Zeng's. It was the General Secretary, Liu Quisan, the leader of China.

"They must be at the Secretary's Palace," Dr. Spencer whispered.

"Good day, General Demidov, General Klegg, Dr. Spencer," Secretary Liu spoke calmly and deliberately, his English not quite as proficient or fluent as General Zeng's. He'd ruled China for the last six years. Liu looked like a leader, with his rimless glasses and straight brushed-back, black hair. "I thought it best to join the conversation. We were concerned about the delay in seeing the data, but that is no longer important. Since you have had more time, what plans have you developed?"

"Good Day, Mr. Secretary." This time Klegg bowed his head in respect to a world political leader. "First, we are preparing our joint forces for any possible assault. However, attacking ships in space is difficult, and there may be little that we can do. Naturally we need your help. Officially, we will be conducting an extended training exercise to test our ability to track and destroy missiles from space-launched platforms. Second, we wish to send a team of linguists and other experts to the ISS, to attempt communications with these aliens should they came to Earth. The Space Station will likely be their first stop."

Klegg detailed what they had done to prepare their militaries, and initiated a hunt for linguists.

Secretary Liu listened attentively until Klegg finished. "So you have not activated ground or sea forces, is that correct?"

"That is correct." Klegg turned to Demidov.

"Our Premier wished to place army units on alert," Demidov said, "but I convinced him that at this time it would not be wise. So, no, Secretary Liu, like the Americans, we have only called up our air and counter missile launch capabilities, ostensibly for a military exercise."

"Then we shall do the same," Liu said. "You said that you need an expert linguist from China?"

"Yes, we feel that with three linguists from the Alliance," Klegg said, "we should have a good base to attempt communications with the aliens."

"You also want a soldier with explosives expertise, to provide security for the Station?"

"Yes, Secretary Liu," Klegg said, "in addition to one that we will provide. Two men trained in small arms and explosives should be adequate to defend, or if necessary, destroy the Station. If these aliens prove hostile, it should not be allowed to fall into their possession."

"If I may say," General Demidov interrupted, "I trust that the Chinese and American fighting men you select will do their best to protect the Russians aboard the Station? If the roster could be larger I would insist on sending a member of our military."

"We are already over the recommended staffing levels for the Station. But you have my word that our man will protect your people as well, General Demidov," Klegg said.

General Zeng hesitated, long enough to glance at the General Secretary. "I agree. Our soldier will help protect everyone on the station."

"We will send you a copy of our tentative roster," Klegg went on. "We still have some names to fill in. I would hope that General Zeng and General Demidov will work with our forces to provide whatever air cover we can. I have assigned General Malcom Brown to command our air defenses. He has been ordered to cooperate with China and Russia on this."

"Who is in charge of this defensive force?" General Zeng's voice held a hint of truculence.

"I have no idea," Klegg said. "I would suggest that General Brown and General Demidov work that out with you or whoever you select. If these aliens are hostile, I really don't care who gives the orders."

General Zeng and the General Secretary exchanged glances. "We will agree to that." The General Secretary seemed satisfied with Klegg's willingness to cede command.

"Thank you, Secretary Liu, General Demidov. Now we can talk about the other billets we have to fill," Klegg said. "We will require some . . ."

The conference room door opened and Major Mitchell entered. Despite Klegg's frown at the interruption, Major Mitchell crossed the room and handed a note to Klegg, who glanced at it, then froze, his eyes widening. "Please excuse me a moment, everyone. Something urgent has occurred. Vivian, please continue the discussion regarding the TO with our Chinese and Russian allies."

Klegg rose and moved to the far end of the conference room, out of view of the cameras. Mitchell followed close behind. "Are you sure of this," Klegg whispered.

Mitchell didn't hesitate. "Yes, Sir. Admiral Goodwin's people deciphered the messages to the lawyer and broke the video file as well. I have a copy with me. The video shows what appears to be a small alien spacecraft, probably a two man ship, resting inside one of the cargo containers originally attached to the *Lady Drake*. With a dead alien inside."

"My God, JovCo found an alien ship and didn't notify anyone?"

"It's complicated," Mitchell said. "The *Lady Drake* survivors were worried about retaliation from JovCo. That's why they contacted the lawyer Ullmann. They wanted him to negotiate a financial settlement with JovCo and provide protection. The two survivors were convinced it was not a fake. They thought the find was worth a fortune."

"And those JovCo bastards have had this ship for what . . . five days?

Mitchell couldn't keep the excitement out of his voice. "There's more. During the fighting aboard the *Lady Drake*, the navigator somehow managed to open the cargo container and videoed the ship inside. While the container was open, apparently the alien vessel sent a burst transmission. The video recorded it. It lasted almost two seconds."

"I want to see the video," Klegg said. "Damn, this could be the most important . . . never mind. Wait here."

Klegg strode back to his chair. Dr. Spencer had just finished describing the linguist selection process when Klegg took his seat.

"Mr. Secretary, General Zeng, General Demidov, I just received new information. Apparently there is an alien ship at the JovCo lunar base with a dead alien still aboard. The vessel appears to have been buried on Io for hundreds, perhaps thousands, of years. At least that's what those who saw it estimated. It's been in JovCo's possession since the shuttle from the *Lady Drake* landed."

Even the usually stoic General Secretary couldn't contain his surprise. "A space ship? An alien? What is the *Lady Drake*?"

General Zeng knew the story about the ore freighter. "I will brief General Secretary Liu about the *Lady Drake*. What else do you know?"

"Not much more than I told you. Our NSA captured several transmissions from the *Drake's* shuttle to a law firm in New York. I have the files here and will transmit them to you now." Klegg nodded to General Zeng. "This time you'll have the data before our President. Mitchell, transmit the files immediately."

"What do you suggest we do about this . . . new development?" General Demidov demanded. "JovCo is a European corporation. They are not members of the Alliance."

At first no one in the Alliance had wanted the stultifyingly slow and overly cautious Europeans involved in making decisions about Earth's security. Later, when the Alliance offered membership to certain European nations, the European Union refused, unwilling to pay the additional expenses or provide support troops.

"We want that ship," Klegg said, "brought back to Earth as soon as possible. And I don't give a damn about JovCo or the European Union." He took a moment to calm down. "General Zeng, your government has two lunar bases. I understand you have a military garrison for security?"

"A small police force," the General Secretary said before Zeng could answer. "It's needed to protect visitors and tourists that visit our sites."

From what? Other visitors and tourists? Klegg knew the Chinese idea of a small police force could be anything from two or three security experts up to a heavily armed combat company. But now was not the time to discuss possible violations of the lunar treaty. "Would it be possible for your police to visit the JovCo base and take charge of the alien ship? Without risking damage to the vessel or its dead pilot? And have them delivered to Earth as soon as possible? We need to examine that craft before the idiots at JovCo screw it up."

"Yes, we can do that," General Zeng said. "We have one shuttle on the Moon large enough to transport our, eh, police force. If the alien ship fits inside a cargo container, we can get it aboard."

"And take it where?" General Demidov's voice sounded hard.

Klegg wanted that ship, Demidov wanted it, and the Chinese wanted it. But only one thing really mattered – who had the best capability to study the vessel. "General Demidov, I think we should let China take the lead on examining the ship. Their launch facility at Jiuquan is probably best equipped to deconstruct the alien spaceship." He turned to the General Secretary. "Provided that your government allows full access to US and Russian scientists. I really hope that we can work together on this, Mr. Secretary, make it a joint Alliance project."

General Zeng's face revealed he wanted to refuse. Giving outsiders, especially technical experts, access to secret military bases went against all tradition. The Chinese, now that they knew about JovCo, would take the ship no matter what. Once they had it, why bother to share its secrets or possible breakthroughs in technology?

But the General Secretary understood the larger picture. "Yes, I agree. General Klegg, General Demidov, you have my word that we will work together. We will prepare Jiuquan to receive the vessel, and each of you may send teams of scientists immediately. I would suggest no more than ten or twelve people in each team. Any more will get in each other's way. If additional resources are needed, we can address the number later."

General Klegg nodded. "Good. General Zeng, when you retrieve the vessel from JovCo, can you send us videos and photographs? We'd like to see the ship and alien in as much detail as possible."

"Yes, we can record it during the voyage to Earth."

Major Mitchell moved into the camera's view and handed Klegg another note. "Sir, you may want to consider this."

No one interrupted or looked annoyed while Klegg scanned the brief note. Dr. Spencer leaned over and read it as well. Klegg sat back in his chair. "General Zeng, I would like to ask another favor. The two *Lady Drake* survivors are at JovCo's base. When your police get there, could you arrange to transport them to the ISS station as you bring the ship back to Earth? After you read the file we're sending, you'll understand why. It happens that one is a medical technician and the other a fully qualified navigator, and both are at home in zero gravity. I think we just identified two more names to fill our station roster."

*   *   *

General Klegg leaned back in his chair. His private briefing of Major Delano had lasted over an hour. The new Marine major and senior linguist for the Alliance now had all the facts he needed to lead the mission.

Delano, his jet-lag and tiredness forgotten, had concentrated on every word. Klegg's attention to detail and even nuance impressed Delano, allowing him to memorize the information without asking more than a handful of questions or repetitions.

When Dr. Vivian Spencer placed a cup of coffee into his hands, Delano scarcely acknowledged the gesture. The General had shared his insights and private conversations with the President and Alliance leaders. A vast world-wide military operation had commenced, one with Alliance complications and the potential for worldwide political and social unrest. Now Joe Delano had received the hot potato, right out of the oven and still smoking. In the words of his Quantico drill instructor, Delano was in for a major screw job.

The intercom on Klegg's desk buzzed, and the General picked up the handset. After a moment he said yes, said it again, and hung up. "The Commandant is outside. First time he's ever been early in his life. Must be dying to know what's going on. My sergeant will give you a new set of orders, assigning you temporarily to Operation Sentinel Star and placing you under my direct command. As I said, you're probably going to end up being the senior officer on the Station, so make sure you keep your mouth shut about what I've told you. Just remember your mission – communicate with these aliens, find out what they want, and ascertain what danger if any they represent." He grunted, as if displeased by another possibility. "Most of all, you make sure the Station and its scientists don't fall into alien hands."

Klegg ignored the shocked look on Delano's face. "You heard

me. Welcome to the team, Major. Don't discuss any of this with the Commandant. He's not cleared for it yet. Dismissed."

The next forty minutes passed in a flurry. Delano and the Commandant of the Marine Corps, Major General Michael O'Sullivan, sat shoulder to shoulder on narrow office chairs dragged in front of the sergeant's desk. The sergeant, hunched over his computer, punched in what seemed like an endless stream of data. Eventually he printed out two sets of orders, as well as the official notification of Delano's promotion to Major. "As of today, Major," the sergeant said, "you're drawing pay at your new rank."

Great news. At least Delano's death benefits would be higher. Neither the Commandant nor the busy sergeant showed the slightest interest in Delano's well-being. General O'Sullivan signed both sets, kept one for himself and handed the other to Delano.

"I'd wish you luck on the mission, Major, but I'm not sure exactly what it is, and that FBI agent sitting over there is watching me to make sure I don't find out. Just do your duty and uphold Marine Corps tradition. I'd hate to court-martial you when this is over, but I will if you fuck up whatever it is they want you to do." He rose and nodded toward a pair of FBI agents sitting by themselves along the wall. One got up, and he and the Commandant walked out the door together.

"OK, Major," the sergeant began, "you've got about five minutes before the FBI agents take you back to Andrews where you'll catch your flight to Holloman Air Force Base. There will be some others riding with you, but you don't say a word to anyone about anything. No phones, no texts, no notes, nothing. If you try to communicate with anyone, General Klegg will have you in a cell in Leavenworth for the rest of your life, no bullshit."

"Camp Pendleton," Delano muttered. "Marines are sent to the brig at Pendleton." He shook his head. One prison was as bad as the other, so what difference did it make? "Why doesn't the Commandant know what's going on? I mean, he's a two-star general."

"Get this straight, Major. For this operation rank don't mean anything. Only the need to know, and he don't need to know. Not yet. He will in a day or two." The sergeant beckoned to the remaining FBI agent. This one, a serious looking jock, wore a running jacket over a black shirt and gray slacks.

"OK, here's your boy. Major, go with . . . whatever his name is. He'll escort you down to the car and out to Andrews. Oh, and during the flight, think about what equipment or clothes you might require on the Station. Make a list and give it to the agent on the plane. Maybe you'll catch a break, and it'll be waiting for you in New Mexico. Good luck."

Yeah, maybe I'll catch a break and the car will crash on the way to the airport and I'll get out of the mission. As far as Delano could see, his luck had turned bad and didn't look likely to improve.

Chapter 5

Day 2: 0130 Zulu Time – JovCo Lunar Base

Peter Tasco sprawled back on the foam slab mattress in his jail cell, relaxed and at ease. He'd never been in a lockup before, but as such establishments went, this one didn't feel too bad. The food arrived warm and tasted OK, better than shipboard meals. Best of all, his new bride, Linda Grayson, occupied the next cell, so he had someone to talk to. The JovCo lunar detention facility had only the two cells – very little crime on the Moon. An annoying but transparent shield separated the two-meter square cages.

Despite that obstacle, he and Linda managed to hold hands by reaching through the aluminum bars at the front of each cell. They could talk, but not much else.

As a skilled navigator and qualified (Second Class) pilot, Peter had worked for JovCo on the Moon to Io run. The Company paid well for those few with the right skills and genetic make-up, especially individuals able to withstand long durations of zero gravity. Peter, thirty-five years old, needed the money to support his ex-wife and their ten years old daughter. He'd contracted with JovCo for the last six years. For the last three years, the mining company management ignored his growing reliance on alcohol. As long as he could function, they didn't care what Peter did to his body.

That problem had disappeared during the crisis aboard the *Lady Drake*, a JovCo ore freighter inbound from Jupiter's moon Io. To conceal a recently discovered and ancient artifact – a long-buried, two-seat alien spaceship and its dead pilot – the *Lady Drake's* captain and a few of his henchmen had killed several of the crew. They left Peter to die outside the ship. Linda Grayson, the ship's med-tech specialist, suffered more personal assaults at the hands of the murderous crew, and would have ended up dead as well. Only the fact that the captain had special plans for an attractive woman kept her alive. After a horrendous struggle, Peter saved himself and rescued Linda. Together they escaped the *Lady Drake* via its shuttle, taking the newly-discovered and quite valuable alien ship with them. By then five of the original nine crew members had died. When the killing ended, so did Peter's interest in booze. They'd both narrowly avoided death, instead finding solace and love in each other's companionship. Saving Linda turned Peter's life around.

Knowing that the alien vessel and its new technology would be worth a fortune to JovCo, the couple needed a way to ensure both their personal safety and stake a claim to some of the artifact's value. JovCo was capable of anything. The Company already had a bad reputation for skirting international law and for its disreputable and callous dealings with its contracted employees. To Peter's relief, Linda possessed an even greater distrust of their employer than he did. She quickly figured out a way to protect themselves from JovCo.

A week before they landed on the Moon, Linda forwarded a complete record of events aboard the *Lady Drake*, sealed and encrypted, to the very exclusive law firm – Rubio, Ullmann, and Lambert. RUL specialized in suing large corporations, class actions, that type of thing. More emails were exchanged, and to Peter's surprise, Ullmann himself agreed to represent them. That agreement probably saved the two survivors from disappearing into the lunar dust, at once closing the book on the *Lady Drake* and eliminating any possible leaks about the alien.

After their long shuttle flight, Peter and Linda landed at the primary JovCo lunar base, bringing with them the alien artifact that had triggered the killing spree aboard the *Lady Drake*. The directors of JovCo needed only one brief inspection to realize the alien spacecraft's value. If they could reverse engineer the ship's drive, billions in credits from the Alliance and every other space-minded country and corporation would be theirs. Eager to benefit from the potentially priceless find, JovCo decided to exploit the alien technology at all costs. JovCo's only problem was keeping secret the existence of the alien craft for six months or so while their engineers figured out what made it tick and the Company lawyers nailed down the patents.

As soon as Peter and Linda disembarked at the JovCo Lunar Refining Facility, the Company's stooges had tossed them in the slam. Located on one of the upper levels of the dome, the jail consisted of a small chamber within an equipment storage area. To

Peter's surprise, neither he nor Linda minded the discomfort. After extended living on an ore freighter or below Io's fiery surface, not much fazed them. They'd had plenty of time for intimacy during their transit to the Moon. Peter asked if he and Linda could share the same cell, since they'd already signed a marriage contract three days before their arrival. The knuckle-dragging jailers refused, citing "safety reasons."

Peter and Linda's incarceration might have lasted until they died of old age or contracted some mysterious and fatal illness. But as soon as Linda informed JovCo's management that Mr. Jerry Ullmann, attorney-at-law, knew all about the *Lady Drake*, the Company had to rethink whatever nefarious plans it might be contemplating for the two newlyweds. Mining "accidents" often befell those who ran afoul of JovCo.

At least he and Linda had time to relax. Peter discovered they still had a lot to talk about. The one thing they didn't discuss was their future, thanks to the snoopy recording devices and cameras staring into each cell. Their fate now rested in the hands of a New York law firm and its senior partner, Jerry Ullmann.

Three days had passed since they reached the Moon. Even Linda's patience had worn thin, and she'd started to worry. "We should have heard something from the lawyer," she declared. "Do you think the Company has blocked Ullmann? It's almost a week since his last email."

Longer than that. Peter didn't bother to point that out. "He may be doing something already, and we just don't know about it." *Or JovCo bought him off and we're screwed.*

The JovCo goons had confiscated their phones and turned off the jail compartment's news feed, so for all Peter and Linda knew, the world might have ended. "Let's give it another day," he said, "before we start banging our plastic cups against the bars."

Before she could reply, the chamber door rattled open. Harry the Hulk, one of the usual jailers – Peter wondered what the man did for his real job – came in and used his communicator to unlock the cells. "Get your stuff," he ordered, "and follow me. Clugston wants you."

Since Peter and Linda didn't have any personal property – their captors had even confiscated Linda's comb, leaving her short blond hair a tangle over her blue eyes – they were on their feet and moving in moments. *At least something is happening*, Peter thought, taking Linda's hand.

JovCo, always busy in its machinations, utilized a full-time lawyer on the Moon. Clugston might be a second-rate legal mind, but for the Company, always interested in cutting expenses, the man proved more than adequate. Far too many employees had their rights trampled under his determinations.

Peter and Linda followed the guard down two tunnels until they reached the executive offices. Both moved with the grace and poise of ballet dancers in the weak lunar gravity, hands slightly extended from the body and taking long, arching steps that covered three meters or more. Neither had ever visited this restricted level before, but its smoother walls and better quality paint proclaimed its higher status. After another fifty meters, the jailer reached a door and opened it for them.

Inside a small conference room, three men awaited their arrival. Peter recognized the Administrator of the JovCo Lunar Mining Operation, Philippe Bontemps. The man sitting beside him looked even sleazier, so Peter guessed that must be Clugston. Both men, dressed in the usual gray and white singlets, sat on the same side of the brown polystyrene table. Opposite sat the third man, this one dressed in expensive safari clothing, which the upscale specialty stores on Earth sold unsuspecting tourists as appropriate lunar garb. Holding on to the table – obviously he hadn't acclimated himself to the one-six gravity – the man rose as they entered. After a moment, Peter recognized Ullmann from the newsfeed images.

"You must be Linda." He shook her hand first, then Peter's, and somehow managed to make the greeting a serious gesture. "I'm Jerry Ullmann, your attorney. Sorry to take so long to get here, but I had to make certain provisions." He glanced at Bontemps. "I hope you've been treating my clients well. If you've done anything . . ."

"Nothing, nothing at all," Clugston answered. "We just wanted to make sure they were safe until we could fully document the . . . events aboard the *Lady Drake*."

"They put us in their tiny jail," Linda countered. "Didn't want to hear anything we had to say. And they took away our communicators." She glared at Bontemps.

Ullmann looked grave. "Removing communications access is a serious infraction of space law, akin to kidnapping, but we'll deal with that later. Please, Mr. and Mrs. Tasco, take your seats. We have a lot to discuss."

Right to business, Peter thought. Somehow the lawyer knew about their marriage. No time would be wasted trying to confer privately with his clients, if such a thing were possible in this facility. Ullmann dropped gracefully back into his seat.

Even in a crowded JovCo teleconference room, Ullmann managed to look dapper and in control, despite the bogus travel gear. Tall, with thick silver hair brushed straight back over his head, he could have stepped onto any Shakespearian stage in the role of King Lear, with a deep baritone voice to match. Peter felt impressed.

He'd read over a dozen articles of background material on the lawyer before they landed on the Moon. Ullmann had dealt with JovCo before. Three years ago his nephew had died on Io. The Company had blamed the young engineer for his own death and that of several others. JovCo also slandered his professional and personal reputation, all tactics designed to lower the insurance payouts.

A long and bitter legal fight followed. But by the time Ullmann finished with JovCo, the boy's family received a full apology and upwards of ten million US dollars had been transferred to their account. An additional five million went into Ullmann's pocket, which to his credit, he donated to charity in the name of his nephew. That legal victory had placed Ullmann at the top of the list for anyone wanting to hire a lawyer tough enough to take on JovCo. And now that same Jerry Ullmann had braved the arduous journey to the Moon, hopefully to rescue Peter and Linda from the Company's clutches.

With so much money at stake – the alien ship's drive alone was priceless – JovCo couldn't ignore the potentially fatal report sitting on Ullmann's New York desk. His unexpected arrival and demand to see his clients threw JovCo's Disaster Containment Team into a flurry of consternation and activity. Exactly what Ullmann intended.

Two minutes passed without a word spoken. Peter glanced around the room, but nobody seemed inclined to talk. He was about to break the silence when the teleconferencing system lit up. A moment later, two men appeared on screen. Peter recognized one – Mathieu Messerly, CEO of European Space Ventures, parent company of JovCo. One of the richest men in Europe, in the world for that matter, Messerly rarely appeared in public. So the *Lady*

Drake problem had reached all the way to the top.

The second man took the lead. "I am Hans Bergman, chief solicitor for ESV. I understand Mr. Ullmann is representing our employees, Peter Tasco and Linda Grayson, both of whom are still under contract to JovCo."

Ullmann waved his regal hand. "Forget about their contract. Once your official representatives, specifically the captain and his first mate, tried to kill Peter and Linda, it ceased to exist. They are no longer your employees. There's a Chinese transport leaving New Beijing tomorrow for Wenchang, and I intend to take Peter and Linda back with me. From there we'll make a connection to New York."

Wenchang remained China's main civilian spaceport, akin to the one in New Mexico.

"Impossible," Clugston whined. "Your clients killed several members of the *Lady Drake's* crew. They'll be charged with murder."

Ullmann, busy pulling his phone out of his travel bag, laughed. "As I see it, the direct representative of your Company, the ship's captain, jettisoned several members of his crew into space, tried to kill Peter several times, and physically kidnapped and assaulted Linda. In effect, your senior JovCo agent aboard the *Lady Drake* attempted to murder my clients. To their credit, and at great risk to their own lives, they heroically saved both the ship and its cargo."

Ullmann finished arranging his phone. "On that portion of the case, I'm ready to proceed to trial immediately. Should I contact the news organizations right now, or wait until I return to New York and hold a live press conference? Perhaps my staff should conduct a poll of public opinion." He tapped his phone. "Is that what you want?"

Clugston turned red, but before he could answer, Herr Bergman cut him off. "I'm sure we can dispense with that. But your clients did sabotage a Company vessel and sent it off on a wild trajectory. It might have never been recovered, along with its valuable cargo. They can be charged with theft of JovCo property, destruction of Company property, and illegal use of Company resources. And they remain liable for any damage to ship or cargo. The *Lady Drake* has yet to reach the Moon. More charges may be added when she does, and we gain access to the ship's computer."

"I've read their statement, backed up by the shuttle's log,"

Ullmann said. "All their actions were taken in self-defense, to escape the homicidal plans of your captain and his co-conspirators. Do you really want to present those logs as evidence in a courtroom?"

Peter smiled at that one. The *Lady Drake's* computer log couldn't be tampered with, at least not by anyone lacking serious computer skills and specific equipment. Only one man aboard the *Lady Drake*, Carl Brock, possessed the necessary skill. Peter had crushed the bastard's skull for what Brock did to Linda. *Too bad, JovCo.*

"Peter killed two members of the crew," Bergman insisted, "and must be held criminally accountable. Linda Grayson may be charged as an accessory."

Ullmann laughed again, this time a raucous sound that sounded out of place coming from a distinguished attorney. "A plea of self-defense will cover every aspect of Peter and Linda's actions."

Peter glanced at the clock on the wall. It took exactly seven minutes before that allegation disappeared as well. He gave Linda's hand a squeeze.

"Nevertheless," Bergman insisted, "Peter violated specific terms of his contract with JovCo. He removed part of the cargo and threatened to destroy it. Our contract is very clear regarding these actions. Our cargo containers are sealed for a reason."

"Oh, you mean the alien spacecraft and its dead pilot," Ullmann countered, "the one JovCo is now concealing on this very base, in complete violation of Alliance directives? I suppose you might make a legal argument over that. Which Alliance country should I contact first, China or Russia? I'm sure either would be more than glad to assist my clients in thoroughly investigating the case."

Peter felt the tension rise in the room the moment the alien issue stepped onto the stage. Under the table, Linda reached over and squeezed his hand. JovCo had no intention of risking that precious piece of technology. The moment they announced the find, the Alliance would demand, rightfully or not, possession of the alien ship. The Company would be out in the cold, no technological breakthroughs, no valuable patents. As long as Ullmann had that to bargain with, JovCo was vulnerable. For the first time since entering the room, Peter let himself relax.

"The alien ship is clearly a fake," Bergman said. "Our engineers say it was constructed on Io. No one takes it seriously."

Ullmann shook his head. "Let's not waste time. If JovCo wants the ship, fine, I don't care. Neither I nor my clients have any responsibility or interest in enforcing the arbitrary rules and directives of the Alliance. JovCo isn't even headquartered in a member nation. If the Company wants to keep the artifact a secret, well, I can look the other way with the best of them. Perhaps we can reach a mutually satisfying agreement?"

Peter winked at Linda. They both leaned back in their chairs. The discussions would drag on, but he knew how it would end. Still, everyone needed to save face. Forty minutes later, the two lawyers reached agreement.

"Let me sum it up," Ullmann said. "First, JovCo agrees to pay my clients five million American dollars each, after taxes. If news about the alien gets out, whatever happens does not affect my clients or this payout. Of course I guarantee neither my clients or RUL will ever divulge any of this."

A sour-looking Bergman grunted acceptance. "Second," Ullmann went on, "JovCo will indemnify Peter and Linda with complete and total immunity from the Company in regard to any and all possible future charges, losses, damages, or disasters, man-made or natural, up to and including the collapse of the sun. No matter what happens, they keep their money. In return, we won't sue you for attempted murder, illegal arrest, and kidnapping."

Ullmann waited, but no one wanted to argue. "Third, since you desire to keep my clients in your employ, you agree to let them work together for as long as they wish, or until you terminate, without prejudice, their contracts. Also, since you want them to work on the alien ship, JovCo will have to insure them. In the event of any unfortunate accidents or death, for any reason, to either of my clients within the next ten years, the Company will immediately forfeit another ten million dollar bond."

Peter saw the JovCo attorneys still didn't like that one.

"Working in space is inherently dangerous," Clugston claimed. "Accidents can and do happen."

"We've been over this," Ullmann said. "Peter and Linda are young and healthy, and as long as you don't send them on foolish ventures or expose them to unnecessary risks, they should easily survive the next ten years. And if they don't, well, it's only money, and everyone knows JovCo has plenty of cash."

Peter's jaw had dropped when he heard that JovCo wanted to keep he and Linda under contract. But it made sense. Since the Company wanted to keep the alien craft for themselves, they realized it would be easier to maintain security if Peter and Linda extended their employment. In fact, their expertise could be useful in studying the alien craft and its pilot. A pilot/navigator and a med-tech would be needed anyway, and why add to the number of people who knew about the alien.

Peter and Linda exchanged glances. In fact, they'd talked about that very possibility on their shuttle voyage. Both wanted to work on the alien project. Since they enjoyed living in space, they agreed to remain with the Company.

In that case, Ullmann had countered, both should receive suitable promotions and substantial increases in pay. Peter became a Pilot/Navigator First Class, and Linda received an already overdue upgrade to her rating, making her the equivalent of a ship-board medical doctor. They also accepted a three day vacation at JovCo's private hotel, to celebrate their marriage.

So Ullmann and Clugston drew up a new document, and both signed it. Clugston also prepared new employment contracts for Peter and Linda, which everyone witnessed and signed. The Company lawyers put on their happy faces, then registered the documents. After that, the transfer of funds occurred, the money moving directly to private accounts at a New York bank, and managed by Rubio, Ullmann, and Lambert. JovCo would have preferred making payment in yuan or rubles, but Ullmann demanded American dollars. The current conversion rate happened to be slightly more favorable.

Peter hugged Linda, as they once again became cheerful and loyal members of the jovial JovCo family, effective immediately. They would return to work after their mini-vacation. In less than three hours, Peter and Linda had transformed from wage slaves to multimillionaires.

Peter saw the resigned smile on Bonetemps' face. In reality, the Company had gotten off easy. JovCo still had its surreptitious asset, and the payments to Ullmann and his clients were insignificant compared to the potential gain. All Peter and Linda had to do was help spin the *Lady Drake* episode as a case of space madness and keep quiet about the alien ship. *That we can do.*

To demonstrate the Company's appreciation for their efforts in safeguarding so valuable an artifact, JovCo also agreed to pay Jerry Ullmann's fees and expenses. He had, after all, undertaken a dangerous and tiring trip to the Moon, risking life and limb to help JovCo preserve its secret. After a bit more haggling, the Company lawyers agreed. For less than a week's work, Ullmann's firm received five million US dollars.

This time a smiling Ullmann shook Peter's hand, and gave Linda the *de rigueur* European kiss. Linda wrapped both arms around him and gave him a hug. A few moments later, the funds cleared. The lawyer offered his congratulations, said his goodbyes, and hastened back to his hired lunar puddle-jumper, heading for New Beijing. He didn't want to miss the transport back to Earth, should it decide to leave early.

*   *   *

Thirty six hours later . . .

Wearing a wonderfully soft white terrycloth robe embroidered with the red and gold JovCo logo, Peter Tasco lounged on the large bed, holding what he called an umbrella drink in his hand. The hotel beverage menu described it as a Luna Colada. Peter had never tasted one until yesterday, when Linda introduced him to the mango-colored drink. Whatever the ingredients, he enjoyed the sweet taste and the hint of alcohol.

Of course, it wasn't real alcohol. As the mantra went, once an alcoholic, always an alcoholic. Upon request, the hotel did serve drinks made from a synthetic blend, the flavoring almost the same as the real thing, but without the addictive reaction. Linda preferred the imitation, so he didn't face the temptation of taking a sip of hers. Even so, he decided to limit himself to two Coladas a day, one at lunch and the other before dinner.

Notwithstanding their new status, neither Peter nor Linda had permission to leave the hotel zone. That slight inconvenience didn't bother them. JovCo's refining complex, most of it deep below the lunar surface, didn't have much worth seeing anyway. If you've seen one ore smelter, you've seen them all. Few lunar travelers went to see the Company's rare-earth mineral processing base, only the occasional stockholder, technical expert, or junketing politician.

Despite infrequent visitors, the five-room hotel possessed every first class amenity. The senior management of JovCo spared no expense to make certain its corporate guests possessed and enjoyed every comfort during their sporadic visits. Now those wonderful fringe benefits were offered to Peter and Linda.

As another hotel perk, the lobby's tiny guest stand, in addition to the usual tourist tee-shirts and trinkets, offered a wide selection of designer, reality-enhancing drugs. Several of these remained illegal on Earth. Neither Peter nor Linda had any interest in those. Both had already experienced one life-altering ordeal, and they didn't need any more stimulation in their lives, artificial or not.

Peter sipped at his drink, ignoring the occasional craving to gulp it down. He didn't intend to ruin his life a second time, especially now that he had Linda and a pile of money big enough to last a lifetime. His teenage daughter on Earth could attend any university in the world, and Peter had a unique opportunity to do some serious exploring and research while he enjoyed life. Nothing like a close brush with death, a lot of cash, and a loving relationship to change a man's view of the future.

Almost two days had passed in ease and comfort. Life was good and about to get even better. Starting tomorrow, they'd have alien technology to study. In a few months they would be back on Earth for a well-deserved three month vacation, relaxing at some resort in the South Pacific. No doubt they'd enjoy pampering massages and discover an equally good and plentiful supply of umbrella drinks.

Linda came out of the bathroom, interrupting Peter's pleasant daydreams and wearing only a blue towel wrapped around her cropped blond hair. Since he first set eyes on her aboard the *Lady Drake*, Peter had never seen her wear makeup. Now a hint of eye shadow enhanced the blue of her eyes, and a trace of red lipstick on her soft lips deepened her smile. Applying what little knowledge of women he'd accumulated in his thirty-five years, Peter deduced that she was definitely in the mood.

Linda placed her hands on her slim hips. "So, what do you think? Too much towel?"

"Oh, no, just perfect. Lovely and dressed to perfection. Prettiest woman on the Moon."

She laughed. "I wish. You're such a romantic. Now, where's my

Luna Colada?"

"On the dresser," Peter said. "Take a sip and come to bed. I'm getting lonely."

She glided over to the table and took two swallows. "I notice something else has come up." Moving with care, she climbed onto the bed, then leaned down and kissed Peter's upturned lips. The kiss lasted some time, and they both forgot about the drinks.

Later, relaxing in each other's arms, Peter decided the experts were right. Sex on the low gravity Moon was the best. No sweating, no straining, no real exertion, just pure pleasure for as long as you wanted. Lunar love making had proved far better than zero gravity, where you had to hold onto something to keep from injuring yourself or bouncing around. Either that, or crawl into a onesie suit together, which could kill the mood faster than anything else Peter had ever seen.

Together they had faced the most horrific kind of nightmare. He had saved Linda from torture and slow death, and she had rescued Peter from the cold of space. That bond, to their surprise, continued growing stronger. Even on the cramped shuttle, alone for over three weeks, they'd never stopped appreciating each other.

Peter kissed her nose. "Honey, it's time we visit the dining room."

"I suppose," Linda said. "Or we could order in?" She snuggled against him. "Maybe some pie, or something with . . ."

Without warning, the hotel room door burst open. Before it swung wide, Peter's feet hit the floor. He'd locked that door himself and supposedly even the hotel staff couldn't open it except in an emergency.

But before Peter could take a step, he recognized an emergency if he'd ever seen one. Two uniformed men, both Chinese, pushed into their chamber. Both moved easily in the lunar gravity. Each held a pistol, one aimed at Peter and the other at Linda. Peter drifted back onto the bed.

A third man followed. He, too, wore a uniform and had a pistol, but it remained holstered at his side. Instead he held photographs in one hand. "You are Peter Tasco? You are Linda Grayson?" His terrible, Chinese-accented English might have sounded humorous under different circumstances. But right now, his curt words and callous demeanor sent a chill through Peter.

"Who are you?" Peter demanded. "How did you . . ."

"Answer now, or my men will shoot."

Linda spoke before Peter could decide to play the hero and possibly get them both killed. "Yes, I'm Linda Grayson, he's Peter Tasco. Who sent you? What do you want?"

The man ignored her questions as he glanced at the photographs, compared them to their faces, then nodded. "You will both get dressed and pack your . . . things. We return Beijing Base soon as our ship loaded with alien vessel. You come with us. You have two minutes."

At first Peter had thought these were Company goons sent to cancel their new contracts by eliminating them permanently. But Chinese soldiers? No, something had gone wrong. They must have learned about the alien ship and decided to seize it by force. Some JovCo idiot must have shot off his mouth.

Even so, using armed military personnel on the Moon, that didn't sound right either. The Chinese seldom resorted to violence. It just wasn't their style. They'd mastered the arts of persuasion and intimidation, backed by the ever-present threat of overwhelming force, to get what they wanted.

Linda swung off the bed and with a single smooth step reached the wardrobe, ignoring the soldiers' appreciative stares at her body. "Just get dressed, Peter. We'll figure it out later."

He hoped she was right. These soldiers looked fit and well trained. They didn't seem worried about JovCo's goons or lawyers or any other legal niceties. All the same, it didn't make sense for Peter to argue with armed military people willing to shoot first and ask questions later. *Geez, I hope our money is safe.*

"I knew it was too good to last," he muttered. Peter stood carefully, keeping his hands in sight as he reached for his clothes. Damn, he hoped he wouldn't have to climb into a space suit again. He'd already had enough extravehicular activity to last a lifetime.

Chapter 6

Day 2: 09:00 AM MST

Delano didn't remember much about the nighttime flight to Holloman Air Force Base. No uncomfortable fighter this time, but instead a luxury Gulfstream, the kind usually reserved for the senior brass. He dropped into the first empty seat and extended the comfortably padded recliner as far as it would go. Two other passengers had taken seats in the rear of the plane, each accompanied by an FBI agent, gold badges prominently displayed. After giving those poor bastards a quick glance, Delano closed his eyes, went right to sleep, and didn't wake up until the wheels touched down in New Mexico.

The three passengers and their trio of FBI agents ended up in a concrete, two-story building a hundred yards from the hangar. Delano's bodyguard, who hadn't said a word since they left the Pentagon, guided Delano into an empty conference room and left him there after closing and locking the door. The other two passengers apparently had equipment traveling with them and the FBI agents wanted it inspected.

Delano spotted a brown leather sofa along the back wall and stretched out. At least this time he had a brief moment to recall Eugenie's love making. Within seconds he fell asleep again, one arm thrown over his eyes to block the lights, still wearing his rumpled uniform.

When he woke, he found someone had draped a blanket over him. Delano struggled to a sitting position. His fellow passengers from the Gulfstream had rejoined him and taken chairs at the head of the table. They must have dimmed the lights so he could sleep. A glance at his watch showed that he'd slept almost an hour.

Delano's mouth felt dry and his back had stiffened up. Regardless, the sleep on the plane and the nap on the sofa had refreshed him, though his stomach felt empty. He stood and stretched, as both men turned toward him.

"Coffee, Captain?" The older of the two men gestured to a pot on a table. "It's fresh. We just made it. The agents said they'd bring us something to eat soon." The man had a Southern drawl, probably from the hill country of southwestern West Virginia.

"God, yes," Delano muttered. He filled a Styrofoam cup and took a sip. It burned his tongue, so he blew on it, then took a few small swallows. He topped off the cup and sat at the table. For the first time he noticed the FBI guys were gone.

"Sorry I didn't catch your names," Delano began. "I'm Captain . . . Major Joe Delano, USMC. Just got promoted. They pulled me out of a . . . party in Paris, so I haven't had much chance to sleep."

"Gunnery Sergeant Jack Stecker, USMC. Force Recon out of Camp Lejeune."

By now Delano had noticed the man's powerful arm and chest muscles. Force Recon marines were as tough as they come. He's seen them train at Camp Lejeune – the kind of men who parachuted into the jungle behind enemy lines with nothing but a knife and a radio. The joke was that sometimes the Marine Corps forgot to issue the knife.

"Nice to meet you, Jack," Delano said. He looked at the other man. Thin, almost emaciated, and very young. Unlike Stecker, this one didn't appear to have a muscle on his body.

"Sergeant First Class Steve Macey. Army Communications, Electronics Command. I'm stationed at the Aberdeen Proving Ground in Maryland."

Steve Macey could pass for a seventeen year old high school student. Christ, he even had a pimple on his cheek. On the table two empty bags of potato chips lay crumpled next to a large coffee cup. Steve must have found a vending machine somewhere in the building, or paid off his FBI guy. Steve's accent placed him somewhere in the New York or New Jersey suburbs.

Delano did the military translation of Macey's rank. An Army Sergeant First Class was an E-7, which meant that technically Macey outranked Stecker's E-6 rank. And what the hell was Electronics Command?

"OK, Steve, nice to meet you, too. I suggest we skip the formalities and just go by our first names. This assignment doesn't appear to be normal military."

"Yes, Sir." Macey's high-pitched voice sounded like a teenager struggling through puberty.

Delano glanced around, looking for the FBI agents. "Where are our friendly bodyguards? Anybody know?"

"Outside, Sir," Steve said. "They've secured this room and are setting up a conference call. We're not sure when it will come, but we have to be ready." Right now the phones are disconnected."

Obviously the agents no longer cared if the trio spoke among themselves. "So both of you know what's going on?"

Jack Stecker nodded. "Yes, Joe. Steve and I got a full brief from General Klegg at the Pentagon yesterday. Even had a few minutes teleconference with some Chinese army brass and a General Demidov in Russia."

"That probably puts you ahead of me, Jack. Klegg talked to me for about an hour, but only Dr. Vance was there, and she didn't say much." Delano took a breath. "You know where we're going?"

"Yes, the ISS. General Klegg said we'd get another briefing either here at Holloman or when we get to Spaceport." Stecker sounded about as perturbed as if he were ambling across the street to the local coffee house for a Danish.

"Why do they want a Marine Recon on the ISS?" Delano's coffee had kicked in and his mind, what was left of it, had started working again. "What's your specialty?"

"Mostly small arms, Joe. I can shoot pretty good," Stecker said, "and I know a little about explosives. Also I'm used to working alone, not like Seal team members. Klegg said my job was to stick close to you, and make sure nothing bad happens."

My bodyguard, Delano decided. Maybe he did need one at that, with possible life-sucking aliens in the equation. "And the explosives?"

"Just in case these aliens try to capture the station. I'm not supposed to let that happen. Me and the Chinese guy."

"Who? What Chinese guy?" Delano heard the tension in his voice and ordered himself to relax. So far he was the senior ranking officer, and he'd better start acting like one. Klegg had mentioned a Table of Organization, but hadn't gone into any detail.

"Don't know anything about him," Stecker said, "just that another shooter would be joining us, some Chinese special forces type."

Jeez, as if a trip to the ISS to meet aliens wasn't bad enough, now Delano had to worry about getting shot or blown to bits in space by his own guys. Lovely, just lovely. He turned to Macey. "What's your field of expertise, Steve?"

"Communications and computers . . . Joe. I'm to establish secure communication links from the Station to the Pentagon and Russia and the Chinese. And I'm supposed to try and tap into whatever communication system the aliens are using."

A computer geek. Well, that sounded useful. Now that he thought about it, Delano realized he was merely part of a team that would try to communicate with these aliens.

"This assignment, Major . . . I mean Joe, what's your specialty?" Steve didn't look as confident as he sounded.

Definitely from northern New Jersey, probably the Paramus/Ridgewood area. "I'm a linguist. I'm to establish communications with the aliens."

Stecker nodded. "Seen any action, Joe?"

The casual question caught Delano off guard. Of course the Recon grunt would want to know about his new, and probably a few years younger, commanding officer who might be nothing more than a desk jockey and likely to get them all killed if trouble broke out. No doubt Stecker hadn't had time to tap into the enlisted buddy network for the hot scoop on his new Commanding Officer.

"Some. I did six months in Yemen," Delano said, "two years back as a Second Lieutenant. I was sent there to work as a translator, but the unit needed a platoon leader, so you know how that goes. A few firefights, and we took some mortars, but nothing too serious. Mostly just running around in the desert."

"I hear ya. I spent time in Yemen, too. At least you know which end of the rifle the bullet comes out," Stecker said. "Not every chair warmer does. If we get time, I can give you and Steve a little catchup training. Know anything about explosives?"

Another seemingly casual but probing question. "No, just what they covered at OCS." That single day of training probably meant less than nothing to an explosives expert.

Stecker took a swallow from his cup. "No problem. I'll take good care of you both."

Delano thought about Stecker's Yemen experience. Delano had not worked with any Recon Marines, but everyone knew about them. They provided the REMFs (Rear Echelon Mother Fuckers) with on-the-ground intel, and junior officers soon learned not to ask where Recon Marines were deployed, what they did, or how they did it.

The door opened and two FBI agents entered, neither of whom Delano had seen before. A third man followed and Delano needed only a glance to realize this overweight, balding man in a yellow plaid shirt was not a member of the Bureau.

"Glad to see you're all awake," one of the FBI men said. "I'm Senior Field Agent Rick Barnes, and my colleague is Senior Field Agent Luis Hernandez. We're here to keep an eye on you and make sure you get whatever it is you need." He turned to the third man. "This is Supervisor Hernando Alviso, from the Spaceport facility. He'll give you the first brief."

Alviso cleared his throat and walked over to a whiteboard. "Nice to meetcha. In about fourteen hours, you three gentlemen will board a spaceplane for a lift up to the ISS. Two Russian men will be landing here in about an hour. An hour after that, two Chinese will arrive, a man and a woman. Spaceport's job is to prepare all seven of you folks for the flight and help you adjust to living and working in a zero gravity environment. Normally that takes at least two months, so all we can do is hit the highlights and hope for the best."

Delano glanced toward the coffee maker. The two FBI agents had congregated there, obviously grateful that they weren't going along for the ride. Lucky bastards.

"So here's how it will work," Alviso went on. "The spaceplane will be load heavy, with seven passengers and all your gear and supplies." He gestured toward Steve. "Sergeant Macey has almost a ton of equipment he's taking with him. Sergeant Stecker is weighing in at over eight hundred pounds. We don't have anything listed for you, Major Delano. Do you need any special equipment?"

Delano thought about that. Linguists generally needed nothing but their tongues and brains, but clearly he would be expected to document his progress, recording everything in whatever language translator he deemed most suitable. "Mr. Alviso, I could use two tablets, fully equipped, some high-quality speakers, and a dozen spiral bound notebooks. Plenty of pens and pencils, too. And I'll need to access my personal language files and translation software. It's customized to my voice. A copy is on my office computer at the Embassy in Paris. Better make a few copies for backup."

One of the FBI agents stood. "Give me your password, and I'll download the contents."

Delano took one look at the man and decided they wouldn't let him do it himself anyway. Thank God he hadn't been there long enough to have anything embarrassing in his files. He wrote his password on the pad in front of him — *thestreetsareguardedbyunitedstatesmarines!11101775* — tore it off and handed it to the agent. "My office is on the third floor . . ."

"We know where it is, Major. We've already had agents searching it for anything interesting. Probably don't even need the password." He didn't smile. "I'll be back with your files in about an hour."

By now they probably knew the name and bra size of every woman he'd ever had sex with, not to mention every stupid move Delano had ever made. Nosy bastards.

Supervisor Alviso went on. "We'll start your training with how to use a space suit, well, really a pressurized flight suit since you won't be doing any EVA. Luckily we have enough spares for all of you. You'll be measured and a suit assigned. It won't be a perfect fit, but it will have to do. Then we'll show you how the WCS – the space toilet – works. That's the first thing you'll be looking for when you reach the station. Until you get there, you'll be wearing a Maximum Absorbency Garment, or MAG. Some call it a diaper, but that's not correct. It's a polymer consisting of sodium polyacrylate crystals and odor absorbing . . ."

While Alviso droned on about the MAG's ability to absorb five hundred to a thousand times its mass in water, Delano decided to call it a fucking diaper and the hell with NASA and their cute acronyms.

"Next," Alviso said, "I'll go over how you can settle in for some sleep, and how to eat and drink. You should expect to throw up a few times, until your stomach figures out which way is up." Alviso laughed at his little joke, a quick burst of sound that sounded hollow in the room.

"We'll spend a little time at the Micro-Gravity Wall and the Multi-Axis Trainer. You'll skip the lunar gravity trainer, since you won't be going to the Moon. At the MGW, you'll be outfitted with harnesses and customized weights which allow you to climb and descend the wall in an almost effortless state. It's good training for how to move in zero gravity. You'll each have a few minutes on the MAT. That's a machine that randomly spins and twirls its occupant in multiple directions and through 360° revolutions. If your body can't handle that, and not everyone's can, you'll probably have a tough time at the Station for the first few days."

So nobody, sick or not, would avoid getting their ticket punched. Delano glanced at Jack Stecker, who appeared as calm and unworried as he could be. Steve Macey looked more like Delano felt. He glimpsed the borderline panic on Steve's face.

"Well, that's the program," Alviso said, "the best we could put together on such short notice. I suggest you visit the restroom now, take a quick shower if you like. Then we'll get started."

The next thirteen hours or so reminded Delano of the non-stop basic training at OCS in Quantico. At least back then he could complain, under his breath, of course, to his fellow officer candidates. As a Marine Officer, he had to prove to his two enlisted team members that he was tough enough to take anything. As soon as Delano saw Stecker in a tee shirt, he knew the gunny was in far better condition, with muscles bulging everywhere.

What saved Delano from appearing clumsy was his near eidetic memory, the same skill that had helped him develop his exceptional language skills. Once he read or heard something, he could almost always remember it.

Delano's parents had honed and intensified that skill, found in many children but seldom cultivated. Though born in Brooklyn, Delano's parents – his father was an Italian translator for a New York investment bank, his mother a teacher from London – spoke only Italian to their son until he was two years old, when they switched to English. Six months later, after he mastered English, they hired a Spanish tutor. That routine continued, language after language, for the next sixteen years, until he left for college. Before he was eighteen years old, Delano could memorize every phonetic sound he heard. His parents also expected him to recall and repeat every syllable exactly and with the proper accent.

Without that skill Delano would have been far behind Stecker. But while the Gunny struggled to remember the proper sequence to don the flight suit, the steps to seal it, how to adjust the oxygen flow, and the myriad of other details associated with using a complex pressure suit, Delano could practice getting in and out of the cumbersome gear. Not that these were full-capacity suits, suitable for extended periods of work in space. For the space rookies, the upgraded flight suits allowed brief exposure to outer space in the event that they needed to move from one ship to another, or transfer to the Station should the spaceplane be unable to dock.

Delano did OK on the spinner, though afterward it did take him a few minutes to get his stomach to stop shaking. The MGW – why couldn't they just call it a rock climbing wall – provided the closest thing to fun. He enjoyed the free floating sensation and climbed up and down the wall almost as fast as the Gunny. Steve, on the other hand, had to be rescued a few times before he made it to the top.

Two hours later, Alviso moved them along to the next segment, while the newly arrived Russians began their training. Delano caught a glimpse of them, and an hour later the two Chinese, as they passed one another in the hall. All four new arrivals appeared haggard, stressed out by jet lag. Delano doubted that he, Gunny, and Steve looked much better. Delano thought the Alliance members would be joining Alviso's lectures, but being several hours behind, they were being trained by other specialists.

Finally, after more than twelve hours, Alviso called it quits in the middle of a topic. Delano wondered why, until the FBI agent came in and led the three exhausted Americans to another, smaller room set up for videoconferencing.

"There's a conference call from General Klegg coming in . . . two minutes. Take your seats facing the cameras." The agent checked over the equipment, making sure the encryption protocols were engaged. As soon as the monitors lit up, the agent left the room. Delano found himself staring at General Klegg and his aide, Major Mitchell. Another man's head, at an odd angle, appeared on the second screen, and Delano realized that signal came from the space Station.

"Good to see you all again," Klegg began. "Also on this call is Air Force Lt. Colonel William Welsh, presently serving on the ISS as a science specialist. I spoke with Colonel Welsh earlier, and he explained the realities of life on the Station. The addition of at least seven space rookies will severely strain the Station's resources. Colonel Welsh will be heavily engaged in his usual activities and has taken over the role of Flight Commander and possibly chief babysitter. He will also be backing up Colonel Kosloff, the Flight Engineer. So he and I have determined Major Delano will assume command of the First Contact mission. The Major has command and combat experience, and will be taking the lead in dealing with the aliens anyhow. Major Delano will make any decisions regarding how the rest of the team are assigned duties. That includes the two Russians, and the two Chinese. Both countries have agreed to this. Any problem with that, Major?"

"No, Sir." Only about ten problems, but the training officers at Quantico stressed that Marine officers never had the slightest problem accepting a command.

"You will, of course, consult with Colonel Welsh as needed," Klegg went on. "If there is a conflict, which I sincerely hope doesn't arise, you will both call me. Is that clear, Major? Sergeants?"

All three answered, almost in unison, "Yes, Sir."

"Good. Now Sergeant Macey, your priorities will be to establish secure, simultaneous communication links with each member nation in the Alliance. We have agreed there will be no delays and no withholding of information and data. You will also record everything seen and said during any contact situations, in extreme detail, at the highest resolution you can. You will compress the data, and burst transmit it as frequently as possible. I want visual and audio of everything. If there is audio or video contact between the two alien ships, you will attempt to tap into their transmissions. If they communicate by any other means, see if you can hack into it."

Klegg paused to allow Sergeant Macey to acknowledge the command. "Gunny Stecker, your role is a little more difficult. You and . . . " Klegg glanced at his notes, "Chief Sergeant Class 4 Shen Zhu of the PLA will provide Station security. You both have the same orders – to make sure that none of the Station's scientific personnel or the Station itself fall into alien hands. That may require some delicacy, since Shen is also providing personal security for the Chinese translator, Dr. Duan Lian. She happens to be the niece of the General Secretary, the daughter of his youngest sister. In a way, that's good, but it may also create certain, uh, challenges. Major Delano, you need to keep an eye on that situation, since Chief Shen will almost certainly have special orders regarding her safety."

Oh, sure, no problem there, Delano figured. "Yes, Sir." No sense asking why they selected her, since she was already here. No sense in complaining either. Marine officer candidates learned that lesson the first day at Quantico.

"Therefore, Major, the initial task you perform upon arrival at the Station is to deploy the explosives. Make certain that in the event of hostilities the Station, its data banks, and key personnel do not fall under alien control. Understood?"

That constituted a direct order. To commit suicide if necessary. "Yes, Sir."

"I've spoken with General Zeng regarding this," Klegg went on, "and he is in agreement, so Chief Shen shouldn't present too many difficulties."

Klegg glanced down at his notes. "Major Delano, keep your tablet handy on the flight to the Station. I'll be sending you some files, and you will want to look them over. The files will include the Table of Organization and the bios of all personnel. Two more members of your team, a medical tech and a navigator, will arrive at the Station shortly after you. They're coming from the Chinese lunar base, but both are civilian contractors at JovCo."

"Yes, Sir." What the hell did JovCo have to do with this?

Klegg shifted his gaze. "Gunny Stecker, for your information, Chief Shen is a member of the Jinan Military Region Special Forces Unit. What they call 'Eagle' soldiers. Are you familiar with the term?"

"Yes, General. As I remember, Eagle soldiers are extremely fit and skilled in hand-to-hand fighting. Much like our Seal teams."

"Shen is also an expert in small arms and explosives. He's probably one of their best. I will transmit his service record, as soon as we finish translating it. But it may have been edited, so take care, Gunny, if you get my meaning."

"I do, Sir."

"Are you boys ready to go?" For the first time, Klegg's voice held some real concern.

"Yes, Sir, we are," Delano said. To his surprise, both Stecker and Macey echoed his words.

"If it means anything, I wish I were going with you," Klegg said. "We will be doing anything and everything we can to support you. Good luck to you all." The Pentagon screen went black.

But Colonel Welsh stayed on. "Major, to fill you in, we are expecting the alien ships to begin braking any time now. That means they will be orbiting Mars in about four hours. We can now estimate they could reach Earth orbit in about twenty-two hours, less if they pushed it. Of course we don't know how long they'll stay at Mars. Hell, some NASA experts think the aliens may like it there and settle down. Somehow I doubt that."

"Thank you, Colonel," Delano said. "Any idea what they might want on Mars?"

"We've been giving that considerable thought, wondering what sophisticated ships such as these might require. One element that Mars has in good quantity is niobium, and its cousin, tantalum. Both are relatively simple to extract from the Martian soil. Niobium, atomic number 41, has properties that make it useful in superconducting materials. Tantalum, atomic number 73, has some interesting aspects as well. One is that tantalum can increase the radioactive yield of nuclear weapons."

Great, just fucking great. Just what we need – bigger, dirtier bombs. But Delano kept his thoughts to himself. "Don't these elements exist on Earth as well?"

"Yes, but only in small quantities, and over the years they've become more difficult to locate and extract," Colonel Welsh said. "Brazil, China, and a few other places remain sources, but most other locations have been tapped out. Today the major source of niobium is Io, where it's mined along with certain other rare earth metals. But it has to be extracted via a cumbersome and time-consuming process. If the Martian bases ever get around to mining operations, niobium and tantalum will be priority items."

Alviso entered the room. "The choppers are waiting, Major."

"Thanks for the update, Colonel Welsh," Delano said. "Anything else? Our handlers are giving me the hurry up sign."

"Copy that," Welsh said. "No, nothing that can't wait. Hope you guys enjoy your first flight into space. See you in about fifteen hours."

The connection went black. Outside, Delano heard the sound of a helicopter starting up. "Looks like our ride to Spaceport is here."

When they left the building, Delano found two choppers waiting for them. The unhappy travelers were divided between them, sitting on jump seats and jammed in among the gray aluminum crates holding their supplies. Delano hadn't realized how much cargo space would be eaten up by the food, water, and oxygen the new arrivals would require, plus all their specialized equipment. Superintendent Alviso had mentioned that the Russians had started prepping a drone to resupply the Station, but it wouldn't be ready for three or four days.

Demitri Timofeyevich Petrov joined the Americans on one chopper. The Russian cultural anthropologist was almost sixty, which made him the oldest in the group. Even so, he looked as strong as the proverbial Russian bear. Delano had read about the famous man's adventures. He had survived several close calls in the jungles of South America, and backpacked in and out of rough country in Mongolia and Kazakhstan for months at a stretch.

They had time for a quick handshake and a brief introduction before the chopper's engine revved up to full power. Delano had hoped to talk with his fellow linguists on the short flight – Spaceport was only ninety-five miles away by air, roughly thirty minutes flight time – but the other two linguists and Sgt. Shen had boarded the second chopper. Besides, the engine noise and vibration made meaningful communication impossible.

With a sigh, Delano closed his eyes and tried to get some more rest. Something told him he was going to need it.

Chapter 7

When they landed at Spaceport, the first thing Delano noticed was the change in altitude. Located almost a mile above sea level, Spaceport offered an ideal location for a launch facility. As the astronauts frequently joked, the first mile is the real bitch.

Local FBI agents, badges displayed on their jackets, herded the space travelers to an impressive two-story structure of aluminum and concrete shaped like a futuristic space ship. Their guides led them through the glass-enclosed lobby and into a luxurious conference room no doubt used to brief VIPs. Large color photographs and paintings of spacecraft decorated the walls, carpeted to reduce the noise. A thick picture window overlooked the runways. Inside Superintendent Alviso waited for them.

"Glad you all made it here safe and sound," he said. "There are bathrooms through that door, and I suggest you use them now, and again in about thirty minutes. After that, use your enema packs and put on your MAG, because the next toilet stop will be on the Station."

Everyone took him up on the offer. Delano, who by chance had chosen the far side of the conference table to dump his things, was the last one out of the room. He witnessed a bit of drama outside the bathrooms. Dr. Duan Lian, the Chinese linguist, started into the ladies room, and her male escort attempted to follow her.

She whirled around and with both hands shoved him away from the door. They exchanged heated words in Mandarin, the dialect of Beijing, which Delano understood. Lian ordered Shen to stop behaving like a child, and go join the other men. Then she slammed the door in his face and Delano heard the click of a latch.

By then Delano had walked past Shen, though he heard the Eagle soldier mutter something in Cantonese. Smiling, Delano pushed through the men's room door. The colorful expression Shen had used translated to something like "crazy bitch," to take the most polite rendition.

Welcome to the party. If Delano survived this insane mission, his chances of ending up inside the Camp Pendleton brig kept increasing. And now he had to worry about an overprotective trained killer and a high-strung woman with serious connections to the General Secretary of China. *Damn, things just kept getting better and better.*

*   *   *

Dr. Duan Lian stared at her reflection in the mirror, and frowned. Despite washing her face and hands, she looked haggard and felt exhausted. The harsh lights in the bathroom didn't help. The long, non-stop trip from Beijing to Holloman had left her jet lagged despite several attempts to sleep. The flight's direction from west to east only made the effect worse. Her uncle had provided a government jet with every conceivable comfort, but nothing really helped. Despite the fact that it carried only two passengers, herself and Sergeant Shen, it barely had the range for the almost eleven thousand kilometer flight.

She reminded herself that she had arrived in the United States, so she better start thinking in miles – close to seven thousand miles. She had landed at an American military base in New Mexico, quite an accomplishment considering her uncle was the General Secretary of the Party's Central Committee, as well as the President of the People's Republic of China. More important, at least to her, Liu Quisan was her uncle, she was his only niece, and she loved him like a father. Her real father had died just after her ninth birthday. Her mother acted as hostess for all of her brother's official functions, and she and Lian lived in his home in Beijing.

Lian had insisted on meeting with him, as soon as she learned of the frantic search going on for linguists. Lian's phone rang in the middle of the night. Her favorite mentor broke the news, and within the hour she received two more calls from colleagues seeking more information. As the search for language specialists continued, Lian wondered why, as one of the top linguists in China, her uncle had not summoned her himself.

Sitting on the edge of the bed, Lian thought about that. Though only twenty-six years old, she had already mastered every Asian dialect in her country, as well as Japanese, Korean, English, French, and Russian, among others. A child prodigy, she had amazed her parents and teacher with the ease with which she learned new

configuration. He sighed. As Italian engineers like to say, *solo un piccolo problema.*

An included picture showed the outer hull. Antennae, sensors, telescopes, experiment boxes, hull cameras, and God knew what else seemingly obscured every square meter of the exterior. NASA had installed the large optical telescope on the top portion of the ship, just behind the Control Room. In this image the scope pointed forward, like the main cannon of a tank.

Now that Delano thought about it, the ship did resemble an armored battle tank, festooned with paraphernalia that covered almost every surface.

Most of the guts of the ship were underneath the air-tight flooring, including the wiring conduits, water pumps, and carbon dioxide filters. Whatever space not taken up with machinery was allocated to storage. Less than a meter separated the outer hull from the floor plates.

The exposed overhead contained the lighting, humidity and temperature controls, scrubbers, and the air delivery systems. The height from deck to overhead was three meters. When NASA completed the conversion, three main corridors ran the length of the ship. Two of them terminated at the Control Room, while the third provided access to and from the two airlocks, both located on the port side of the Station.

Compartments were dedicated to specific functions, such as oxygen storage and water tanks. These had been part of the ship's original construction, and NASA hadn't bothered to modify them. Before turning over the ship, JovCo had removed two of the three air processing units and gutted the engine room, which was now used mainly for storage of waste and trash.

That explained why the Station could support only a limited number of people. If the air processors hadn't been removed, another twenty or thirty specialists could have been accommodated. *Plus de malchance.*

Three science laboratories of various sizes had been installed, plus one dedicated to biology and plant experimentation. A small medical lab, machine shop, and exercise room completed the layout. A good sized loading dock permitted the delivery of larger scientific components. Every remaining compartment was used for food, oxygen, and supply storage.

Obviously NASA hadn't been willing to expend any extra funds on modifications, and over the years the various crews had repurposed (translated: cannibalized) equipment and compartments as need dictated.

The Control Room, which protruded ten meters from the main body of the Station, possessed a large viewport. Filled with computer workstations, the Control Room computers and monitors managed the Station's daily maintenance. When not sleeping or working in the science labs, the NASA specialists spent most of their time in the Lounge or the Control Room. The Lounge also included some communication and monitoring workstations, along with the usual chairs, tables, and food serving equipment.

Studying the data, he concentrated on the areas of the ship modified for scientific functions. When he finished, Delano had a good idea of the Station's layout, and the names and purposes of each compartment.

Unfortunately, the document contained nothing about meeting and greeting aliens.

He read everyone's bio at least twice, including those of the late additions from the lunar base and the crew already on the Station. Delano saved the lengthy emails sent by Grayson and Tasco to the lawyer on Earth for last, assuming they would be the least critical. Two paragraphs in Delano realized how wrong that assumption was.

The emails made for compelling reading, and he studied the video recording Peter Tasco had made of the container, its contents, and the dead pilot, who Tasco referred to as 'Star Rider.' The alien ship sent a burst transmission during the recording. Damn, this Tasco guy might be the idiot who triggered the aliens' awareness of our planet and their subsequent arrival.

When Delano finished, nearly three hours had passed. He'd memorized most of the information and some of it might even prove useful. Delano's stomach kept acting up, but he ignored it. Instead he decided to check on his team, despite the risks and against the pilot's orders.

Delano unbuckled himself, then tried to get out of his seat. Fortunately he hung onto the chair and saved himself from slamming into the bulkhead above. His feet kept moving, flailing around with a will of their own. Demitri Petrov extended a hand to help Delano regain his balance. He took a moment to catch his breath. Alviso had warned about this, suggesting that the new space travelers make small, controllable motions and always keep a hand on something to prevent injury. Easy to say, but harder to do.

Delano thanked Petrov, who watched him closely, no doubt wondering why the stupid American Major was moving about.

"Are you feeling alright, Dr. Petrov?" Delano kept his voice calm despite the turmoil in his stomach and inner ears.

"Yes, thank you, Major Delano." Petrov could still smile. "I am very much enjoying this . . . adventure. Exciting, is it not?"

Yeah, sure. Some fucking exciting adventure. Delano nodded and moved to the next row. Lian's seat was behind Delano's. The Chinese girl – he now knew she was twenty-six years old, had two Ph.D.'s in language studies, and two Master's degrees, one in English Literature from UCLA – looked pale. She kept swallowing, and he noticed that her barf bag was sealed, indicating that she had thrown up at least once. And had done so without making a sound. Tough girl, he decided, with plenty of determination.

"Dr. Duan, are you okay?" Delano asked in Chinese, to make sure she didn't misunderstand anything.

"Yes, Major." She replied in the same language, then swallowed again. "I am attempting to keep my stomach under control."

"It's difficult," Delano agreed. "Is there anything I can do?"

She switched to English. "No, but would you please check on Sergeant Shen? I think he is having a bad reaction. I would go myself, but I'm afraid I might throw up on him."

Sympathetic vomiting happened all too often, Alviso had warned them, especially in the confines of a spaceplane or the Station. "I will, Dr. Duan."

She spoke perfect English, with the slower paced usage of Southern California. Well, she had spent two years at UCLA in Los Angeles. Not quite the party capital of California universities – perennial winner Santa Barbara held that title – but a close second.

Delano, moving with care, reached over and shifted his grip to the arm of Steve Macey's chair. "Steve, you OK?"

"Feel like . . . crap, Joe. My head is pounding, and I keep thinking I'm falling."

"Well, they warned us," Delano said. "How's your stomach?"

"No problem there, Sir. Haven't thrown up yet, or even felt like it."

All the junk food Steve probably wolfed down with his coffee must have permanently desensitized his stomach. "Good for you. Hang in there."

Clutching the headrests, Delano pulled himself to the next row, taking care not to bang into anyone's head. Dr. Stepanov was clearly still in distress, his face pale and his hands trembling. Beads of sweat lined his forehead, and Delano saw one break off and float in the air. The vein in Stepanov's neck throbbed and Delano could see the Russian's heart was racing.

"Dr. Stepanov? Feeling any better?" Delano leaned closer and read the vitals on the man's arm monitor. Blood pressure up, heart rate ninety-two beats per minute. Not good for a man in a zero-gravity environment and stationary.

"I am sorry to say I am not, Major Delano." Stepanov's words came slowly, as if the man had to concentrate to get them out. "I've thrown up three times and my stomach is completely empty." He coughed and started to vomit. He clapped the bag over his mouth just in time. When the convulsion stopped, Stepanov let his head loll back on the headrest. "You see how it is."

"I'm sorry, Doctor. Just try to hold on until we reach the Station. They'll take care of you much better there."

Feeling foolish at his empty words, Delano shifted to Gunny Stecker's chair. Looking relaxed and at ease, Stecker just gave him the thumbs up sign.

Delano acknowledged the gesture and moved to the last member of the team, Sergeant Shen.

"Sergeant, how are you doing?" Delano spoke slowly, to make sure Shen wouldn't misunderstand. The man looked pale, and he, too, had thrown up a few times.

"I am well, Major Delano." Shen kept his eyes straight ahead. "There is no problem."

"Sergeant Shen, each of us is having trouble adjusting. It is expected. I will not . . . no one will think less of you, but as team leader I must know your real condition."

The Chinese soldier swallowed. "In that case, my stomach is twisted and my head hurts. If I move it, I think I am falling."

"I'm feeling the same way, Sergeant. Remember what they said, that it takes one to three days to acclimate yourself to zero gravity. This will pass, and we should be on the Station in a few hours. Is there anything you need before then?"

"No, Major Delano. I can last that long. Is Dr. Duan well?"

"A little better than you. Dr. Stepanov is having the most difficulty."

Moving cautiously, Delano dragged his way back to his seat and settled down, breathing a sigh when he snapped the first fastener closed.

The cockpit door opened and Colonel Hatcher glided over to Delano's seat, halting his progress by grabbing the chair's arm. "You shouldn't be moving around, Major. I told you to stay buckled in."

So Hatcher was keeping an eye on them from the cockpit. Delano ignored the rebuke. Marine leaders were expected to see to their squad's needs first. "Just checking on my team, Colonel. Stepanov's getting worse. Can you give him something to ease the nausea, maybe put him to sleep for a few hours?"

Hatcher hesitated. "I've been watching his vitals and I've already spoken to the doctors at Spaceport, told them I've given him the maximum dose. He's fifty-six years old and they won't recommend anything more at this time. Two tablets are supposed to last for eight hours."

Delano glanced at his watch. Eight hours had passed since liftoff, but Stepanov hadn't been given the meds until almost two hours into the flight. "Alright, let's wait another hour, that should be close enough. Then give him a second dose."

"Sounds good," Hatcher said. "I'll be back in . . . sixty-five minutes." He went down the aisle, checked everyone's readings, and returned to the cockpit.

Opening his tablet, Delano stared again at the files, then pulled up the medical bios for each member. Everyone's genetics had been examined. No one possessed a gene combination that indicated a high risk of space sickness. Nevertheless, some people got sick and others didn't, so obviously the gene test wasn't infallible.

He started through the information again, this time taking care to memorize anything that might be important. Hatcher returned and administered another pill to Stepanov. Dr. Duan asked for and accepted something to calm her stomach, and so did Steve Macey. Delano wanted one but refused to take anything that might dull or slow his thoughts.

He ignored his fluttering stomach and continued reading. The sooner they reached the Station, the better. Two hours later, he set the tablet aside. Delano wanted to sleep, but his mind kept racing, thinking about the bios of those aboard the spaceplane and waiting on the Station. Suddenly the enormity of the situation hit him. These men and women were his team, his command, and he now had responsibility for each and every one of their lives. The decisions he would make might kill them all. Even worse, he could make some dumb mistake that left everyone dead, and accomplish nothing for planet Earth.

The tough lessons Delano had learned in Yemen washed over him. No matter how hard you might plan, no matter what advantage you had in men or material or equipment, the enemy remained resourceful and adaptable. A good plan might last only seconds once the bullets started flying.

He chased the grim thoughts from his mind. Aliens awaited him, aliens with sufficient firepower to level the Station in the blink of an eye. All Delano had was his mouth. He might end up talking while the aliens started shooting, and there would be nothing he could do. People would die and the blame would be his, whether he survived or not. That was the final onus, no matter how good his intentions or his decisions. It was, he remembered, an unfair world.

Delano pushed the gloom away. He would do his best, and damn his critics. By now his eyes had grown heavy, and he didn't have to close them for long before he drifted into an uneasy sleep.

*   *   *

Lian, seated behind Major Delano, watched his head slump forward. She had dozed off earlier, for about twenty minutes. Not enough to refresh her, but more than enough to keep her thoughts racing. Her stomach continued to knot and her head hurt. Since she couldn't sleep, Lian forced herself to consider her situation. She would soon be on the International Space Station, and this American would be in charge of communication with the alien species.

Of course the Americans and Russians had agreed to cooperate with China, but now all three linguists were in the field and circumstances could easily change. Her uncle had warned her about that possibility and advised that she insist on an equal position with the other Alliance members. If necessary, she could call on Sergeant Shen for support. The Eagle soldier, she had learned, was one of the most dangerous fighters in all of China, let alone their military. From hand-to-hand combat to firearms to knives and even throwing stars, Shen had mastered them all. His personal bag contained a pair of fighting knives and three stars.

If she hadn't read Sergeant Stecker's file, she might have thought the slow-moving and easy-going American Marine, the one they called 'Gunny,' would not last ten seconds in a contest with Shen. But Stecker had earned a red and black checkered belt from the Shorin-Rhu school of fighting, which made him a Master. Perhaps as important, he had several independent missions, what the Americans called operations, to his credit, which meant he could think on his own. General Klegg must have considered Stecker capable, or he would not be aboard. Aside from speaking Spanish and a little Chinese, he had no language skills. His knowledge of explosives matched Sergeant Shen's.

As for Major Delano, he might be a Marine, but he was far from a professional fighting man. Nor did his rank, including the recent promotion, inspire confidence. As her uncle frequently said, being an officer in the military does not necessarily make a man a leader. Leadership is proved only in a crisis, never in an office or on a committee.

Lian knew most of these concerns would be answered in the next forty-eight hours. How well she, Delano, and Stepanov would work together might prove critical. If dissension arose, the mission could fail, and Earth could suffer the consequences. Fortunately, if she encountered any difficulties, a quick transmission to her uncle would bring immediate results. It did help to have friends, or in her case relatives, in high places.

Still, she knew it would be better to avoid such situations. In her entire life, she had never asked her uncle for any help or favors, though he had many times offered to assist her. Instead she had often argued with him over her career choices. Now the roles had reversed. He was depending on her to tell him what these aliens wanted, and what danger they represented. Lian would not let him down.

With a sigh, she closed her eyes, certain she would not be able to rest. A moment later, she fell asleep.

Chapter 8

Day 3: 2340 Zulu Time

Once again buckled in tight with helmet on, Delano waited as the long flight to the Station drew to a close. Less than eleven hours after departing Spaceport, the spaceplane had approached close enough to the Station to see a blinking white light on the camera feed. Colonel Hatcher, or maybe the unknown and still unseen copilot, had guided *Jumper 1* so precisely that only two small course corrections, each less than ten seconds, had been needed. Now the craft drifted slowly toward the Station's docking bay, a large hatch on the Station's lower deck, a few meters aft of the docking boom.

Colonel Hatcher announced he had shut down the Skylon engine and would use maneuvering jets for the final docking. Meter by meter the spaceplane drifted toward its destination. Contact came with a start, as the craft gently bumped against the shock absorbers on the freighter's hull. A small robotic arm guided from inside the Station reached out and grabbed *Jumper 1* on the first try. Centimeter by centimeter the two vessels merged, aligning the entry hatch of the spaceplane flush against that of the Station.

One last clanging of metal, then all sense of motion within the spaceplane ceased. A dull thumping penetrated *Jumper 1* through its hull. Hatcher exited the cockpit and unsealed the outer door but didn't open it. He stood beside the main hatchway, waiting. Hatcher, taking no chances, kept his helmet on. A light beside the opening turned green. The pilot pulled down on the two latching mechanisms, and then dragged the big door inward. A hiss of air signaled the equalization of pressure between the two crafts.

A figure in a regulation spacesuit, not the simple pressure versions worn by Delano and his team, glided into the spaceplane's main compartment. He and Hatcher doubled checked the readouts beside the door, then the stranger unlatched his helmet. Delano recognized Lt. Colonel Welsh. After one final check, Hatcher removed his as well, then turned to the passengers and signaled they could do the same.

Delano worked the latches and pulled his helmet off, glad to get away from breathing the thick air inside the suit. Distasteful odors had leaked from his diaper and fouled the air. He heard the same sighs of relief from the rest of the team.

"Welcome to the Station," Welsh said. "I'm sure you want to get out of those suits. We'll escort you through the docking collar into the Station two at a time, starting with Major Delano."

By now Delano had loosened the restraints keeping him in place. He drifted above the seat, but kept a firm grip on one of the fastenings. He did not intend to go floating off like a clumsy idiot. "No," he said, "the first two to leave *Jumper 1* will be Dr. Stepanov and Dr. Duan Lian. Dr. Stepanov is ill and requires medical attention. Lian needs to prepare herself and begin planning for the alien encounter."

Colonel Welsh, caught by surprise at the challenge to his order, stared for a moment. Hatcher glanced away, amused by the situation, but kept his mouth shut. He was, as he would cheerfully testify at any subsequent court-martial, not involved.

Delano wasn't finished. "After Lian has freshened up, I want her to be the first on the elliptical for at least fifteen minutes. A little exercise for everyone will help clear our heads. We've been flying or sitting around for the last few days, and the flight here hasn't helped."

Delano glanced toward the rear of the plane. "The next two out will be Gunny Stecker and Sergeant Shen. They'll need help transporting their equipment, which comes off first, before any of the regular supplies. Can they utilize one of the storage chambers, unless they are unavailable?"

By now Colonel Welsh had recovered. "Of course, Major. Engine Storage Compartment A is almost empty. We can clear it out."

"Good. Then please take Dr. Stepanov inside and see that someone helps him until the Med Tech arrives. Dr. Petrov, Sergeant Macey, and I will go last. After that, you can start unloading the food and water supplies."

Delano turned to Colonel Hatcher, who grasped the situation. Once *Jumper 1* had reached the Station, and as long as it remained docked, Major Delano commanded the mission. Everyone's orders had been clear about that, thanks to General Klegg. Delano could read the pilot's mind – a fucking asshole Marine had taken charge of the Station and its crew, and immediately started pushing his weight around.

"Yes, Major," Hatcher said. He pulled himself over to Dr. Stepanov's chair and began unbuckling the sick linguist's straps.

Delano turned to face Lian. He moved too quickly and nearly lost his grip on the harness. "Dr. Duan, Colonel Welsh will escort you to the main toilet. It's in Compartment 12. The exercise equipment is in Compartment 7. After you finish your cardio exercise, please proceed to the Station's main Control Room and check it out. I think that is where we want to set up our equipment. All Station communications pass through that chamber. It also has the only viewport on the Station. Unless you find the room isn't suitable."

By now she had finished extricating herself from the seat. She floated up, and would have banged into what would normally be the plane's overhead. Delano caught her arm and steadied her. Her other hand went to her mouth. "Stomach," she said, barely moving her lips.

Colonel Welsh floated over the top of Delano's seat. "Hang on to me, Dr. Duan. I'll escort you to the toilet."

Delano moved over to Gunny Stecker's chair. Sergeant Shen had already unbuckled himself. "You two will make sure that all of your equipment gets to the storage room and is locked inside. After you've finished cleaning up and doing some cardio, I want you to inspect every piece of your gear. Test everything. As soon as I get time, we'll make a detailed inspection of the ship, and you will select the best locations to place the explosive charges. Also see if you can identify some possible defensive positions. Did you get all that, Sergeant Shen? Your English is very good, but I can repeat it in Chinese."

"Very clear, Major. Thank you."

Shen definitely looked better. Either he was adjusting to zero gravity or the second pill had kicked in.

Welsh returned, bringing with him another man that Delano recognized as the young British biologist, Darrell Parrish. "I left Dr. Duan with Mission Commander Susan York," Welsh said. "Thought she might be more comfortable with a woman assisting her."

"Yes, thank you, Colonel. Now if you can help Gunny Stecker move his gear? And please be careful. The contents are very . . . fragile."

Delano had thought it would take two or three trips to move all the special cargo. But Welsh pulled bungee cords from one of his baggy pockets and hooked everything together. The four men soon had the supplies on the move.

Delano turned to Sergeant Macey. "Ok, Steve, your program is pretty much the same. There's an empty berth near the Control Room. Stowe all your gear in there. Then get cleaned up and do some cardio. After that, test your equipment. We pulled some serious gees, and I want to be certain everything is still functioning. You'll want to spend most of your time with Colonel Kosloff. He's the man who makes everything up here work, and he knows the most about the Station's communication capabilities. Oh, and please see to it that whatever Dr. Duan wants, she gets."

"Yes, Major."

That left Dr. Petrov, the Russian anthropologist. "Dr. Petrov, I would appreciate it if you would use the toilets and cardio last. You appear to be taking zero gravity better than any of us."

"Of course, Major. But please call me Demitri. Dr. Petrov seems too formal for what we are doing."

Delano nodded. "Yes, Demitri. You can call me Delano. Since we don't know anything about these aliens, we probably won't need you until they arrive. Could I impose on you to assist us in some other ways?"

"Of course, Major. What can I do to help?"

"You know we have explosives and weapons on board. I would like you to keep an eye on that storage room until everything settles down, and Gunny Stecker and Sergeant Shen can take over. I don't want to leave that stuff alone."

"I don't know anything about explosives, Major . . . Delano. I am, however, an excellent marksman with a pistol and rifle. One of the weapons wouldn't be a Makarov pistol, would it?"

"No, sorry, just the usual Glocks. Your skill with a pistol wasn't in your file, but I'm glad to hear it. All I want you to do is guard Storage Compartment A until Stecker and Shen get up to speed. Once their gear is inside, nobody else but those two go in, not even you. If you want to help out after that, even better."

Before Demitri could reply, Colonel Welsh swam into the plane. Two others followed him, and Delano recognized the Russian physicist, Maks, and Colonel Kosloff.

"Time to go, Major," Welsh said.

Delano pulled himself back to his seat, grabbed his backpack with one hand and let Welsh take his other arm. A strange sensation came over Delano, as he floated along. In a way, it did feel like he was swimming. At least it took his mind off his stomach.

They reached the toilet area first. Gunny Stecker had just finished. Colonel Welsh suggested that Delano take advantage of the opportunity. Feeling a little guilty about jumping the line, Delano went in. Welsh stood in the doorway while Delano fumbled his way out of the flight suit, banging around a few times. Whenever that happened, Welsh held him steady, politely ignoring the stink from the MAG.

Once he had the thick garment off, Delano removed his sneakers and tee shirt. Now only the foul-smelling garment remained.

Colonel Welsh extracted a black plastic bag from a box mounted on the bulkhead. "Dump the MAG in the bag," Welsh explained, "then wash yourself off with those moist towels. When you're clean, they go in the bag, too. Seal it tight. You know how to use the toilet?"

"Geez, I hope so," Delano said. "I really have to go."

"If you get stuck, knock on the door and I'll come help you. It may be harder than you think."

"Thanks, Colonel," Delano said. Naked by now, he sat down on the toilet. Ignoring the straps that would fasten him to the seat, he held on with both hands until he emptied his bladder.

Ten minutes later, dressed in a clean tee shirt and cargo shorts, Delano exited the toilet, wearing the lightweight deck shoes they'd given him at Holloman. He shoved the black bag containing the diaper and other soiled garments into another larger one, which Colonel Welsh sealed and set aside. Those bags would be returning to Earth on the spaceplane. The Station crew missed no opportunity to get trash and waste off the Station.

Delano headed toward the forward end of the Station, aware now of the loud voices emanating from that direction. Handholds along the corridor walls helped him, and he managed to glide into the Control Room almost unnoticed. The whoosh of air flowing through the vents made plenty of noise as the air conditioner tried to keep up with the crowd inside the chamber.

Kosloff, Parrish the biologist, and Maks were there, along with

Commander Susan York and Dr. Duan. Welsh and Hatcher were in each other's faces, raising their voices.

"I don't give a damn what your orders say, Welsh. We just got here, and we need a few hours rest before we return. It's in the Regulations, for God's sake!"

Welsh shook his head. "In ninety minutes, a shuttle from the Moon is arriving and we need the docking platform. You've got until then to disengage. You can park a kilometer away and take as much time as you need to recover."

"I am not getting on that spaceplane," Commander Susan York announced. "I'm Mission Commander here, and I'm not leaving. Only NASA can order me down. This could be the chance of a lifetime, to make contact with an alien race."

"I'm sorry, Susan, but that's what General Klegg's orders state." Colonel Welsh noticed Delano floating inside the room and maintaining his hold on a hand stanchion. "Major Delano, we're having a problem. Colonel Hatcher wants at least eight hours to rest before he departs, and Commander York . . ."

"I heard it, Colonel Welsh." Delano kept his voice low but firm. He knew the best way to be heard when everyone was shouting was to speak in a normal voice. Everyone turned to face him.

"Commander York," Delano said, "my orders come directly from General Klegg, the head of Operation Sentinel Star by order of the President. You are to return immediately to Earth. Your presence is desired at NASA, and this Station is now considered expendable. So please, gather any personal effects and prepare for the return flight. You have ninety minutes."

Delano turned to Colonel Hatcher. "Sorry, Hatcher, but you've got the same ninety minutes to prep your ship and get out of here. If you're not gone by then, I will disengage the airlock myself. A vessel is coming from the Moon, and you need to be out of here before it arrives. Is that clear, Colonel Hatcher?"

The pilot of *Jumper 1* wanted to argue, but he did know his orders and all about the chain of command. At least Delano hadn't threatened him with a court martial.

"Yes, Major. But I'll need help off-loading the two unused booster rockets. Can't try reentry with those attached."

Delano remembered the boosters had to be removed. He glanced at Colonel Welsh.

"I'll suit up and help Captain Hatcher," Welsh offered. "Kosloff, can you lend a hand?"

Hatcher muttered something under his breath, but Delano decided not to hear it. Swearing at your commanding officer, under Article Eighty-Nine, could rate a court martial. "If you need help unloading the cargo, let me or Colonel Welsh know."

Hatcher launched himself toward the door without another word.

"As for you, Commander York, I'd hate to put you in restraints, but I have two marines with me who will do just that." Delano turned to Derrell Parrish. "Dr. Parrish, this Station may be a dangerous place if the aliens do come, but General Klegg hopes you will remain aboard to help us figure out what these aliens are about. But you can leave with Commander York if you wish."

Parrish shrugged. "I'll stay, Major. As Commander York said, this is the chance of a lifetime."

"That's one way to look at it," Delano agreed. "The rest of you, please leave the Control Room. I need to speak with Dr. Duan."

Before anyone started moving, a chime sounded from the communications control panel. Kosloff floated over to the console and studied the monitor. "It's from General Klegg," Kosloff announced, then activated the channel, this one a voice-only.

"Yes, General Klegg. Colonel Kosloff speaking."

"Good, glad to hear your voice, Colonel. Is Major Delano there?"

Delano pulled himself over to the comm station. "Yes, Sir, I'm here."

"I'll make this quick," Klegg said. "We just received an encrypted message from Mars Base. The alien ships arrived in orbit almost five hours ago. The base went dark two hours before that, hoping the aliens wouldn't notice them. One ship descended and landed near or inside Mons Olympus. Mars Base reopened communications when the aliens left orbit. If they're headed your way, you have between twelve and eighteen hours."

"We'll keep watch for them, Sir," Delano said.

"Good, Major. Are you are making your preparations?"

"Just getting started, Sir. The spaceplane will depart in less than ninety minutes with one passenger. Commander York will be aboard. Doctor Parrish has volunteered to stay with us."

"Good. General Zeng informed us that the Chinese shuttle is

approaching the Station and should be docking within the hour. Did you read the files I sent? You understand what she's carrying?"

"Copy that, General, but I haven't had a chance to share the information with the others."

"Do so as soon as you can. Everything else under control?"

Translated, that meant: have you taken charge? "Yes, Sir."

"Contact me every three hours from now on. I'm your main point of communication for the Alliance. Lots of people down here are interested in what's going on up there. Otherwise I'll try to stay out of your hair. Klegg out."

Still an abrupt bastard. No good luck, no friendly goodbye. Maybe Klegg had already written off the Station and everyone on it. Delano turned to face the others. "The Chinese shuttle is carrying the last two members of our team, a medical technician and a navigator. It's also carrying a small, scout-sized alien spacecraft with a dead pilot on board. The ship was discovered on Jupiter's moon, Io, almost eight weeks ago. That craft is now the most valuable cargo ever transported back to Earth. It's headed for the Chinese launch facility at Jiuquan, for study by an Alliance team of scientists and engineers."

Stunned surprise greeted Delano's words. He let that sink in. "I'm ready to tell you what little I know about this alien ship. But if you can wait another hour or two, you can hear the whole story direct from our new team members, the two people who delivered the ship to JovCo's base."

Delano glanced around, but nobody seemed eager to know more. "OK, thanks for waiting. Now I need everyone to leave the Control Room. Dr. Duan and I have some things to discuss."

When the last person floated out, Delano swung the starboard hatch closed, then paused to look around. Equipment, monitors, and electronics covered every square inch of wall surface, with a few controls even dangling from the overhead. The center of the compartment was relatively empty, except for the two workstations in the center. Four acceleration couches served as chairs.

He glanced at the viewport, but saw nothing but dull gray glass instead of stars. It took a moment before Delano realized that a metal panel outside the Station covered the glass. *I've been in space for almost a day, and I still haven't seen a single star.*

Pulling himself over to the nearest couch, he strapped himself in with a sigh. "OK, Doctor . . ."

Dr. Duan took the adjoining couch and faced him. "Please call me Lian, Major Delano. I do not think we need to be so formal."

"Yes, Doctor . . . . Lian. And I don't think it will hurt military morale if you call me Joe or Delano. I read your bio on the spaceplane, and I must say it's impressive. With Dr. Stepanov ill, I'm thinking you should take the lead in any communication efforts."

"Thank you, Joe. Your resume was interesting as well."

Interesting? Well, she did speak more languages. He wondered what Klegg had shared with the Chinese. "Now, what do you think of this room? It does have the only viewport on the Station."

The viewport measured two and a half meters wide by one meter tall, cast from four inches of metallic glass. More than enough to stop a fifty caliber bullet. But this glass had been exposed to space for almost thirteen years, and who knew how strong it remained. Delano had no idea how long it would last against a laser, particle beam weapon, or even a sharp fingernail.

"Will we be communicating through the viewport?"

"No, I expect we'll be using video cameras for communications. Sergeant Macey . . . Steve, will be working on that. But it might be useful to watch their ship, and for them to see inside ours. It may help them decide we're not hostile. Besides, I'd like to see some stars while I'm here."

She smiled. "I agree. We can set up three chairs facing the viewport. I saw a table long enough for us in the Lounge."

"It may be only the two of us," Delano said. "Dr. Stepanov is still experiencing difficulties and may not be able to help."

"I spoke with him for a few minutes," Lian said. "He is determined to do whatever he can. Even if he is not ready when the aliens arrive, he may be better in a day or two."

"Yes, that's possible," Delano said. "I was considering sending him back on the spaceplane, but I suppose he should stay. He's come this far."

"You mentioned that a medical technician is arriving?"

"Yes, Linda Grayson. At least you won't be the only woman aboard."

She looked at him for a moment, then turned away. Delano realized he'd said something politically incorrect, demeaning in fact.

"Sorry, I didn't mean that the way it sounded."

"This medical person may be able to help Dr. Stepanov," she said, giving him another quick smile. "But how can a navigator help us?"

"I'm not sure, Lian. We can ask him when he gets here. But General Klegg wanted a navigator, and so far he's put together a good team." Delano changed the subject. "You know that the ISS is considered expendable. I may have to blow up the Station to prevent the aliens from capturing us."

Lian sighed. "Yes, my Uncle didn't want me to come because of that. But I insisted that I was the best qualified linguist in China. He finally agreed, because he knows he can trust me to tell him the truth." She met his gaze. "I do not know exactly what Sergeant Shen's orders are regarding me."

Delano shrugged. "Probably the same as Gunny Stecker's regarding me. Don't let any specialists fall into alien hands. But I'm sure Sergeant Shen and Gunny Stecker will try to keep us both alive for as long as possible, and I've no problem with that." He shook his head. "Maybe it won't get that bad."

"Yes, let us hope. For the first time in history, we are facing something bigger than ourselves and our countries. Perhaps this will be a time of optimism."

"Yes, as we say in the Marines, hope for the best, but prepare for the worst," Delano said. *And it's almost always the worst.* "Can I ask you to work with Sergeant Macey to set up the Control Room? I need to help Gunny Stecker and Sergeant Shen. I'll be back as soon as possible."

"Yes, of course. Good luck to you . . . Joe."

"Good luck to you, Lian, and to all of us."

Delano, despite having the Station's schematics in his head, managed to lose his way only once. With a little help from Colonel Kosloff, after a near collision, Delano reached the engine storage room. That turned out to be about twenty-five meters from where the spaceplane had docked. The hatch was closed, so he pounded on it with his fist. The reaction sent him spinning away. After that, Delano learned to hold onto the door lever while he knocked.

Sergeant Shen opened the hatch and helped Delano inside. Gunny Stecker, attached by a packing strap to the floor, sat with a container cover doubling as a desk on his lap, going over his notes.

Stecker nodded in greeting. "We've unpacked everything. All the explosives are in that corner, still in their original cartons to minimize vibration. We're checking the lists. So far nothing is missing and everything is in good shape."

"I have been studying the Station's construction plans," Sergeant Shen said. "I believe there are three places we should place the explosives. The detonation of any two should blow the Station apart."

Delano glanced around. Explosives, detonators, firearms, shooting equipment, duct tape, personal weapons, ammo, all neatly set out and fastened down so that no sudden jolt or bump could send anything floating away. Someone had packed double-sided tape with this situation in mind. All the containers, boxes, and devices had labels in Chinese and English. Klegg's staff knew what they were doing.

"You've both done well," Delano said. "When you're ready, I'll send Colonel Kosloff in to review your placements. He might suggest a few other locations."

"Good idea," Stecker said.

"And when you do plant the explosives, place them out of view. I don't want the sight of bombs making our people nervous. It also occurred to me that these aliens, if they do show up, might want to inspect the Station. If so, I don't want them discovering what we've prepared."

Sergeant Shen looked surprised. "Why allow them to board?"

"I might have to. If they claim to be peaceful, it might be diplomatic to agree. Or they may have weapons on their ships that can stun or kill us through the walls. In that case, I want those charges to go off. Rig as many detonators as you can, so that any of us can blow the Station if things get dicey. And I'll want one of you with me in the Control Room at all times, just in case."

"Think it might go bad?" Gunny Stecker sounded more curious than concerned.

Delano shrugged. "Who knows? I just want us prepared for anything. So while you're both working, think about what might go wrong. Like maybe they jam radio transmissions and the detonators won't work. Or they burn a hole through the hull with their particle beam weapon. Rapid decompression would kill us all, but leave our bodies and the Station intact."

"We will consider such things, Major," Shen said.

"I like the 'we' part, Sergeant Shen. We're all in this together now." Delano glanced at the crate labeled 'Firearms.' "Are those Glocks enough firepower if it comes to that? And why no rifles?"

"No rifles, no automatic weapons," Stecker said. "Too much recoil. With the Glocks, you can hang on with one hand and shoot with the other. These are match pistols with longer barrels and smooth actions, already broken in. I got them from a buddy of mine. He's with the Marine Corps Pistol Team at Quantico. The ammo is hot-loaded, too. The pistols will probably jam up after a few hundred rounds. But they'll provide the most stopping power with the least recoil."

Delano knew a standard 9mm round traveled about 1,250 feet per second. A hot load and a longer barrel would bump that up to 1,400 or 1,500 feet per second. At close range, the impact energy imparted would be around 450 to 550 foot pounds, concentrated on an area less than a half inch wide. He decided that should be ample to take down a target. If the aliens could withstand that . . . game over.

"We can convert two of them to rifles, with the conversion kits," Sergeant Shen said. "That would be useful from a fixed, defensive position."

"Are you familiar with the Glocks, Sergeant?" Delano knew the Chinese usually preferred their own weapons.

"Yes, I am qualified with most military and civilian pistols. The Glock is a simple, basic weapon, and a good choice for this mission. And I prefer being called 'Shen.' It is what I am used to."

Delano smiled. "I understand. I prefer being called 'Delano,' and we'll forget about rank while we're up here." He took another look around. "OK, sounds like you two have it under control. Let me know when you want Kosloff. Can you lock this compartment?"

"Yes, we brought three locks with us in case we had to store items in different locations."

"Good. If you need an extra pair of hands, Demitri Petrov has volunteered to help. He's familiar with firearms and willing to guard the door while you're moving about." Delano turned around and drifted through the hatch. Time to see the spaceplane and its passenger off.

Twenty minutes later at the entry hatchway, Delano watched as a tight-lipped Susan York glided past him, trailing two backpacks, without a word or even a look. Colonel Hatcher came next. He extended his hand. "Good luck to you, Major. You've a lot to deal with. We off-loaded the two spare booster rockets. Kosloff didn't want to waste time securing them, so we just tied them to the Station's hull."

"You're sure you can't take them with you?" Delano didn't like the idea of booster rockets hanging off the Station.

Hatcher shook his head. "Too risky. The heat buildup during descent might set them off."

Delano shrugged. "Thanks, Colonel. But maybe the aliens won't even come here. We may all be wasting our time. But if I were you, I'd get back to Spaceport ASAP. Take good care of your reluctant passenger. Tell her I'm sorry she couldn't stay."

"Will do. I think she'll calm down when she thinks it over."

"Hey, I never got to thank your copilot. He never came aboard."

"My copilot and navigator, she doesn't much like socializing. For a quick trip like this, Debbie would rather just stay in the cockpit and read."

Delano wondered just how much reading Debbie and Hatcher had done on the flight up to the Station. Not that it was any of his business. "Give her my thanks anyway."

Hatcher floated into the spaceplane and closed the hatch. Delano swung around and found Kosloff behind him. "I need to seal the airlock from our side, Major," Kosloff said. "Welsh says the Chinese shuttle is coming in fast, and is only about twenty minutes out."

"Thank you." Delano launched himself toward the Control Room. He almost made it the length of the passageway before he bumped into the bulkhead, this time bashing against a section joint that hurt his shoulder. Unless he stopped colliding with hard objects, he would soon be black and blue.

In the compartment he found Lian and Steve huddled together at the two meter long and newly relocated table from the Lounge. Someone had already fastened it and three lounge chairs to the deck, all facing the viewport.

Steve saw Delano first. "Hello, Major. I mean Joe. Lian and I were deciding where to place the cameras. Then I have to start running cables. Colonel Kosloff said he would lend a hand." Steve looked as excited as a kid on his first date.

"Dr. Mironov was looking for you, Joe," Lian said. "You must have missed him in the corridor."

"Must have," Delano said. "I keep getting lost. I'm so busy concentrating on not bouncing off the walls I forget where I'm going. Did Maks say what it was about?"

Just then Maks entered the Control Room, with Kosloff right behind. "Ah, Major Delano, we've just received an update on the aliens from Mars base. Klegg gave them our security code and told them to fill us in. The aliens left an hour ago and are headed toward Earth. When they arrived at Mars orbit, one of the ships landed inside the Mons Olympus crater. Well, really on the eastern escarpment. It remained there for just over two hours, and apparently extracted something from the surface, minerals maybe. Then the alien returned to orbit and rendezvoused with the second ship for more than forty minutes."

Delano felt his heart racing. So they were coming after all. He kept his voice calm. "Why did Mars wait so long before contacting Earth?"

"They went radio silent when the ships approached," Maks said. "They didn't want to call attention to themselves, though any quick scan of the surface would have spotted the research facility. But that's why Mars waited until the ships were well on their way."

Delano decided he would have done the same. Why risk getting vaporized just to get a message off a few hours earlier?

"OK, Maks, if you can, track their approach. We need to know how soon before they arrive in Earth orbit." Delano turned to Steve and Kosloff. "As soon as we're certain they're coming toward Earth, I want to broadcast a signal aimed right at them. Low power, nothing that might cause alarm. We want them to come here, not the Moon or Earth."

"What kind of signal, Major? I have no idea what to broadcast."

"I can help, Major," Colonel Welsh said. "We can send them a visual picture of a circle, and at the same time transmit the signal for π, 3.14159265. You know, $C = 2\pi r$. Any intelligent race will recognize that."

Mathematics is the one universal language, Delano thought, and you don't develop space travel without it. "OK, let's think about follow-up messages."

"As they approach, they'll be bombarded with video broadcasts from Earth, so they should figure out how our transmissions work," Steve said. "If I can focus a specific channel at them, we can transmit on that. Then I can send another frequency but leave it empty, so they can send us video and audio on the second channel. I'll find some unused frequencies in the 800 MHz band. That way no one on Earth will be likely to pick it up, unless they know what to look for."

General Klegg had stressed the need to keep the alien visit a secret for as long as possible.

"I will return to the spectrometer and continue tracking their approach," Maks said. "Maybe I can get them on the telescope, too."

"I'd like any information as soon as you have it, Maks," Delano said.

He sat down with Lian at the table and opened his tablet. "All my notes are here, Lian, and my translation software. See if there's anything you can use. And remind Steve to set up recording devices."

Delano worked with Lian, going over her preparations. She used the same program and had her own database, which kept everything standard. Both databases could be linked, another plus. Dr. Stepanov remained ill and probably would not be much help for the next day or two. Fortunately, Lian had organized some of the data on the flight up, and she soon had her notes, visual aids, and language translators working. The software would be a big help in establishing a database of words, sounds, videos, even facial expressions and gestures.

Once he saw she had the situation in hand, Delano left to check the status of the explosives. But before he reached the engine storage room, his name sounded on the Station intercom. "Major Delano, the shuttle from the Moon is arriving."

Damn, time moved quickly. Delano managed a few words with Stecker and Shen, then moved to the Station's main hatch. Before the ship's conversion into the Station, an escape vessel occupied the space above the hatchway. The conversion crew had widened the opening to handle larger cargoes and installed an inner airlock door.

Delano found Colonel Welsh and Derrell Parrish waiting for

him.

"Thought you might want to see this, Major." Welsh pointed to the monitor beside the door. "The Chinese shuttle is here, and it's not slowing down much."

The screen showed the starry sky outside the hatch. At first glance Delano couldn't see anything, but then he noticed a small twinkle of light moving toward them. Unlike the spaceplane, which had crept up to the Station, this craft appeared to be moving much faster.

"What if he hits us?" Delano asked.

"Not sure, but we're three times his size," Welsh said, "so most of us should survive. But I hope we don't have to find out."

"Welsh, are you there?" The voice came from a speaker mounted beside the monitor.

"Yes, Kosloff, we're here," Welsh answered.

"I just spoke with Wu Ji, the captain of the *Chan Juan*. He says he's in a rush and does not intend to dock. He'll decelerate to match our orbital speed, but our guests will be dumped out a kilometer or so away. They'll ride a raft to our hatch."

Delano thought about the *Chan Juan*. The name could be translated as graceful or ladylike.

"Then I'll open up the small airlock's outer door," Welsh answered. "If that's OK with you."

"Roger that, Welsh, you have a go." Kosloff's excitement was obvious even through the speaker. "Let me know when they're aboard."

"Why doesn't the captain want to dock with us?" Delano asked. "Isn't that the usual procedure?"

"Yes. We've never received crewmen this way," Welsh said. "It's more dangerous, but saves Captain Wu at least an hour. It also avoids any possibility of a collision. Probably the *Chan Juan* has orders to get to Earth as quickly as possible. He's already set a speed record for getting from the Moon to here. Probably he'll have to refuel in low orbit, to make certain he has plenty of fuel for a slow and safe descent. The Chinese wouldn't be happy if their shuttle and its special cargo burn up in the atmosphere."

"What happens if our new team members can't make it to the hatch?"

"One of us, probably me," Welsh said, "will jump into a suit, and I'll go rescue them. But if these two contractors have been working on the Io run, they probably know their way around."

Delano observed a bright light appear on the *Chan Juan*. The craft's outer airlock door opened. He saw two figures in space suits standing in the doorway. They took a moment to check their equipment, then pushed off from the *Chan Juan*. A puff of air from their maneuvering packs got them angled toward the Station, and he saw the two lying side by side on what looked like a toboggan sled coming toward the Station's airlock. To Delano's eye, they seemed to be hurtling toward him, but Welsh didn't appear concerned. Delano wondered if he would have the courage to jump off a spaceship like that.

They came in fast. About a hundred meters away, a longer puff of air slowed them, and thirty seconds later they drifted through the center of the airlock and out of the camera's view. Right on the money, Delano thought.

He heard the heavy sounds of the outer hatch being closed and locked tight. Air flowed into the chamber. Twenty seconds later, a green light appeared on the panel. Welsh banged on the inner door three times, and heard the same number from the other side.

"They're good," Welsh said. He grabbed the stanchion with one hand, and with the other, exerting some force, released the latch. Delano helped swing the hatch open.

The two travelers drifted in. They waited until Welsh sealed the inner door before removing their helmets. Delano decided they were being extra cautious, which must be a survival trait of every experienced space traveler.

The first helmet came off, and Delano saw a narrow face with deep set brown eyes, close-cut brown hair, and stubble of black beard – Peter Tasco. The second helmet took longer, but when removed it revealed a tangle of blond hair protruding from beneath a red skull cap, blue eyes, and a cute but determined face – Linda Grayson.

"Welcome aboard," Welsh said, introducing himself. "This is Major Delano. He's temporarily in charge of the Station."

"Are you the asshole that got us pulled out of JovCo Base?" Linda glared at Delano, her voice anything but friendly. "We were on our honeymoon."

"Blame General Klegg for that," Delano said. "I never heard of you until a few hours ago. But I'm pleased to meet you. You can complain about me later. Right now, we have a sick man on board, one of our linguists, and we're hoping you can help him."

Her attitude quickly changed from angry newlywed to medical professional. "Of course. I don't have my medical kit with me, but I assume there's one on the station."

"There is," Welsh said. "If you'll let me help you remove that suit, I'll take you to our patient."

While they'd been speaking, Peter Tasco worked his way out of his suit, pulling his arms from the heavy sleeves and stepping carefully out of the semi-rigid legs. Delano waited until he finished. "Sorry about your honeymoon," Delano said. "But apparently as soon as General Klegg saw your report, he wanted you on the mission team. We needed a med tech or doctor anyway, and they wanted a navigator as well."

"I don't know anything about aliens," Peter said. "How did you even find out about us? I can't believe anyone at JovCo would leak that information. Or our lawyer."

"As soon as Earth got word about the space battle out by Jupiter's moons, the NSA began checking all things relating to Jupiter."

"Space battle?" Peter's brow furrowed. "What space battle?"

"We'll fill you in later. But to answer your first question, the NSA intercepted your message to the lawyer and decrypted it."

"Those bastards. Well, if they got the report, you don't need us," Peter said. "Everything we saw and did was in it. Why would they want a navigator?"

"As I read Klegg's report, these aliens must have come from a different solar system, and the General wanted someone here who might be able to reconcile star charts."

Peter shrugged. "Good luck with that. But as long as Linda's here, I'll do what I can."

"Then first thing is for you to give a briefing on what happened on the *Lady Drake*. I dropped the news about your alien ship and its pilot about an hour ago but didn't give any details. If you can fill everyone in, that would be a big help."

"Sure. What's your role in this, Major? Are you some Special Forces type?"

Delano grinned. "No. I'm a linguist."

Chapter 9

Day 4: 0150 Zulu

The captain of the Chinese shuttle didn't bother sticking around to see if his passengers arrived safely on the Station. Without a word he continued his flight to Earth. Delano, meanwhile, turned Peter and Linda over to Colonel Welsh, who assigned the newlyweds to the now vacant compartment formerly used by Commander Susan York. Delano spent the next forty minutes with Shen and Stecker, then returned to the sleeping compartments as Linda emerged from examining Dr. Stepanov.

Delano managed to stop his progress without crashing into her. "Linda, how's Dr. Stepanov? We could really use his help."

Linda shook her head. "Not going to happen. He won't be able to leave his bunk for at least two days, maybe longer. Dr. Stepanov has a serious case of space sickness, one of the most acute I've ever seen. He might even get worse. I've given him meds that may or may not help him. In fact, he'll need to be monitored closely until he starts to recover."

Delano grimaced at the bad news. Alien ships would arrive soon, and he'd already lost a linguist.

"If there was a way to get him back to Earth," Linda said, "I'd recommend that. But for now he's stuck here. I ran an EGG on his stomach and . . ."

"What's an EGG?" Delano's military experience taught him a thousand three letter acronyms, but he didn't recognize that one.

"It's a test, a device, really, that measures the stomach's electrical activity during motion sickness. Been around since the early days of space flight. Dr. Stepanov's stomach is dysrhythmic, with about 75% spectral power in the bradygastic and tachygastic frequency ranges."

Bradygastic? She might not have meant to confuse him, but one language Delano did not speak was medical jargon. "How about explaining that in words I can understand?"

"Sorry," Linda said. "His stomach isn't functioning, and it's not going to work for the next few days. In a day or so he may be able to keep some water down, but for now he needs an IV for nourishment and hydration, which I've given him. Good thing the Station is well supplied. I can't make a guess when he might recover."

"Isn't there something else you can give him, maybe let him work from his bed?"

"No, unless you want to risk him having an aneurism," Linda said. "And the rest of your team, I need to examine each one. I can already see that everyone is exhibiting early signs of dehydration. If you're not careful, you'll all be sick soon. I'll have to check out each of you, starting with you, Major Delano."

"I don't have time for that right now," Delano said. "Maybe later . . ."

"You'll make time, or I'll remove you from your command. As Senior Medical Officer, I have the authority to do that. You can't perform your duties optimally if you're sick."

Delano's anger welled up. Everyone had been kicking him around since Paris. He stared at her, the 'Drill Instructor' stare he learned in boot camp. "First, Linda, let me make this clear." He kept his voice low. No one else needed to hear. "By order of the President of the United States under the Emergency Powers Act, commanded by General Klegg, you and your husband are now members of the military. You do not have any authority over me or my team. Whatever JovCo policies or procedures you're used to don't matter here. Let me remind you that aliens are on their way, and we may all be dead in a few hours. So if you get in the way or disobey orders, I'll confine you to a compartment and you can spend the rest of your honeymoon alone. Are we clear?"

Linda held his gaze while he spoke, but now she glanced away. "Yes, that's clear."

"Good. Thanks for checking on Dr. Stepanov. And as soon as I can spare the time, I'd appreciate it if you examine me. But first I want you in the Lounge. I've promised the team that you and Peter will tell your story, and I expect plenty of questions. It will give me a chance to drink some water. After that, you can start your exams."

Linda accepted the nebulous apology. Delano followed her back to the Lounge. She moved easily through the corridors and even pulled him along by his arm when he started drifting. Which was nice. She could have let him bash into something. Or maybe she didn't want to patch him up if he broke something.

Her file indicated she possessed the 'good' gravity gene, the one that practically made her immune from gravity sickness. Peter Tasco had the same gene. The two could probably honeymoon in space for months without a stomach twitch.

When Delano and Linda arrived, everyone was there except Stepanov. "Peter and Linda have a story to tell," Delano began. "I've read their report of what happened aboard the *Lady Drake*, and I'll upload it to the server so you can all read it, but you should hear the facts from them. Some parts are painful, but I've asked them to give us everything they can."

Linda and Peter exchanged glances. Their personal horror story was going public. "I'll start," she said. "As soon as the *Lady Drake* left Io on the Moon run, we knew something was wrong."

For the next thirty minutes, she and Peter described the harrowing voyage of the *Drake*, including the murders and the desperate fight aboard and outside the freighter to a fascinated audience. When they finished, Delano displayed on his tablet pictures of the scout ship and the Star Rider. Since Peter and Linda knew little about the alien ship or its pilot, there weren't many questions.

"That's why General Klegg wanted Peter and Linda on the Station," Delano said. "Aside from their qualifications and their long experience in zero and low gravity environments, they know how to think fast and act decisively. If the aliens do come, we will need team members like them."

"What's this about a space battle," Linda said, wanting to put the *Lady Drake* episode behind them.

That took Welsh another twenty minutes to describe, including the follow-up activities. Delano and Lian added what they learned, and Kosloff described the technical details of the recording equipment as well as their assessment.

Delano, sipping from a water bottle, filled in with some info about Klegg and his efforts to get the project underway as soon as possible. Lian, to Sergeant Shen's astonishment, revealed all the information she possessed about the Chinese reaction to the news, the initial distrust and the hesitation to work together with the Alliance.

"There was still some suspicion when I left China," Lian said, "but I believe that now my Uncle and the Ruling Committee have put that aside. Otherwise they would never have allowed the United States and Russia to send experts to the Jiuquan Space Center to study the scout ship. I also know General Zeng gave Sergeant Shen orders to protect everyone aboard the Station, and he has given me his word he will do so."

"If the aliens come here," Delano said, "we'll have to work together. Something bigger than a First Contact is going on. There are four dead ships floating in space near Jupiter. We're in the middle of someone's shooting war and if that's the case, we may end up being innocent casualties. What we do next might be a turning point in Earth's history."

"Major," Welsh said, "don't forget, you've got a call coming in from General Klegg in thirty minutes."

"Everyone! I have some news." Maks lifted his head from the console and waved his tablet. "I've located the two alien ships and plotted their course and time of arrival. They are coming toward Earth."

"How long?" Delano got the question in first.

"Eight or nine hours. When they left Mars, they accelerated continuously for almost four and half hours before they cut their drives."

Obviously the aliens were in a bigger hurry to get to Earth than they had been to reach Mars. "Well, at least we know they're coming," Delano said. "Though we'll have less time to prepare."

"And if I may suggest," Maks said, "we should begin transmitting our signal to them."

"Ok, Steve, looks like you and Kosloff are up. Start sending. Lian, I'd like you and Maks to join me on the call with General Klegg."

"Let's get started on those exams," Linda said. "You look like hell, Major."

Delano shrugged. "OK, Dr. Duan is next."

Lian cleared her throat, and all eyes turned toward her. "After our exams, I believe that Major Delano and I should get some rest. A few hours of sleep might be a good idea."

Delano started to protest, then thought better of it. Except for some restless sleep on the flight to Holloman and a nap on the spaceplane, he'd been awake for most of three days. If he were exhausted when the aliens arrived, he wouldn't be able to think straight. Let alone decipher an alien language, assuming they actually spoke one.

"Colonel Welsh, will you brief Klegg when he calls? Tell him Dr. Duan and I are going to bed." Delano realized that sounded odd. "Not together, of course."

That elicited a few smiles from the team. It turned out that they did go to bed together. After their examinations, Linda gave them both a mild sedative. "This will let you sleep for about four hours. If you don't wake on your own, I'll get you up."

Delano and Lian lay down in the same sleeping compartment, each in their own bunk. He felt grateful for the chance to close his eyes. Whatever Linda had given him, he barely finished fastening the bunk's nylon strap across his chest before the pills kicked in and his eyes closed.

When he awoke, Delano realized something was wrong. His eyes felt gummy, and his brain didn't want him to move. Damn those sleeping pills. A glance at his watch startled him awake. Shit! He'd slept for almost six hours. Damn that Med Tech bitch.

He tried to get up, but the strap held him to the bunk. He struggled to loosen it, but at first his fingers wouldn't cooperate. When he finally floated free, he saw Lian still sleeping on the other bunk. If Linda had given her the same dosage as he'd received, Lian with her smaller weight would be out for at least another hour. Damn. He should have told Gunny Stecker to make sure he was awake after four hours. Delano wondered if he would ever learn to prepare for all possible contingencies.

He slipped out of the chamber, closed the door behind him, and moved along the corridor to the toilet. After relieving himself, he washed his face and hands with a wet wipe and ventured out, moving to the Control Room. Five people were there: Steve, Gunny, Shen, Kosloff, and Welsh. They looked up as Delano entered.

"Anything new?" His voice sounded hoarse. Delano dragged his water bottle from his pack and took a drink.

"Nothing," Welsh said. "The aliens are still on schedule, about two hours out. Maks figures they've been decelerating for about that long."

"What did General Klegg say? How's the situation down there?"

"Not real good. The Alliance is trying to stay ahead of the story," Welsh said, "but it's beginning to leak. As more people find out, there will be worldwide panic. Other than that good news, there isn't much else. I told Klegg you had everything under control, and you and Dr. Duan were getting some rest. Since you two weren't on the call, he didn't seem too interested in hearing from the rest of us. I told him . . ." Welsh glanced at his watch, "you would call back in thirty minutes, and he said to make sure that you did. The Gunny was about to wake you up."

Better late than never. The med tech must have told everyone he would be out for at least six hours, damn her. He resisted the urge to rip her a new one. "OK, that gives me a chance to catch up. How are our preparations coming, Gunny Stecker?"

"Working together, Shen and I have placed all the charges," Stecker said, "and concealed them as much as possible. You can find them, but you have to look. We've connected three different sets of detonators, and we're preparing for the last resort scenarios – detonation by concussion and dead man switches. No matter what happens, we can blow the Station. Now that there's some time, I'd like to familiarize Colonel Welsh, Dr. Petrov, and Steve with the Glock pistols. They have some experience with firearms, so that shouldn't take too long. Dr. Duan, Linda Grayson, and Peter Tasco don't, so we'll work with them last if we can fit them in."

"Good. Once you get that underway," Delano said, "start setting up defensible positions. Better assume the Control Room is gone, and the entry hatches are compromised."

Delano turned to Steve. "Are the comms in place?"

"Yes, Sir," Steve said. "I can start broadcasting on the 800 MHz frequencies whenever an alien ship gets in range. Maks and Colonel Kosloff will help with that. We also have three narrow-beam channels aimed at various satellites, one Russian, one Chinese, and one American. The heads of the Alliance will see and hear everything two seconds after it happens. Also I've linked the tablets, yours and Lian's, to the Station's computer, which Colonel Kosloff has linked to the NSA system in Washington. That, by the way, is a first for the NSA, authorizing outsiders a link into their computers. If you need any information, you'll have access to every database in the world through their mainframe. Plus the latest in translation software, if yours isn't up to date."

That would be useful. Delano regretted he hadn't suggested the idea. The information of the entire planet would be at his fingertips. All he needed to do was figure out the right questions. *Meet aliens, ask questions, get answers. Right.*

Steve hadn't finished. "I've also set up a second monitoring station. That way Dr. Petrov, Dr. Parrish, Peter Tasco, and Linda Grayson can monitor everything you and the aliens say. You and Lian will have earbuds so our guys can communicate with you if they spot something."

Another good idea. "I'm impressed, Steve. Good work. But why not for Colonel Welsh and the others?"

Steve nodded at Welsh. "Kosloff and Maks and myself," Welsh said, "we would like to be in the Control Room, in the background, so to speak. We won't say or do anything, we'll just look busy. We figure the aliens won't be interested in the rest of the crew, and they'll know there has to be more than two or three people on the Station."

Logically, the aliens would know their presence had been observed and their arrival expected. They would assume preparations for communications would have been made.

"In that case," Delano said, "let's put the Gunny or Sergeant Shen at one of the consoles. They can take turns. But while one is in here, the other is on duty in the engine room." He turned to Steve. "Make sure there's a monitor and communications there as well."

Ready to blow us all to hell. Delano kept that thought to himself. "Let's go, people."

Everyone worked feverishly for the next thirty minutes. Delano kept moving from room to room, even checking on Dr. Stepanov, now sedated and getting nourishment and water through an IV. Lian joined them, yawning, but seeming surprisingly refreshed. She had combed her hair into a pony tail again and put on a clean tee shirt. She looked almost ready to go out on a date.

When the call came in, General Klegg appeared on the monitor, sharing a split screen with three others – China's General Secretary, Russian General Demidov, and NASA's Director McChesney. In the Station's Control Room, Delano, Lian, and Dr. Maksim Mironov sat shoulder to shoulder facing the camera. Klegg started talking the moment the connection went live.

"This won't take long," Klegg said, "and you're busy enough without our interruptions. First, the story has started to leak. Some French online reporter in Moscow found out somehow, and it went worldwide before the Russians could shut him down. Our official position is denial, but that will change in about three hours. President Clark will announce a sudden press conference and reveal some details of the alien contact. He will not mention the ship on its way to Jiuquan, not at this time. After that, some people all over the world will start to panic. I've suggested that General Secretary Liu do the same. In Russia, General Demidov is arranging to be at the Premier's side to answer questions."

Klegg leaned back in his chair. "Secretary Liu?"

The General Secretary again sat beside General Zeng. "We will make a similar announcement at the same time as your President," Liu said. "More important, our lunar shuttle carrying the alien ship is on final approach and should touchdown within the hour. Extreme care is being taken to make sure nothing happens during descent. A team of scientists is ready to receive the ship. Russian engineers are on the way to Jiuquan. We have just received word from Dr. McChesney that four propulsion designers took flight from Los Angeles, so they should arrive at Jiuquan in about fourteen hours."

"That is correct," McChesney said. "Meanwhile we've set up three teams at Houston for analysis of the data from Jupiter picked up by the Station. The largest will focus on the power signatures of the ships. Another will examine the maneuvering capability of the vessels, and the third will study the aberrations in local space that occurred near Jupiter. Since our equipment in Houston is some of the latest, I've invited China and Russia to join us in this analysis. That way we will have links to the technical experts in all members of the Alliance. I'm sure other areas of study will arise once the scout ship is examined. That's all I have for now. If anything noteworthy is discovered, we will of course let everyone know at once."

General Demidov took over. "Our astrophysists have noted some unusual readings from the alien ships as they departed Mars space . . . constant fluctuations in the energy readings. The observed changes are small but detectable. We are developing theories about why and the cause. We would welcome any assistance, of course."

Delano felt a poke in his ribs from Maks. "Go ahead, Dr.

Mironov."

"General Demidov, I would suggest that our scientists consider the possibility that these ships possess and utilize some type of energy shield, both for defense and for high speed travel through space. The Station's instruments have detected the same anomaly as the aliens approach Earth. It may be that they cannot travel even through normal space without some type of plasma shield, which might strengthen or supplement the hull. That is all I can suggest, Sir."

"I will make sure they consider your idea."

No one else on Earth had anything else to contribute. "If that's all we have for now," Klegg said, "we will communicate again as soon as the First Contact is completed."

"I would like to speak with my niece," General Secretary Liu said, and switched to Chinese. Everyone on the conference call spoke Chinese. But most scientific conferences and documents still used English, the language that expressed complex ideas in the clearest and briefest fashion. For Alliance meetings, English took precedence. So the Secretary's words would be personal.

"Lian, is there anything you need, or you think should be done?"

"We are doing everything we can, Uncle," Lian said. "The preparations are thorough, and Major Delano is exercising thoughtful leadership."

"Would you give me a personal report for your mother? Is there anything you wish to tell her?"

The subtle question gave Lian a chance to say whatever she wished. Delano had no doubt that her choice of terms included some secret code words, but he didn't intend to worry about that.

"No, Uncle," Lian said. "Tell my mother that all is well, and I am adapting to zero gravity. Major Delano has taken all the proper steps to prepare for the alien arrival. He and I are working together, and he solicits ideas and suggestions from all members of the team. Hopefully Dr. Stepanov can rejoin us soon. Also Sergeant Shen is doing an excellent job. He and I have spoken several times, and he understands his role. I am sure you can confirm this, Uncle."

General Secretary Liu let a smile cross his face. "Yes, of course. I will send a message to Sergeant Shen, thanking him for his diligence and reminding him at all times to follow your directives."

"Thank you, Uncle," Lian said.

So that would cut out any special orders General Zeng might have given Shen, Delano decided. Good. Divided loyalties up here could mean disaster.

"Anyone else?" General Klegg asked. No one spoke. "Then we're finished. Good luck to all of you. Klegg out."

Delano turned to Steve. "End the call. And get with Kosloff. Start transmitting the greeting." As soon as Steve left, Delano turned to Maks. "Why would ships need a plasma field to travel through space?"

Maks laughed. "Perhaps they don't. But perhaps they don't need a hull, either. A plasma field could form a barrier to open space, eliminating the extra weight of airlocks and thick doors. If they use such a field to strengthen a physical hull, it would open up all sorts of interesting possibilities. When you have a free hour, I can explain the theory to you."

Delano shook his head. It sounded like a force field, always a staple in the science fiction vids. "Maybe later, Maks." He smiled. "Right now I don't have time for a lecture in physics."

In fact, he didn't have time for anything. He had aliens rapidly approaching and no doubt by now they had picked up the Station's signals. Delano had barely enough time for one last inspection before the balloon went up, as they used to say.

Lian watched Delano push off, trying to glide his way back to the engine room without banging into the bulkheads. Unlike the Station regulars, he looked clumsy and uncoordinated, though Lian doubted whether she could do much better. He hadn't glanced at her while she spoke to her uncle, and if he had any concerns about her passing information along, he didn't show it.

No, she decided, Delano had too many other things on his mind. First, of course, were the preparations to destroy the Station should the aliens prove unfriendly. That heavy responsibility would weigh down anyone's shoulders, and Lian felt glad that she didn't have to make the decision. Second, he had to coordinate each person's activities and make sure everyone had what they needed for the coming encounter. Third, he had to ensure that the Station's systems were ready for the aliens' arrival. Just as important, he had to maintain communication with the Alliance members on Earth, all of whom would soon be attempting to exert as much control of the contact as possible.

Her uncle would support her, of course, but Delano had no particular connection to General Klegg. Neither man had any real reason to trust each other. Lt. Colonel Welsh technically outranked Delano. Lian knew how important military men deemed the chain of command.

Well, Major Delano had been fair to her so far. He had accepted all of her suggestions, and indicated that he would be willing to work at her direction, especially if Professor Stepanov remained ill. Lian hoped the control issues would fade away once the aliens reached the Station. Otherwise, sooner or later, conflicts would arise.

In a way, she actually felt sorry for Delano. If anything went wrong, he would take the blame. She hoped he wouldn't do anything foolish that might jeopardize the mission. Lian decided to keep a close eye on him. He needed help, and she needed to accept as much responsibility for the First Contact as he did. They would work together to establish communications with the aliens. Whatever happened, Lian did not intend to hide behind her Uncle.

Chapter 10

Delano, seated in what he now called the new alien communication center (basically a six foot long table and three chairs from the crew's Lounge), stared out of the Control Room's viewport at the vast expanse of space. The stunning vista, which he'd scarcely had a moment to enjoy, displayed the full splendor of the Milky Way, a shower of silvery stars. He found himself holding his breath, as if the least movement might cause the magical sight to disappear.

Against that background, he couldn't see much else, but Delano knew the alien ships approaching the Station had started decelerating. Earlier Colonel Welsh had pointed out the direction from which they would appear. Steve and Kosloff had mounted three monitors below the viewport's thick glass in preparation for Delano and Lian's upcoming alien encounter.

Right now, two of those monitors were blank, but the third replicated the feed from the 1.5 meter optical telescope mounted above the Station's hull. A smaller, forty-five centimeter telescope, normally used for Earth observations, acted as a backup. The monitor feed allowed Delano and Lian to see the alien ships coming toward the Station, without having to move to the Physics lab. Two computer workstations in Lab One controlled the telescope and its related equipment. All Delano could see were two fuzzy reddish dots, which didn't seem impressive given the size of the telescope.

"About 500 kilometers out," Welsh's voice, piped in from the navigation workstation, came through the earbud in Delano's left ear. Seated beside him, Lian heard the same message. Both made final adjustments to the volume. Too loud would be distracting, even irritating, but too soft might mean a critical message went unheard.

Six meters behind Delano and Lian, Welsh, Kosloff, and Steve sat behind the Control Room's main workstation. Their roles consisted of looking busy, but prepared to respond to questions and keep the comm links up. Farthest away, Sergeant Shen had bolted another lounge chair to a floor mount next to the atmosphere control workstation. Shen had a Glock attached by a magnet beneath the monitor, and another in the small of his back concealed by a loose vest.

Gunny Stecker and Peter Tasco were in engine storage compartment A, with the interior hatch dogged tight. Stecker wore his flight suit, while Tasco wore his borrowed command suit, one capable of powered flight. Both kept their helmets close at hand and had practiced donning them. In an emergency, they could be breathing canned air in less than ten seconds.

Kosloff had also linked two video feeds to their tablets. Stecker's displayed a wide angle picture of the Control Room, so he could see if anything weird happened. Peter Tasco monitored the bandwidth frequencies assigned to the aliens, if and when they decided to transmit.

In the Lounge, Derrell, Linda, Dr. Petrov, and Maks huddled around two tablets, now functioning as temporary monitors, that would display any alien transmissions. Steve had set up a small network that also allowed them to radio suggestions or comments to the earbuds that Lian and Delano wore. Hopefully the aliens would not be able to pick up the weak signal that powered the earbuds.

"They've stopped," Welsh said. "About 400 kilometers away."

"Are we still transmitting the π signal?" Delano refused to let his excitement, or maybe fear, sound in his voice.

"Roger that, Joe. Signal is good." Steve spoke a little louder than needed. The microphones at his station would pick up the slightest whisper and relay it to the other compartments.

Ten minutes ticked by. The two ships didn't move. Their images on the primary optical telescope wavered and flickered slightly, which prevented Delano from making out any details. To his eye they appeared to be moving.

But Welsh had them on his instruments. "No movement," he repeated. "We watch them, and they watch us."

For ships that had raced around the planets, this sudden hesitation seemed strange. Why stop now? Delano visualized the 1.5 meter telescope, over thirteen meters long and mounted atop the Station. It could easily be mistaken for a weapon.

"Kosloff, we're pointing the optical scope right at them, aren't we? We're not really seeing much, and maybe to them it looks like a weapon. Should we angle it away?"

"Damn, you're right. I'll move it 90 degrees." Kosloff swam

out of the Control Room, headed for the Physics lab and the telescope's controls.

Kosloff needed almost two minutes to get the unit moving. Then Delano felt a small vibration, almost a hum, as the telescope turned away from the alien spacecraft. Fifty seconds later, a shout from Kosloff indicated the motion had ceased.

"Optical scope now pointed away from alien ships," Welsh announced, as much for the benefit of the team members as for those watching and listening on Earth.

Minutes passed, while Delano drummed his fingers on the desk. *Dammit, do something. You haven't come this far to stop now.*

"One of the ships is moving in!" The excitement in Welsh's voice made Delano smile. Welsh had the usual pilot's keen interest in unfamiliar aircraft.

Two minutes later, Delano detected movement through the viewport. The blurry vessel advanced slowly. "I'll bet 400 kilometers is the maximum effective range of their weapons."

"Roger that," Welsh agreed. "Even so that's awfully accurate for a beamed weapon. By the way, the second vessel isn't moving."

Apparently the aliens could blast the Station out of existence from almost 250 miles away. Delano wondered how long the retired ore freighter's hull would stand up to a phased particle beam weapon at that distance. Ten seconds? Five? He made a mental note to start counting if it happened. It might be the last fact he ever learned. *Focus, you idiot.*

The approaching ship drew closer and now Delano could see details. Two squat domes sat atop the hull, one forward and one slightly higher and located near the ship's center. Four thick metallic rods extended about two meters beyond the flickering screen, two forward and two aft.

"I've got ranging data from the docking camera," Kosloff said. "The ship is approximately 90 meters in length, and 50 wide. About 24 meters from top of hull to bottom."

About the same length as the Station, but built like a tank, Delano thought. Those numbers approximated the size ratio of large American and Russian tanks. Almost certainly a fighting vessel, he decided. That design offered the least amount of usable interior space but provided a low profile, highly desirable if you're ducking beam weapons. If a space-faring species wanted to carry people or cargo, the design would be considerably different.

The ship continued to approach and now Delano saw it clearly through the viewport. The shimmering effect increased, or perhaps merely become more noticeable. The ship's forward weapon, assuming that's what it was, pointed directly at the bow of the Station.

Right where I'm sitting, Delano thought. "Anyone know what a plasma field looks like?"

"No science lab has ever produced one so large, Major," Maks answered. "What we're seeing might be a plasma *window*, some gas heated to a high enough temperature, then molded and shaped by magnetic forces. Theoretically, a plasma window could prevent matter from passing through it. Or it could be something else entirely."

Still sounds like a force field, Delano noted. Why couldn't the damn scientists just call it that?

"I'm getting a signal!" Steve's voice rose another octave. "It's on the correct frequency!"

The blank monitor in front of Delano lit up, displaying a random static pattern. The image twisted and rolled, then black and white lines ran diagonally across the screen. After a minute or so the motion stopped, the screen went to a uniform black and gray pattern. Delano picked out shadows moving within the display. The black and white images shifted and changed to color, the palette rising in intensity.

Suddenly the vague pattern took on shapes. Two fuzzy images of something or someone stood hunched over what looked like the back of a console. The color became sharper and the image resolution improved. Two creatures were working on whatever device they used as a video camera.

Delano and Lian, by the tiniest fraction of a second, had just become the first humans to see living aliens. The focus blurred again, then sharpened, as the two creatures lifted their eyes and stared into the lens. Both gazed at him, probably as curious about his origins as he about theirs.

Assuming their color transmission was correct, both beings were a light chestnut brown. That coloring – it had to be a coat of hair – covered most of their bodies, leaving only the faces, arms, and upper chests relatively bare. Wide brown eyes, much larger and set farther apart than human, stared into the camera, examining the two linguists. Long and narrow heads displayed a large mouth with broad, flat teeth and thin lips. A generous tuft of unruly hair covered the top of each head. The nose, if that's what it was, consisted of a flush double opening just below the eyes. Slender, pointed ears on either side of the head flicked back and forth, like a racehorse at the starting gate. Each being wore a loose fitting vest fastened at the front, with at least six pockets.

At first glance both creatures looked identical. But the more Delano stared at them, the more he noticed slight differences. One lifted its arm and reached above the camera, the image momentarily showing nothing but the arm and hand, as it adjusted something. The hand possessed three fat fingers. A thumb, thicker and almost as long, completed the appendages. But two arms and two legs seemed a good sign. Humans and aliens had at least that much in common.

The creatures moved their mouths, and Delano guessed they were speaking. But no sound came through. "Steve, are we getting sound?"

"Nothing coming in on the line. We're sending audio, so watch what you say," Steve said. "I don't think they've figured out the sound frequencies as yet. They may be using an older or different type of audio technology."

"Older than what? What are we sending?"

"We're transmitting a VHD composite, about 10k resolution, with the sound on a separate track. Nothing new, no 3-D, just a basic image-sound mix. Been around for years. Easy to manipulate. It should be obvious to anyone."

Said the team's nerd. Perhaps these creatures were not technology junkies. Delano was about to suggest that Steve dumb down the transmission, when a high-pitched screech erupted from the speakers. Delano and Lian flinched. He reached out to adjust the volume control, but the aliens were faster. The volume dropped, the screech became a squeal, which quickly faded. Then a low-pitched rumbling came through the speakers. The aliens were speaking.

At least that's what it sounded like. The creatures conversed among themselves, perhaps arguing over how to adjust the camera and sound controls. The creature on the left of Delano's screen apparently won. He made another adjustment, then backed away from the camera, a long rumbling sound coming from his chest.

"I think they've figured it out and optimized their signal," Steve said. "My meters are showing a strong signal, clear and sharp, in the human audio range. They can hear us, and we can hear them without major adjustments."

Well, there's only so much you can do with air flow and a mouth, whatever the shape, Delano thought. Definitely humanoid, with a spoken language. Good news. At least they're not bats, communicating at very high frequencies, or whales, using very low ones.

Before he could think further, another, harsher voice joined the mix. The second creature hunched forward, giving plenty of room to the third alien. The alien who had corrected the signal nodded its head and moved off camera. The new arrival appeared bigger with thick arms and a strong muscle pattern across its chest. Head and jaw were larger, and Delano guessed the creature stood a foot taller than the first two.

He heard a click in his right ear, as Lian cut the sound transmitter. "Could that be a male? Could the first two be females? This one a male?"

If they even had sexes. None wore clothing except for the vests, and Delano couldn't see any genitalia. He reminded himself to take nothing at face value. Genitalia didn't need to be external. "Male or not, this new guy is giving orders. Maybe he's the captain." Every ship needed a leader. Hopefully he isn't the gunnery control officer with his finger on a trigger.

The big guy stared at the camera, then spoke. RUMBLE RUMBLE RUMBLE. A wave of his arm punctuated its words, and then the hand pointed directly at the camera. To Delano, the large hand seemed only inches from his face. RUMBLE RUMBLE. The smaller creature, huddled at the edge of the camera's field of view, pointed at something out of sight. RUMBLE RUMBLE RUMBLE RUMBLE.

Then the large male glided smoothly away from the camera in two long strides and returned to what might be a captain's chair mounted in the center of a raised platform, just partially visible on the edge of the screen. Delano noticed the back sides of what appeared to be monitors and other electronic equipment.

"Voice is definitely two octaves lower, perhaps three," Lian said. "It seems like . . ."

"My God!" Maks cut in, his voice almost painful in Delano's ear. "Did you see that? Did you . . . it's walking!" Maks couldn't control his excitement. "Walking! There's some form of artificial gravity on that ship."

Delano, concentrating on the alien's physiology and voice, hadn't noticed. But the Russian was correct. The creature moved as if within a gravity field. Even Delano knew that generating an artificial gravity field remained theoretically impossible, according to Earth's best scientists. *Well, they got that one wrong.*

Another voice cut in, that of Dr. Petrov. "Based on the creature's size, I would guess they evolved on a higher gravity planet than Earth. Look at . . ."

"Everyone quiet," Delano ordered. The smaller alien had moved farther away from the camera, and Delano could now see its entire body. Powerful legs supported an upper body that canted forward, giving the appearance of a not-quite erect upper half. Nevertheless, what looked like an awkward carriage seemed smooth and graceful. Part bear, part horse, Delano guessed.

The alien tapped its chest with its right hand. "Ahvin. Ahvin. Ahh-vinn." With each repetition, the alien tapped its chest again.

Lian's elbow brushed Delano's side. "You first. Look authoritative, but not threatening."

Yeah, right. Don't threaten the aliens with the big space cannons. Delano stood, one hand holding onto the table to keep himself anchored. "De-lann-oh. De-lann-oh. Delano." Lian followed his example. "Li-ann. Li-ann. Li-ann."

Mankind's first communications with an extraterrestrial species had begun.

Ahvin stared for a moment. "Ahvin. Duh-land-do." The alien pointed its finger at the camera. "Duh-land-do."

Delano decided that Ahvin was female, at least until evidence to the contrary appeared. He touched his chest. "De-lann-oh." He pointed at the camera. "Ahvin."

Ahvin thumped its (her) chest with approval. "Ahvin." She pointed again. "De-lann-oh."

The accent was off, but he recognized his name. He nodded, and Ahvin responded with the same movement.

She moved to the console, momentarily filling the screen, picked up some type of tablet and a stylus, and returned to her original position. At that distance from the camera, Ahvin filled the screen from top to bottom. She touched the tablet's surface, and an image of a three-fingered hand appeared. "Grek. Grek. Ahvin ss grek."

So "grek" was a hand, and "ss grek" was Ahvin's hand. Delano started to point to his hand, but Ahvin had already moved on. Fingers, arms, legs, feet, head, a whole list of body parts followed. Delano repeated the words, often getting the pronunciation right on the first try. With each of his successes, Ahvin appeared pleased, and he could already interpret some of her facial expression as an indication of approval.

Twice Delano tried to bring Lian into the process, but Ahvin showed no interest in dealing with a smaller or female human. Possibly she didn't intend to waste her time teaching two humans when one would do.

Whatever the reason, the lesson proceeded rapidly. After the basic body parts had been learned, Ahvin started on numbers. The first eight were distinct sounds, but the ninth required a lifting of a finger and a vocal change to accompany the word. Ahvin stopped the series at forty-eight. Delano didn't need Maks's voice in his ear telling him it was an octal or base eight system.

With the basic numbers nailed down, Ahvin began naming objects, beginning with her tablet, the stylus, the desk, the chair, everything she could put a hand on or point to in her ship's control room. Then Ahvin moved on to the harder stuff – verbs.

Verbs, of course, were the most challenging part of any language. You might know the word for various items, but without verbs, no real communication was possible.

Delano felt the elation, and knew Lian experienced the same excitement. Ahvin might be an alien, but her species seemed quite similar to humans relative to basic tools and communication. Her language could be learned, and he and Lian would learn it.

While Delano mimicked and memorized sounds, Lian worked her computer tablet and translation software, entering data and recording special sequences. The software would create a database of nouns and verbs, and once it grew sufficiently large, it would first assist, then become an integral part of the communication process. Each personal exchange would be matched later to Steve's video record, to make certain no mistakes were made.

Two hours passed, and Delano had learned at least a hundred words and the forty-eight numbers. Either the strain began to show on his face, or perhaps Ahvin had tired, though he could see no sign of that. She muttered the sounds and hand gesture for the number thirty-six several times. Then she leaned forward and switched off the camera. Abrupt end of lesson.

Delano slumped in his chair, and would have floated off if he weren't belted in. He felt exhausted from the strain of focusing on every sound and action, and committing them to memory. But he had no time to rest.

He took a deep breath, released his seat buckle, and pushed himself away from the chair. "Everyone in the Lounge, right now." He collected his notes and floated to the Lounge. Everyone except Stepanov was already there. Delano slipped into the last empty chair.

"OK, people, what have we got?" As Delano hooked his leg around the chair, Lian pushed a container of cold coffee into his hand and he gulped it down. He'd seen her fill it before the session started. "Come on, talk to me."

"I think it's critical that they have artificial gravity," Maks said. "We need to find out how it works, especially in a ship so small. It could change . . ."

"Later for that," Delano interrupted. "Any thoughts on the aliens?"

"I have a question about their language," Dr. Petrov said. "When they speak to each other, we hear that rumbling sound. But Ahvin's language with you seems different, almost guttural. She had to struggle to articulate some of the words, as if her vocal chords weren't designed for them. Are there two languages? Perhaps one for themselves and a different one for other species?"

"Yes, I think so," Lian said. "And I don't think this is a first contact situation for them. The idea of meeting aliens doesn't seem to trouble them. Ahvin shows little curiosity. They had a tutor ready, and I think she followed prepared notes of her own."

Petrov and the others agreed that Ahvin might be female.

Delano had noticed the issue of the two languages, but it hadn't seemed important. All of a sudden, it might matter a great deal. "You know, when the Romans established their empire, every country they ruled had to learn to speak Latin if they wanted to work with their conquerors. When those countries had to speak amongst themselves, they used what they called a lingua franca, a common trade language. It was a bridge between countries other than Rome itself, and eventually it grew and contained words from many different cultures."

"That would explain why Ahvin had to struggle with some of the words she taught us," Lian said. "Those words are not native to her species."

"American Indians used a form of sign language to converse among tribes," Colonel Welsh said.

"That would mean there might be many cultures besides this one," Dr. Petrov said. "I would expect aliens to be as curious of us as we are of them, but these people . . . creatures . . . seem almost uninterested."

"Yeah, they didn't waste a moment on learning anything we might have to say," Delano agreed. "As the visitors to our solar system, you'd think they might want to learn our language. Instead they expect us to learn theirs."

"So it follows there may be many more aliens out there," Petrov said. "If there were only two or three species, one dialect would have been chosen."

"Which might explain the battle off Jupiter," Kosloff said. "Different species perhaps, different interests, different ships?"

"OK, we'll save that for later, when Lian and I can examine our notes," Delano said. "What else have we got?"

"Their numbering system seems to be octal based," Maks said.

"Octal, that means eight, doesn't it?" Delano remembered something from a computer class about an octal machine language.

"Not quite correct," Kosloff said. "The eight numbers are zero thru seven. Then the zero is combined with the next sequence of numbers, to count from eight to fifteen, and so forth."

"What about Ahvin's last statement," Delano said. "Thirty-six what?"

"It probably means a length of time," Steve Macey said. "Like we would say see you in thirty minutes, with each minute containing sixty seconds. When they come back on, we'll know a bit more about how they keep time."

"So who do we think this Ahvin is?" Dr. Petrov raised the question. "Is she a low level member of the crew? One assigned to train new species?"

Delano thought about that. "No, they can't be encountering that many alien cultures. If they did, they'd use something better than sketch pads. It's probably a subset of her duties. You know, she might be a clerk or a cook, but also required to perform language training as needed."

"Yes, that is plausible," Petrov agreed.

"I have a question," Derrell Parrish said. "No one has commented on how humanoid these aliens are. Eyes, ears, nose, mouth for speaking, two arms and legs. Even a spoken language. Same thing for their ship – chairs, workstations, monitors. Does anyone think this is a coincidence, that the first extraterrestrial race we encounter is so much like us that we can quickly establish communications with them?"

"It does seem very much against the odds," Dr. Petrov said. "Yet here they are. Perhaps this may prove to be a case of parallel evolution."

"As a biologist, I don't believe it," Parrish said. "The odds of meeting an extraterrestrial life form so similar to our own have to be almost zero. I need to see a sample of their DNA. It's possible that our species and theirs are related."

"We're a long way from asking them for that." Delano had to remind himself that Parrish might be the smartest man on the Station, despite his age. He'd already proved his courage by volunteering to remain on the Station. Delano glanced at his watch. "What does Earth have to say?" Almost twenty minutes had passed since the session ended, and he and Lian might be called back at any moment.

"Not a peep from Earth," Steve said. "That's odd."

Odd was not the word, Delano thought. General Klegg and the other leaders should be chomping at the bit. "Find out what they think and why they haven't contacted us. Any problem with the equipment?"

"No, everything worked fine last time I checked." Steve understood the look on Delano's face. "I'll go check again."

"I'll go with you," Kosloff said. "We should have heard something by now."

Delano nodded. "Gunny, Shen, anything you guys picked up?"

"No visible weapons," Gunny Stecker said. "Still, they might not need much. Did you see the size of the captain's arms? He could pick up a tree trunk and probably kill all of us. Or throw a stone and brain anyone."

"A club was the weapon of choice until the Bronze Age," Sergeant Shen said. "Humans killed each other with clubs for tens of thousands of years."

"Major Delano," Derrell Parrish said, "another point about alien biology. I would guess they evolved on a higher gravity planet or moon. It might be twenty-five to fifty percent more massive than Earth. Those leg muscles wouldn't look out of place on a racehorse. Judging by their relatively small incisors, I don't think they're purely carnivorous either. They probably can eat plant and animal life, just like us. A mixed diet of plants and animals favors a species' evolution."

Delano really didn't care what they ate for lunch. "OK, that's it for now. Lian and I need to prepare for the next session. Thank you all."

They swam their way back to the Control Room, both careful to move slowly. Once at the table, they took their seats and belted themselves in. Delano felt thankful he hadn't banged into something on the way.

"For a first session," Lian said, "we have made remarkable progress, better than we could have hoped."

Delano turned to her. "What do you suggest?

"I think you must continue to be the main contact. For whatever reason, Ahvin is not interested in speaking with me. Perhaps it is only your visible authority, your height, even the depth of your voice. She and the male, if that's what he is, had no male-female issues that I could see. They spoke as equals. If you were not here, I think she would speak with me."

"Yes, I agree. We'll try to get you involved later. Ahvin used her sketchpad for basic drawings. We need to do that as well, only using our tablets. I'm pretty sure the next lesson will involve more complex expressions, and we may need images of our own. Can you follow up with that? Steve can help if you need him."

"No, I can handle it," Lian said. "But I think you should call the next break. Two hours is far too long. We should not allow ourselves to be considered subservient to their schedule."

"Well, they do have several weapons pointed at us," Delano

said, "but I take your point. I couldn't have lasted much longer anyway."

"You must not work to exhaustion," she said. "You're needed for the review sessions."

"Excuse me," Kosloff said, floating over from the Comm workstation. "The reason we haven't heard from Earth is because our transmission frequencies are blocked."

"Blocked? How could they do that? We're talking to them." Delano heard his voice rising and told himself to calm down.

"Possibly they extended a plasma field from their ship around the Station," Kosloff said. "We're transmitting fine, except that our signal isn't penetrating. Maks is checking that now. I'm not exactly sure how that could work. It might not affect the ship-to-ship transmissions, those within the field, that is. I could try to measure its strength."

"OK, and see if you can find a way to punch through," Delano said. "Maybe something simple like extending an antenna. Besides, they must know we're in contact with our leaders on Earth. Why would they want to prevent that?"

"Your General Klegg and the others will be worried about us," Lian said. "What will they do?"

"Nothing yet. They have telescopes, so they can see we're still here," Delano mused. "As long as nobody starts moving or shooting, they'll wait and see what happens."

Kosloff didn't have any suggestions, and Delano decided that it didn't matter right now. "Steve, work with Lian to see if you can help put some images together, or maybe a video that shows us communicating with Earth. I don't intend to sketch words on a pad to communicate, not when we've got all this computer power at our disposal."

Delano had time to review his notes and take one practice run of his newly-acquired vocabulary before the alien transmission resumed. He checked his watch – forty-two minutes had elapsed since the first session ended.

Ahvin started right in, and Delano could see that she had prepared some new sketches. This time she pointed to herself. "Ahvin." She gestured again. "Ta," then repeated the sequence two more times. "Ta mar tar." This time she pointed to the a spot on the deck about two meters away, and with exaggerated steps, moved over to the place she had indicated. "Ta mar tar," and pointed back to her original position.

"I go there," Lian whispered. "She's starting on the verbs."

Ahvin repeated the sequence, moving back and forth along the deck. When she decided Delano understood the phrase, Ahvin started on the next pronoun, which Delano and Lian knew would be 'you.' Ahvin pointed at the camera, "az mar tar." Then she indicated the same location as before.

"You go there," Lian said, speaking softly into the translator.

This was good progress, Delano knew. Already they had two pronouns and an important verb. Next would come the pronoun for he, she, or it, then the verb 'to be,' a key component of any language. With the verbs "go" and "to be," you could do a lot, including a rough future tense.

Delano kept checking his watch, and when thirty five minutes had passed, he held up his palm toward the camera. By now Ahvin understood this to mean pause or stop.

"Show her the video."

Lian held up her tablet and tapped the screen. An animation video started, one that showed two ships in space, facing each other, with Earth and Moon in the background. Surrounding the alien ship was a rainbow of colored lines, wavering and flickering slightly. Then the rainbow extended outward from Ahvin's ship to enclose the Station.

The thirty second animation that Steve and Lian had created had a marked effect. Ahvin's eyes widened, and Delano read that facial reaction to show surprise as well as interest. He guessed these aliens did not have this type of animation technology. When Ahvin recovered from her shock, she turned away and called out something in her native language, speaking to the 'Captain.' A moment later the big male returned.

Lian replayed the video. The male, too, showed surprise. Lian ran it for him three times before he lost interest. He said something to Ahvin, then glided back to his command workstation.

"So that's a negative, I guess," Delano said. "Kosloff, any change in the plasma field?"

"No, nothing yet," Kosloff said. "Still can't receive or transmit."

"It seems we've learned another phrase of their native

language," Lian said. "No way."

"It's break time, Lian. Give her the screen."

Lian pulled up a second animation. This one showed a ticking clock with seventy-two seconds instead of the human sixty. Then Lian spoke the number 'thirty-six' several times. Before Ahvin could say or do anything, Delano cut the transmission.

Even without a call to Earth, Delano and Lian had plenty to do. Again they reviewed their notes and what they had learned. The second session with Ahvin had provided some additional information. By now they, especially Lian, had a good understanding of Ahvin's body language. Whether she was happy, satisfied, or disappointed, could be inferred from her facial expressions, ear movements, and body posture. That constituted real communication as well.

When Delano leaned back to take a break, he found Kosloff waiting for him. "Major, we increased the power of our transmission to Earth, but we still cannot get a signal through the field or receive one. The edge of the field, on Earth side, is about eighty meters away, which is too far for us to extend any of our antennas. We could have someone suit up and give it a try, but we don't really know how close we can get to the plasma field without risking some exposure."

Delano shook his head. "No, you're right, too risky. Besides the aliens might not like that. Leave it for now."

"Time to go on the air, Major," Steve said. "Shall I open the channel?"

Back to work. "Yes, thank you, Steve."

For the next six hours, Delano and Lian struggled through five more lessons. By now they had established quite a vocabulary of nouns, pronouns, and verbs. By studying Ahvin's body language and facial expressions – always an important part of learning any language – he sensed that Ahvin felt satisfied with his progress.

At this rate Delano figured in another six or eight hours they might be able to carry on a real conversation. Lian had grasped the training as fast as he, and she also created several more animations that speeded up the exchange of ideas and deeper understanding of concepts. Without her help, Delano knew he would not be half as far along. He had never worked this closely with another translator before, but realized her skills surpassed his in some areas.

As soon as the eighth session began, Delano sensed a change. Ahvin's eye and drooping ear movements showed some distress. At first Delano thought it might be caused by the intensity of the sessions, but then he realized the lesson content had changed, and not to Ahvin's liking.

She held up the sketch pad. It showed only a single drawing. A small dot inside a circle, with another dot on the circle itself. Definitely not a verb.

"It's a simplified representation of the hydrogen atom, Major." The voice in Delano's earbud belonged to Maks, also following the session. "You might want to respond with the helium atom."

Delano glanced down at Lian and saw she had already pulled up a periodic table app on her tablet. A moment later she launched a far more sophisticated representation of the helium atom, its nucleus made up of two protons and two neutrons, surrounded by two electrons. She let Ahvin study it for a few moment, then Lian set the electrons in motion, swirling in a blur around the nucleus.

Once again Ahvin registered surprise at the simple imagery. A glance and a word toward the 'Captain' brought him over and he examined it carefully before nodding. He spoke to Ahvin, and this time he remained beside her.

"You go." Ahvin pointed to Delano while she spoke. "You go." She gestured toward Lian.

"Lithium is next, Lian," Maks said.

By now Lian had full control of the app's interface. One after another, she produced animations of lithium, beryllium, boron, carbon, nitrogen, and oxygen in their proper order, showing protons and neutrons within the nucleus.

As soon as Lian displayed the oxygen atom, Ahvin held up her hand. She went back to her sketch pad and worked on it for a moment. When she finished, she held it up to the camera.

Delano studied it, but didn't recognize the image.

Maks helped him out again. "Major, that drawing is a representation of helium-3, an isotope of helium that contains two protons instead of one, with a single neutron in the nucleus. It is still helium, with only two electrons."

Delano shrugged. He didn't know much about atoms and less about isotopes, except that they tended to be much rarer than their regular counterparts. That's all he remembered from high school chemistry. He looked at Ahvin and made the gesture that meant something between *I don't understand* and *so what*.

Ahvin's captain didn't like that reply. He grew impatient, pointed to the sketch, and spoke to Ahvin. She stepped away, but returned almost at once dragging into view a tall and narrow metal container which looked exactly like an oxygen tank. It even had some type of valve on the top. Setting it on the deck, she went to the sketch pad. and displayed the helium-3 atom again. She spoke the number twenty-five. With her other hand, Ahvin pointed to the tank, and made gestures that simulated filling it.

So that's what the captain – by now Delano had decided the big male was in command – wanted. His visit to Earth wasn't a social one. The captain needed twenty-five containers of helium-3, each about six feet tall and maybe a foot in diameter. "Maks, I think they want helium-3. Do we have any?"

"On the Station? No, of course not," Maks said. "We'd have to get it from Earth, and it's in very short supply. Half of the Chinese mining efforts on the Moon are aimed at extracting helium-3 from the regolith. For the last ten years the lunar mines have been the major source of helium-3. JovCo's mines on Io also extract small quantities, as a by-product of their rare earth extractions. They sell almost all of that to Russia and the United States."

Great, just great. Naturally the aliens want something in short supply. Still, that wasn't his problem. The Alliance could work that out. "What's helium-3 used for?"

"As I recall, it has two major uses," Maks said. "One is for medical imagining technology, MRI equipment, specialized electronics and so forth. The other is for use in fueling and utilizing fusion reactors."

"Major Delano," this time it was Kosloff's voice, "this may be a clue to the alien space drive. With Niobium to increase the superconductive process and an enhanced fusion drive, that might be a way to explain their plasma shields and propulsion system."

"Fine." Right now Delano didn't care if they pedaled around the solar system on bicycles. "That's another problem for the Alliance. I'm sure they can come up with a few cylinders of helium."

"Don't be so sure," Maks said. "Depending on the pressure in those tanks, twenty-five tanks could hold thousands of liters of helium-3. At one atmosphere, a liter of helium-3 would weight approximately a quarter of a gram."

"Yes, it all depends on the strength of the cylinder," Kosloff said. "We would need to examine one, to determine its maximum pressure strength."

A quarter of a gram? That didn't sound so bad. "OK, enough for now." Delano swung around back to Lian. "If they want helium-3, we need to talk to Earth. Can you whip up another animation?"

She smiled. "Yes, give me a few minutes."

It took almost five, but it was worth the wait. Earlier Lian had captured an image of the captain and shrunk it down to avatar size. She played it for Delano first, showing the plasma field surrounding the ship, then removing it. The next sequence involved an empty cylinder being moved to the Station.

Lian ran the animation for Ahvin and her captain, who studied it carefully. Lian started to run it again, but the captain had seen enough. He pointed to the tank sitting beside him, then to the camera.

Ahvin spoke and Delano struggled to catch her meaning. "He go you Station." The captain wanted to bring the cylinder aboard the Station.

"Oh, shit," Delano muttered. "I just gave them an excuse to board us." He motioned toward Ahvin. "We rest now – thirty-six. Talk later." He turned to Steve. "Cut the signal."

Chapter 11

Day 4: 1942 Zulu

Delano did a double-check to make certain the connection had ended, then turned away from the camera. For his first screw-up, he'd selected a big one. It might even be his last. "All right, time for another conference. Everybody in the Lounge."

Three minutes later, Delano sipped from a hot cup of coffee, thanks to Steve who apparently could not function without a steady supply of the black stimulant. The Lounge had filled up, with people sitting or just hanging in the air, a foot or an arm hooked over something solid to prevent them from floating away in the ventilator breezes.

"OK, team, the captain, or maybe one of his men," Delano began, "wants to come on board, ostensibly to deliver a canister, but they probably will want to look around. I'm inclined to say yes to their request. So unless anyone has strong objections, when we go back on the air, I'll tell them only two can come inside. I don't think we could resist more than that, if they get pushy."

"Can they breathe our air?" Steve sounded dubious. "I mean, what do they breathe?"

"Not sure. We haven't discussed life support yet."

"We can send them the makeup of our air supply," Kosloff said. "78 nitrogen atoms and 20 oxygen. If they can't breathe that, then they'll have to bring their own suits."

"What about the pressure?" Maks again.

"They look bigger and stronger than we are," Delano said, "so I'm assuming they can handle our atmosphere. Kosloff tells me the air in here is at sea level pressures, roughly 15 psi, and 21% oxygen. And they know we have no gravity generator."

"Letting them on is OK," Welsh said, "but I would insist that they restore communications with Earth."

"I agree. By now Klegg must be freaking out," Delano said. "We'll let them on board only after we've spoken to Earth."

"Can you communicate with Ahvin that well?" Derrell Parrish, the biologist asked. "Doesn't look like you've made enough progress to initiate bargaining."

"We should be able to convey our reluctance," Lian said. "We're close to the point of grasping the essentials of their language. As we learn more, progress will proceed faster."

Delano glanced at Gunny Stecker. "You and Shen ready for a visit?"

"As long as there are only two," Stecker said, "I think we can handle them. Don't get too close, keep the Glocks handy, that sort of thing. I'm supposing that if they do something threatening, we shoot, right?"

Welsh turned to the Gunny. "Will those 9mm slugs take them down?"

"One in the head will do the job," Stecker said. "Unless their skulls are stronger than a half inch of steel." Shen nodded his agreement.

Assuming their brains are in their heads. Now Delano had to worry about starting an interstellar war. He chose his next words with care. "Yes, you are authorized to shoot, but only as a last resort." He turned to Colonel Welsh. "Can you stay with the explosives and be ready with a detonator? In case the rest of us are . . . neutralized?"

"Wouldn't be my favorite duty station," Welsh said, "but if it comes to that, I'll do it, I'll push the button."

"Thanks. I hate delegating something like this," Delano said. "OK, now let's get back to work."

Delano and Lian prepared a short list of key issues for their next communication session with the aliens. The first item was the removal of the plasma field. Second was a forty-two minute break so Delano could converse with Earth. Third was the visit of two, and only two, aliens aboard the Station, with said visit to last not more than another 42 minutes.

The next session began. Using her tablet, Lian coordinated the visual display while Delano made sure Ahvin understood what he wanted. They went through the list, then returned to the first item and waited.

Ahvin wanted to discuss the visit, but Delano kept pointing to item number one. Finally she moved away from the camera. Almost ten minutes passed before she returned. "Plasma will go," she repeated several times.

Moments later, Maks's voice sounded in Delano's ear. "The field is gone, Major. Steve has already sent the first data burst, and we're reestablishing communications."

Steve had compressed every minute of contact with the aliens, and transmitted it to General Klegg in the first three seconds after the links were restored.

Lian brought up item number two, the forty-two minute break. Ahvin appeared unhappy about the additional delay, but nodded acceptance. Delano cut the link and moved over to the communications console. Lian perched on the edge of his chair.

Major Mitchell's voice boomed from the speaker. "My God, are you ok? You've been off the air for almost ten hours."

"Everything is fine up here," Delano said. "Can you get General Klegg?"

"Already on his way. He was sleeping down the hall. The Chinese and Russians will be on the line in a minute. We've kept the Alliance comm channels open."

"Steve sent a data burst," Delano said. "It's a full recording of everything since they arrived."

"Already processing it," Mitchell said. "Here's General Klegg."

Klegg sat down, pulling on his jacket. "What happened? Why were you out of contact?"

Delano explained the situation with the plasma screen. "That's not important now, Sir. What is important is that they want us to give them twenty-five canisters of helium-3. We think they need it to fuel their ships. Probably won't want to talk about anything else until they know it's on its way. Their leader appears to be under considerable pressure."

By now Lian's uncle had joined the briefing. "Lian, are you well?"

"Yes, Uncle," she said. "All is well. We have made significant progress. The aliens are much like us, so we are rapidly learning their language."

General Demidov, holding a glass of something that did not look like tea, came on. "What is this about helium-3? How much do they want?"

"We're not sure yet," Kosloff answered. "However the tank they showed us is about two meters tall and looks quite thick. We will try to find out that information during Major Delano and Dr.

Duan's next session. But I estimate ten to fifteen atmospheres of pressure for each tank. Possibly more."

"I'm checking on our stockpile now," Klegg said. "What happens if we don't deliver it? What are they offering in exchange?"

"So far as we know," Delano said, "nothing. They do have one of their space cannons pointed at us."

"There is that," Klegg agreed. "Try to find out why they want it. They can't expect us to just cough it up. Maybe they'd be willing to trade for it. God knows they have plenty of technology we could use." He covered the microphone for a moment, speaking to someone off-camera. "Our NASA guys say that we don't have anything near that quantity of helium-3 on hand. China has the largest stockpile."

"I am investigating that now, General Klegg," Secretary Liu said. "But I am told we need to know the exact size and capacity of the cylinders."

"We will get that information in our upcoming session," Lian said. "They will bring an empty tank with them when they come on board the station. So far, the aliens do not appear hostile. I'm sure they understand that if they attack us, they will not receive any helium-3."

Everyone on the link started talking at once, and the only thing Delano got out of the jumble of voices was that no one wanted to allow the aliens on board the Station. The conversation collapsed into a confusion of speakers, each one offering suggestions or giving orders. Finally Delano decided he'd had enough.

"General Klegg, everyone, please stop talking," Delano said firmly. "Lian and I need to prepare for our next session. We don't have to make a decision on them boarding the Station right now. We'll call again when we have more information." He turned to Steve. "End the call."

Steve nodded, and a moment later, with the leaders of the Alliance still talking, the connection went dead.

"OK, that's the last time we try that," Delano said. "Next conference call, I'll decide who speaks."

"Klegg won't like that," Welsh said. "He won't like being cut off, either."

"I'm sure he won't," Delano said. "But he's not up here, and he's not attempting to converse with space aliens."

The next session started almost five minutes late, the first time Ahvin had failed to open a channel at the agreed-upon time. Right away Delano noticed something amiss. Ahvin appeared nervous, almost ill-prepared. She stood at her station, working on another sketch. Usually she had one prepared.

"Look at the captain," Lian whispered. "Something's happened. Even the lighting is lower."

The captain stood behind his consoles, but his body language had changed. Before he had seemed tense, abrupt in his movements, curt with Ahvin, and uncaring about Delano and Lian. Now the captain appeared at ease. The alien ship's interior lighting had decreased at least thirty percent. Delano saw only a single crewmember at the main station. Previously at least two and sometimes three males had worked the consoles.

Ahvin lifted her sketch pad. The image depicted another life form, slender, with large eyes even bigger than those of Ahvin's race. Humans apparently had not been gifted by genetics with good eyesight, at least compared to other sentients.

"Talmak comes." She repeated the phrase, emphasizing the new word.

Now what? "Somebody is coming," Delano said to Lian. "Did you get that word?"

"No. She's never used it before. A title, perhaps?"

Ahvin worked at her pad. This time the sketch took only a few moments.

Delano gazed at a rough image of the solar system. She pointed to Jupiter, jabbing at the planet until Delano nodded recognition. Then she drew a line from Jupiter to Earth. "Talmak comes here. Talmak comes to Earth."

"Who is Talmak?" Delano asked.

"One who leads. One who speaks. One who knows. One who travels. Talmak."

A traveler? A senior leader? Delano thought that was what Ahvin meant. Perhaps another ship had arrived off Jupiter's moons. He studied the drawing.

"Major, this is Peter Tasco. Linda and I have been examining Ahvin's drawing of the Talmak. It's similar to the alien body we found in the ship."

"Another race of space aliens?" Just what Delano needed.

"Not sure, Major." This time Linda spoke. "I don't think it's the same species. If Ahvin's sketch is accurate, there are some significant differences, like the position of the ears and nasal openings. I'd say similar, but not the same. Cousins perhaps?"

"OK, good. Thanks." Delano took a breath. "Steve, get Klegg on the line. Ask him if anyone is monitoring Jupiter, and warn him that we may have a new alien ship, maybe a new species, inbound to Earth."

"Lian, can you pull up a star map of the galaxy? It's time to find out where these extraterrestrials are coming from."

Delano turned his gaze to Ahvin. "Talk to me of Talmak."

                    *   *   *

Day 5: 0845 Zulu

That discussion occupied the first of the next twelve hours. At Delano's insistence, the schedule moved at a slower pace. Every forty-two minute session was followed by a forty-two minute period with no contact. That gave Delano and Lian time to add more data to the translation software and practice their pronunciation. In an emergency, such as Delano and Lian being unavailable, already the software would work for basic communications with the aliens. After three more sessions, Delano insisted on the equivalent of two hours' rest. That gave him time to report to Klegg and catch an hour of sleep.

The preparation for the Talmak's arrival proceeded. Ahvin continued introducing Delano and Lian to more sophisticated concepts, and both sides needed to ensure that the two species understood each other. Each new concept required prolonged dialog, to make certain that words such as leader, planner, ship, captain, battle, and dozens more meant the same thing to Ahvin as they did to Delano. Critical words such as invasion, attack, defense, and resistance were thoroughly reviewed. Use of verbs had grown more erudite as well. Delano and Lian now had a useable past and future tense.

When the twelve hours had passed, Delano and Lian reported once again to the leaders of the Alliance. By now their understanding of the Ktarran language – that was the name of the trade dialect – had increased significantly, to the level where an actual conversation could be conducted.

"General, this Talmak should be arriving soon," Delano said. "When he does, assuming he is male, we'll be able to converse with him using the Ktarran trade language. This time we will insist Lian be a part of all contacts, and we've stressed that with Ahvin as well. She agreed to work with Lian, as soon as Ahvin feels I am up to speed. She also agreed to teach us the Halkin language if there is time. That's what they call themselves, the Halkins."

"Why wouldn't there be time?"

"Ahvin says her captain – his name is Horath, and she refers to him as One Who Leads – knows the Ktarrans are on their way here. Which is why he wants the helium-3, so the Halkins can fuel up and get out of Dodge or at least put up a fight. Oh, Ahvin's leader – we call him the captain and he is male – wants the helium-3 no later than fifteen hours from now. Can you give me an update on the status of the helium-3?"

Klegg turned to General Secretary Liu, letting him answer the question. "Major Delano, it's going to take a little longer than fifteen hours. And if we give them every liter of helium-3 we possess, either on the Moon or here on Earth, we can fill approximately fourteen containers at ten atmospheres of pressure. If more is required, it will have to come from other sources."

"The United States can produce five containers at that pressure," Klegg said, "and General Demidov indicated Russia can contribute four more. But if we give so much helium-3 to them, we'll have almost nothing left for ourselves. It might take months, even years to replace. Have you discussed the size and pressure of those tanks?"

"No, Ahvin's focus has shifted to teaching us as much as possible so that we can speak with the Talmak. Apparently it is both a title and a name, and he is some type of overall leader of his species, with much more knowledge of the Ktarrans and their plans. Ahvin seems to be in awe of the Talmak."

"And the Ktarrans?" Klegg seemed skeptical. "What have you learned about them?"

Delano corrected Klegg's mis-pronunciation, distinctly enunciating the hard 'KITtarr-ans' accent for the General. If Earth ended up fighting these aliens, we might as well get their name right.

"According to Ahvin," Delano went on, "the Ktarrans are a warlike species that want to kill and enslave other worlds. One of their ships pursued and attacked the five Halkin vessels off Jupiter. Apparently a battle had been fought and lost somewhere else. The Halkins tried to escape but the one Ktarran ship pursued them through the wormhole."

"If I may," General Demidov said, "my staff has discussed the option of giving these Halkins nothing. After all, we may be better off not supplying them. If these Ktarrans come, they may take any gifts to the Halkins as an unfriendly act."

Delano glanced at Lian. "We've considered that as well. Apparently Ahvin's captain is no longer concerned that the Ktarrans will arrive in the next few days. He's also decided to leave all negotiations up to the Talmak. So within the next thirty six hours, if the talks go well, we should have much more knowledge of the situation. But I suggest you prepare to provide the helium-3 as quickly as possible."

"Major Delano," Secretary Liu said, "it seems to us that this Talmak and the Halkins will simply reinforce their mutual point of view. Perhaps we should leave ourselves open to discussions with the Ktarrans, if and when they come. Do you agree with that, Lian?"

"Yes, of course," she said. "Major Delano and I are aware that we are hearing only one side of the story. We have discussed another option. Perhaps we can tell the Halkins that we have only ten cylinders of helium-3. It seems likely that they requested more than they actually need. Perhaps we give them just enough to leave our solar system."

"And these Ktarrans may not come at all," Demidov said. "Our astrophysists believe that the wormhole near Jupiter may be an unstable one. It may lie dormant for months or years, even decades, until conditions are suitable for it to exist. Maks, we are sending you a summary of the work done here at Star City for you to review."

Maks leaned closer to the shared microphone. "Yes, General. That will be useful."

"General Klegg," Delano said, "Kosloff has been tracking the Talmak's ship, and it has begun braking maneuvers. It will be here in about three hours. Once he arrives, Lian and I believe we are far enough along to begin a real conversation. A few hours after that, we should know a lot more about everyone's intentions. I suggest we wait until then before making any decision on the helium-3."

"I agree with that suggestion," Lian said. "We will be in a better position in the next twelve hours or less. But we should continue to collect the helium."

Klegg glanced at the other members of the Alliance. They all seemed resigned to the delay.

"All right, Major," Klegg said, "you've got the ball. Just don't give away the planet without consulting us."

"Understood, Sir," Delano said. "You and the other Alliance members will be getting a live feed of our talks with the Talmak. That should help speed up the process."

"Good. Meanwhile find out about the size and pressure of those storage tanks," Klegg said. "And see if you can get some of their technology as well. We would all like to know how their space drive works, and how to create those plasma fields. As for artificial gravity, that's worth more than anything. Make sure they understand we're not just giving away the helium. Obtaining their technology may prove to be the most important part of these negotiations."

No, General, getting off this Station in one piece is more important. "Agreed," Delano said. "Lian and I will do our best. Now if you'll excuse us, we need to get some rest."

Chapter 12

Day 5: 2315 Zulu

When their next session with Ahvin ended forty-five minutes later, Delano felt drained of energy and emotion. He sat slumped in the chair, held down by a seat belt. "God, I'm exhausted."

Lian handed him her bottle of coffee. "Here. I saved this for you. Only an ounce or so is needed to stimulate the brain without impacting the nervous system."

Delano took two swallows, all that remained. Cold or not, the coffee helped. "Thanks. This is getting to be a habit, Lian. Your coffee is saving my life."

She laughed. "The more I save for you, the less I drink. I never drank coffee until I left China. First Paris, then Los Angeles. No one in either city drinks tea. They hooked me on coffee." She glanced around the empty Control Room. "I think they're expecting us in the Lounge. Are you ready, or do you need a few more minutes?"

Suck it up, Marine, Delano thought. "Steve better have made fresh coffee." He released the seat belt, and pulled his way out of the Control Room and into the Lounge. Everyone waited there and he saw two monitors connecting the Station to Earth, both active.

He moved to the head of the table and hooked his foot around one of chair legs. Despite the jolt from Lian's strong coffee, Delano's stomach had settled down, and zero gravity had become almost relaxing. Steve handed him a fresh brewed container, still warm. Delano managed two sips before General Klegg started in.

"We watched your session with the aliens," Klegg said. "Can you provide any new insight?"

At least Klegg didn't chew him out for cutting short the previous call. "Yes, Sir, this was by far the most productive discussion," Delano said. "Ahvin showed us their approximate location in the galaxy. Peter Tasco says they're from the outlying end of the Orion Arm. We think that's where she was pointing."

"Why couldn't she be more exact?" Klegg's voice sounded more curious than suspicious.

"Well, I don't think Ahvin is very technical. And she obviously had no intention of asking Horath to provide more specifics. She acts a little nervous when dealing with him. We'll know more when the Talmak arrives. Apparently he's a member of another species – Ahvin called them the Tarlons – and one of the leaders in the war against the Ktarrans. Ahvin's captain now wants him to take charge of negotiating with us, so Horath will wait until the Talmak gets here before he concedes anything. But Horath still insists on the delivery of the helium-3."

"If I may interrupt, General," Secretary Liu said, "we've had our resources on the Moon monitoring the Jovian region, and they tracked the Talmak's sudden arrival. A significant distortion in that area's gravity waves preceded it. Then our scientists tracked the ship by its energy signature. It is moving toward us at a high rate of speed. They will continue doing analysis and forward any new information to us as soon as possible."

"Uncle, Ahvin told us in the last session the Talmak would reach Earth in about twelve hours," Lian said. "What may be of more importance is that the Halkin somehow learned about his arrival at least two hours before the gravity disruptions near Jupiter occurred."

"So they received word before the Talmak's ship arrived in our solar system," Klegg observed. "Wonder how they managed that?"

"General Klegg, if I may," Kosloff said, "if the Talmak can reach Earth orbit so quickly, then he will be traveling even faster than the Halkin ships did on their run from Mars to Earth."

"That might mean a faster ship," Welsh said, "or more fuel to burn."

"Let's hope this Talmak doesn't want another twenty-five canisters of helium-3," Klegg said, "because he won't get it. Speaking of helium, we discovered that JovCo and some other corporations in Europe had a supply. We, uh, asked them to loan it to us, and they agreed."

Rather than face a Russian airborne force landing in Zurich and kicking down doors. Still, not Delano's problem. After reading Peter Tasco's report, anything that happened to JovCo and its management was fine with Delano.

*   *   *

Day 6: 2230 Zulu

Through the Station's viewport, Delano watched the approach of the Talmak's vessel as it drew near the Halkin ship. Both ships had a similar design and shape. The Talmak's appeared about a third larger and included one more weapon turret – if that's what they were – for a total of three. The newest visitor to the solar system ceased its traveling and took position about a hundred meters from the Halkin ship, which actually placed it closer to the Station.

As with the Halkin ships, the Talmak's vessel twinkled against the starry background, though its plasma shield displayed more blue and green when contrasted to that of the Halkin.

"This looks like a serious warship," Delano said. "If the Halkin ship is the equivalent of a destroyer, this is a step up, like a guided missile cruiser. I wonder what other weapons besides particle beams it has on board?"

"It should not concern us," Lian said. "The Halkins could easily destroy us, and by now they must see that we possess no weapons, let alone any that could penetrate their force field."

The monitor displaying the video feed from the Halkin ship started broadcasting, and Delano watched Ahvin center herself within her camera's field of view.

"Greeting. Talmak has spoken with Horath several times during his journey," Ahvin said. "He is happy to meet with you. He thinks your . . . progress . . . learning language is very fast."

"Ahvin is good teacher," Delano said. "When do we speak with Talmak?"

"Soon. Leader Horath and I go now Talmak's ship. Talk from there. Go now."

The screen went dark and five minutes passed. Then, as Delano and Lian watched the alien ships through the viewport, they saw a sudden flicker around the Halkin ship. A small vessel about the size of a family recreational vehicle detached itself from the hull. It passed through the Halkin plasma screen, and the tiny shuttle crossed the gap between the two ships, penetrated the Talmak's vessel's shield, and disappeared.

Nothing happened after that for forty minutes. Delano found himself dozing off until the Halkin broadcast resumed, this time coming from the Talmak's ship.

"I wondered if they carried the communications gear with

them," Delano said. "Wouldn't it have been easier for the Talmak to board Ahvin's ship?"

"Major, this is Steve. This new link is a higher quality than Ahvin's. So I think the Talmak has better or more flexible comm gear."

"Thanks, Steve." Delano glanced at Lian. Neither of them had noticed any deficiency in the Halkin broadcast signal. He watched the camera reveal a small chamber, filled with four aliens – Ahvin, her Captain Horath and two new and quite similar faces – the species of the Tarlons.

Ahvin began the session. "Delano, this is Talmak." She gestured toward one of the aliens. "He also speak for Halkin."

Ahvin's rough sketch had not done the alien justice. Where the Halkins projected bulk and strength, the Tarlons were tall and almost gaunt, more sinew than muscle. Their heads looked humanoid in shape, but devoid of facial hair or visible eyelids. The skin resembled aged leather, crisscrossed with lines and whorls. The top of the skull appeared to be almost a different texture, with perceptible seams where it bonded with the face.

Interesting, Delano thought. Perhaps like the human skull, the top of the head hardened into bone well after birth. A similar development in the Tarlon species might have resulted in a different layer of skin. The eyes were closer together, and the nose, another piece of aged leather, seemed almost too small for the face. Ears, mouth, lips, all looked humanoid.

Both Tarlons wore loose jackets with several pockets. The one seated beside Horath seemed older somehow. His hands, extended toward the camera, appeared larger than they probably were, but nevertheless the long fingers looked flexible and strong. One thumb and four fingers.

"Major, this is Darrell. I'm not believing what I'm seeing. These Tarlons are even more humanoid than the Halkin. You must obtain some DNA at once. I need to examine it."

Damn, the kid was pushy. "Not now, Dr. Parrish. When I get a chance, I will." Delano stared at the camera. The Tarlon bodies gave the impression of being more symmetrical, more erect than that of the Halkins. However Darrell Parrish had hit on something. Biologists expected aliens to be, well, alien, not variations on the human theme.

"It is curious, Joe." Lian kept her voice to a whisper. "Dr. Parrish may be correct. We should obtain a DNA sample."

"We'll find a way . . ." The audio link came on, and Delano saw the Talmak and his guests watching him. "Greetings. I am Delano," he pointed to himself, "and this is Lian. We will speak with you."

Expecting some polite reply, Delano was surprised by the Talmak's first words.

"When does helium-3 arrive? How many segments?"

By now Delano knew a segment equated to forty-two minutes. "Helium will arrive in 68 segments. Helium-3 scarce. May not have enough to fill tanks."

"Must have in seventy-five segments. Ktarrans arrive in one hundred thirty segments. Must have."

OK, fuck you, too. Delano felt his annoyance growing. "We have questions. First question. What do you offer us in exchange?"

"What do you want from Tarlons?"

"We want to understand your power plants and gravity generators," Delano said, stating the two most urgent requests from the Alliance.

The Talmak showed no hesitation. "Will give you plans when helium-3 arrives. What else do you want from Tarlons?"

Caught off guard by the casual offer, Delano hesitated. Lian spoke up. "We want a sample of your . . . skin."

The Talmak apparently had no problem speaking with a female. "Why you want that?"

"Tarlon, Halkin, human," Lian said, "all appear to be same . . . family. We want to explore differences."

Delano didn't have enough experience with the Talmak to read his body language, but he guessed the first reaction was surprise, followed by puzzlement.

"Why humans want to know? You understand meaning of life?"

At least Delano translated it that way. (Later Lian interpreted it as 'force of living.') Mankind had searched for the meaning of life for centuries, with no luck so far. But almost certainly the Talmak was thinking of DNA, the magic code which defined and replicated life.

"Yes. Want to study your life material," Lian answered. "And that of Halkins."

The Talmak shifted his gaze to Ahvin and spoke for some length of time to her. But the language he used was not the Ktarran language or the Halkin. Obviously the Halkins understood the Talmak's native tongue.

"Will give life material." The leader of the Tarlons seemed unconcerned about DNA samples.

That seemed too easy, and Delano distrusted anything so valuable given away for a few cans of helium gas. But maybe these aliens had no equivalent of the Star Trek Prime Directive and didn't mind revealing technological advances to a less developed species.

"What happens if we do not provide helium?"

"Commander Horath will destroy bases on your moon. He holds energy for that. Then he and his ships will attempt to avoid destruction by hiding."

"And what will Talmak, the Tarlons do?"

"We have enough . . . fuel to return to home world. We depart your . . . system."

"You would allow Horath to destroy our bases?"

"Is his foolish gesture," The Talmak said. "But Horath is quick to anger. He wants to destroy your bases. Do not be concerned. They do not matter. The Ktarrans will destroy them, will destroy your world when they arrive."

Well, that put a different tone to the conversation. Delano decided the time had come to talk about the Ktarrans.

"You will tell us of the Ktarrans."

"Talk when you come to ship," The Talmak said. "Horath bring you over. You come now."

Delano glanced at Lian. She nodded. "We will come."

"Are you sure you want to do this, Delano?" Colonel Welsh's voice revealed his concern. "What happens if they decide to keep you?"

Delano and Lian continued donning their flight suits. "You'll be on your own," Delano said. "You've got copies of our translation software. Do whatever you think best."

"I'm not supposed to let anything happen to you," Gunny Stecker said. "General Klegg said no one was to be taken alive by the aliens."

"First, we're not being taken. As I remember the orders," Delano said, "you are not to let the Station or the scientists fall into alien hands. Lian and I know nothing technical, certainly nothing useful to them. Our only value is as translators, which means it will be in their interest to keep us alive and cooperative, unless they want to schedule more training sessions and start over. Besides, if what they say is true, the Ktarrans are the real danger and they're already on their way. So we don't have time to argue about this."

"I cannot let Dr. Duan be taken," Sergeant Shen said. "You can go by yourself. She can stay behind and monitor from here."

"I'm not staying behind," Lian declared. "You will not interfere."

"Delano, you should talk with Klegg first," Welsh said. "Let him decide."

Delano grinned. "That's why we're not calling him. He might say no."

Across the Control Room, Kosloff lifted his eyes from the workstation. "Halkin shuttle craft is on the way. If you're going, better get down to the airlock. I've turned on the outside lights, so Horath will know where to go."

"Suppose you can't breathe their air?" Steve sounded as worried as the Gunny.

"If the Halkins can breathe it, and we're all related, then we can breathe it," Delano reasoned, zipping up the final closure on the suit. "Don't worry, I'll test it first, just to be sure." He tapped a zippered pocket on his jacket to make sure he had the atmosphere tester Kosloff had provided him.

Delano picked up his helmet with one hand and the backpack containing his gear with the other. "Time to go. We'll try to keep the audio channel open. Now if someone will just help us down to the airlock?"

Maks and Welsh did the honors, guiding Lian and Delano through the corridor and back to the same airlock where Peter and Linda had recently boarded. Welsh did the final run-through on their suits, checked the hatch, then opened the inner door. Delano and Lian stepped through, linked arms, and each grasped one of the stanchions.

"Remember, don't open the outer door until I exhaust the air," Kosloff said. "Otherwise you might get blown out."

"Got it," Delano said. He turned to Lian and peered into her helmet. "Are you as scared as I am?"

"Yes, really scared." But she smiled at him through the metallic glass of her helmet.

"Major, Horath is outside the lock." Kosloff's voice came through the suit's headphones. "He says to open the outer door."

"Are you ready, Lian?"

"Yes. Open the hatch."

He took one last look to check her suit. "Hang on."

Tightening his grip on the stanchion, Delano pulled down the release mechanism. With a puff of escaping air, the door swung inward, moving slowly until it clanged against the hull. Delano stared at the alien shuttle, only a meter or two away. He saw Horath standing at the edge of his craft. There was no hatch on his airlock, and the Halkin wore no helmet or suit. Suddenly the space craft edged closer until it nearly touched the hull of the Station. Horath reached out an arm and gestured for Delano and Lian to cross over.

Delano hesitated. He saw a shimmering inside the opening to the alien vessel, some kind of force field keeping the air in and vacuum out. But Horath's hand reached through the shimmer. Damn these aliens with their blunt, impatient ways. Gritting his teeth, Delano extended his arm and clasped the creature's hand, letting Horath draw him across the half-meter of open space and into the Halkin shuttle. Lian, holding tight to Delano's other hand, came with him.

They had boarded an alien space craft. Delano realized he'd been holding his breath, and released it.

Horath adjusted something beside the door and the view of the Station vanished, as the entrance became opaque. The Halkin said something, then realized that his visitors couldn't hear him. He made motions indicating that they should remove their helmets.

While Delano hesitated, Lian reached for the latches. He caught her hand. "Wait a moment." He pulled the air quality tester from his pocket, and pushed the button, waving the air collector around as Kosloff had showed him. The meter took only a few seconds to display its analysis – oxygen 17%, nitrogen 80%, and one percent each for carbon monoxide, water vapor, and argon.

However Delano cared only for the green display with the word 'breathable' showing. The air within the Halkin ship was safe for humans.

"Kosloff, the Halkin air mix is safe," Delano said, nodding at the same time to Lian.

She had her helmet off before he did. A sharp hiss as the pressure equalized made Delano flinch. Undoing the fasteners of his helmet, he took a quick breath. His first reaction was that the air was moist and warm, a refreshing difference from the dryer air of the Station. A few more breaths confirmed what the Halkin obviously knew – the air was breathable for this alien species – the humans.

Lian had already taken a cautious breath.

"I think it's OK," Delano said. His voice sounded higher, and he guessed the air pressure was much lower inside the tiny shuttle. But definitely breathable.

Horath waited patiently while the two travelers adjusted. When he realized they were not removing their suits, he grunted, the sound apparently indicating his disapproval.

"Follow me." The voice sounded harsh, almost brutal, when heard live instead of through the comm speakers. Horath touched a panel that slid aside, and motioned to benches on either side of the ship. "Sit. Wait."

Horath glided toward a pair of couches at the forward end of the shuttle. He pulled into one and worked the controls. The shuttle broke away from the Station. In moments, they reached the Tarlon vessel. He docked against a shimmering rectangle that turned into another force field the moment the shuttle ceased moving. The entire journey from one vessel to another had taken less than sixty seconds.

"Follow," Horath ordered, and he led the way into the Tarlon ship.

This time Delano didn't bother to check the air. The moment his feet touched the deck he felt the welcome pull of gravity. Though not Earth gravity – probably less than half that – it reassured his body and let his brain operate more efficiently. Even so Delano and Lian moved with care. Neither had any training in a low gravity environment, and it would be easy to stumble and fall. Pulling off his gloves, he shoved them into his pocket.

Now is not the time to break your neck. Without thinking, Delano took Lian's hand in his as they followed Horath deeper inside the Tarlon ship. A narrow corridor, the walls curving into the overhead and deck panels, stretched in either direction. Every few meters control or communication panels interrupted the smooth surface. Horath turned to the left, moving slowly in consideration of his visitors. A steep ramp led up to what Delano guessed was the vessel's main level. Power and storage below, living and working on the upper deck.

Indirect lighting from some unseen source illuminated the passageway, though the light seemed quite a bit weaker than what humans preferred. The bulkhead, deck, and overhead looked the same, all the surfaces covered with a light gray material that seemed to have some flex to it. Whatever it was, it provided more than enough friction for Delano and Lian to walk, though they moved with care.

When they reached the second level, Horath needed only a few of his long strides to reach an open doorway. He halted, then abruptly waved Delano and Lian inside.

Déjà vu all over again. Delano couldn't resist a smile. The furnishings consisted of an elliptical table about three meters long by one meter wide, with six chairs – really stools with low backs – grouped around it. Four on one side, and two on the other. Well, that made it simple. *Another damn conference room, and another damned meeting.* A few more meetings and Delano's head would explode. The only things missing were the pitcher of water, a coffee urn, and some empty Styrofoam cups.

Two Tarlons sat side-by-side on the inner side of the table. Ahvin sat next to them, and Horath took the chair beside her.

"Please sit," Ahvin said, pointing to the two remaining chairs. "Are you good?"

"Yes, Ahvin," Lian answered. "We are good."

Chapter 13

Day 6: 2357 Zulu

After removing their flight suits, Delano and Lian settled into their chairs, moving with care at what felt like one third of Earth's gravity. After days of zero gravity, the sensation of weight seemed unnatural. The uncomfortable chairs didn't help. The Tarlons' anatomy didn't quite fit Delano's spine, and the thin gray cushions added little to the humans' ease. Horath looked even more uncomfortable, shifting his weight a few times before settling in.

Horath's discomfort didn't trouble Delano. His stomach relaxed and he enjoyed the steady equilibrium in his ears. The items he placed on the table remained where he put them. Pens didn't float away, propelled by the slightest air circulation. The air aboard had a soothing floral scent, though he didn't recognize the particular flower, quite unlike the dry recycled air on the Station that always smelled like warm motor oil. The human sense of smell had no problem adapting to this environment. At first Delano hooked his feet under the chair from habit, and had to remind himself to let his legs stretch out. *Ah, the simple pleasures of life.*

He glanced at Lian, and saw her enjoying the sensation of gravity as well. She smiled at their hosts. Hopefully they wouldn't take the display of teeth as a hostile threat.

For an alien spacecraft, the Talmak's ship appeared far more inviting and comfortable than did the interior of the Station, with its wires and electronics dangling from every surface. Without the world crisis hanging over their heads, Delano guessed he would enjoy spending time with these creatures. With a start, he realized he'd just accomplished another first for mankind – he and Lian were the first humans to board an alien ship.

He lifted his gaze and met the Talmak's brown eyes, large and tinted with pink. Delano studied the slender nose, large cheekbones, and expressive mouth with its two rows of small, even teeth. The body color seemed different from what the camera transmitted, a light tan that went well with the black desktop and gray-lined wall behind him. The Talmak returned the stare, regarding two humans with equal interest. First Contact meetings apparently needed some time for the participants to adjust to the strangeness of the new sentients.

"Greetings, Talmak," Delano spoke in the Ktarran tongue, and Lian echoed the welcoming phrase. "The helium-3 is being processed and should be arriving soon."

Lian converted the time to segments, using her tablet. "26 segments."

"We thank Delano and Lian. When you depart," Talmak said, "we give you plans and diagrams of power plants and gravity . . . device." He turned to his companion. "This is Celeck. . . teacher, one who studies, one who communicates. He assist you."

The Talmak showed no concern about turning over what might be valuable information. Delano wondered what else he should have asked for. Part of him didn't trust either the Talmak or Horath. A large part of that distrust came from the use of the Ktarran trade language, which provided little more than basic communication in words and math. It lacked the subtle nuances that gave depth to advanced languages. Both Delano and Lian coveted the chance to speak to the Talmak in his native tongue.

"Talmak," Delano began, "since we have time before helium arrives, we wish to learn your language. We want to understand you and others like you, talk direct, not use Ktarran words. Will you teach us your words?"

The Talmak shifted in his seat. and Delano guessed his request had caught the alien by surprise.

"Not time for learning," Talmak said. "Ktarrans come soon, perhaps forty segments, perhaps fifty segments. Then you . . . your world is destroyed."

Delano felt his jaw drop. Destroy Earth? He wanted to ask how the Talmak knew the arrival time with such certainty. But that question had to wait. "Why would Ktarrans destroy my world?"

The Talmak lifted his slender arms. "They are Ktarrans. They are destroyer of worlds, of species. They destroy most of your cities, establish places for food." He let his hands fall to the table.

Well, that sounds final enough. Case closed, sit back and relax, nothing to worry about here, the Ktarrans will destroy Earth. "What will happen to Tarlons, to Halkin, if Ktarrans destroy Earth?"

"We leave this place. With helium-3, we return to gate. Leave this system. Fight Ktarrans another place, another time."

So they called it a gate. Interesting.

"Talmak, what are places for food?" Lian leaned forward. She had continued entering information on her tablet, analyzing the conversation.

Delano had skipped over the mention of food places, but Lian had picked up on the vague reply.

"Food places are places where species . . . humans . . . turned into food, into . . ." Talmak searched for a word, but couldn't find anything better "into food for Ktarrans."

Cannibals? Delano glanced at Lian. An advanced space-going race of cannibals? He didn't believe it. Well, later for that.

"If Earth cities are destroyed." Delano chose his words with care, "power plants, gravity machine of no use."

The Talmak bowed his head in agreement. "No use to you. All you ships, bases on moons, all destroyed."

Delano leaned back in his chair, an even more uncomfortable position considering the differences in human and alien physiology. Right now he enjoyed the minor discomfort, anything to keep his anger in check, to keep away the thought of Earth being ravaged and conquered. Horath watched him, and Delano realized his fists were clenched. He took a deep breath of the perfumed air, let it out, and relaxed his hands.

This wasn't working. The Ktarran trade language had too many limitations. Already he and Lian had identified and cataloged over eight hundred nouns and almost forty verbs. While adequate for basic communications, the Ktarran lingua franca, at least what they knew of it, couldn't convey complex ideas and emotions. A more than adequate vehicle for a first contact, but it certainly couldn't be the basis for a discussion on the whys and hows of human destruction or planetary defense, let alone cannibalism by one species on another. No, not cannibals, but predators, carnivores – those who ate raw animal flesh and enjoyed the taste. He repressed the urge to shiver.

Delano turned to Lian, and when he spoke, his words were Chinese. "Lian, this process isn't going to work. The Ktarran language can't tell us what we need to know to help Earth. I think we must learn to speak the Tarlon language."

She nodded. "That would be best, but do we have time to learn an advanced language? If what the Talmak says is true, the Ktarrans will be here in fifty to sixty segments . . . that's as little as thirty-five hours, maybe a little longer. To fully grasp their language, that's not enough time."

She was right, of course. To really achieve fluency in a language, you had to know certain things about their culture, history, literature, all the subtleties that made up a unique heritage. Without that knowledge, true comprehension and higher level communication couldn't take place.

"Then we're out of luck," Delano said. "We might as well pack it in now."

"Perhaps not," she said. "You may have the right idea, now that I think about it. After all, there are two of us, and we have the translators. If the Talmak could be persuaded to help us, really pitch in, we might be able to do it. The Ktarran language gives us a substantial head start."

Anytime a linguist had to learn a new language, if both sides spoke a second, separate lingua franca, communication always developed faster.

"If these Tarlons are leaders," Delano said, almost speaking to himself, "then they may be proficient in teaching others their language. Look at the Halkins . . . look at Horath. He understands the Tarlon language well enough. Perhaps the Talmak has his own translator software."

"If they cooperated with us," Lian said, warming to the idea, "we might learn even faster. We could ask them."

Delano shook his head. "No, not asking. We'll demand it. If they don't, they can kiss their helium goodbye."

"Yes, why should we bother helping them and risk antagonizing the Ktarrans? If our cities are to be destroyed, what matters who does it."

He smiled at the resolve in her voice. "Then I think you should tell them what we've decided. That way they'll know we're both determined to get what we want."

"Are you sure? You've been taking the lead in all the negotiations so far."

"So far I've done nothing but agree to everything they wanted." Delano smiled. "Time for a new sheriff to take charge."

Lian turned toward Talmak, fixed her eyes on his and held them.

"Talmak, I am Lian." She had switched back to the Ktarran tongue. "We want to learn your language. Need to speak to you direct. Ktarran language not good enough."

"There is no time for you to learn our language."

Lian shook her head emphatically. "There is time. Delano and I learn fast. Have good machines." She tapped her tablet. "Talmak must help, work hard. If you help, we can learn in twenty segments."

The Talmak glanced at his companion before replying. "If you do not learn?"

"Then no helium-3 for Tarlons or Halkins."

That statement caught the Talmak's attention. Horath, too, bristled at the threat.

"We have power to destroy many cities," Horath said, speaking for the first time. "Do not forget you are aboard our ship."

Lian refused to be daunted. "We are aboard Talmak's ship. Horath will not waste little power he has on cities or moon bases. Not think Talmak will kill innocent. If he kills, then the Tarlons no better than Ktarran. We, Earth, will offer peace to Ktarrans."

A good answer, Delano thought, briefer and better than what he could have come up with. Prove to us that you're the good guys, or we'll take our chances.

The Talmak turned his eyes toward Delano. "Does Lian speak for Earth? Do you speak for Earth?"

"We *both* speak for Earth," Delano said. "You will teach us your language. Show us your writings, images, all things to help us learn and understand the Tarlons. And the Ktarrans."

The Talmak glanced at Horath. The two spoke but now they were the ones who wanted privacy, so the language used was the Tarlon tongue. When the conversation ended, the Talmak turned back to Delano, but this time he included Lian in his gaze. "Horath very angry. He will destroy your ship, destroy bases on your moon if no helium."

Delano leaned closer to Lian and whispered in her ear. "It's time to shove all the chips into the pot." He realized she might not understand the idiom. "Call his bluff."

She nodded, then leaned forward as far as the table allowed, and spoke to Horath. "Then we are finished. No helium for Horath. Let him destroy our ship. Better we die, our ship die than give him helium and the power to destroy even more."

Lian leaned back in the chair and crossed her arms. The aliens had no difficulty understanding what that dismissive gesture meant.

Delano watched the Halkins. Horath's thick fingers trembled, and no doubt he wanted to reach over the table and crush Lian into pulp. Ahvin's reaction revealed her emotions – she showed fear in her hunched shoulders. But that didn't stop her from reaching out and holding Horath's arm.

Either the Talmak wasn't watching, or didn't concern himself with Horath's problem.

"Does Delano agree with Lian? Is she not . . . under your command?"

"No. Lian and I are equal. We both speak for Earth. Help us learn your language. We can learn very fast if you help."

"We will learn language," Lian said, "and we must talk to our Station while we learn. Must talk to leaders on Earth, tell what we are doing. They must know of Ktarran danger."

The Talmak shook his head. "Talk to planet dangerous. Too much power needed. Ktarrans may hear."

"Must talk with Earth first," Lian insisted. "Or no helium."

"Must also have food and machines from Station," Delano added. Might as well get it all out on the table. "Prepare for hard work learning Tarlon language. Also want skin samples now."

The Talmak didn't like it. Horath's reaction was even worse.

"I destroy your Station, your base on Moon, if you not provide Helium." He banged his large hand on the table.

Delano wished he knew the Ktarran equivalent for "fuck you," but if there was one, Ahvin hadn't taught it to them. He turned away from Horath, to face the Talmak. "Talmak is leader, or not?"

Lian didn't wait for the reply. "We return to Station now. Talk to Earth leaders. Warn them of Ktarrans, warn them of Horath. You lower the plasma screen. We return in one segment and begin learning. Or no helium."

Delano rose, moving fast enough in the light gravity for his feet to leave the floor for a moment. "We go now." Lian scooped up her tablet and pushed it into her bag.

For a long moment, no one moved. Then the Talmak turned to Horath and started talking. Delano couldn't understand what Talmak said, but Horath made another fist. This time he managed not to pound on the table.

When their brief conversation ended, Horath stood. Now he moved too quickly, knocking his chair backward. Ahvin reached down and lifted the chair back to its proper place. "Come." He stalked out of the chamber, leaving Ahvin behind.

Delano nodded to the Talmak and followed. Lian moved right behind him, showing no fear. Delano decided it was even money as to whether Horath intended to take them back to the Station or dump their bodies in space. They shared a look. They had said what needed to be said, and now they just had to swallow their fear as they entered Horath's shuttle craft.

During the brief ride, from the glare Horath gave him, Delano thought the Halkin had indeed decided to toss them through the hatch. When the Halkin ship reached the Station, Horath practically shoved them through the plasma field and into the airlock. By the time Delano and Lian removed their suits and reached the Lounge, everyone on the Station waited there for the returning heroes.

Delano gave everyone the highlights, but he knew he needed to speak with General Klegg as soon as possible. Klegg had called earlier, and according to Welsh, the General had lost his usual calm demeanor when he heard Lian and Delano had left the Station.

Kosloff established the connection to Earth, while Delano and Lian settled down in front of the monitor. Delano had no trouble seeing the anger on Klegg's chiseled face. China and Russia were already on the line, and Delano saw a new member had joined the call. Splitting a screen with General Demidov, Delano recognized the frowning face of the President of Russia, Iosif Alekseyevich Garanin.

Great, just what he needed, another asshole telling him what to do.

Delano guessed none of the Alliance members had wandered far from their transmitters in case anything happened. The fireworks started at once, and in five seconds the call turned into a shouting match. Klegg's booming baritone won out.

"You had no authority to leave the Station, Major." Klegg's voice echoed throughout the Control Room. "You put yourself and Dr. Duan at risk. You both might have been captured."

Delano, still excited from the visit to the Talmak's ship, reminded himself to stay calm. "Sir, we, both of us, felt the risk was minimal. If we hadn't gone to speak to the Talmak, we wouldn't have learned that the Ktarrans are coming. According to the Talmak, as soon as they arrive they will establish control of our solar system by the destruction of most of Earth's cities and all off-world bases. Apparently that's normal procedure for Ktarrans when they encounter a new species. They cripple the planet, then take over, either with their surrogates or through any of the planet's rulers willing to go along with the slaughter. For a planet like Earth, the Talmak thinks they'll destroy eighty percent of our population centers to start. Meanwhile the Halkins want the helium-3, or they have threatened to destroy the lunar bases. Apparently they have enough fuel and firepower remaining for that."

"You believe this Talmak?" Klegg leaned forward and growled into his microphone. "What makes you think he's telling the truth? Maybe he's the criminal and these Ktarrans are trying to capture him and the Halkins."

"We don't believe him, not completely, but we have two different species saying the same thing," Delano said, attempting to soothe the General. All the other faces on the call looked just as angry, in particular the Chinese General Secretary, who no doubt had worried about Lian.

"That's why we must go back and learn the Tarlon dialect before the Ktarrans arrive," Delano said. "Lian and I believe the only way to know the truth is to converse with them in their own language, examine their records and history. If we don't like what we see, then we don't turn over the helium, and we take our chances with the Ktarrans."

"You are not going back to their ship, Major, and that is a direct order." Klegg had his voice under control, but the threat came through nonetheless. "If you need further contact, you can do it from the Station, just as you did with the Halkins."

Before Delano could answer, Lian leaned closer to the microphone. "Even if Major Delano is not allowed to return to the Talmak's ship, I will still go. The only way this negotiation will work is if we learn their language in time, and we must do that together on their ship, face-to-face, with their help and resources. We do not have time to waste."

Before a startled Klegg could reply, General Secretary Liu cut in. "You will not return to that ship. I forbid it. Do your work from the Station. If someone must go, Major Delano is fully qualified."

Well, thank you. At least the Chinese had no problem risking Delano's capture and life for that matter.

Lian started to protest, but her uncle interrupted. "Sergeant Shen, you will ensure that Lian does not leave the Station."

General Demidov cut in. "May I remind everyone that those who volunteered for this mission were considered expendable. We need to obtain as much knowledge as possible about these aliens, and if risks must be taken to get that information, so be it. Even if Major Delano and Dr. Duan are taken captive, that will be equally instructive."

Not so good for us, but it works for you.

"May I remind everyone that it was agreed I would direct the mission." Klegg's voice had risen sharply. "I'm sure Major Delano and Lian can conduct . . ."

"General Klegg," Delano cut in before the shouting could resume, "we both have to return. Otherwise there is no way to learn their language fast enough to determine the truth about these Ktarrans. They're already on their way here, and with luck, Lian and I can learn what you need to know. Otherwise . . ."

"I agree. I am returning to the ship with you." Lian's voice had a hard edge, almost as sharp as her Uncle's.

"Major, I am relieving you of command," Klegg said. "Colonel Welsh, you will assume command of the Station and this mission. Make certain Major Delano continues his work from the Station."

Delano rapped his fist on the table, hard enough to carry through the microphone. "General Klegg, you did not give me a mission. You gave me a command and now I am giving the orders until the mission is completed. You're thousands of miles away and not in the best position to evaluate the situation or make First Contact decisions. On the Talmak's ship, we can examine their technology, ask questions, talk to others. And we'll make certain that everything is transmitted to the Station. After that, after we've established full communications with the aliens, you can relieve me. Meanwhile we're losing precious time."

"I'll do more than relieve you, Major," Klegg said. "Colonel Welsh, did you hear my orders?"

Delano turned to Welsh, who looked uncomfortable. Everyone in the Station waited. The moment of truth had arrived.

"Sir," Welsh said, "I believe Major Delano should remain in charge. We need to know who to trust, the Talmak or the Ktarrans. From what I've seen of the process, we can't get that information working from the Station, not without the full cooperation of Delano and Lian, not in the little time we have. So with all due respect, no, I will not relieve the Major."

Delano clenched his jaw. Not only had he disobeyed orders, he'd started a mutiny, and in front of Alliance partners no less. Now Welsh was hip-deep in it, too. *Just fucking great.*

Klegg sat there for a moment, his lower lip between his teeth, struggling to keep his temper reined in. Seconds ticked by before he spoke, but he had his voice under control. His facial expression and body language, no so much. "All right, Major, since you won't follow orders, all I can do is try to support you and hope for the best. For now. Secretary Liu? General Demidov?"

The leader of China had to be as upset as Klegg. But China's leader had a lifetime of experience in keeping his emotions under control. "If Lian is determined to do this, I suppose I must agree also. But Lian, take all possible care."

"I will, Uncle."

"Make certain you provide regular reports," Demidov said. "We have other duties to perform besides waiting for you to schedule a call."

Klegg hesitated a moment, to allow President Garanin to speak. But the dour Russian apparently had nothing to add. "Report in as often as you can, Major."

"Yes, Sir. Secretary Liu, General Klegg, General Demidov, President Garanin, we will both take care," Delano said. "We'll establish contact when we're on the Talmak's ship. You'll know soon enough if anything goes wrong."

Chapter 14

Day 7: 0124 Zulu

Delano and Lian wanted to return to the Talmak's ship as soon as possible, but when they contacted Ahvin to request a ride, she informed them that Horath had duties to perform, and the Tarlon Celeck needed some time to prepare training materials. Delano fumed at the delay, but Lian convinced him that they could use some sleep. Colonel Welsh and the others agreed, so Linda injected them with one of the new benzodiazepines. She called it a mild sedative, and agreed to wake the linguists in two hours.

This time Delano made sure Welsh understood that meant exactly two hours before he let Linda near him. For the second time, Delano and Lian climbed into their bunks. Before he could strap himself down, Linda shot the dose into his upper arm. He was asleep before his head hit the pillow.

When Delano woke, he found Linda bending over him.

"Welcome back to the land of the living," Linda said as she put away her equipment. "Exactly two hours and twenty minutes of sleep, just what the doctor – that would be me – ordered."

Delano sat up. Aside from a mild headache, he felt as if he'd just had ten hours of sleep. In fact he felt too good. "What else did you give me?" He tried to snarl at her, but couldn't.

"Nothing bad, Major," she said. "Just a little ephedrine and some happy juice. And the IV, of course. You'll be fully recovered in a few minutes, more than enough time for you to get ready for the Tarlons."

"An IV?" Delano knew he should be angry, but somehow he couldn't summon up the emotion. He glanced down at his forearm and saw a Band-Aid. "What did I need an IV for?"

"You and Lian looked a little dehydrated," Linda said. "The IV took care of that, and I also added some liquid protein, so your food intake will be in balance."

He shook his head. "Damn you. Why didn't you tell me first?"

"You'd waste too much time arguing. Lian didn't mind at all."

Delano glanced at the other bunk. "Where's Lian?"

"Already gone, Major," the Med-Tech announced. "She needed a smaller dose to wake up. Oh, by the way, you may want to visit the WCS before you have an accident." She grinned. "Need any help?"

When Horath returned to the Station again to pick up Lian and Delano for their second shuttle ride, the big Halkin appeared as annoyed as the last time they'd seen him. Horath's body language remained intimidating, and Delano took pains not to antagonize him. Horath had two ships and crews to worry about, and it might not take much to send him over the edge.

But Delano no longer cared much about the Halkins. The Talmak and his people remained the key, not only because of their superior technology, but because they had mastered the languages of many species. That meant they possessed records, written or recorded in some fashion, that could verify their claims about themselves and the Ktarrans.

Nevertheless, Delano and Lian had not yet reached that stage of communication, so they had collected all the equipment and supplies they would need once on board the Tarlon ship – each had their own tablet, radio, and backup power. They also carried energy bars, water, and Lian had the bottle of pep pills Med Tech Linda had prepared for them. Under that burden, they struggled in zero gravity to manipulate all their equipment.

Privately Delano and Lian had agreed that neither would return to the Station until they achieved complete and accurate communication with the Tarlons. Hopefully before the Ktarrans arrived.

As soon as they boarded the Halkin shuttle, Horath jetted away from the Station, and in moments, deposited them in the same airlock aboard the Talmak's ship. A Tarlon waited to escort them to the communication room they had used before. At least this alien proved himself friendly by carrying Lian's equipment.

Inside the tiny conference room, they found Celeck waiting for them. The communication specialist for the Tarlons sat behind a thick stack of what had to be teaching paraphernalia. He watched with interest as Delano set up the tablets, established a link to the Station's mainframe, and opened a comm link as well.

Delano intended to have everything they did and said recorded on the Station and transmitted to Earth as soon as possible. They took their time setting up and checking their computers. Then Delano signaled that Celeck could begin.

"This is how Tarlons teach our children, or when we encounter new species." Celeck began, in the Ktarran trade language. He handed them what looked like a thick brown clipboard without the clip. A child-sized recessed button activated the display and revealed a brightly colored picture of a garden scene, with trees, flowers, bushes, and several other objects Delano didn't recognize.

The display proved simple enough to operate. Touch the object, and a soothing voice identified it. For a few of the more complex words, the voice also provided a phonetic pronunciation. Human children learned on much the same type of toys.

Delano and Lian, sharing the display, took extra time to enter the data into their translation software. They had decided Lian would take charge of inputting the phonetics, since her voice better approximated the tones of the Tarlons. She repeated the name of the object, reproducing the sound as best she could, until Celeck nodded approval.

Then a tap on Lian's screen, and the sound repeated. The first time that happened Celeck seemed both surprised and impressed with the tablet's operation. Once again Delano noticed the Tarlons lacked the advanced computer hardware and software skills common on Earth.

When Delano and Lian had mastered the first display, she pushed the button a second time, and a different scene appeared. This one showed a two-story dwelling with open rooms. Lian and Delano processed the second display much faster. Both repeated the new words and mimicked the sounds. When Celeck assented, they entered each word or phrase into their translation software. Then they advanced to the third scene.

This third slate – for want of a better word – included the fundamentals of pronouns and the simplest verbs. Slate four introduced basic grammar rules. Always difficult, Delano knew. Human children learned grammar and tenses by hearing adults speak, so those subjects rarely needed to be taught at such a young age. But fortunately Celeck had a few displays to address the issue, and Delano guessed these would be used for the most precocious progeny.

Each screen added another hundred or so words to the database. More than an hour later, they finished the ten scenes. Lian had logged over eight hundred nouns properly identified, attached to an English phonetic spelling, and with each word's correct pronunciation in the Tarlon language.

They worked for another hour before Delano suggested a break. He and Lian split an energy bar, and they both finished their first bottle of water. As Linda warned, it was all too easy to become dehydrated in space. Celeck had offered them water and nourishment from Tarlon supplies, but for now Delano preferred to stick with what they'd brought aboard. No sense risking a stomach ache, Montezuma's revenge, or something worse.

The snack finished, they resumed work. Two hours later, they had added more than two thousand words into the database, including over a hundred verbs. As their skill and familiarity with the language increased, the lessons proceeded faster. By the time another two hours had passed, the database held four thousand words. That roughly equaled the vocabulary of any bright five or six year old human child. They took a another quick break, but both wanted to keep working.

Three hours later, Delano checked the software's word count. To his surprise they had entered over seven thousand words. That, he knew, was about what the average news media or blog reader needed to fully comprehend another person. On Earth that would be more than enough for any basic conversation. But Delano wanted more, and with Celeck's help, they were absorbing the Tarlon language at top speed.

When Delano and Lian had started the learning, he hadn't been certain that even working together, they could master the new language in time. But now, thanks to Celeck, Delano felt more confident. Celeck's linguistic and teaching talents proved very good, and he guided the lessons with skill and efficiency. In effect, there were now three sentients working hard to teach the humans the Tarlon language.

When Delano glanced at his watch, almost ten hours had passed. He and Lian had grasped the basic language. What they might have forgotten remained safely stored in the translation computer. Only the materials Celeck had provided made this feat of learning possible, that and the power of Earth's state of the art computer tablets and translation software. Without Celeck's active participation, it would have taken at least two days to reach this level. Now they needed to get more technical.

First they needed a break. Delano and Lian decided to get some sleep, so he explained the problem to Celeck, who didn't seem tired at all. But he understood the requirement. Two minutes later, Delano and Lian curled up together and fell asleep on the deck, using their packs as pillows.

Lian's tablet woke them. They'd slept for little more than an hour, but both felt refreshed. Zero gravity had something to do with that, Delano knew. They shared another snack, and each took one of Linda's pep pills, a different formulary that the Med Tech claimed would keep them going and improve cognitive functioning. Both had to stay sharp. Delano didn't think he needed one yet, but adrenalin could only keep you going for so long before you crashed. Besides, better to take them early than try to pull yourself out of low energy state.

Delano readied himself for the next phase. He nodded respectfully to Celeck when the Tarlon returned to the conference room. Delano explained how they would like to proceed. Celeck arranged for another Tarlon to join them, this one named Jarendo. He arrived carrying several displays, star charts, and maintenance documents.

Delano learned that Jarendo was the second in command of the Tarlon ship. If the captain, or what the Tarlons called the War Leader – the Talmak's ship was indeed a fighting vessel – was killed or incapacitated, those duties would fall to Jarendo. While the Talmak directed the ship's political purpose and defined the mission, the War Leader commanded the ship's daily operations and made tactical decisions.

Communicating with Jarendo represented a major leap forward, and Delano was determined to extract all the technical vocabulary for a fighting warship – guns, beams, cannons, maneuvering, navigation, compartments, shuttles, weapons, fighting skills. In short, all the specific terms and expressions needed to conduct a military operation, recall one from the past for analysis, or plan one in the future. Celeck, aware of his pupils' capabilities, proved as skillful explaining Jarendo's technical concepts.

After another three hours of continuous work – almost twenty-two hours had passed since they came aboard – Jarendo took Lian and Delano for a tour of the ship, beginning with the Tarlon control room. They carried their tablets, and Delano took images of everything he saw, including the overall layout. Jarendo guided them from station to station, identifying the function of each – navigation, power, plasma control, gravity, ship integrity. Delano was surprised to learn that task required two positions, each manned by two crewmen. The tour continued until Delano had recorded sixteen separate functions, including several he didn't fully comprehend.

About halfway through the tour, Delano realized he was conversing with Jarendo and referring to the tablet only to record new words or concepts.

Delano glanced at Lian. "I'm starting to understand without having to translate."

"Yes, me too. We're making good progress. They are accomplished teachers."

They smiled. Both had spoken in the Tarlon language. Still, they had no time to celebrate the moment, that magical moment when a linguist realized he was not only speaking but thinking in a new and different language.

The half-dozen Tarlon crew members scattered about watched with curiosity as Delano and Lian recorded the technical words needed to control a starship. Even the War Leader, an older Tarlon named Kaneel, paused to observe the visitors wandering about his control room.

An hour later Delano and Lian had absorbed all they could from the control room visit. They returned to the conference room. A glance at the translation software revealed the addition of almost a thousand new words. Celeck, meanwhile, had kept busy. He prepared a new slate that contained the diagrams and a simplified explanation of the Tarlon's power drive.

That discussion lasted another hour. Jarendo, with Celeck's help, explained the basic functioning of the ship's drive. The engine turned out to be only partly a fusion drive. Anti-matter extracted from empty space provided the primary source of energy. Jarendo tried to explain the concept, even offered to bring in a more technical member of the crew, but Delano knew a more detailed explanation would be wasted on him. A good physicist, someone like Maks, might be able to follow along, but Delano didn't have the time to waste.

By now Delano's head hurt, and Lian didn't look much better. They took another break and gulped more pills. Since coming aboard, they had worked for over twenty-five hours, with only one brief nap. If the Talmak's estimate of how soon the Ktarrans might arrive still held, they might show up off Jupiter in less than twenty-four hours. Delano questioned Celeck about that time window, but the Tarlon had no new update. How long before they reached Earth remained an unknown factor.

Delano had ignored the Station's three attempts to contact him, turning off the communicator after the last attempt. Now he opened up a channel and soon had Kosloff on the line.

"Major, what is your status? Everyone here is worried about you and Lian. Is everything all right?"

"Yes, we're both fine, and we're making excellent progress. We're almost ready for full communication with the Talmak. Is Colonel Welsh there?"

"Yes, just arriving," Kosloff said.

"Welsh," Delano said, "can you hear me? We're fine here."

"Damn you, Delano, Klegg's been on my ass for hours. You'd better get back here and speak to him. Or I can patch you through to Earth."

"No time," Delano said. "We're about ready to open negotiations. Lian has collected over eight thousand Tarlon words in the database. Tell that to Klegg. What's the status on the helium-3?"

"A shuttle lifted off two hours ago with twelve tanks of helium," Welsh said. "Another shuttle will depart the Moon shortly. It's carrying nine canisters and should reach the Station in about twelve hours. That's all the Alliance could round up without delaying its arrival. Are our new friends being helpful?"

"Yes, we have the basic concepts on the power drive, and we're working on understanding the weapon systems and wormhole travel. I'm sending over a file for Maks to look at. Maybe he can understand how you can scoop up antimatter particles from empty space. They tried twice to explain it, but we don't have a clue. We'll be bringing back some training tutorials the Tarlons use to explain the basic propulsion. Something to do with the separation of matter and antimatter scooped from subspace. Sounds crazy to me. If there's time, Maks can ask a few questions later on. Oh, and tell Parrish we have Tarlon and Halkin DNA samples for him to play with."

"Good to hear all that, Delano. But you need to talk to Klegg. He's demanding a conference. They're all going ballistic down there. The country is in a panic and the President is preparing to declare martial law. The news broke that aliens are at the Station, and that the Alliance has a team trying to establish communications with these aliens. Hell, they even have your name and Lian's. At least give Klegg a few minutes. I can connect you right now?"

Right now Delano didn't care if Klegg's head exploded. "No, not yet. We'll probably be back on the Station in about six hours. Tell Linda her pills are working fine. Oh, and Lian says she just transmitted our updated language database to your mainframe. Make sure you back that up and send it to Earth. That may keep Klegg off our backs."

"Will do. But you're asking for it, Delano," Welsh said. "Klegg's going to turn you into hamburger when this is over. Probably me, too. Good luck over there."

So the Camp Pendleton brig had reentered the picture. "Talk to you in a few hours," Delano said, "and thanks. We need all the luck we can get."

Delano helped Lian finish up the last entries going into the database. The time had come for serious negotiations with the Talmak.

Delano and Lian notified Celeck that they were ready to meet with the Talmak as soon as he was available. That turned out to be twenty minutes, so they took their time setting up the equipment, then treated themselves to another break. Delano did some stretching, and Lian performed a series of Tai-chi moves. He noticed that she looked quite graceful as she held the poses. Both had to move carefully in the low gravity. They split a bottle of water, ate another energy bar, and checked the software.

They were as ready as they would ever be. The entire purpose of the last fifty-plus hours had been to prepare them for this moment. Delano and Lian would have appreciated more time to immerse themselves in the language, but with the arrival of the Ktarrans still on the horizon, they had run out of time.

"Lian, would you mind leading the conversation?" Delano asked in Chinese. They had used English to communicate in all of their training. He didn't know if the Tarlons were recording them or might even be trying to learn English. Better safe than sorry.

She looked at him in surprise. "Of course, but you've been doing most of the speaking. Why change now?"

"I want you to watch the Talmak during the talks. You seem better at reading body language and facial expressions than I am. We have to be sure he's telling the truth."

"You think I can read his expressions? We haven't gotten too far with that yet."

"It should be easier now," he said, "and it's worth a try. We can match everything to the video record later, if there's time."

"He may have objections to dealing with a female. The Halkins certainly do."

He shrugged. "He'll get over it. Besides, it may look better to the Alliance. Your uncle believes in you."

She smiled. "I've always been his favorite niece, especially because he never had any daughters. He and my mother are very close."

Sounds from the corridor indicated the time for small talk had ended. A moment later the Talmak, Celeck, Jarendo, Horath, and Ahvin entered the compartment. This time another Halkin joined them – Captain Morad, who commanded the second Halkin ship. The six crowded around one side of the table, leaving Delano and Lian alone on the other.

Seeing Ahvin caught Delano by surprise. He hadn't expected her to be present, but perhaps this opportunity for learning more of the Tarlon language couldn't be passed up. Or maybe her role aboard the Halkin ship had increased in importance. Captain Morad appeared so much like Horath that Delano wondered if they might be brothers.

"Celeck informs me," the Talmak began in his own language after he settled into his chair, "that you have progressed rapidly in your learning. In fact, we have no record of any species learning our language as fast."

Delano glanced down at the software, which had captured the Talmak's opening words and converted them to English. The text on the screen matched exactly to what Delano had understood. *So far, so good.*

"All of you have been most helpful." Lian spoke the words in English into the hooded translation microphone. Because of the number of people and the size of the room, the hood helped filter out extraneous sounds, and prevented the speaker's words from affecting the translation or creating confusing feedback. The software converted her words into English text and entered that into the tablet. A fraction of a second later, the machine reiterated Lian's translated words, in the Tarlon language, through the speaker.

Delano watched as the Talmak's eyes shifted to the table and stared at the white speaker, a square block less than three inches on a side. The quality was good, and the words sounded as if Lian had spoken them herself. Delano might not fully understand the Talmak's body language, but he felt certain his reaction registered surprise. The alien had watched as Delano and Lian entered data into the machine, but he had never heard it speak sentences before or grasped its potential.

Lian saw the reaction, too. "Our translation machine has stored all the words we have learned, along with basic rules of grammar and syntax. We can speak into the machine in our language, and it translates what we say into yours. But for now, we will only use it when you speak. It will translate your words and display them on the screen. That way, we can compare what we see to what we heard. If the machine matches, then we are confident we understand your meaning. If not, we must discuss with Celeck."

She had everyone's interest. What had previously been regarded by the Tarlons as a mere teaching and learning tool had now morphed into something significant.

"How many words of our language does your . . . machine know?" The Talmak spoke slowly, as if to give them extra time to comprehend.

"Almost eight thousand, including many technical words that describe the ship and its operation. It is enough for simple communication. And there is no need to speak slowly. The machine can keep up."

It damn well better keep up, Delano thought. It's the best we have.

The Talmak nodded in approval. He turned to Celeck. "You

have done well to teach them so fast."

"The **gratification/satisfaction/joy/pleasure** belongs to them," Celeck said.

Whatever word Celeck had used, the software didn't fully recognize it. But it had pulled words that had appeared in similar context. Lian made no comment about the word. It was too trivial to matter, and she didn't intend to waste time just to learn another word.

Celeck had more. "I have worked with Delano and Lian to equate some of their mathematics to our systems. When we speak of distances or time periods, I will convert to their mode. This will be useful when they report to their leaders on Earth."

Earlier Delano had shown Celeck the metric system, using a ruler displayed on the tablet to detail one-quarter of a meter. He'd also given Celeck his watch, so that the Tarlon could work with both time and distance. Whether Celeck had accomplished it alone, or handed the task to another, the Tarlon teacher now understood basic human measurements and had saved everyone hours of valuable time.

"The recording device," Lian pointed to the camera placed on the desk between them, "records all our words. It transmits them to our Station, which relays the images and sounds to Earth. Humans and Tarlons can now communicate with each other, as long as we use simple words and brief sentences."

The fact that his words and image would be recorded didn't appear to bother the Talmak. "Good. Then let us begin. What do you wish to know?"

Lian never hesitated. "Tell us about the Ktarrans."

"The Ktarrans." Talmak leaned back in his chair, a very humanoid gesture. "Before one can talk about them, we must speak of the Ancient Ones. About . . ." he turned to Celeck.

"About three million of your solar cycles ago, or years as you call them," Celeck explained.

"About that time," the Talmak continued, "the first species of sentients arose in this region of the galaxy, a species that in time grew so superior to all others that it became the most **strong/dominant/powerful** and intelligent in the galaxy. We call them the Ancient Ones. In time, they discovered the space drive and **gate/wormhole/portals**. They were wise and gentle beings. In their wisdom and love of all living things, they decided to help speed up the cycle of life developing on many planets throughout this sector of the galaxy. They wanted to spread their love for the universe to as many beings as possible. For many thousands of your solar cycles they took their life material and inserted it on countless planets where they believed life might someday arise and grow. That is why your life material is so similar to that of Tarlon and the Halkin and many others. We are all descendants of the Ancient Ones."

Lian nodded. "And where are these Ancient Ones today?"

"We do not know," the Talmak replied, a hint of sadness in his voice. "They have **left/abandoned/departed** this quadrant . . ." he glanced at Celeck, to make certain the humans understood the stellar reference. "It may be they have left this galaxy. We believe the Ancient Ones could not bear to see the suffering caused by the Ktarrans, a species they had helped develop."

Delano leaned forward. "The Ktarrans are also descended from the Ancient Ones?"

"No, they are a separate species, a kind of hunting animal that had come to dominate its home planet. The first Ktarrans were ruthless, savage, and extremely intelligent for a creature that ate the flesh of its victims. A very bad combination. The Ancient Ones **gave/imparted/introduced** their life material into the Ktarrans. In their pride, the Ancient Ones thought to make the Ktarrans more **gentle/peaceful/docile** to speed their **evolution/growth/path** to higher intelligence. But the basic Ktarran life material proved too strong. It absorbed only some of the life material of the Ancient Ones, enough so that the Ktarrans became sentient, but retained their hunter ways. Somehow they **hid/disguised/concealed** their true nature from the Ancient Ones, always begging for more knowledge, more machines. But deep within their **hearts/souls/minds** the Ktarrans remained **savage/brutal/killers** and eaters of flesh."

"Why did the Ancient Ones not destroy the Ktarrans?" Lian hesitated. "To correct their mistake?"

"That was not their way," Talmak said. "To them, all sentient life is **sacred/precious/important**. They would not kill the evil they had created, or they did not know how. Perhaps they thought the Ktarrans merely required more time to evolve. They watched for many cycles as the Ktarrans increased in strength and numbers. At first, the Ktarrans were deceivers. They hid their true ways. But when they grew strong, they **attacked/conquered/invaded** other worlds and stole technology to add to their own. At the end, the Ancient Ones pleaded with the Ktarrans. But by then, the Ktarrans had spread to several worlds and increased their power and strength. They had **developed/created/acquired** many weapons and ships, and become far too powerful even for the Ancients to destroy. Ktarrans killed some of the Ancient Ones and ate their flesh, in a celebration of their authority."

"Talmak, that is the second time you spoke of Ktarrans eating flesh," Lian said. "Do you mean they actually eat those they fight?"

"Yes. You may ask Horath what became of his species, those we could not save."

Horath clenched his fist. "Truth. I have seen the splintered bones that remain of our kin. My brother, Captain Morad, also saw it." The language software processed the Halkin's words, despite the fact that his voice and tone were so different from that of the Tarlons. "What they did to our world they will do to yours. You will be destroyed. That is why you must give us the helium, so we can leave this place."

So Horath's brother commanded the second Halkin ship. Interesting, Delano thought. Perhaps whole families of fighters?

Lian turned back to the Talmak for confirmation. "You know this to be true?"

"Yes, it is as Horath says," the Talmak replied. "Celeck **tells/informs/advises** that your planet Earth has nine billion humans. In the last thousand cycles we have never found a world so populated with life as yours, one with so many sentients. Now you have taken the first steps into space. The Ktarrans will see Earth as a potential threat and as a source of . . ." He turned to Celeck.

"**Building/creating/constructing** of things," Celeck said. "They always need new ships and raw materials. And slaves."

"If they destroy our world," Lian asked, "how will that help them?"

"Not all of your world. They will deliver death to probably eight billion of your species," the Talmak said, "to achieve a manageable number. Then they will use the survivors as **slaves/laborers/workers/builders** for them. The Ktarrans will bring in their own species as rulers and their race of slaves . . . slaves who will be your masters. They will rule you and force you to rebuild anything of value to them that has been destroyed, anything that they require. Whatever is not needed for their purposes will be destroyed. Your only purpose will be to work and create for them, or be turned into food animals."

A look of revulsion crossed the Talmak's features. Obviously the eating of flesh, human or otherwise, was disgusting to him. Delano wondered what General Klegg and the Alliance members, listening over the comm link, thought about that.

"Then we cannot . . . speak with the Ktarrans?" Lian asked.

"They do not **talk/deal/negotiate/reason** with other species. Other species are only slaves, builders, or suppliers of food."

Well, that sounds bad, Delano thought. He saw Lian didn't like this revelation either. "Then there is no way to reason with them?"

"I have lived for over three hundred of your cycles," the Talmak said. "In that time, the Tarlons have lost three worlds. Others have lost as many or more. Never have we heard of anyone . . . reason with them."

"Earth will not allow so many to die," Lian said. "We will fight."

"If you fight, even more of you will be destroyed. Your people will soon understand that. A few will save themselves. They will **sacrifice/give up/yield** many of their own kind to survive and accept their roles as Ktarran slaves. It has always been so."

Lian turned to Delano. "Do you believe him?" She asked in Chinese, but kept her voice calm. "I do."

"Yes," Delano answered in the same language. "The Talmak is resigned to our destruction. The Halkins want only to escape. They want nothing else from us. If this were an elaborate lie, they would be asking for something in exchange, something more valuable than a few canisters of helium."

"They know we will try and negotiate with the Ktarrans when they arrive," she said. "They will be gone, and the Ktarrans, if they are not these bloodthirsty monsters, will talk to us. They will not kill billions because we gave the Halkins a few tanks of helium."

He nodded agreement, then turned toward the Talmak. "If the Ktarrans attack, Earth will fight. So you must tell us about their weapons and how they fight. But first, you must tell us when they will come."

The Talmak glanced at Celeck, indicating he should answer.

"We expect them to arrive near . . . Jupiter in about," he took a moment to convert the time period, "twenty of your hours. That will have given them enough time to gather sufficient force. But they know they must hurry. The gate will be closing soon."

Delano's jaw dropped. The wormhole was closing? *Was it on a fucking schedule, like a fucking train?* But he kept his voice under control. "Can you explain to us how the wormhole works? Until a few days ago, we did not know of its existence. We do not know how to use it."

This time the Talmak looked toward Jarendo to answer the question. "What you call the wormhole . . . we call it a **gate/portal/door** . . . it is very difficult to explain. The Ancient Ones, their scientists, were the first to discover their existence. They used their knowledge of mathematics and physics, after they had studied wormholes for many cycles, to learn how to find or create them. That enabled the Ancient Ones to travel among the stars."

"But each wormhole is unique," Jarendo went on. "Some permit travel for great distances, others for shorter distances. Some are stable. Others, like this one, are only open part of the time. When your Jupiter and its moons align in a certain way, and the nearby stars are in suitable positions, gravity waves line up and the wormhole is open. But this wormhole, when Jupiter moves, it closes again. The gate is open now, but it will close in about . . ." Jarendo had to work on his calculator to convert the data, "in about twelve of your planet's rotations, what you call days. After that, it will remain closed for . . ." another delay, "for at least five hundred ten rotations, until Jupiter and its moons once again move somewhat . . . together."

Delano did the calculation. The wormhole would be closed for seventeen months. *Damn, that was good news.* If they could somehow keep the Ktarrans out of the solar system for the next twelve days, Earth would have almost a year and a half to prepare its defenses.

"Do the Ktarrans know this information?"

"Of course," Jarendo said. "The Ktarrans can detect the growing and weakening of the gate. Their technical slaves know when it will open or close, with only a . . . small error."

The word Jarendo lacked was 'approximately.' Delano didn't care. "Then you must help us against the Ktarrans. Earth can do much if it has time to prepare its defenses."

The Talmak shook his head. "The Ktarrans already know there has been fighting at this gate. They will send a force strong enough to defeat any remaining Halkin ships that might linger or seek refuge here. Ktarrans have lost one ship, and will be ready for resistance. Without ships of your own and plasma fields for defense, your planet cannot resist."

Delano wanted to argue the point, but that could wait a few more minutes. "How will the Ktarrans attack? How many ships will they send?"

Jarendo paused to consider. "I think the Ktarrans will send at least three or four . . . **big/large/powerful** ships through the gate. That will be more than sufficient to defeat any remaining Halkin ships. The Ktarrans may already know there is a rich planet here to be **taken/captured/attacked**, so they will come in force, seize control, and establish their power. After that, most will depart through the gate. Once your planet is destroyed, one ship will be more than enough to rule here until the gate reopens. Then many more Ktarrans and their followers will come."

We'll see about that, Delano thought. "How many ships do the Ktarrans have?"

"We are not sure. Possibly as many as two hundred, but most are scattered across the quadrant, enforcing their **rules/laws/orders**."

"How many ships do the Tarlons and the Halkins have?" Delano asked.

"The Tarlons and the Halkins have about twenty ships," the Talmak said, "but all are smaller than those of the Ktarrans. Other **friends/allies/helpers** have about the same number. So perhaps in total a hundred ships that can fight. But each world defends its own. All hope that the next Ktarran advance will leave **alone/bypass/ignore** them. All prefer peace to war. So they do not band together to resist, knowing that would draw the wrath of the Ktarrans upon them."

Delano knew his military history. Large and aggressive countries eager to expand could pick and choose from among their smaller neighbors, offering alliances to some, but attacking each in turn with overwhelming force. Exactly what the Japanese and Nazi Germany had done in World War II.

"Earth has seen many wars in our past," Delano told the Talmak.

"We are at peace now, but we still possess many weapons. We have atomic weapons – fusion and fission – mounted on flying machines and missiles."

Delano's mention of atomic weapons required a consult with both Celeck and Jarendo, until they understood the terms, and the Tarlon equivalent words were entered in the database.

"Atomics are of little use against ships in space," Jarendo declared. "Long before one could get close enough to penetrate the Ktarran shields, the weapon would be vaporized."

"We have missiles that can launch ten or more independent missiles. Can the Ktarrans stop so many?"

"What they do not vaporize with beam weapons will be stopped by their shields. Plasma shields are very strong."

"Do your ships carry atomic weapons?" Delano already guessed the answer, but always better to verify.

"No, none of our ships carry such weapons. Too many would be required and would take up too much space. Also special control and safety systems would be needed to guide them. Beam weapons draw their power from the anti-matter engines. As long as the ship is moving, unlimited power is available."

"Do the Ktarrans carry atomic weapons?"

"We do not think so," Jarendo said. "We have never seen them used against us, or any planets they have conquered. A beam weapon can do almost as much damage, and it will not turn the ground or air . . . radioactive."

That last word took several tries before Lian entered it into the database. Delano waited until she finished, then spoke to her in Chinese. "I don't believe the Tarlons have much experience with atomic weapons. In space battles, ship-to-ship, they probably are not practical. But to defend Earth, I think they could be used. Klegg and the Alliance are already mobilizing their air defenses."

"Even if the Alliance can launch them," Lian answered in the same language, "won't the Ktarrans just shoot them down?"

"I don't know if it's that simple, but you're right, we need more information." Delano turned back to Jarendo. "When the Ktarrans arrive at Jupiter, what will they do?"

Jarendo thought for a few moments. "When they leave the gate and enter into Jupiter's space, they will form a defensive group. After they are satisfied there is no immediate threat, they will probably destroy your outpost on the inner moon."

"How will they know there is an outpost there?"

"The residue trails from your **inefficient/old/wasteful** fusion engines linger in space for many . . . years. The Halkins and our ship noticed them. It will be simple to follow the residue trails to the first moon of Jupiter. After the outpost there is destroyed, they will come to this planet, your Earth and your moon. The Moon will offer little of value to them, so they will destroy your outposts there, to make sure there is no threat behind them. Then they will come for your Earth."

So first Io, then the lunar bases, Delano thought. "How close must these ships be to use their beam weapons?"

"That answer varies on the power output of the weapons. The closer they are, the more effective. For your planet, I would say that they would orbit about . . ."

That required another discussion among Jarendo, Celeck, and Horath. Jarendo did some calculations, evidently to satisfy Horath. Some additional data were required, and then the resulting answers translated into human terms.

"We believe they would take position about 400 of your kilometers above the planet. If they encountered no resistance, they would drop lower, into an orbit between 250 to 300 kilometers above the surface. This is what they have done to other worlds they have destroyed. To penetrate your atmosphere with optimal efficiency, their beam weapons would be most powerful at that distance."

"Jarendo, Lian and I thank you," Delano said. "You have worked very hard to help us learn your language, and understand the weapons of war in space."

Delano's military background lacked any real knowledge of missiles or how far they would be effective. Satellites could be shot down easily enough, but most of them were located much closer to the Earth's surface. "I need to speak to the Station," Delano said. Without waiting for permission, he opened a connection. "Delano here. Is Welsh there?"

A moment later, excited voices blasted from the speaker. "Delano, are you alright? Damn you, we lost the connection. It's been hours since . . ."

"No time to talk now. We're both fine. Welsh, I need to know how far above the atmosphere an aircraft-launched nuclear missile can reach, what's the best height for launch at a target, say four hundred kilometers above Earth? Also how fast would it be going?"

The feed from the Station went silent while the listeners digested Delano's words. Then Welsh spoke. "An aircraft could launch a satellite killer missile at about fifty thousand feet, say ten kilometers. An Am-Ram III missile launched at that height could probably reach a target that high. It would be traveling at Mach 3.5 or 4.0, depending on the warhead weight. So it would take about three hundred seconds to reach an altitude of 200 kilometers. But its fuel would be gone and it would have to coast the last two hundred or more kilometers. Say five or six minutes?"

That sounded like a long time to Delano. While he thought about it, Welsh went on. "These numbers are off-the-cuff, Delano. Lots of variables involved, and within the Alliance, there are many different types of missiles. Some would be faster, others slower. You would need to define the mission precisely. Then we could determine the appropriate missiles."

Yeah, I'll get right on that. Let Klegg earn a few dollars more of his monthly pay. "I understand," Delano said. "You're giving me the extreme outer range of what we need. Tell Klegg to get the engineers working out the best method to deliver a nuclear warhead on target at four hundred kilometers. What's more, I don't think it can be coasting up to the Ktarran ships. Oh, the Ktarrans may not know we have atomic weapons. Apparently not many species mastered their use, or miniaturized them enough to fit on a missile. Delano out."

He took a breath. "Jarendo, Horath, our weapons can reach that far above the atmosphere. If the Ktarrans attack Earth, and they come within range, when can we launch atomic missiles at them?"

"Ktarran weapon . . . **specialists/operators/experts** will destroy your missiles before they can come in range," Jarendo said. "To penetrate a Ktarran shield at full power, your atomic missile would have to explode within a . . . half kilometer to cause damage, and even closer to **overwhelm/stress/crack** the plasma shield. Otherwise damage will be minimal. You might overload some of their sensors at longer distances, but that would be all your atomic weapons could achieve."

"I understand," Delano said. "However if we combined our

missiles with an attack by your ship, could we not defeat them?"

"If there were one ship," Jarendo began, "perhaps the three of us could engage it. The odds would be against us. But if they send three ships, there will be at least two attacking your planet. We could not attempt to fight that. The moment they detect our ships, they will abandon their attack on Earth and concentrate their efforts on destroying us. When they finish with us, the Ktarrans will return to continue their attack on Earth."

Delano caught a glimpse of Horath's face. The Halkin did not like even the discussion of attacking Ktarran ships. Then Delano thought about Jarendo's words. "You say two ships will attack Earth. What will the third be doing?"

"I believe the third ship, which will probably be the command craft, will be observing from this orbit, your Station as you call it. Ktarrans like to keep a ship in reserve, either to direct or to support an attack. After they finish with your moon, they will come here, just as we did. If you broadcast to them in Ktarran, they will want to capture you, **question/interrogate/torture** you to learn about your planet, and how you learned to speak their language."

Delano hadn't thought about that. Of course they would come to investigate the Station first, before blasting it out of existence. Maybe it was time to bug out and get back to Earth. Or maybe that fact could be used against the invaders.

He turned toward the Talmak. "What you have told us has been very helpful to Lian and me. We would like to return to the Station for a time, to review what we have discussed. After that, if is permitted, we would like to return for a final talk."

"That is acceptable," the Talmak said. "Tell your leaders we would help your species if we could."

Delano bowed. "That gives us hope. My people believe that any enemy can be defeated with the right plan. We still have time. Perhaps we can find one."

Chapter 15

Day 7: 2220 Zulu

The grim discussion with the Talmak added to the weight on Delano's shoulders. He felt weary from head to toe. The stimulants had worn off and now the inevitable crash loomed. He and Lian both needed some real sleep, at least enough to clear their heads.

Delano and Lian collected their equipment, donned their flight suits, and followed Horath through the Tarlon ship until they reached the Halkin shuttle. This time they stepped with confidence through the flickering plasma shield which served the little craft as an airlock. The slight tingling feeling passed almost unnoticed as they entered the Halkin vessel. Delano started to sit in his usual place but then changed his mind and pulled his way forward to the nose section, where Horath sat at the controls.

"Horath, would the Ktarrans use a ship like this to board the Station?"

"Not like this," Horath said. "Not as efficient as Halkin. But Ktarran transport, what you call shuttle, is larger. Can carry at least twenty slaves, plus slave masters and pilot."

Delano reminded himself the Halkins were very precise in their use of words. Looking around, he decided the Halkin shuttle could probably accommodate six humans in suits. Delano observed the process as Horath took the controls and with a blast of some pressurized gas, guided the shuttle away from the Talmak's ship.

"But they would board Station from a transport? Not bring main ship alongside?"

"No, they use shuttle. For you few humans, would send maybe ten or twelve guards and slave masters. One Ktarran, maybe two. One pilot."

"How would they know how many humans aboard station?"

Horath stared at Delano as if amazed at his ignorance. "Can detect living creatures if ship close enough. Humans not have such device?"

Delano knew electronics existed that could sense people or movement through walls, but nothing that would function in space or through a metal hull. "No, we have no such device on Station. Maybe on Earth."

By then they had reached the Station airlock. Delano stepped to the plasma shield, reached through, and activated the outer door mechanism. With a puff of air it swung slowly inward. They floated through the entrance.

"Never thought this place could seem like home." Delano closed the hatch and started re-pressurizing the airlock.

"I'm already missing the artificial gravity," Lian said. "It's a pleasure just to sit without holding on to something. What are we going to do now?"

The air pressure equalized with the Station's interior and they floated inside. He closed the inner hatch and secured it.

"We have to come up with a plan," Delano said, "something good enough to convince the Talmak to risk his ship to help Earth."

"The Halkins won't help," she said. "Horath does not want this fight."

"I think he'll be easier to convince than the Talmak. Horath may not be human, but I've known men like him before. Sometimes the ones who don't want to fight turn out to be the toughest warriors. We can work on him."

They finished shedding their flight suits and headed straight to the Control Room. Everyone was waiting for them, and Colonel Welsh jabbed his finger toward the comm link to Earth. Delano frowned. That meant Klegg was already on the other end. *Time to pay the piper.*

"You all heard our talk with the Talmak?" Delano didn't intend to waste any time.

"Yes, we did," Colonel Welsh said. "Except for what you said on the Tarlon bridge. That connection kept breaking up for some reason"

General Klegg's voice resounded through the Control Room. "Major Delano, you are relieved of command. You will take your orders from Colonel Welsh starting now. Do you understand?"

"Yes, General, I understand." *Great, just fucking great.* They had the translation software and they didn't need him anymore.

"Uncle, are you there?" Lian edged closer to the microphone.

"Yes, Lian, I am here. We were very worried. You spent so much time on the Talmak's ship. Are you sure you are well?"

"Very well, Uncle. The Tarlons, that is the name of their species, are most gracious. If Major Delano is removed from command of this mission, then I too must be relieved, since he and I have done what we think is best for the Station and for Earth. We planned to return to the Talmak's ship after we reviewed our options with the team, but you can cancel that, or send someone else to speak to the Talmak. Perhaps that person will negotiate with him more effectively."

The link from Earth cut out. Some member of the Alliance had pushed the mute button. I wonder who, Delano thought – Klegg or her uncle? Or Demidov. No, not him. The Russian would have no qualms about sacrificing either Lian or Delano.

Delano, as stunned as anyone in the Control Room, glanced around. Expressions varied from grins to astonishment. Welsh couldn't restrain his smile as he shook his head.

"While we're waiting for them to come back," Delano said, "we should start thinking about how we're going to stop these Ktarrans. You all heard the Talmak. Anyone believe he's conning us, and that the Ktarrans are good guys willing to negotiate?"

"No, I believe they will most certainly attack Earth," Colonel Kosloff said.

"As do I," Demitri Petrov said. "We Russians know when the worst is coming. It's in our blood."

Heads nodded in agreement. "By the way," Delano said, "I don't know if the Tarlons are able to lie."

"It doesn't matter," Welsh said. "If the Ktarrans come through the gate and attack Io, then we'll know they are hostile. No attacking force wants to leave a base, either military or mining, in their rear. No matter how small or defenseless it may be. So if they discover the camp on Io, which you say is likely, and don't attack it, then maybe we can negotiate with them."

"Gunny, Sergeant Shen, what do you think about the Ktarrans?" Delano had a pretty good idea of how his men would respond. "We may have to fight these guys."

"I'd bet a hundred bucks on the Talmak telling the truth," Gunny Stecker said. "He sounded like someone you could trust. The Halkins trust and respect him enough to let him decide what to do next."

Before Delano could canvass the rest of the crew, the Earth

comm link reconnected. This time it was the Chinese General Secretary. "Lian, what do you suggest?"

"Uncle, I suggest we be allowed to continue. We must find a way to resist these Ktarrans, and that can only be accomplished with the help of the Talmak and the Halkins."

"We may be able to develop a strategy here," her uncle said. "Our soldiers . . . the Alliance soldiers . . . know the capabilities of our weapons."

"Any plan must include the Talmak and his ship," she said. "He will need to be convinced. The hours we spent with him and his crew have built a trust, a relationship. He will not rely on a voice coming from a speaker, or even anyone else here on the Station."

"What type of plan do you have in mind?" The General Secretary's voice remained calm. No doubt he wanted to soothe the feelings of General Klegg.

"I do not know yet, Uncle. Major Delano has an idea. That is why we returned to the Station, to discuss it with the team."

"I need a moment, Lian." The General Secretary sounded resigned. The mute button light came on again.

"Jeez, Delano, what the hell have you started?" Colonel Welsh shook his head. "I'll bet a hundred of my own that Klegg is about to get overruled by the Chinese."

"Maybe. Right now I don't care," Delano said. "Here's the bottom line. Ktarran ships are coming, and they'll arrive off Jupiter in a few hours. We don't know how long they'll hang around Jupiter and Io, or even if they'll stop there. If they send five ships, there's probably nothing we or the Talmak can do. The usual Ktarran procedure is to leave one of their ships to guard the gate and prevent any hostile ships from entering or leaving the system. That would leave four of their battleships to attack Earth, and if that many come to Earth orbit, we won't be able to stop them."

"Then we have to assume that they will send less than five," Welsh said. "That's a big assumption."

"Yes," Delano said, "but we need some luck now. If they only arrive with a fleet of four ships, and eliminating one left behind to guard the gate, that leaves three inbound to Earth. One will probably stop at the Station," Delano said. "We'll be broadcasting in Ktarran that we're unarmed and have no weapons. Since we speak the language well enough to communicate, they will probably want to capture and examine the Station while they interrogate us. At least that's what the Tarlons say is standard Ktarran M.O. We can use that to buy some time. If we can take out or seriously damage the ship that comes to the Station, only two ships will be left to attack Earth."

"You think the Talmak can take two battleships?" Welsh sounded skeptical.

"No, not a chance," Delano agreed. "Based on the Ktarran playbook, they'll arrive with plenty of firepower. These ships will be powerful, probably larger than the one the Halkins destroyed. And the Ktarrans will be ready for trouble. They know that their other ship didn't return from this system."

"So what do . . ."

The chime signaled the mute button was off. The next voice they heard was General Klegg's.

"Major Delano, I'm withdrawing my order relieving you of command." Klegg's voice still held a hint of anger. "As you said, you're the tip of the spear, and we aren't. We discussed matters, and the Alliance agreed that you should remain in charge of the mission and continue the negotiations with the Talmak."

"Yes, Sir, I understand." Delano hoped his relief didn't translate through the microphone. A charge of mutiny in the face of the enemy might mean life imprisonment. "We're already discussing a possible scenario, but we could use input on what weapons, nuclear and otherwise, are available to defend Earth."

"We have that ready. I can transmit that data to the Station now."

"Thank you, Sir. It will help when dealing with the Talmak. And it's time to send the escape module back to Earth. Dr. Stepanov is still ill, and must not fall into Ktarran hands. Also I believe Maks, Dr. Parrish, Dr. Petrov, Linda, and Sergeant Macey should also leave. I'd send Lian back as well, but she insists on staying. General Secretary, I do need her here to facilitate the talks with the Talmak."

"I understand, Major Delano." The General Secretary's voice held quiet resignation. "Lian has always been . . . difficult to convince."

"Then if you will excuse us, I need to meet with the team," Delano said. "We'll get back to you in an hour or so. We can't return to the Talmak until all of us know what to expect."

"Very well, Major. Good luck. Klegg out."

The comm line went dark. Delano sighed. *Well, Marine, you wanted the mission, now you've got it.*

"I'm staying on the Station," Sergeant Macey said. "No matter what happens, you'll need communications."

"I, too, will stay," Demitri Petrov said. "If you are going to fight these aliens, you will need as much firepower as you can get."

"I think I will also stay," Maks said. "There is still much to be learned and . . ."

"No, Maks, you're the one person who mustn't fall into Ktarran hands. In fact, before you go, I need you and Steve to scrub the computers and files. I don't want the Ktarrans picking up anything useful."

Delano waited until Maks grudgingly acknowledged the decision, then turned toward Peter and Linda, holding hands as they floated in the air. "Peter, I can't force you to stay, but we could use someone with your skills."

Peter looked uncomfortable. Clearly he wanted to return to Earth with his wife.

"Major, Linda and I just managed to survive one fight in space," Peter said. "I don't think we are ready for another one. Neither of us knows anything about guns or fighting."

"No need to decide now," Delano said, "but we definitely want your input. We have to figure out a way to defeat or drive out these Ktarrans."

"I'm staying," Linda declared. "You may need medical help." She didn't look at Peter.

Peter swore under his breath. "Then I guess I'm staying as well. Wouldn't want to miss the party."

Ten minutes later, everyone gathered around the table in the Lounge. Delano started the session. "From what I've seen of the Tarlons and the Halkins, I doubt either of their species is especially suited for all-out, strategic warfare. War was forced upon them and they reacted. They fight when they have to, and according to the historical summary Celeck gave us, almost always defensively. That's why they've been steadily losing for hundreds of years."

"The Halkins did all right against that ship out by Jupiter," Welsh countered. "They're probably good fighters in ship-to-ship encounters. Although now that I think about it, they should have known they might be pursued. When they came out of the wormhole, it would have been good tactics to turn around and see if they were being followed, maybe ambush any hostile ships coming through behind them."

"Let's consider a possible scenario," Delano said. "If the Ktarrans send five or more ships, there's probably nothing we can do. But let's suppose only four Ktarran ships enter our solar system through the wormhole. One remains at Jupiter to guard the gate. The three remaining come to Earth, to take over the planet. One captures the Station, while two continue on to attack Earth."

"Still a big assumption," Welsh argued.

"Maybe not so much," Delano said. "Celeck told us that the more ships they send, the more they have to split the spoils. So they may send just enough ships to eliminate any resistance. But maybe Earth isn't another pushover world. Don't forget, the Alliance has enough nuclear weapons to blow apart the planet. They just need to get close enough to use them. Maks, you've seen our notes on the beam weapons. The Talmak said the Ktarrans would blast Earth's cities and industrial areas from space. How low would they need to be to do that?"

"The Halkin, I think it was Horath," Maks said, "mentioned something like four hundred kilometers. Beam weapons eventually disperse, so the closer to the target, the more effective. At four hundred kilometers, the beam would probably be about eight or ten meters wide. Depending on the power behind the beam, it would vaporize pretty much anything it touches."

"Won't the atmosphere weaken the beam?" Delano had wondered about that before. "It's traveling through a lot of air."

"Energy loss will be negligible," Maks said. "Probably less than one percent of the output power."

"Colonel Welsh," Delano said, "how effective would our missiles be attacking targets at four hundred kilometers?"

"So, that's about two hundred fifty miles, not a lot of distance for a missile traveling at Mach 2 or faster, and launched at fifty thousand feet. Say six to eight minutes, depending on the missile, speed of the aircraft, launch altitude, angle of attack, and a few other variables. If the Ktarrans can track them, and the Tarlons say they can, it's not likely our missiles will be very effective."

"If the Talmak is right, the Ktarrans will detect the missiles and shoot them down," Kosloff said. "A beam weapon could lock on to three or four targets per minute, perhaps more. How hardened are these missiles? Can they resist the beam weapon long enough to pass through the beam, get close?"

"No idea." Delano shrugged. "The Tarlons might know, but I don't think they have much experience with missile technology or guidance systems. So maybe we need more missiles. A lot more. That's Klegg's problem. The Alliance has hundreds of planes and thousands of missiles. The trick is to get the Ktarran ships down below four hundred kilometers, at least to three hundred. What does that do to missile flight time?"

"If the target is at three hundred kilometers, using air-launched missiles from fifty thousand feet or even higher – that eliminates the first fifteen kilometers . . ." Welsh pushed out his lips while he did the mental calculation. "With missiles traveling at least Mach 3, you probably reduce the flight time to under five minutes."

"So we might have a chance," Delano said. "Good."

"As I understand these Ktarran beam weapons, assuming they are similar to the ones the Tarlons and Halkin have," Maks said, "they are not computer controlled?"

"No, not directly," Delano said. "They have some simple targeting screens with computational capability, but they rely heavily on the skill of the gunner and the flexibility of the weapon. But Jarendo said the Ktarran sensors are very good."

"I'll bet the best way to get the Ktarrans down to two or three hundred kilometers is to do nothing," Welsh said. "Like any attack aircraft, you begin at high altitude. If there's no resistance, you descend lower and lower to improve your accuracy and lessen the time to target."

"The beam weapons will become increasingly deadly at lower altitudes," Maks said. "You're asking for a lot of on-the-ground damage."

"Yes, but the lower the Ktarrans come, the faster our missiles can reach them," Welsh said. "If we can get the Ktarrans down to three hundred kilometers or less, and we throw enough nuclear missiles at them, some should get through, at least enough to destroy or damage their ships. We may save more lives in the long run."

"Perhaps we can coat the missiles with some material, a mirrored surface, that would reflect the beams," Maks said. "We must have good thermal barrier coatings available. If the missile could survive a beam weapon for a tenth of a second, it might escape damage, remain on course, and continue to its target."

Delano had never heard of thermal barrier coatings. "OK, that's enough about planes and missiles for now." He glanced at his watch. "Klegg's desk jockeys can figure all that out. Welsh, suppose the Tarlon and the Halkin ships were parked on the Moon, out of sight. They could take off, fly right at Earth, and hit the Ktarrans from behind."

"I don't think there is a 'behind' in space," Welsh said. "You're in a three dimensional environment, and warships monitor in all directions. But if the Ktarrans were busy destroying Earth's cities and military bases, the Talmak might get close enough. Continuous acceleration from the Moon at, say, a constant four or five gravities . . . Maks would have to run the math for that. But probably fifteen or twenty minutes for the Talmak's ship to reach Earth orbit."

Delano shook his head in astonishment. *Almost a quarter of a million miles in fifteen minutes? Still not fast enough.* "Then Klegg has two problems to solve. First, lure the ships down to three hundred kilometers or less, and second, keep the Ktarrans too busy to look in their rear view mirror."

"Traveling at that velocity," Welsh said, "they will only get one pass at the target. They'll be moving so fast . . . can they hit anything at that speed?"

"We'll have to find out," Delano said. "Meanwhile, start the ball rolling with Klegg. If the Alliance can't pull together on this, all our planning will be for nothing. Lian and I are returning to the Talmak's ship. For now, I'd like Gunny and Shen to figure out how we can neutralize any Ktarrans that they send to board us. And how to destroy their ship before it starts bombarding Earth."

Gunny Stecker glanced at Sergeant Shen. Both men laughed. "Sure, no problem," Stecker said. "Should be easy to eliminate a boarding party and blow up an alien battleship."

Shen nodded in all seriousness. "The first part shouldn't be too difficult. For any aliens that board the Station we do have weapons and explosives. They won't be expecting trouble, so we'll have the element of surprise. Welsh, Kosloff, and Steve can help. We'll think of ways to improve the odds. But as for the ship, I don't know."

"Let us think about it," Stecker said. "Maybe we can come up with something."

"Sorry to dump a problem like that on you guys," Delano said, "but we have to get back to the Talmak's ship. "Steve, call the Halkin ship and I'll tell them we need a lift."

Now comes the hard part.

Gunny Stecker watched Delano and Lian head toward the airlock. Stecker waited a few moments, but no one said anything. He looked around at all seven of those remaining in the Lounge. Delano had handed them an impossible task, and it was up to Stecker and Shen to make it work.

"OK, people, let's start with the Ktarrans," Stecker said. "What do we know about them that might prove useful?"

"They're big, ugly, and arrogant," Welsh said. "They've been kicking ass across the galaxy for hundreds of years and no world has come close to stopping them."

"Score one for the bad guys," Peter said.

"Think positive!" Linda jabbed him in his ribs with her elbow.

"We know that they will arrive with several ships," Petrov said. "They will expect to destroy any resistance and establish control of Earth. As they have done on other worlds. They will assume that Earth will fall, just as the others did."

"They also possess more powerful weapons, hand lasers and stunners," Shen said. "They will board the Station, and probably stun anyone they encounter."

"We've got the C-4," Steve said. "Why can't we lure them aboard and blow them up?"

Both Gunny Stecker and Shen shook their heads. "Our explosives are meant to destroy the Station," Stecker said. "If we try to use them as antipersonnel weapons, we are just as likely to blow ourselves up. Speaking of that, what happens to the Station if something does explode, or we punch a hole through the hull?"

"This Station was once a ship," Kosloff said, "with every door an airtight hatch for safety." He took a moment to pull up a schematic of the Station on his tablet. "NASA decided we didn't need such security, so many of the internal hatches were removed. That's when the floor plates were installed. But in the event of an emergency, the Station can still be sealed into three major sections. The Control Room is Section One. Both entry hatches are air tight, and will automatically close and seal if there is a drop in pressure anywhere on the Station."

Everyone crowded around, to study the Station schematic. "Section Two includes everything from the small airlock forward to the Control Room," Kosloff said. "Section Three covers the main airlock to the food and water storage compartments." He pointed to the various locations on the diagram. "The hatches in Sections Two and Three will also automatically close if there is a loss of air pressure. The important thing, in the event of a breach, is to have access to the spacesuits."

"And an airlock," Welsh added.

"So if we blast a big hole in the Station," Stecker said, "we could lose an entire section."

"That is likely," Kosloff said. "And a large explosion might completely destroy the Station."

"That eliminates trying to blow up any aliens," Stecker said. "Looks too dangerous."

"This Station is old," Shen agreed. "Besides, what explosives we do possess would have no impact on a large Ktarran battleship. Stopping the boarding party won't do us any good if the alien ship isn't destroyed as well."

"We'll have to use the Glocks on the boarding party," Stecker said. "If they only send ten or twelve aliens and a few Ktarrans, we should be able to take them out, if we can find a way to neutralize their stunners."

"How do you propose to do that?" Peter Tasco, sitting close to Linda, allowed the disbelief to sound in his voice. "Are you guys crazy enough to think we might actually resist these super aliens? With handguns?"

"Shen and I are pretty good shots," Stecker said. "Plus we've got Major Delano and Colonel Welsh. They are familiar with firearms. As I understand it, most of the lot coming to collect us will be those alien slaves, and I doubt they'll be very good at close-in fighting."

"Don't forget that I know how to use a pistol," Petrov said. "My marksmanship is quite good."

"Are these Glocks are up to the task?" Welsh seemed skeptical. "They're pretty low tech if you ask me."

"They'll do the job," Stecker said. "Shen, what do you think?"

"These are not basic Glocks," Shen agreed. "These are modified, match-quality weapons with longer barrels. The extra length increases the bullet's velocity. The armor piercing +P ammunition is quite powerful as well."

Welsh still appeared doubtful.

"I understand that all the slave races have eyes and brains," Stecker said. "The Station is large, but the longest shot we might have to take is only about twenty-five meters. At such close range, Shen and I should be able to take them out with head shots."

"You're assuming they have heads," Peter said. "Suppose they don't?"

"We know of three aliens species," Stecker said, "and they all have heads and eyes. Shen and I can put three rounds on target in less than two seconds. Unless our visitors are wearing armored suits, the AP rounds will punch through almost anything."

"Even if they can't penetrate," Shen added, "the shock of the bullet will be transferred to the target. Consider being hit with a sledgehammer weighing four hundred and fifty pounds, with all that weight concentrated in an area equal to the cross-section of a bullet. It's going to hurt and it will knock them off balance for at least a few seconds."

"They'll have their own weapons," Welsh argued.

"Yeah, that's true. We need to know more about them, what they can do," Stecker said. "The Halkins must have a laser weapon of their own. Do the Ktarrans have any experience with slug-throwers? Maybe they've never heard of or seen a gun before. Delano will have to get more info about that, and possible alien weapons."

"What does this Ktarran stun weapon do?" The question came from Linda.

"As I understand it," Welsh said, "it sends a brief but powerful electrical charge through the body, almost like a mini-lightning strike. Worse than being hit with a taser. The nervous system is jolted, and the reaction is pure pain throughout the victim. The effect can last for fifteen or twenty seconds."

"I can mix up some drugs that will deaden the pain big time," the resident Med Tech declared, "if that would help."

"The stun weapon also emits sound waves," Welsh added. "Apparently very loud and intense, that adds to the disorientation."

"Hell, we can block that," Stecker said. "The special ops ear plugs we brought with us can compensate for any number of decibels, over multiple audio levels. Shen says China's special forces use the same ones."

"I have an idea," Kosloff said. "I was thinking about your C-4, and it occurred to me that we do have some serious explosives of our own on the Station."

Welsh stared at him, then rapped the table with his fist. "Damn, of course we do. The booster rockets! Sixteen hundred pounds of rocket fuel. I'll bet that would put a dent in a Ktarran battleship!"

"If we can get them there," Kosloff said. "We'll have to find a way to deliver them."

Stecker glanced from Welsh to Kosloff. "What are you guys talking about?"

Welsh explained about the extra booster rockets and the shuttle pilot's decision to leave the booster at the Station. "They're still attached to the hull, in front of the portside cargo boom.

"You know, I'll bet we can brainstorm some ideas of our own to disorient the bad guys," Steve said. "We've got plenty of audio equipment that we could direct at them. Maybe we can rig some lights, too."

"Sounds like we have some ideas," Stecker said with a grin. "Everyone keep thinking. Shen and I will start the pistol training. We'll set up a short distance range in the engine room. After we get that going, I'd like to take a look at these booster rockets. Good thing we brought plenty of detonators."

"While you're doing that," Welsh said, "I'll work with Steve and Kosloff to see what other dirty tricks we can come up with. Peter, Linda, Petrov, think about anything else we could do. Maybe low tech might just work at that."

"Yes, if we can anticipate what the Ktarrans will most likely do when they first arrive," Stecker said, "we can make some real plans. Steve, get on the radio and call Delano. Tell him to get as much info as possible about Ktarran weapons, tactics, and first contact procedures. Ask if the Ktarrans even have any experience with firearms. The Tarlons have been through this before. They must know how things will go down."

"Then we are agreed," Shen said. "We will resist and find some way to destroy the battleship."

"All you people are crazy," Peter said, shaking his head. "But what the hell, what other choice do we have? We'll figure something out. Hopefully it won't get us all killed."

Linda leaned over and gave him a kiss. "That's the spirit. You took out a crazy killer in space before, and you can do it again."

Peter made a face at her. "Why do I love you so much?"

"Because I convince you to do what you already know is right," Linda said. "Now get to work."

Chapter 16

Day 8: 0112 Zulu

Delano and Lian suited up outside the airlock. He waited until Lian finished donning her suit, except for the helmet. "Lian, I'm not sure when we'll get a chance to talk, but I want to thank you for what you said on the call. Without you, I'd be facing jail time. Once we got back safely to the Station, I didn't expect Klegg to be so angry."

"I'm sure my Uncle and General Demidov were just as upset," she said. "But I believe you can persuade the Talmak to help us. No one else here or on Earth can do that."

"You could do it," he said.

"Perhaps. But I didn't think of it. It takes a soldier to come up with a military plan, what you call an operation."

"It won't be much of an operation," he said. "Anything we come up with will be a long shot."

They entered the airlock and closed the inner door.

"Joe, I wanted to ask you earlier, but so much was happening," Lian continued. "What did Jarendo mean when he said the Ancient Ones learned to create wormholes? I thought wormholes just were . . . well, there, and the Ancients figured out how to exploit them. Can they be created?"

He had to close his eyes to recall that part of the conversation. But Delano's eidetic memory found it. Jarendo had indeed used the term 'create.' He might have simply chosen the wrong word. Still, Delano in his excitement had missed it entirely. Lian hadn't.

"I don't know, Lian," Delano said. "It may be important. We need to ask him exactly what he meant. Even if we can't use it, the more our scientists understand about wormholes the better."

Kosloff's voice over the Station's loudspeaker interrupted them. "Major, your ride is here. Joe, Lian, good luck."

Delano and Lian inspected each other's suits one last time, to make certain the monitoring and integrity lights were all in the green. Then he cycled the outer door. *I'm really getting the hang of this zero gravity stuff.*

The Halkin shuttle awaited them. They pushed off from the airlock and floated through the plasma shield, feeling the slight sucking sensation as they passed through the field. Then they were once again inside the small craft. Horath sat at the controls, the only one onboard. After the last session, Delano had expected the irritated Halkin to send someone else.

"Wait, Horath," Delano said as he unlatched his helmet. "Before you start, I would like to see how you pilot this vessel."

"Why?"

Blunt as ever. "I want to know how difficult it is to maneuver . . ." That word didn't translate, he realized. "How difficult to guide the ship from one vessel to another."

Horath waved his hands in a gesture that Delano knew meant annoyance. But the Halkin obliged nevertheless.

"Not difficult. Break contact with ship." He flipped a lever that cut the magnetic field keeping the ships in contact. "Then use jets to move away, and guide shuttle to other ship. Watch."

He went through the steps, and Delano memorized every movement. It didn't look difficult, but he'd never flown anything in his life, not even a drone. As they approached the Talmak's ship, another idea popped into his head.

"Horath, can you please fly around . . . circle the Talmak's ship?"

"Why? Waste more time."

"It would help me understand how your ships work. If you would, please tell me what I'm seeing."

Horath glared at him, then linked to the Tarlon control room and explained that the stupid humans wanted to see their ship. At least that's what it sounded like.

Stupid human is right. Otherwise I wouldn't be out here risking my neck.

The Tarlon vessel gave its approval, and Horath swung slowly around the ship. The plasma field continued to sparkle, but at a very low level, since the ship remained motionless. As the shuttle traveled down the side, Delano noticed dozens of various types of antennae and sensors protruding through the plasma and extending above it, some as high as five or six meters. *That made sense.* If the plasma field were strengthened, it must expand in size. Most of the protrusions were slender masts, but a few were thicker. "What are those?"

"Sensors. Must extend beyond plasma. If inside, cannot function."

OK, that seemed logical, Delano reasoned. If nothing can get through the plasma, they'd be flying blind.

As they approached the stern of the vessel, Delano saw a very large tube that also extended through the shield. He remembered there had been one forward, just behind the bow of the ship. He pointed. "What are thick tubes?"

Horath responded, but realized the phrase didn't translate, and tried again. "Glass. Fused glass. Coated with . . . *something*?" The word didn't translate either. "For passage through wormhole. Ship must not touch inside of wormhole."

By the time the brief tour ended, Delano had figured out the word 'insulator.' So the ship had to be protected from touching the sides of the wormhole during the journey. Which meant a wormhole was not just an empty tube, but some kind of energy conduit. Interesting. He wondered what Maks would make of that fact.

As they settled against the Talmak's ship, the shuttle smoothly fitting over the airlock, Horath initiated docking, and the two ships joined with a distinct click that reverberated through the shuttle's hull. Delano hadn't noticed the sound before. The Halkin had flown the small ship without bothering to suit up, and only utilized two controls. Now he pointed to another switch on the console. "Or push **return/automatic/home** to get back to mothership."

Delano needed a moment to comprehend. "You mean . . . if you wanted to return to Halkin ship, you activate control and ship flies . . . guides itself?"

"Yes. My ship, the *Meseka*, like most ships have beacon. Shuttle will pilot itself back to my beacon, to *Meseka*. Only use in case of emergency or injury. Otherwise too slow."

"Do Ktarran shuttles have beacon?"

Horath made the gesture that indicated uncertainty. "Not sure, but likely. Would be useful to return shuttle back to ship after dropping off people or cargo."

"Thank you, Horath." Delano turned to go and saw that Lian had recorded everything on her tablet. She took an extra moment to pan the camera over the control panel.

"Lian, you read my mind," Delano began, "and I appreciate you more and more each minute. If we get out of this alive, I'll take you out to dinner."

She replaced the tablet and slung the bag over her shoulder. "Joe, are you asking me out on a date?" Lian laughed at the look on his face. "I accept." She placed her gloved hand on his arm. "I know a great Persian restaurant in L.A."

Back in the Tarlon conference room, everyone settled into the same uncomfortable seats as before. Delano and Lian set up their equipment, and Delano started right in.

"Talmak, I have many questions, but first want to say that helium is on its way."

"That is good," Jarendo said, speaking for the dour Halkin. "We thank those on your planet."

Delano nodded. Time to being. "Talmak, Earth, my planet, intends to resist the Ktarrans. I need you to give us more information about their weapons and **tactics/battle-skills/fighting**. I have link to Station, and Maks, our scientist, will listen. He will understand theory and has translation machine."

The Talmak glanced at Jarendo. Both looked resigned. "What do you wish to know?"

"Most important, we must know more about the plasma shields you and the Halkins possess. Do the Ktarrans have the same screen?"

Jarendo leaned forward. "Yes. Perhaps small differences. There is no single screen. What you call plasma field is made up of four separate layers."

Great. Of course it had to get complicated in the first thirty seconds. "Please go on, Jarendo. We will record."

"Outermost layer is highly-charged plasma window," Jarendo said. "Very hot, superheated to vaporize metals or meteors. This layer allows ships to travel at high speed, not worry about small meteors or dust. Second layer is **curtain/screen/material** of many, many high energy laser beams. All beams crisscross many times to create . . . lattice." Jarendo intertwined his fingers to explain the word. "Anything passing through lattice is heated to vapor, made harmless."

After Delano was certain he had correct translations for lattice, curtain, and plasma, he said, "We understand you. Please continue."

"Third layer is single layer of atoms that are photochromatic. Since other layers allow light to pass, this needed to stop laser and particle beams. Turns dark when struck by light or lasers or particle beams. Is primary defense against beam weapons. During battle, power is reduced to first and second screen, and sent to photochromatic layer."

Photochromatic? Even Maks needed almost ten minutes to figure out the word. Another lengthy discussion was required to comprehend the language and theory of photochromatic atoms. But with the Russian physicist's help, Delano and Lian finally grasped the concept.

Delano thought about that. If power could be directed to the various layers, then it might take a very powerful beam to punch through the photochromatic shield. Interesting.

Jarendo went on. "Fourth layer is lattice of single carbon atoms. Very hard. Create screen that very strong. Can resist anything that might get through the outer layers." Jarendo waited while Delano and Lian had another, not so brief conversation with Maks aboard the Station.

"I think he's talking about carbon nanotubes," Maks announced at last. "It's theoretically possible. We can't do it, but if they can create and weave the nanotubes, it would explain why their ships are so strong without having thick hulls, and why they can resist the particle beam weapons, at least for a few seconds."

"OK, Maks, that's enough for now." Delano turned toward the Talmak. "What about your beam weapons? How do they work, and what do they consist of?"

"Our primary weapons are very simple," Jarendo said. "An accelerator is used to send protons into an electrostatic lens. The particles are focused and accelerated again and again. Particles have much kinetic energy, which they impart to any matter they touch. That causes nearly instantaneous and catastrophic superheating. The protons themselves are collected from space, so there is never any shortage of material. All that is needed is power."

As soon as Jarendo said the beam technology was very simple, Delano knew he was in over his head. Jarendo's 'simple' explanation required almost thirty minutes of translation and discussion before Maks declared he understood the basic concept. Delano glanced at Lian, and she made a face, which he interpreted to mean 'not a clue.'

But that discussion point paled compared to the next topic – what energy source powered the Tarlon ship?

Delano, feeling like an idiot, tried to translate Jarendo's terms into something that Maks could understand. Celeck's help got them through it. Delano and Lian, hearing it all, didn't understand more than a few words. After more than an hour, Maks tried to simplify it for the two linguists.

"As I understand it," Maks said, "the Tarlons use vacuum energy. Space, as you know, isn't really empty. It's actually a sea of particles and antiparticles that flash briefly into and out of existence. That's in addition to the random number of cosmic rays or neutrinos or gravity waves passing through every cubic meter at any given time. The aliens have discovered a way to harness these temporary particles. They are scooped up, separated into matter and antimatter chambers, concentrated, and then allowed to annihilate each other. The resulting energy bursts are collected and stored, or sent directly to various systems. The theory is actually pretty simple. The engineering is the hard part."

Oh, yeah, simple. Delano, who had never heard of vacuum energy or particles that flashed into or out of existence, glanced at Lian. She understood about as much as he did. "I'm glad you understand it, Maks," Delano said. "So as I hear it, these Ktarran ships collect these non-existent particles, and use them to power their weapons, shields, and propulsion systems. Is that it?"

"Yes, that's pretty much how it works," Maks said. "But the amount of energy collected is still finite. Only a small amount can be safely stored. The rest has to be used. So the Ktarrans feed it directly to the engines or plasma shields. Or they can close some of the scoops."

"Wait a minute," Delano said. "Are you saying that if they send all that generated power to the shields, there's nothing left for propulsion or life support or weapons?"

"Not sure, but I think so. At least I think that's what Jarendo meant to say," Maks answered. "He's really doing very well explaining their advanced technology."

"That seems like a weakness to me," Delano said. "If we can overload the Ktarran screens, they wouldn't have power for the weapons."

"Nuclear bombs could . . . might overload them," Maks said, "but you'd probably need more than one."

"Get that information down to Klegg, and make sure he understands the concept." Delano added his observations of the wormhole insulators.

With Maks off the line, Delano and Lian started on the next topic. "Jarendo, what will Ktarrans do when they reach Station?"

Jarendo had to think about that. "First they see how many humans on Station. For small number like you, they send shuttle to collect humans and return everyone to Ktarran ship. Then destroy Station. When humans arrive, some humans will be eaten, others killed and . . . inspected. Learn human weaknesses, how to kill, how to control. Language speakers will probably be allowed to live, if work with Ktarrans."

Dissected, that was the word Jarendo wanted. Or more likely, vivisected. Why work on a dead body when you have a planet filled with billions of live ones? Just strap one down, start cutting, and ignore the screams and blood. After experimenting on a few dozen victims, the Ktarrans would learn all about human biology and its weaknesses. At least all they needed to know.

"How many Ktarrans will they send to Station? To collect us?"

"One. Perhaps two." Jarendo saw the look of surprise on Delano's face. "Rest will be slaves."

Delano remembered hearing about slave species, but this was the first he'd heard about slaves serving aboard Ktarran ships. "Who are slaves?"

"Ktarrans have two slave sentients, act as helpers," answered the Talmak. "One is for labor or simple tasks. And for fighting. They are called Dalvaks. Other is for technical tasks. They are most numerous on Ktarran ship, and are called Peltors. Most of crew is Peltors. Large Ktarran ship will only have twenty to thirty Ktarrans, but fifty to sixty Peltors, perhaps ten or fifteen Dalvaks."

OK, got that. Dalvaks for grunt labor, guard duty, and security. Peltors for the complex tasks, like running a ship. "How many of each will come to Station?"

The Talmak and Jarendo turned to Horath, who must have more

recent knowledge. "Your Station have thirteen humans. For so few, they send two, three Ktarrans. One or two Peltors. Eight or ten Dalvaks. With stun weapons. More than enough to capture all humans."

For the next fifteen minutes, Delano probed the Halkin about Ktarran weapons and tactics, trying to get as much information as possible for Gunny Stecker and Sgt. Shen. Then Delano asked about how the Ktarrans would take possession of the Station and capture the humans, should they resist. When he'd collected everything he could think of from Horath and Jarendo, Delano sat back in the uncomfortable chair. *The time for the big sell had arrived.*

"Talmak, we need your help," Delano began. "Humans are skilled in fighting and in creating weapons. Also skilled in knowing how to win wars. If you help us, we can help you in your war with the Ktarrans. If you help save our planet, we will help you. With our knowledge and resources, you can win, put an end to Ktarran advances."

Delano turned to Horath. "I know Horath . . . unwilling to challenge Ktarrans. We do not ask him to stay and fight. It is best that he escapes while he can."

With those words, Delano brushed off the Halkin and turned his attention back to the Talmak and Jarendo. "Think about what I say. If you can help drive off the Ktarrans, you will have made an ally with a planet of more than eight billion people, all skilled at construction of weapons and machines."

"Even if we could help you now," the Talmak said, "the Ktarrans will return with even greater force."

"You said not for seventeen months." Delano felt his determination increasing. "In that time, Earth will be ready for them. New weapons, new tactics, new ships, new defenses, all designed to defeat Ktarrans. We will find ways to stop them. Then Earth will go on offensive. In our wars, we hunt down and destroy those who attack us. We will fight alongside the Tarlons and your allies. Even the Halkins."

A growl came from Horath and his fists were clenched. Twice his courage had been impugned and he didn't like it, especially in front of the Talmak.

"One ship cannot stand up to the Ktarrans," the Talmak said.

"We understand, not ask that," Delano countered. "But at the height of the attack, one ship could attack the Ktarran rear, and disable or weaken their power generators for a few moments. With that help our atomic missiles will finish them. Meanwhile, I will destroy whatever Ktarran ship comes to this Station."

Talmak glanced at Jarendo, then back to Delano. "How will you do that?"

"We are working on a plan," Delano lied. "We have some weapons and explosives. With what you have told us about the Ktarrans, we will find a way. Talmak need only help destroy the ships that will be attacking Earth. Already humans on Earth are preparing defenses. Remember, if Halkin had not come to our world, then perhaps the Ktarrans might never have found Earth."

Once again Delano had insulted Horath by not including him and the information he had supplied. Now Delano, in front of the Tarlons, blamed the Halkin for Earth's predicament. Which was exactly what Delano intended.

The Talmak hesitated, thinking about the risk. "What do you think, Jarendo? Would you risk the ship, our lives, to help these humans?"

Jarendo, too, had to pause and consider his words. "Talmak, I grow tired of running from the Ktarrans. They advance, we fight, many die, and they push us back, until we abandon another planet to them. Perhaps it is time to think about winning. With a planet of so many billions and so much industry, the humans could build many ships, hundreds, perhaps thousands. With our help, they would have the weapons to fight."

"Are you sure your planet will do what you say?" The Talmak eyed Delano. "Will fight the Ktarrans? Planet may face complete destruction."

"A terrible end is better than terror without end," Delano said. That phrase needed some consultation before the Talmak nodded his understanding. "We will have no choice," Delano continued. "Once we resist, we are committed. We fight the Ktarrans, or we are destroyed and enslaved. I will talk to my leaders. They will pledge their support."

The Talmak nodded. "I must consult with War Leader Kaneel and Horath. Then we will talk again."

"Can you give us life materials?" Lian had remembered to ask.

"Yes. Already prepared," Jarendo said.

"Lian and I must return to the Station."

Lian put her hand on Delano's arm. "Jarendo, earlier you said something about 'creating' wormholes. Did I not understand?"

Jarendo, about to rise, settled back in his chair. "Possible to create wormhole, but requires much power to do, and can only maintain for a few . . . seconds? Not useful for travel between stars. No ship can generate enough power. But for short distances or in emergency, can be done."

She glanced at Delano. "How short a distance?"

"Not sure," Jarendo said. "This ship has never attempted the . . . journey. Would need many calculations. Take much time."

Delano glanced at her, then turned back to Jarendo. "Still it is possible. We must think about this and talk to Maks." He turned to Horath. "Can you take us back to Station?"

"No. I will stay and talk with Talmak and Kaneel." Horath's anger resonated in his voice. "You prepare your plan. If Talmak fights, if risk is not too great, Halkins will fight beside the Talmak."

Delano and Lian stood and bowed. "Your help is most welcome. We will find a way to victory." He turned to the Talmak. "Can you return us to the Station?"

After the humans left the ship, War Leader Kaneel joined the group in the conference room. He had monitored the sessions from the control room, and now he took the seat Delano had used and faced the Talmak. "So, the one named Delano wants us to remain behind and attack the Ktarrans?"

"Yes, that is what he wants," the Talmak said. "He says that his world will help us in our fight, and that they only need time to prepare. With the technology we have given them, it may be possible they can alter the balance of power in the quadrant. They are a remarkable species. You have scanned their world. Their numbers, their cities . . . quite astonishing."

"You are considering this?" Kaneel gazed at each in turn.

"I have observed their technology, their devices," Celeck said. "Their language machines . . . we have nothing to equal that, and they treat it like a useful tool, something of little consequence. Who knows what other surprises humans might have? They have learned two languages in a brief time, faster than any species has ever done."

"But no screens, no beam weapons," Kaneel said, "no ships capable of traveling between the stars. Nothing that will stop the Ktarrans."

"They have just begun their journey into space," Jarendo argued, "and they have not yet needed such things. Now that they know they exist, they will build them. With the threat of the Ktarrans, they will build them quickly. A species such as this could stand against the Ktarrans. Remember, the Ktarrans once dwelt on a single world. They had to steal the technology of the Ancients to rise above so many others."

Kaneel turned to Horath. "What do the Halkins say? Would you risk your lives, your ships for these humans? Do you not need every ship you have to defend the Halkin home world?"

Horath looked unsettled. "I did not want to aid these humans. But the Delano is right, we brought Ktarrans to this system." For a moment he clenched his fist on the table. "Two more ships will not save Halkin. But if we can defeat the Ktarrans here, their incursion into Halkin space may be slowed. If the Talmak says to fight, then the Halkin will fight beside him."

"What do you say, Kaneel?" the Talmak said. "You would have to lead the ship, including the Halkin ships. Would you risk your life, all our lives, for this species?"

"The humans only ask for one pass of our ships," Jarendo spoke first, before Kaneel could reply. "We could attack, and then head for the gate. Even if the Ktarrans leave a ship to guard it, with three ships, we might fight our way past it and into the wormhole. At least some of us."

"If we all survive the battle," Kaneel pointed out, "it would be our seven beam weapons against ten or twelve on a Ktarran battle cruiser."

Horath grunted. "When have we not outgunned the Peltor slaves? When have we fought that we were not outnumbered?"

Kaneel made the gesture of resignation. "I will lead the ship against the Ktarrans, to help the humans. But only if you agree, Talmak. You speak for the Ruling Council, our leaders. If you think this is worthy . . ."

"If there is a chance to change the course of the Great War," the Talmak said, "then we must take the risk. Otherwise we know our ultimate ending. First the Halkins, then others, finally the last of the

Tarlon worlds. With each advance of the Ktarrans, they grow stronger and we will grow weaker. Soon whole worlds will submit, sacrifice many to save a few, who will live as Ktarran slaves." He stared at Kaneel. "To prevent that future, yes, I want to save these humans, if possible. No matter what the risk to ourselves."

Kaneel studied the faces around the table. Jarendo, Celeck, they wanted to fight. Even Horath, not long ago ready to rip Delano into pieces, had volunteered his ships. Now the Talmak had claimed the moral authority to give the command. Kaneel could protest the decision, and some aboard would take his side. But that was not what Kaneel wanted.

"I think these humans are a dangerous species," Kaneel said, "to have won over so many of us so quickly. But I agree, the reward may be worth the risk. But only one pass. We will not engage in a fight against Ktarrans here, not when we will still need to break through at the gate. One pass, and after that, the human battle will be over for us, one way or another. One pass and we head for the gate."

"One pass," the Talmak agreed. "Then you and Jarendo must study the plan of the Delano and the leaders on their planet, and work with him to increase the chance of success."

"That will not take long," Kaneel said. "It isn't much of a plan."

The Talmak agreed. The odds of his death had just increased greatly, but to his surprise, he felt satisfied, purposeful. There comes a time and a place when one must dare greatly to win a victory. Perhaps the time had come to strike back at the Ktarrans.

Chapter 17

Day 8: 0400 Zulu

Derrell Parrish hovered at the hatchway, his body twisting and twitching while the airlock slowly cycled. He hated waiting. He'd volunteered to join the NASA expedition for one reason – to gain experience that few others in his profession had. Zero gravity research would make fellow-scientists take him seriously. It might even help him get some dates when he returned to Earth. With his adolescent features, he needed all the help he could get.

At last the light turned green, and he helped Kosloff swing the heavy door inward and admit the returning linguists. The moment Parrish had the hatch open, he extended his hand, unable to conceal his excitement.

A surprised Delano, still in his suit, handed over the sealed specimen box. Without a word the biologist snatched the precious container and swam back through the Station, heading for his lab in the agricultural experiments chamber. Everyone else would gather in the Lounge to discuss the latest information and plan for the coming conflict, but Parrish had more important matters on his mind.

Once inside, he closed the inner door to make certain he wasn't disturbed, though few bothered to visit the lab. Hard science specialists like Maks and Colonel Welsh had no interest in biology. Parrish attached the specimen box to the work table. Earlier he'd cleared the surface of his other research, shoving long hours of work carelessly into bins or fastening the growing containers to the nearest surface. Parrish had spent a full hour prepping his lab, stopping his other analysis and readying the equipment he would need to examine the alien DNA.

Not that he had everything he wanted. The Agricultural Section of the Station was designed for biology, not genetic research. But in the past NASA scientists had conducted many trials on genetic material aboard the Station, and much of that equipment remained. Parrish had dredged up every useful instrument from storage and re-arranged the lab. He also inspected and tested the equipment, then readied whatever else he needed.

When he finished his preparations, he'd collected enough tools to examine and test DNA samples. These devices included a DNA extractor, the Vortex centrifuge and tube racks, an older model comparison microscope, and a second, even older centrifuge capable of going over 6,000g. A small polymerase chain reaction (PCR) machine with PCR Beads, coated slides, and pipettes stood ready, awaiting the samples.

Opening the precious box, Parrish inspected the three DNA packs resting within. He removed the one labeled 'Halkin' in Delano's careless handwriting. The Major might be an excellent linguist, but Parrish didn't trust the man's handling procedures for biological specimens. Nevertheless a close examination showed the seals intact. Some unknown alien on the Tarlon ship had packed the material properly.

The Halkin genetic tissue interested Parrish the most. While humans appeared closer to the Tarlons than to the Halkins, Parrish knew DNA could tell a different tale. After his observations of Halkin behavior, he was willing to bet humans and Halkins would prove to be related. He noted the date and time in his tablet log, belted himself into his chair, turned on the video recorder, and began his examination.

He worked with all possible precautions to insure he used the least amount of the sample possible. Parrish doubted the aliens would donate more of their DNA in the foreseeable future, and his analysis would have to be repeated for verification back on Earth. Not to mention the swarm of genetic scientists and researchers there who would line up, pushing and shoving, to get a glimpse of this alien DNA. They wouldn't trust conclusions reached by a mere eighteen year old biologist, despite his credentials. Even though biology had fathered the science of genetics, the child had long ago outgrown the parent in importance.

So Parrish labored over each step, using his tablet and the Station's mainframe to ensure that he followed and documented every procedure in the analytic protocol.

An hour later, Parrish sealed his pipettes, slides, and sample cases with a sigh of satisfaction. He leaned back and reviewed his data read-outs, numerical and graphic, which proved to him the Halkin and the human race shared a common ancestor. On Earth, humans and chimps duplicated 98.1% of their DNA. Gorillas matched to 98.2%. The Halkin tissue revealed a match of 92.4%. Any result above 50% would be enough to indicate a relationship between the two species. No wonder the two alpha-males, Horath and Delano, didn't get along. Parrish let out a sigh. Phase One complete. He sipped some water, then cleaned and prepped his equipment again. Time to begin on Phase Two – the Tarlon DNA specimen.

That sample had come with a half-dozen charts and images from the Tarlon scientists, along with their DNA. Much as he wanted to study those charts, Parrish ignored them for now. Instead he worked strictly from the genetic material, following each stage of the protocol and documenting every result. Only when he completed his analysis did he pick up the Tarlon documents. Using them, he confirmed what he'd examined matched the Tarlons' claims.

The tests confirmed his guess – match of 90.8%. Parrish now knew for certain that humans and Tarlons also shared a common ancestry. With the evidence he had just obtained, Parrish believed somewhere in the past, perhaps as few as three or four million years ago, a yet unknown species had possessed and spread its basic DNA to all three species. That conclusion would be debated on Earth, probably for years, but the data supported the conclusion. In the end, the evidence for a common ancestry would prove irrefutable. The data matched, and he felt certain that no alien could have falsified the material without leaving traces of meddling.

Parrish stared at the remaining sample – Phase Three. Not a tissue sample but instead a few grams of artificially created DNA material of the Ktarran genetic substance. Not even the Tarlons would likely be traveling around the galaxy with spare Ktarran tissue, but someone had mapped the sequence, and the Tarlons had a copy. It wouldn't be considered positive proof, but until Earth's geneticists had a real Ktarran sample, it would have to do.

On to Phase Four. Using his tablet, he lined up the three sets of genetic material – human, Tarlon and Halkin. All three revealed marked similarities. When he tried to overlay the map of the Ktarran genes on the human genome, he saw immediately that it wouldn't be possible. If this map were a true representation of a Ktarran genome, then there was little relation, less than 17%. The Ktarrans were a completely different species, with different DNA markers, protein molecules and even cellular construction.

The Ktarrans might not be the alien monsters the Tarlons and Halkin claimed, but they were definitely not related to anything remotely human. For the first time he took a close look at the image of the dead Ktarran the Tarlons had provided. Parrish hadn't wanted to study it until he'd finished his analysis. He shivered. The Ktarran looked like something out of a nightmare, part beast, part reptile, completely alien.

Parrish shrugged. The Ktarrans weren't his problem. He finalized his conclusions, wrote a few paragraphs describing what steps he'd taken, and bullet-pointed his summary. He made backup copies of everything, keeping one flash drive in his pocket. That would stay in his possession until he reached Earth. When he finished, he glanced at his watch. Almost four hours had passed.

Unbuckling himself, Parrish floated up and out of the chair. He resealed the original specimen box and stored it within a locker. That box had to be returned to Earth as soon as possible. He left the lab and negotiated his way toward the Control Room. When he arrived, another of the endless conference calls with General Klegg had just begun. He found a convenient place to observe and hooked a foot around a unused table leg.

After a few moments of listening to Klegg argue with Colonel Welsh, Parrish had heard enough. He raised his voice and interrupted. "Colonel Welsh, would you like to hear the results of the genetic testing?"

Welsh shook his head. "Later. We're still trying . . ."

"I would very much like to hear Doctor Parrish's findings," General Demidov cut in. "Our scientists are extremely interested."

Welsh shrugged. "Alright, Parrish, what did you find?"

"I've completed my analysis of the Halkin and Tarlon DNA." He flipped one of the backup drives in Welsh's direction, but Kosloff reached out and snared it. "My original theory that we and the Halkin are related has proved correct. And we're related to the Tarlons as well. Both match our DNA by more than 91%. I've just given my data to Colonel Kosloff for transmission to NASA. There's still enough genetic material available to confirm my conclusions, if we ever get it to a lab on Earth."

He might as well have dropped a bomb inside Klegg's command center. The normal two second transmission delay stretched on and on.

The Director of NASA broke the silence. "Dr. Parrish, this is Dr. McChesney. Are you sure about the DNA? I mean, could you be mistaken? You don't have all the proper equipment . . ."

"I'm certain," Parrish said. McChesney might be the first skeptic, but he wouldn't be the last. "The samples are viable and the data is plain. Genetically, we are related to the Halkins and the Tarlons. They are our cousins. More testing would be useful, but not really necessary for confirmation." Those on Earth who might fear aliens would find no support in his data. It's hard to hate a close relative.

"What about these Ktarrans?" Klegg's voice sounded curious.

"I don't have a sample for them, but the Tarlons gave me a copy from their records. If what they provided is accurate, the Ktarrans are a totally alien species, different biology, cell construction, proteins, and DNA."

"That would bolster the Tarlons' Ktarran threat argument," Klegg said. "Could they have given you false data, just to have you come to that conclusion?"

"Perhaps." Parrish didn't really care about the Ktarrans. "Of course it will be easy to prove or disprove when we confront them. A good visual image would be convincing. A skin sample should confirm it."

"Please send the data as soon as possible, Dr. Parrish," McChesney said. "We need to review it."

Parrish glanced at Kosloff, who had inserted the drive into his tablet. "I believe Colonel Kosloff is sending my analysis and findings as we speak."

"I suppose it may matter," Klegg said, "but right now I want to know why Delano and Dr. Duan are still out of touch. They've been aboard the alien ship for almost three hours."

So the two linguists had returned to the Talmak's ship. Parrish hadn't noticed they were missing. Nor did he care.

Derrell Parrish settled back and ignored the rest of the conversation. He'd secured his place in history – the first scientist to study true alien DNA. After this, no one could smile at his youth or point to his inexperience. From now on, when Derrell Parrish spoke, everyone would listen. Even if he didn't survive the coming encounter, at least he'd earned that distinction. He hoped it wouldn't be written on his tombstone any time soon.

Chapter 18

Day 8: 0400 Zulu

By the time Delano reached the Lounge, he'd forgotten all about Parrish and his DNA samples. With the exception of the biologist and Dr. Stepanov, everyone crowded around Lian and Delano. For once the lack of gravity allowed every member of the team to sit, float, or hang in close proximity to the two linguists.

Lian recapped the meetings with the Talmak, his crew, and the Halkins. Everybody had questions, and answering them properly would have taken hours. "So, people, you'll have to hold the questions for now," Delano said. "We may be able to convince the Talmak and the Halkins to stay and fight, but only if we can come up with a real plan, one that has a chance for success. They won't help us in a hopeless battle."

"How can we plan a battle," Welsh said, "when we don't know how strong, or how many, enemy ships they'll send against us?"

Delano had already thought about that. "Look, we can't win this fight if they show up with five or ten ships. But Jarendo and Horath didn't think they would send that many. For these kinds of first contact invasions, they may only send three or four ships, possibly five. The more ships they assign to this world, the more they have to divvy up the spoils. Apparently they don't like that idea too much."

"Even so, when you invade an inferior species," Petrov said, "you want a show of force, to convince the locals that resistance is futile. Do you know what types of ships they have?"

"According to the Tarlons," Lian said. "The Ktarrans use mostly large ships, with between eight and twelve beam weapons each. That much armament requires a significant amount of energy. I didn't really understand that part, how their greater size actually lets them generate more power to the beam weapons. I now get their preferences for outsized ships – they can minimize Ktarran crew numbers, and rely more on their slave followers."

Delano shrugged. "I've been thinking about these enormous

Ktarrans ships as battle cruisers, built for combat only. The Tarlons and others prefer smaller ships that are capable of search, rescue, transport, and rapid movement as well as the occasional enemy encounter."

"So it's like battleships against destroyers," Gunny Stecker said. "In World War II a battleship, with more powerful guns and greater armor, could challenge any number of destroyers. Maybe the Halkins knew what they were doing after all."

Welsh shook his head. "Horath lost three ships – even if they did save most of the crew from the damaged vessel – which doesn't sound like a good tactical operation result to me."

"Horath admits that the Ktarran ship they destroyed wasn't one of their largest," Delano added. "I think they got lucky, or maybe the Ktarran captain wasn't too bright. We can't count on that combo happening again."

"How many of these battleships," Shen asked, "can China . . . I mean the Alliance, defeat?"

"I'm thinking General Klegg and the Alliance can muster enough planes and missiles to take out two or three, but no more." Delano had considered that question, too. "And these ships have to be destroyed quickly. If we only destroy one, Jarendo said the remaining Ktarrans will simply remain in high orbit and continue reducing Earth to rubble. It may take a little more time, but they're in no rush."

"Okay, then," Welsh said, "we have to maximize our advantages. We've got nuclear bombs in missiles, and the Alliance has a significant number of aircraft. If we can get the Ktarrans to descend to low-earth orbit, then hit them with everything we've got, we should be able to get a couple of nukes through. Maks, can these plasma screens survive a hit from a nuke?"

"A direct contact," the Russian physicist said, "not likely. But these plasma defenses are very strong, and the missile would have to get close, say within one or two hundred meters. An explosion at that distance would probably overload the plasma containment field, at least for a time. Remember, in space the explosion will be spherical, with no air or ground to enhance or channel the blast. So only a portion of the energy would be directed at the ship."

"What about non-nuclear missiles?" With all the talk of beams and nukes, Delano had almost dismissed conventional warheads.

"What happens if one of them gets in close?"

"An air-to-ship missile weighs about three thousand pounds, with approximately a thousand pounds of RDX or HMX material. It usually carries a shaped charge, to funnel most of the destructive force forward," Welsh said. "They don't even need to hit the target. The warhead can be detonated magnetically about ten meters from the hull, and almost all of the explosive energy goes forward."

"We showed the Tarlons images of some of our missiles," Lian said. "Jarendo was not impressed. He said they were too slow, and that the beam weapons would obliterate our rockets long before they came close to the Ktarran battle cruisers."

"Let's see how it might go," Welsh said. "Each beam weapon can probably destroy five missiles per minute. Ten weapons equals fifty hits. If it takes two or three minutes for the missile to reach its target, that's one hundred fifty missiles destroyed."

"And at the first sign of serious resistance, the Ktarrans will change course and climb back to a higher orbit," Delano said. "At four hundred kilometers or higher, they are out of effective range of anything we've got."

"So it's like an ambush," Gunny Stecker said. "We have to sacrifice territory or troops to lure them down, then have the Tarlons distract them with an attack. If the Tarlons can keep the Ktarrans' attention for a few minutes, we might have a window to launch the missiles."

Delano nodded. "Without help from the Tarlons and Halkins, Earth will not win this fight."

"That means we must convince them to join our fight," Lian said. "Somehow."

"First we have to get the Alliance to agree to throw everything they have at these invaders," Delano said. "Welsh, I'll leave that up to you. Oh, and you better start prepping the Station's escape vehicle for the flight to Earth. We need to get Stepanov and the others off the ISS."

"Yeah, thanks, Delano," Welsh said. "I hope we end up in adjoining cells."

"Sorry, different prisons," Delano said. "Maybe we can text."

Lian and Delano returned to the Talmak's ship, their third trip. This time they were not kept waiting. Their arrival at the little conference room filled it to capacity. The Talmak, War Leader Kaneel, Jarendo, Celeck, Horath, Ahvin, and Morad, the Captain of the second Halkin ship. Delano didn't consider himself a good reader of alien physiology, but the faces and body language of all those present looked gloomy.

If Lian noticed the tension, she didn't let it show. "We thank you again, Talmak, and you also, Horath. We have begun the planning to resist and destroy the Ktarrans. We ask your help in our struggle."

The Talmak spoke first, and directly to the point. "What is this plan?"

Lian glanced at Delano, signaling him to respond. Delano leaned forward. "Our plan is still being designed by our weapon masters on Earth. It assumes no more than three or four large Ktarran ships coming to Earth. When they begin the attack, Earth will not resist very much. We hope to lure them down to a lower orbit, where they will be in range of our missile weapons. If your ship and those of the Halkins can hide on the Moon and attack at that time, distract them for a few moments, we will then launch every missile we have, hundreds of them. Many of them will be atomic devices. After your attack, you can continue on to the gate and escape."

Delano spent the next fifteen minutes giving them the remaining few details he possessed, repeating several times that more specifics would be coming. When he finished, no one spoke. Delano realized how thin the plan sounded. Too many assumptions and not enough firepower.

"What of the Ktarran ship that comes to your Station?" The Talmak broke the silence.

"We will use explosives that we possess to delay or destroy that ship," Delano said. "We will sacrifice ourselves if necessary. We will not be captured."

The Talmak paused a moment. "Your courage is commendable, but there is much that can go wrong with your plan." He glanced around the table, but no one spoke. "You must work with War Leader Kaneel and Jarendo, and your leaders on Earth, to show us the details. We will tell you what we can do. If War Leader Kaneel decides there is little possibility of success, then we will leave this system. But if there is a reasonable chance for victory, the Tarlons and the Halkins will do what they can to help you."

Delano felt a weight lift from his shoulders. "We thank you for the people of Earth. Perhaps one day in the future, we can help the Tarlons and Halkins defeat the Ktarrans once and for all."

Chapter 19

Day 8: 1615 Zulu

General Klegg eased himself into the conference room chair. In the last forty eight hours, he'd spent most of his time in this stuffy room, surrounded by the world's best communications equipment. He'd snatched some sleep, an hour here and there. But aside from a few meetings in his Pentagon office, Klegg had done most of his work in this teleconference room located in the bowels of the building. Even President Clark had bowed to necessity and come to the Pentagon, to this facility, to be briefed.

Klegg wasn't the only one pushing himself to the limit. General Demidov's face seemed painted onto the Russian monitor, and he'd spent more time on camera than anyone. He carried a double load – military planner and public communications. The ham-fisted President of Russia had panicked his country, setting off repercussions within his satellite countries. Garanin's arrogant rhetoric about the aliens threatened to undo General Demidov's reassuring announcements. Klegg never ceased to be amazed how such incompetent people rose to positions of authority.

In the US, Dr. Vivian Spencer, the National Security Advisor, had taken on the role of the public face of the crisis, and her calm words had helped maintain order. By her directives, all stock markets and electronic trading system were frozen, pending resolution of the current crisis. In China, General Secretary Liu had twice spoken to his countrymen about the need to maintain order, leaving General Zeng in charge of Alliance military preparations.

General Malcolm S. Brown had joined the group as well. As STATCOM's commander, Brown was doing the actual planning and coordinating of US and Alliance military resources alongside Klegg and the NSA Director, Admiral Goodwin. Because Klegg had jumped on the ball so promptly, the US had moved its resources faster and more efficiently than either China or Russia. With that head start, the Pentagon's communication systems guided the Alliance, creating a combined command center to direct the coming alien assault.

Klegg's team had fleshed out Delano's pitiful excuse for a plan and allocated the men and resources needed. Klegg didn't like it, hell, nobody liked it. He'd bet the farm the Tarlons didn't care much for it either, after Delano presented it to them. But somehow they continued to help, and no one could think of anything better. So Klegg's team had worked out the logistics and begun putting the essential detachments in place.

And now four large Ktarran spaceships had appeared in Jupiter's space. Instruments on the Moon had transmitted that information a few minutes earlier, but the International Space Station had detected them as well, thanks to a heads-up from the Tarlons. The Ktarran ships hadn't moved yet, but they certainly hadn't arrived to take in the local sights, no matter how interesting Jupiter might appear to be.

By now all the Alliance leaders believed the Ktarrans would strike Earth. Delano, Lian, everyone on the Station trusted the Talmak's words. Klegg had watched the faces of Secretary Liu, General Zeng, and General Demidov as they listened to the recording Lian had made and forwarded to the Station. Even through the translator, no one who heard it doubted the danger, regardless of how much they wanted to believe otherwise.

But most of the world's population would never learn of it. That information would terrify everyone. At the mere mention of alien spaceships, panic had already swept across the country, across the world. Within every government on Earth, the struggle to maintain calm had reached a crisis point. Police, National Guard, regular military and active reserves, every unit had been called up and sent into the streets and instructed to maintain order at all costs. Looters or trouble-makers were being shot on sight. Anything less than drastic measures would send the planet reeling into chaos.

Less than nine hours after the news of the Halkins first approaching the Station burst upon the world, the information about the space battle off Jupiter had leaked, from Brazil of all places. By then virtually every telescope on Earth had turned its eye onto the Station. First the Halkins, then the Talmak's arrival had all been recorded and reported on. Now the entire planet knew that attempts to communicate with alien species had begun.

All over the world, people who mistrusted government pronouncements added to the rumors. Real disruptions would occur when the people of Earth discovered that a third species of aliens, the Ktarrans, had arrived near Jupiter. Total panic would erupt if the bases on Io were attacked, and there was no chance of withholding that information. After all, if the mining bases on Io could be destroyed, why not cities on Earth?

Across the globe, people started leaving the metropolitan areas. For more than a hundred years, people had seen television shows and videos about malign aliens coming to destroy Earth. Already the doomsday preppers and zombie apocalypse believers were pulling out of the cities and heading for their safe houses in the countryside. No one called them fools any longer.

Right now, Klegg had no time to worry about the civic unrest erupting worldwide. He had to fight these aliens, based on a wish and hope from Delano, Lian, and a few others on the Station. They had cobbled together a rough tactical plan, and somehow convinced the Talmak and Halkins to join the fight. But the brunt of the encounter would fall on Earth's forces, and that meant Klegg and the Alliance had better get it right. He knew they would only get the one chance.

Six hours earlier, the President and the Joint Chiefs had jumped all over Klegg. Everyone wanted to know what he was going to do and how he intended to defeat the aliens, should they prove hostile. They had already criticized his actions, but of course, no one had any better suggestions or seemed willing to accept any responsibility for the coming encounter. Vicious criticism, rather than constructive ideas, sprang up in every meeting.

President Clark had reacted to the bleak news pretty much as Klegg expected. The President's first instinct was to remove Klegg, as if that would solve the alien problem. But a few minutes on the line with China's General Secretary eradicated that idea. Essentially Secretary Liu told the President to grow a backbone and emphasized that neither he nor the Russians trusted anyone else in the US military, and certainly not one of President Clark's political allies. Klegg still offered to resign, but the suggestion was refused. If he departed, the President and his cronies would have no one to blame.

Dr. Spencer, who also understood what was at stake, supported General Klegg and threatened to go public if he were removed. Stunned by the hard line opposition, the American President had folded. In fact, Clark had broadcast a message to the country, placing all the responsibility in Klegg's hands and implying that if anything went wrong, Klegg would be to blame.

Dr. Spencer's horrified reaction to the scientific explanation of beam weapons, initially prepared by the Station's crew and enhanced by NASA's experts, revealed how civilians would likely be affected. The scientists, working from Maks' notes, explained what a phased particle beam, traveling at near the speed of light and with a kinetic energy range of fifty to sixty gigajoules, would do to anything it touched. Vivian had gone pale as the scientists equated that to fifteen barrels of gasoline being combusted in less than a tenth of a second. One specialist casually mentioned that a barrel of gasoline weighed three hundred pounds.

The resulting explosion and fireball would vaporize anything. Worse, the beam was continuous and could sweep a steady path of destruction. Focused on a given area, say a hardened underground bunker for five or ten seconds, anyone could do the math. The beam had the capacity to obliterate anything it touched.

No wonder the aliens didn't bother with atomic weapons. Beam weapons could indeed do more damage, precisely guided damage at that, and without the downsides of nuclear processes. The Tarlon ship possessed only three of these beam weapons. The larger Ktarran vessels might be armed with nine, ten, or more. Worst of all, from Klegg's viewpoint, beam weapons might operate for long periods of time, with endless power being supplied from the annihilation of antimatter scooped continuously from space. The potential damage one such ship would do to Earth's cities sent shivers down everyone's spine.

Klegg now knew how Winston Churchill had felt as he watched the destruction of the City of Coventry. Klegg didn't dare release the preliminary strategy that Generals Brown, Demidov, and Zeng had cobbled together. Now Klegg sat there, a copy of General Brown's final operational plan in his hand. Zeng and Demidov had received the same document about two hours ago. The time had arrived – they must accept or reject it.

"You've all read the report," Klegg began. "Anyone want to comment on General Brown's assessment?"

"If we understand this," General Zeng said, "then the alien ships are invulnerable at four hundred kilometers and above. Our missiles won't survive to reach them at that altitude."

General Brown glanced at Klegg, then answered. "Yes, that is correct. The analysis by Dr. Mironov, working with the Tarlon-supplied data, is quite definite. Assuming, of course, that the figures from the Tarlons are correct. But we recorded the weapons used off Jupiter, and the energy readings measured by the Station are consistent with the Tarlon numbers. We have to trust them. Mironov and Colonel Welsh said the Tarlons didn't seem too impressed with the speed of our missiles. Apparently the Ktarran beam weapons can operate effectively at that altitude. The weapons have the capability to destroy any number of missiles coming toward them at a constant, or in Earth's environs, a decelerating rate of speed. The beams can be adjusted to sweep a wide area, and a single touch of the particles on any missile will either vaporize it, detonate the warhead, or alter the trajectory. Our missile experts and scientists have confirmed this analysis."

Zeng muttered something, but General Demidov's hoarse voice sounded loud and clear. "We, too, performed the same analysis and reached the same conclusion. If we attack them at four hundred kilometers, they might simply move to a higher orbit. Their beams would be weaker, but they would have plenty of time. Our only hope is to get the aliens down to a lower altitude, no more than three hundred kilometers. Two hundred and fifty would be better. At that distance, launching enough AARAM missiles, some should get through the beams' defenses."

That meant, Klegg knew, that missiles launched at fifteen kilometers, or roughly fifty thousand feet, would accelerate up to Mach 3.5 or Mach 4, and reach the target in approximately four to six minutes. That might be fast in air-to-air combat, but it remained a significant time to cover so many kilometers. And these alien ships had demonstrated extremely powerful engines. If they detected a slew of missiles on approach, they might accelerate away, and Alliance missiles, unable to redirect themselves, would be useless.

"So unless someone has a super-fast missile that can climb to four hundred kilometers," Klegg said, "adjust its course as necessary, and hit a target dead on, we can't touch these ships."

"The odds of a such a hit seem poor," General Zeng agreed. "We must somehow entice them to drop below three hundred kilometers to have a chance of success."

"That means we must get them to descend to lower orbits, then hope the Tarlon and Halkin ships can keep the Ktarrans down for a few minutes, long enough to get sufficient nukes on target." Klegg shook his head. "If there are three or more alien ships, our odds are lousy of getting all of them."

"We agree," General Secretary Liu said. "So we must hope no more than three attack Earth, as Major Delano and Lian have suggested. But there are already four Ktarran ships in our solar system."

"Without better intelligence on their capabilities," General Brown said, "what other choice do we have? Secretary Liu, I know you are a bridge player. If there is only one layout of cards that will allow you to win, you have to play the hand accordingly and hope for the best. Otherwise, we just give up."

Liu managed a brief smile. "Perhaps you are right. But what of Major Delano? Do we assume his plan to take out whatever ship comes to the Station will work?"

"It's a forlorn hope," Klegg said. "But again, it's all we've got."

Klegg had dismissed all thoughts of relieving Major Delano. Not only were Demidov and Secretary Liu against the idea, but the Chinese president had placed all his trust in his niece. If she remained satisfied with Delano's decisions, nothing Klegg said to the contrary would matter. And so Delano and his hare-brained scheme for defending Earth and the Station took precedence. Still, no one in the Alliance had come up with anything better.

"Regrettably we are in agreement," General Demidov said. "We will not launch the real counterstrike until the Ktarrans descend below three hundred kilometers."

General Zeng turned to face the President of China, who nodded approval. "We will follow General Brown's plan. It is a hard decision, but it must be done."

And that was as much as anyone wanted to discuss the unspoken flaw in General Brown's plan. Earth had only one way to lure the Ktarrans to a lower altitude – offer no resistance. Sacrifice major cities and millions of lives. Not an easy decision.

"Then we can get started," Klegg said. "I'll send the final draft of the plan to the Station, and Delano and Lian can provide the specifics to the Talmak. I hope he still buys into it."

"Major Delano and Lian are very persuasive," Secretary Liu said. "You will see to the command structure?"

"As you suggested, we'll take charge of Alliance communications," Klegg said, "and coordinate the defense of the planet. Good luck to us all. Operation Sentinel Star is initiated."

The Chinese and Russians broke the connections. Klegg slumped in his chair as Brown collected his things and hurried out of the conference room. He would depart for the command center in the West Virginia hills to direct the combined forces of the Alliance.

As the screens went dark, only Klegg and Vivian Spencer remained. For a few moments, they had nothing else to do.

"It's going to be bad," Vivian reached out and placed her hand on his. "Isn't it?"

"Millions will die," Klegg answered. Her touch softened the bitterness in his words. "That's in the best case scenario. If things don't work out . . ."

"We might lose most of the planet," she said. "And those poor people who decided to remain on the Station? The Secretary's niece?"

"I don't think . . . the Station, the people up there are not going to survive," Klegg said. "Maybe they'll damage one of the ships, but that's about all they can do. They have no real weapons. Maybe it's all we can hope for."

Klegg kept his next thought to himself. The poor bastards probably didn't even have a chance of slowing them down. They were all dead men up there. A quick death might be their best hope.

Chapter 20

Huairen Air Base, China

Day 9: 1245 Zulu

Major Peng Qilang, Chinese Air Force, managed to grab the last empty chair in the pilots' ready room at the Huairen Air Base. For more than two days, Peng had been flying high altitude training missions, his fighter jet armed with various types of air-to-air missiles. He'd hoped to get some rest after today's flight session, which had pressed every bird and pilot to the limit. In his eight years of flying, he'd never seen such intensity, not even when he flew combat missions over Somalia and India.

Ten minutes earlier he'd sat on his bunk, laying out fresh clothes and getting ready for a relaxing shower, when the barrack's loudspeakers, at full volume, ordered all pilots and navigators to report to the ready room at once. Most of the pilots responded with groans and curses. Peng would have joined in, but he detected something in the announcer's voice, nerves or excitement, so he quickly pulled on clean shorts and tee shirt, and slipped into his leather flight jacket.

Now sitting in the ready room, he would learn what new scenarios Air Command had dreamt up to ruin his evening. Still and all, Peng had no place to go. Four days earlier, the General in charge of the Huairen facility had restricted pilots and support crews to the base indefinitely. No exceptions.

The briefing room overflowed with pilots and navigators, thirty-two of them, and Peng felt grateful he'd found a seat. Especially when nothing happened for another twenty minutes, until the base commander arrived with his aide.

Peng took one look at the man's face and knew something serious was up. After a casual greeting to the assembly, the commander took his seat facing the larger monitor that dominated the forward wall. His aide fiddled with the controls. At last the blank screen lit up, revealing the face of Senior Colonel Jang, the second highest officer in the Chinese Air Force. Jang reported directly to

General Zeng, who answered only to Secretary Liu.

From the size of the carved wood desk and impressive red curtains, Peng knew Senior Colonel Jang's transmission originated from his office in Beijing. His stern face stared grimly into the camera, as if he could actually see each of the pilots facing him. After a quick greeting, Jang came right to the point. "All pilots and navigators are to prepare for immediate combat missions. This is not a drill. Failure to obey orders will not be tolerated. You will also not disclose what you hear today with anyone, except your fellow pilots." Jang glared into the camera as if to reinforce his orders. "My aide, Captain Chiew Chuntao, will deliver the preflight briefing."

Short and full-figured, Captain Chiew brushed back her black hair. "This briefing is being delivered to all fighter bases within the Jingjinji and the national capital region. All orders are to be followed precisely. No changes are permitted, and no requests for clarification or modification of orders are allowed."

Chiew droned on for almost an hour, going over each sector, naming the planes and pilots and giving them a detailed list of instructions intended to address every aspect of each mission.

Peng scarcely noticed the passage of time or the hard wooden chair pressing against his back. Instead he concentrated on the startling news coming from the monitor, where Colonel Jang's efficient aide produced and displayed various pre-flight charts and operational documents. An attack from space by aliens? Alien space ships? Mining camps on Io already destroyed. Lunar facilities being bombarded and now out of communication with Chinese Space Command. How could this happen?

Captain Chiew concluded her briefing. "A full scramble has been declared, with every pilot ordered to prepare his plane. Written copies of your orders should be ready for distribution when you leave. Your planes will be armed with either conventional or nuclear warheads, depending on the squadron. Good luck and good hunting." She turned to Jang for further instructions, but he waved her away.

Part of Major Peng Qilang wondered if this might be some new drill, some test of pilot reliability and attention to orders. But the hard eyes staring down on him from the screen refuted that idea. Colonel Jang had far too much seniority to be involved in a drill.

"To summarize," Senior Colonel Jang said as his aide stepped aside, "we expect between two and four of these alien spacecraft to attack Earth. They will likely concentrate on major population and industrial centers. China will be among the first targets. We and the Alliance will respond to this threat with everything we have. Only aircraft capable of operating at extreme altitude and launching our most powerful missiles will be utilized. That means we have less than a hundred planes available for the mission. Many of the missiles have been specifically modified for an upper orbit target. The Americans will be coordinating the overall defense of the planet, since they possess the most sophisticated detection and communications equipment. We expect the Americans or possibly the Russians to be attacked at the same time, depending on the number of alien ships."

Jang squinted at his notes, providing the thirty-two pilots in the briefing room the opportunity to exchange quick glances.

"Since the Beijing area is considered a primary target in China," Jang continued, "communications regarding this operation will be issued from Chengdu Air Base, in case Beijing Command is knocked out. All messages from Chengdu or Beijing will be preceded by the code word 'LION.' If Chengdu is destroyed or unable to communicate, you will receive instructions from Guangzhou base. Their code word is 'DRAGON.' Communications from the Americans will begin with the word 'EAGLE.' You will obey all orders, especially from the Americans. The order of precedent for commands is EAGLE, DRAGON, then LION. In other words, if the Americans issue you an order, even if it conflicts with prior instructions, you will obey it. Do you understand?"

"Yes, Colonel." The shocked response came from every person in the room.

"Good. For this mission it is critical you follow orders. There is to be no improvisation at the pilot level. You may be airborne for many hours, so prepare yourselves. Your country's survival, your planet's survival, will depend on each of you. Your plane, even your own life, is to be sacrificed for the mission if necessary. Is that understood?"

Another chorus of agreement, more muted this time. In his eight years of flying, Peng Qilang had never received nor heard of such orders before.

"Then you may proceed to your aircraft, and good hunting,"

Colonel Jang said. He again referred to his notes. "Major Peng Qilang of Huairen Base will remain to receive special orders. The rest of you are dismissed."

Peng, about to rise, slumped back on the chair, surprised at being singled out. A few of the other pilots eyed him with curiosity before hurrying out of the room, snatching their orders from the base commander's aide as they left. On the screen, Senior Colonel Jang's aides removed the briefing material and charts.

"You are Major Peng Qilang?" The Colonel's stern voice cut into Peng's thoughts.

"Yes, Sir."

"Move closer to the camera, Major, so I can see you better."

Peng swore under his breath. His short stature, lank hair, and slim build did not look imposing in a video transmission. Only his strong chin hinted at something more than what met the eye. Jang would not be impressed.

By the time Peng scrambled up onto the raised platform, Colonel Jang had arranged his notes. A second, even more officious female aide stood behind him, holding additional documents.

"Sit down, Major. Your orders are slightly different . . . no, that is not accurate. Your orders are significantly different from those of the other pilots. You will be carrying two VLRAAM (Very Long Range Air To Air Missile) nuclear missiles, each with a warhead of three megatons. The missiles are being modified as we speak to produce a massive electromagnetic pulse. When the attack comes, you will be given special target coordinates to feed into your Strike Fighter's guidance system. You will do your utmost to climb as high and fast as you can before you release your missiles. That is critical. Now listen closely. The coordinates you receive will seem to be in error. They are not. Wherever the enemy target is, you will be aiming for a different point. It is vital that you target the missiles exactly where we, or possibly the Americans, instruct you. Do you understand, Major?"

"Yes, Sir." Flight orders directly from the Air Wing Commander? Or possibly the Americans? Peng knew no pilot had ever received orders like these. Still, the instructions were clear enough. And he understood what would happen to his career or possibly his life, if he failed to follow such specific directives.

"You have been chosen for this specific mission because your commander believes you are the best pilot he has for this operation, are fully trained on the Strike Fighter, and you can follow orders. You will fly this mission alone, without any wingman, because these are the only two missiles our scientists have had time to modify. We, especially the Americans, are hoping that a single fighter away from the others is less likely to be noticed or targeted. Your call sign for this mission is 'FOX.' You will attack only when you receive specific orders. Not before. Understood?"

"Yes, Sir. I will ignore all attack orders unless preceded by the call sign FOX."

"Remember that. You are dismissed." Senior Colonel Jang started to rise, but his aide leaned over and whispered something. "Oh, you will be supported by a dedicated refueling aircraft, in case you are required to remain airborne for several hours. You will take your position five kilometers above the tanker."

Another first. Tankers, always in short supply, supported as many fighters as possible.

The connection dissolved into a blank screen. Peng rose, and found his base commander waiting for him. "You have your orders, Peng. Better get going."

He went to his locker and collected his helmet and other gear. Taking his time, he made certain the flight jacket fit properly. In a long flight, even a single wrinkle could prove distracting. When Peng trotted out of the barracks, he found the base commander's Yongshi vehicle with a driver waiting for him, another first. The SUV took him not out to the fighters warming up on the crowded tarmac, but to Hanger Nine, a small and today heavily guarded facility at the far end of the base. Inside he found one of China's fastest and most powerful planes, the J-23 Strike Fighter.

Two small panel trucks, both displaying the international atomic symbol, were parked just behind the fighter, their engines running. A few steps away helmeted soldiers armed with rifles surrounded a team of technicians wearing white coats and working on the VLRAAMs. Both missiles rested on canvas mats with the innards of the nose cones exposed. As Peng stared in fascination, a technician closed up one of the weapon's access panels, using a small electric screwdriver to seal it. The missiles looked different from the regular payloads, longer and thicker, each painted an ugly shade of white instead of the usual gray.

An army lieutenant, wearing the insignia that belonged to the PLA Rocket Force, strode up to Peng. "You are the pilot?" He didn't bother to salute.

"Yes, I'm . . ."

"These weapons are much heavier your usual payload. Be aware you will not be able to climb as high. Modifications to the missiles are almost finished. You will take off as soon as they are attached. Make sure you subject the devices to as little stress and movement as possible. The changes being made have never been tested, and two safety mechanisms have been removed. It is possible the missiles are unstable."

An unstable nuclear warhead? He'd be sitting on two atomic bombs, each capable of turning a good-sized city into radioactive rubble? Peng started to ask about that but the surly Lieutenant had moved away. Members of the Rocket Force, tasked with the security of China's nuclear weapons, tended to lord it over the regular military.

Cursing under his breath, Peng began his preflight check list. The chief mechanic had already signed off and reported the bird was in perfect condition.

Twenty minutes later, Peng eased the overweight J-23 out to the airstrip. The rest of the squadron had already launched, so he simply rolled onto the runway and started accelerating. Normally he would push the aircraft hard during takeoff, to identify any problems early, but the nuclear expert's words had shaken Peng out of that idea. Instead he took off leisurely, climbed slowly to ten kilometers, found the tanker, and began flying the same figure eight pattern, only a few kilometers above.

Now the hardest part of the mission began – the waiting. Doubts and worries would creep into his thoughts, attempting to weaken his resolve. To kill time, Peng rang through his checklist again, though he'd done so only a few minutes before. Yes, he hated the waiting. Hopefully it wouldn't last too long.

Chapter 21

Day 9: 1420 Zulu

General Klegg sat in the Air Command bunker, buried in the hills of West Virginia just over two hundred miles from the Pentagon. He and Dr. Spencer had made their arrangements and departed the Pentagon two hours after General Brown. From this new command center, Klegg and his staff, augmented by a force of Air Police and technicians, would coordinate the response of the Alliance if, or rather when, the Ktarrans attacked the planet.

Klegg hadn't asked for operational control, but the Russians didn't trust the Chinese that much and preferred the Americans, so Klegg found himself representing the Alliance as overall commander. General Zeng, aside from his habitual frown, offered no protest. No doubt he, too, had moved past petty bickering. Planetary warfare had come to Earth, and for once individual and national interests were set aside.

No one in the Alliance any longer doubted the attack was coming. Less than an hour after the four Ktarran spaceships arrived through the Jupiter wormhole, they shifted position and soon hovered over Jupiter's moon, Io. Klegg and the others had listened to the pleas for mercy from the two bases on Io. The message, dictated by Delano and broadcast in the Ktarran language, declared the mining operations had no weapons and wanted only peace. But the battle cruisers – each with an energy signature larger than the ship destroyed by the Halkins – had ignored the efforts to communicate. Instead the aliens blasted the two sites into rubble in less than one minute.

Afterward, the Ktarrans hadn't lingered. Klegg, as frustrated and angry as Delano at the destruction and slaughter of helpless miners, didn't know if any of them had survived. Delano, speaking for the Alliance and JovCo, had warned them earlier to dig in. Hope remained, but without a speedy rescue mission, any survivors clinging to life beneath the surface would be dead soon enough.

The attack on Io had occurred almost twenty hours ago. After completing the destruction there, three Ktarran ships headed straight for Earth orbit, with the Moon as the likely next target. One Ktarran remained behind, orbiting near the gas giant, apparently guarding the entry vector of the wormhole. Any incoming Tarlon or Halkin ships arriving would immediately be attacked.

Klegg expected the Ktarrans to repeat the merciless bombardment on the lunar bases. Once again Klegg and the Alliance could do nothing to save them, except advise the lunar settlers to abandon the domes and seek shelter in the mines, caves, transports, and vehicles. When the Ktarrans finished with the lunar settlements, the Station riding in high orbit above Earth would be next. After that, they would turn their weapons against the planet itself.

The Alliance used the hours remaining to prepare. Thanks to General Klegg's immediate push to ready planetary defenses, most of the pieces had fallen into place. Missiles and aircraft had been modified, pilots briefed, and public services alerted. Worldwide panic had erupted with the attack on Io. But the military and civil defenses of the Alliance had immediately moved into the major cities and key facilities. That kept the chaos from spreading. For now.

The camera feeds showed cheerless faces of Klegg's counterparts – General Zeng in a bunker somewhere outside of Beijing, and General Demidov in one of the underground blast chambers at the launch pad in Star City. The US President had taken refuge at Camp David, in the bomb-proof underground facility there. Strong enough to withstand multiple nuclear hits, President Clarke, his friends, and bodyguards would ride out any Ktarran attack. Officially, he'd taken control of all US forces, civilian and military. Unofficially, he was out of the loop. Klegg and Dr. Spencer retained operational control.

Klegg, coordinating with the Russians, watched a colonel hand Demidov a note. The Russian read the message but said nothing.

For a few moments, Demidov seemed lost in thought. Then he rose. "Excuse me," he said, "I must attend to something." He moved outside the camera's view, and one of his colonels took his place.

Klegg wondered about Demidov. Usually when he left any joint conference, Demidov informed his counterparts how long he expected to be gone. But Klegg had bigger problems to worry about. He and the Alliance were gambling now, following Delano's sketchy playbook. So far, the linguist had guessed right. Delano and the Tarlons had believed – hoped might be a better word – that the Ktarrans would hold back one ship to guard the wormhole, and they had done exactly that.

Now the real test would come. Would the Ktarrans again keep one ship at the Station while the other two attacked Earth? With the help of the Tarlon and Halkin ships joining the defense, Klegg believed the Alliance had at least a chance to defeat two Ktarran ships. But if all three alien vessels decided to finish whatever business they might have with Delano and the Station's crew, and then move to attack the planet, Earth's defenses would be in trouble.

Since Klegg was acting as coordinator for the Alliance, his problem was straightforward. He didn't know if the Alliance could handle three ships attacking Earth at the same time. Two would be a stretch. Also, Klegg didn't know exactly when or where this unknown number of ships would strike. That meant Klegg had to keep the counterstrike scenarios fluid, positioning and shifting Alliance aircraft and missiles as conditions changed. Adjusting the defense plans became a full-time effort.

He and the others had already made the first hard decision. No non-Alliance countries would be defended. Klegg didn't like it, and had argued that industrialized Europe should be included. But China and Russia wanted none of it. They didn't intend to waste a single aircraft or missile on Europe's defense, and Klegg reluctantly agreed. With the rise of the Alliance and its de facto guarantee of stability, Europe and parts of Asia, Africa, and the Middle East had abandoned their military capacity. Now they would pay the price.

The second decision proved far more difficult. Klegg insisted that no nuclear missiles be launched against the alien ships until they dropped below three hundred kilometers. According to Delano and Lian, the Ktarrans could commence their attack at four hundred kilometers or higher, but their weapons would create the most destruction if utilized at under three hundred.

Consequently Klegg, Zeng, and Demidov had decided that, except for a number of conventional missiles to be fired as decoys, the real counterstrike would not be launched against the aliens until they dropped below three hundred kilometers.

The logic for this came from Delano and Lian's information, collected from the Talmak and Halkins, about the capabilities of the Ktarran beam weapons. Entire populations would be sacrificed to build up the enemy's confidence and lure them into a lower orbit.

At first General Zeng, worried about China's heavily populated cities, argued against it, but finally Secretary Liu had overruled him and accepted the plan. It meant many cities and lives would be lost without more than token resistance, but everyone understood they would get only one shot at these battle cruisers. If the Ktarrans decided Earth was too tough, they would just stay high above the planet or call in more reinforcements.

Untold numbers of innocent and helpless civilians were going to die because of Klegg's decision. He wondered if he would ever be able to look himself in the mirror again.

On the monitor, Klegg listened as General Zeng finished with his assistants. "We will stand ready to defend Beijing, Shanghai, and Guangzhou in less than two hours. Hong Kong and the other cities in China will have to wait until we regroup and can refit our fighters."

For the US, General Malcom Brown established the primary air fleet at Offutt Air Force Base in Nebraska. He'd staged other fighters at regional bases and made preparations to defend the major cities on both coasts.

General Demidov had fewer large cities in Russia to protect, and he had volunteered to assist in the defense of the United States. In return Klegg agreed to provide coverage for Moscow, St. Petersburg, and Novgorod in case the orbital assault began in Russia. What plan would actually be used depended on where the aliens decided to attack.

The planes stood ready. Now only a few details remained unresolved. China achieved readiness first and General Zeng passed the control baton to Klegg. The Americans, too, had completed their preparations. Only the Russians hadn't finalized their plans.

Klegg tried to reach Demidov. But the Russian monitor had gone dark ten minutes ago, and Klegg couldn't get through. Perhaps some technical issue had arisen. The three Ktarran cruisers were less than two hours away, and now was not the time for the Russians to be out of touch.

Klegg needed to confirm the operational plan with Russia. "Damnit, where the hell is Demidov?"

*   *   *

General Demidov's stomach turned after he read the note his aide had handed him. He found the news distasteful, but did not allow his face to reveal any of his thoughts. Russian President Iosif Garanin's plane was landing at the Star City complex and he would arrive at the bunker in less than thirty minutes. No doubt Garanin had decided the Star City bunker would prove much safer than Moscow's bomb shelter.

Three hours earlier, Demidov had spoken with his President, and the conversation had not gone well. Garanin declared the Alliance decision on deploying Russian air defenses needed what he called "oversight." Translated, Garanin had resolved to take charge. Not to mention that if Moscow were attacked, Garanin preferred to be elsewhere.

Unfortunately, Garanin had no military experience, having risen to power through the ranks of the internal security services. He knew a great deal about spying on Russians, eliminating dissidents, and Swiss bank accounts, but he had never worn a military uniform or faced personal danger. Nor could he always conceal his contempt for those who had.

Two years earlier Garanin had floated the idea of withdrawing from the Alliance. Only the opposition of everyone in his inner circle kept him from making that disastrous mistake. For the last twenty-five years, China's unofficial operating doctrine declared that any major power not part of the Alliance could be considered a threat. Russia and China shared a border of over forty-two hundred kilometers. To leave the Alliance would place much of that territory, filled with mineral wealth, at risk.

Thankfully, Garanin had backed off the notion, but hadn't given it up completely. The fool might think the current crisis provided an opportunity to act without repercussions. His arrival at the Star City bunker could only mean trouble, and Demidov had a good idea of what his president intended.

And so Demidov broke the communication link to the West Virginia bunker. He turned to his subordinate. "Our President is arriving soon. I must go to my office and prepare." Rising to his feet and trailed by his personal security guard, Demidov left the bunker complex. As he passed through the thick steel door, he ordered the three guards to make sure that, from now on, it remained closed at all times.

He took the elevator up four levels to the administrative offices. Demidov strode down the corridor, ignoring those few he encountered and entered his office.

His bodyguard, Pavel Lazarev, accompanied him. Demidov went to his desk, opened one of the drawers and removed the key to his private bathroom. He kept it locked at all times. Otherwise half the officers and soldiers stationed on the floor would be using it in his absence.

"Make some fresh tea, Pavel," Demidov said. "We could both use it."

Pavel had been Demidov's bodyguard for seven years, ever since Demidov had taken the assignment as Chief of Russian Space Command. The two had become close in that time, and Pavel frequently dined with the Demidov family, often bringing his two young girls. But in Russia, a friend could also be a spy, and in Pavel's case, that happened to be true.

Demidov had suspected it almost from the beginning. A quiet favor from a grateful colonel in the security services confirmed it. Pavel Lazarev reported in secret to a special division officer, who reported directly to the President.

For eight years, ever since President Garanin had taken charge of Russia, Demidov had been nothing but loyal, and he knew that Garanin considered his Space Command general a faithful lapdog. But Demidov appreciated Russian history, and past presidents had invariably ended up putting down even their most trusted lapdogs. Sooner or later, Josef Stalin's pitiless advice proved its worth – kill anyone at the first sign of disloyalty.

Demidov had prepared as well as he could for the day Garanin decided he no longer needed his dutiful Air Force general. However this alien crisis turned out, Demidov knew he would eliminated. Garanin's pride allowed no subordinate to grow too powerful or even too popular.

He picked up the Star City base newspaper from the desk, still printed and distributed in hard copy for the senior staff, and tucked it under his arm. "I may be a while, Pavel." He unlocked the thick door to the lavatory and pulled it closed behind him. It had a latch to insure privacy, but Demidov didn't bother to use it. Pavel had never interrupted his superior in the lavatory.

Demidov let his trousers drop and the heavy belt buckle clanked against the gray tile floor. *While I'm here,* he pushed his underwear down and sat. He reached into his pocket and removed his keys. Attached to the key ring was a tiny Swiss Army knife. The four centimeter blade was useful for cleaning your nails, but little else. However it would do for Demidov's purposes.

By leaning forward, he could reach the towel rack. He pushed aside the rough white cloth and fitted the blade of his knife into a tiny crack at the base of the center tile. A slight pressure lifted up the tile, and he carefully pulled the loosened square off the wall.

The small recess inside contained four items. Ignoring a plastic case that contained a poison pill, Demidov withdrew a small box of ammunition and an empty magazine for the fourth item, a Russian P-96S automatic pistol. He'd carried the old 9mm weapon for many years, until he attained the rank of General. It remained reliable despite years of use, and Demidov had no doubts that it would function properly. He'd used more than a sufficient amount of lubricating oil before he placed the weapon in the wall four years earlier.

A glance at the weapon's magazine revealed some rust spots on the spring, but it still pushed back against his finger with what should be sufficient tension. Nevertheless, he loaded only three cartridges. If he needed more than that, he would already be dead.

He inserted the magazine into the butt of the gun, quietly racked the weapon, then checked to see if the top cartridge had fed properly into the chamber. Satisfied, he replaced the spare ammunition, shoved the tile back in place and centered the towel over the bar. Even someone using the towel might not notice the loose tile, though that was probably something he didn't need to concern himself about. If Demidov survived, he would have it repaired properly.

He sat back for a moment and realized that he did indeed need to move his bowels. A few seconds later, the remnants of last night's greasy dinner, eaten in the bunker and washed down with nine ounces of vodka, splashed into the stained and cracked porcelain bowl. Relieved, he grunted loudly in satisfaction.

A few moments later, Demidov dressed, washed his hands, wrapped the newspaper around the compact gun and shoved it into his jacket pocket. He opened the door and stepped back into his office. Pavel was seated on the sofa on the other side of the room, perusing some article or book on his electronic reader.

His bodyguard stood, his nose wrinkling. Demidov knew from years of experience that the smell from the poorly-ventilated lavatory would linger in the office for some time. "Definitely a good one, Pavel," Demidov said, sipping tea from the glass Pavel handed him. "For an old man like myself, it takes longer and longer each time."

In spite of his words, Demidov felt younger than his sixty-six years. Perhaps the familiar friend in his pocket had something to do with it. Today would be a day of choices, and not just for Demidov.

They rode the elevator down to the bunker. "I still find it hard to believe," Pavel marveled. "Aliens from space are preparing to attack our planet. Can we stop them?"

Demidov grunted. "You know what happens to those who attack Russia." They entered and he reminded the guards to keep the door closed, to be opened only by his order or for the President. Demidov returned to his command station, took his seat, and nodded to his senior advisor.

By the time he and Pavel resumed their places in the command center, the aliens had arrived in Earth orbit.

"General Demidov, the three Ktarran vessels stopped at the Station," his assistant informed him. "One remains there, at thirty-six thousand kilometers, but the other two descended to low orbit, and are taking position about five hundred kilometers above Earth. One is moving toward the western Pacific, and the other toward the North American West Coast. General Klegg has recommended Attack Plan C and insists on speaking with you."

Demidov required a few moments to grasp the tactical situation. Plan C meant China and America would face the brunt of the aliens' orbital attacks.

"Launch the tankers, and scramble the fighters," Demidov ordered. "Tell their commanders Attack Plan C. Move them into position for a strike across the North Pole."

He watched his staff dispatch the order, then turned to his console. The moment Demidov flicked the switch, he found General Klegg waiting for him.

"I thought you had abandoned us, General Demidov," Klegg snapped. "The attack is about to start."

"We are tracking them," Demidov said. "We're still shifting forces ourselves, and are moving our lead aircraft into position. Within forty minutes our first counterstrike can begin. The first two missiles will be the HAMPs (High Altitude Magnetic Pulse)."

"I understand," Klegg said. "We're not quite ready ourselves. General Zeng continues to position his aircraft."

"These aliens will select the major population centers as their first targets," Demidov said. "There will be plenty of casualties." He had expected nothing less. Hopefully Moscow would be spared from this first assault.

"President Garanin is in the elevator," Demidov's aide called out.

"Unlock the door," Demidov ordered over his shoulder. "Secure it after the President enters."

The blast-proof door to the command center swung open, and the President of Russia, Iosif Garanin, strode into the room, a bodyguard preceding him and another just behind. Short and overweight, Garanin had already started sweating even in the air conditioned bunker.

Demidov observed three or four additional guards in the hall before the thick door swung closed. With a flip of his finger, Demidov casually broke the connection to General Klegg, interrupting him in mid-sentence. Demidov rose and faced his President.

"Mr. President." Demidov bowed properly but did not come to attention. The newspaper in his pocket might have fallen out.

"What is the latest status?" Garanin, his face flushed from the long walk through the building, did not like to waste words or especially his time. "Are the aliens coming?"

"Yes, Mr. President," Demidov said, pointing to the largest wall graphic that displayed the alien ships and the Russian forces. "It appears that they will first attack the Eastern Coast of China and the West Coast of the United States. Our fighters have lifted off, and we are ready to support the Americans."

Garanin studied the board for a moment, pretending he understood the blue lines and flashing white symbols. "Recall them. We will not waste our fighters defending the United States. We will need all we have to defend Moscow."

The room went silent, and every set of eyes went to Demidov.

Everyone knew the counter strike required all Alliance fighters to work together.

"Mr. President," Demidov began, "we made a commitment to the Alliance to support each other. If these aliens came to Russia first, the Americans and Chinese committed to aid us. If we fail to do the same, the Alliance will turn upon us."

"Nonsense." Garanin's voice was firm. "They wouldn't dare. We still have our defenses. It may even be possible to deal with these aliens once the Chinese and Americans are destroyed. Recall our fighters."

"You will be responsible for Russia's destruction." Despite the risk, Demidov had raised his voice so that everyone could hear. "Even if Beijing and Washington are obliterated, the Alliance will launch their missiles against us. They will know we betrayed them."

Garanin's face showed surprise at the outburst, then anger. "Are you disobeying a direct order, Demidov?"

Demidov let his shoulders sag and lowered his head. "No, of course not, Mr. President. But before we issue the recall, you should see the alien attack pattern. We may want to shift the fighters to protect St. Petersburg." Demidov moved around his command station, stepping over to one of the monitoring consoles.

Curious, Garanin followed him.

"Here, see the flight plan." Demidov reached the console first, pointed his finger, then moved aside to allow Garanin to study the monitor. The President leaned forward and squinted at the screen.

"I don't see . . ."

As Demidov turned sideways, his right side was blocked by Garanin's body from the eyes of the President or his bodyguards. In a smooth motion, Demidov slipped the pistol from his pocket, shoved it against the back of Garanin's head and pulled the trigger.

The sharp crack of the firearm in the closed room echoed off the concrete walls. As the President slumped forward, Demidov dropped the P-96S and raised his hands.

"This was necessary to save Mother Russia," he shouted.

As Demidov spoke, both of Garanin's guards, stunned surprise on their faces, drew their weapons and pointed them at General Demidov. For a moment, no one moved.

Demidov kept talking. "Do not shoot! The President would have betrayed our country and Russia would have been destroyed."

Outside the bunker, more guards, both Garanin's and base security personnel, pounded on the thick door.

"You traitor!" Garanin's senior bodyguard shouted.

Demidov saw his death standing in front of him, as the gun aimed at his chest. Two quick gunshots reverberated inside the command center. Demidov flinched and waited for the pain, but it never came. Instead Garanin's thugs, both shot in the head, slumped to the floor. Demidov saw Pavel, his military Makarov pistol still directed at the two bodies. The second guard twitched for a moment, then went limp.

Pavel was an excellent marksman.

Demidov found himself holding his breath, and let it out. "Do not open the door!" That order was for the guard stationed beside the entrance, his hand reaching for the unlocking lever. "Garanin would have brought us to ruin. He had to be stopped. I will not issue the recall order."

Everyone in the room stared at Pavel, who now held the fate of all of them in his hand. The pounding on the bunker door continued, but once closed, it could only be opened from inside.

Pavel lowered his Makarov. "No, of course not, General Demidov. Garanin was a traitor and was assassinated by his guards. Is that not so?" With a hard look on his face, he glared around the chamber.

The nine assistants in the room took only a brief time to react. Then heads began to nod in assent.

"I suggest that you remember that fact," Demidov snapped. "Each of you was busy working at your station. You did not see which guard fired the first shot. Does everyone understand?"

A chorus of "Yes, General" rang out. These men, highly trained and carefully selected, did comprehend the full threat of the alien attack.

"Good. Then I am temporarily assuming command of the military operation against the aliens," Demidov announced. "Until a new election can be called, of course." He turned to Pavel. "You are a hero of the State, Pavel Lazarev, for killing the assassins. As my first official act, you are promoted to the rank of Senior Lieutenant. Please contact our security forces and have them arrest the remainder of Garanin's guards. More of them may prove to be traitors. Until we are certain of their loyalty, put them in the base prison."

"Yes, General Demidov." Pavel saluted crisply and picked up a phone.

Ignoring the pounding on the door, Demidov returned to his command station, sank gratefully into the cushioned leather. He reactivated the uplink to General Klegg. It took three tries. His hands still shook and his face felt flushed.

"Where the hell have you been?" Klegg demanded. "Are the Russian fighters on the way? The West Coast is getting pounded."

"The order was given," Demidov glanced at the large digital clock mounted on the wall, "five minutes ago. They should be on your screens any moment. Good luck, General Klegg."

"Thank you, General Demidov," Klegg snarled. "I was beginning to wonder if you were going to help."

"Be assured," Demidov declared, "Russia will be at your side."

Demidov sagged back in his chair. His heart still hammered in his chest from the excitement and shootings. Today had been a day of choices. He had gambled, as most Russians loved to do, and won, at least for now. Pavel, faced with a sudden choice in loyalties and with Garanin dead, had risen to the occasion. Now it only remained to defeat the aliens. If the Alliance couldn't stop them, and Russian cities were attacked, he and Pavel would both probably be stood against some wall and shot as traitors to the Motherland.

Even so, Demidov wished that Klegg had contrived a better stratagem. But all in the past, that. Nothing short of an Alliance victory could save them now.

Chapter 22

New International Space Station

Day 9: 1445 Zulu

"Well, here they are," Delano said, gazing through the viewport at the three immense Ktarran ships drifting effortlessly toward the Station. In space, without the usual reference points, he'd had trouble gauging objects' size and range. Not so with these. When the Ktarran vessels halted, less than a kilometer separated them from Delano's viewport. These latest visitors to the Station looked huge. The sensors confirmed it. Even the smallest behemoth was over three times the size of the Talmak's vessel. No wonder the Tarlons and Halkins wanted nothing to do with facing such battleships.

Not that it mattered. All the hurried planning, the desperate preparation and training, the studying, and likely Delano's life would soon be put to the test. Not only his own life. Because of him, the other nine people remaining aboard the Station might die as well. Delano hated the responsibility, but the time for doubts and worries had passed.

Unlike the cautious Halkins, who had remained hundreds of kilometers away when they first approached, the Ktarrans showed no fear of drawing near to the Station. All three ships blazed with the power of their plasma shields, flickering fields of blue, red, and purple that resembled a pulsating evil creature.

The stunning, almost hypnotic effect caught and held the eye, a terrifying display quite unlike the Halkins' or Talmak's. What little could be glimpsed through the plasma fields only added to the image of nightmarish horror. The ships' beam weapon turrets appeared malevolent, like multiple bulbous eyes protruding from the face of a giant beast of prey. Each weapon seemed to be pointed at the Station.

Idly, Delano started counting the beam weapons of each ship. One ship showed nine beam projectors, the second eleven, and the largest vessel of the three displayed twelve. If these beams produced as much destructive power as the Tarlon devices, the Ktarrans had arrived with more than enough armaments to destroy as many of

Earth's cities as they wished.

"Look upon my works, ye Mighty, and despair!" Delano shook his head.

"Quoting Shelley." Lian stood beside Delano, holding onto his arm. "I'm impressed. By you, not the Ktarrans." She lowered her voice. "They are enormous, much larger than I expected."

"That's the impression they want," he said. "With battleships like these, you have machines that are instruments of terror, plain and simple. You could probably build three or four destroyers for the same price and effort, with the same firepower. These ships are meant to strike fear into the minds of their subjects."

"And they also want to show their indifference," Lian said. "They obviously know we puny humans have nothing that can harm them."

"We'll see about that," Delano said. "Who knows, we may get lucky."

"Big ugly brutes," Kosloff added as he gazed at the unwelcome guests. "Maybe we should have gotten out when we had the chance."

Delano, thinking much the same thing, shrugged in resignation. In any case the automated escape shuttle couldn't have taken all of them. It departed hours ago, carrying only three aboard – Darrell Parrish, Maks, and the still very sick Dr. Stepanov. Parrish had protested vehemently, to Delano's surprise. He'd had to tell the brave young biologist that he knew far too much about human physiology to risk capture.

The others had decided to remain and fight. Of those choosing to stay, the most unexpected was Peter's wife, Linda. Her husband had openly urged her to return to Earth, but she refused to even consider it. Despite the danger, Peter set aside his own misgivings. He had no intention of leaving his new bride's side.

The team's response had touched Delano, though now he had the added worry of so many people. "Steve, any response on the open channel?"

"Nothing, and we're still broadcasting," Steve called out from the communications console. "The Halkins figured out our comm channel in less than an hour. These bastards have been listening for half a day."

Which meant they didn't give a damn. Another twenty minutes passed. Delano and Lian remained in front of the viewport window, almost directly facing the largest ship. If the Ktarrans possessed a telescope or binoculars, they could see them moving about. So why didn't they answer? Why didn't they at least signal that they were aware of the crew's existence? He guessed the Ktarrans were studying Earth and the Station, sizing up their new conquest.

The answer came without warning. Two beams of pulsing light burst into existence, not from the big ship, but from the one to Delano's right. Instinctively he closed his eyes and threw up his hands. There was no explosion but the Station shook and rattled when fragments of equipment and metal, blasted off the exterior surface, struck the hull. As portions of the Station's frame expanded and shattered from the sudden heat of the Ktarran weapons, Delano heard a noise unlike anything he'd ever heard before – the screeching sound of twisting metal and bursting seams coming through the steel bulkheads. The anguished cry of a wounded ship.

Well, that was fast. Delano braced himself for the hull's collapse, but seconds passed and nothing happened. The Station remained intact.

"Derr`mo, the telescope is gone!" Colonel Kosloff shouted, slipping into Russian. "Sliced off the hull."

Delano automatically translated the coarse phrase – *shit*! The big telescope did look like a weapon, though it faced away from the Ktarran ships. But from their point of view, why take a chance?

More bad news arrived when Welsh's voice came through the Station's intercom. "Major, half the Engine compartment is gone! Fucking gone! I can see it on the camera. The beam sliced it off."

"Welsh, you guys OK?" Delano had to force himself to speak softly.

"Yeah, so far. Give me a minute."

"Major, this is Stecker. What the hell happened? Something banged against the compartment's inner wall. There's a big fucking dent."

Before Delano could answer, Welsh's voice cut in. "Delano, a big chunk of the engine section is missing. Carved off. The hull is breached. The only thing we've got keeping out the vacuum from the Exercise compartment is an interior hatch that happened to be closed."

Derr`mo it is, Delano thought, and we're in it up to our eyeballs.

But the Station remained in one piece, so obviously the Ktarrans hadn't wanted to kill them. No, these were precise beam blasts to demonstrate both Ktarran accuracy and power.

"Welsh, did we lose the rockets?" Delano tried to keep the worry out of his voice. If the booster rockets were gone, most of his defense plan had vanished with them.

"I'll have to reposition a different hull camera to get a look at the portside boom," Welsh said. "Give me a minute."

Delano used his intercom. "Gunny, is your team OK?"

"Yeah, Linda and Petrov are here. We're still breathing. What happened?"

"The Ktarrans took a shot at us," Delano said. "Just to show us what they can do."

More than a minute ticked by. Nobody talked. Delano felt the sweat under his arms, despite the cooling air. Then the comm came back to life.

"Delano, this is Welsh. The hull camera shows the boosters still attached to the portside cargo boom. Another three or four meters . . . if they'd been hit by the Ktarran beam, we'd all be dead. But the rear of the Station is mostly gone. The beam cut through both Water Tank compartments, Atmosphere Control, and Engineering Control. Parts of the Station are open to vacuum. Fortunately the pressure doors on C-corridor and E-corridor automatically slammed shut. The Exercise compartment wasn't touched. Everything else appears to be holding. For now."

Stecker and his team were in Engine Storage compartment A, and the two booster rockets were attached to the cargo boom right behind them. Apparently the Ktarran beam had cut through the Station at a slight angle. Otherwise, Welsh's team and the Gunny's would be gone, even if the booster rockets hadn't exploded.

"Got it," Delano replied. "Welsh, Gunny, seems like everyone is OK. Welsh, can you still follow the plan?"

"Yes, we should be all right. Peter and I were already inside, setting up. We just got all our gear moved in. Peter says the Exercise compartment walls are holding. Thank God that compartment has two access doors. So we're still good to go."

"Great. Hang in there." Delano took a deep breath and let it out slow. *Stay calm.* If you let yourself show your nerves, the others will begin to doubt, too.

"Major! The Ktarrans are on the open comm channel!" Steve shouted in his excitement. "I'm getting a feed."

Slipping into the same chair he'd used when talking with the Halkins, Delano peered at the primary monitor. A flickering of colors gradually disappeared. Then he was looking into what had to be the bridge of the alien ship.

The Ktarran wide angle camera revealed a cavernous chamber with about fifteen creatures sitting or standing at various stations. A quick glance showed at least three different species. Farthest from the camera, an imposing Ktarran wearing a dull red garment sat on what appeared to be a raised control chair with wide arms.

The Tarlons had not exaggerated their description of the Ktarran life form. Nor had their pictures and images done it justice. Satan on his black throne would not have looked as evil or menacing. If they wanted to frighten the humans on the Station, they had succeeded.

The Ktarran tech working their camera tightened its focus and zoomed in for a close-up of the grandiose chair. The being seated on it had to be the ship's captain.

The creature resembled a great bear with a powerful protruding jaw. Short arms supported two formidable hands, easily twice the size of Gunny Stecker's. A thumb and three fingers, each tipped with a thick black claw, added to the image of a hunting animal. The hands did not hang at the creature's side, or rest on its thighs. They hovered in the air a few inches away from the chest, as if ready to rend and tear the flesh of its prey.

Delano decided his bear comparison was wrong. Instead of fur, the Ktarran had a thick hide that resembled cured leather, light brown with random patches of deep green. Natural tropical camouflage, so it probably started as a jungle beast. Bright red eyes with yellow pupils glowered into the camera. Delano couldn't see any hair, but the form-fitting vest with four loose pockets might account for that.

All sentients, Delano decided, needed pockets and places to carry their cigarettes and phones. *Focus, you idiot*!

Delano bowed to the camera. "We are unarmed. We have no defensive screens. We wish only peace." He bowed again.

"What are you called?" The high pitched voice sounded out of place coming from so massive a creature. When it spoke, its large mouth exposed a jaw filled with sharp tipped, gleaming yellow teeth. The harsh gutturals of the Ktarran language flowed smoothly from its mouth.

Even so, Delano had to think to translate. The Ktarran language, as spoken by a Ktarran, sounded different, more effortless than the way the Halkins spoke it. "I am called Delano. We want . . ."

"What are you called? All animals have a name for themselves."

Always start with an insult must be Ktarran first contact doctrine. "We are known as humans. Our planet is Earth. What is your name?"

"I am Turhan of the Sineval Clan, Subduer of the Xon and Shuggren. Your planet now belongs to me, as does every living animal on it. You will obey our commands." Turhan paused, to let that sink in. "How did you learn to speak our language?"

"Halkins visited this place seven of your cycles ago," Delano said, using the Ktarran thirty-two hour equivalent for an Earth day. "They were our first contact with other life forms. They threatened to attack our planet. To prevent that we gave them some slight assistance, and in the process learned your language."

"Where are the Halkins now?" Turhan showed no concern that Halkin ships might be lurking nearby, only curiosity.

"They left two cycles ago," Delano said. "We do not know where they went."

"The punishment for helping any of our animals escape is death," Turhan said, his teeth flashing.

That jaw could rip my arm right off. Delano resisted the urge to shudder. "We did not know they were your enemy . . . your animals," he said, doing his best to grovel. "We wish only friendship with other species." A message from Steve appeared on the other monitor. *Earth still receiving the feed.*

Obviously the Ktarrans weren't worried that the Station's radio transmissions to Earth continued.

Turhan uttered a guttural sound that might be laughter, though his long claws twitched as if in anticipation. "Ktarrans have no need for friends, only slaves and food animals. Your planet must be punished."

So much for the friendly alien, we come in peace option. The leaders of the Alliance would get the message. It would be war. Just the same, if there were any chance to save Earth, Delano had to keep trying. "We humans have much to offer in trade and . . ."

But the Ktarran had lost interest in talking to "his" new animals. "You will come aboard my ship now for examination. Bring four others. Leave now, before I destroy your ship."

"We have no transport . . . no small craft," Delano said. "Our only means of returning to the planet left a cycle ago."

Turhan the Subduer didn't like hearing that. He turned aside and spoke to one of his crew, but Delano couldn't make out the words. After listening to a response, Turhan turned back toward the Ktarran camera. "I will send a transport craft to bring you here. Obey all orders from the inspection team. If you've lied, if you resist, you will all die."

"We have no ship, and we will not resist," Delano said. "There are only ten of us, and we have no weapons."

But Turhan had moved on. He said something to one of his crew, and a moment later the Ktarran end of the alien Ship-to-Station transmission link shut down.

Delano recognized Turhan's unspoken message. The Germans had the precise word for it – *Verachtung* – complete and total contempt.

Delano glanced at Lian. "What did he say? Did you catch that last sentence?"

"I think he ordered the other ships to proceed with the attack," she said. "Look, they're leaving. Both of them."

Without wasting a moment. Damn, they really are confident. The Ktarran ships, no doubt expecting the order, moved gracefully away from the Station and started their descent toward the planet. They would be in attack range within minutes.

"Cut our link to the Ktarran ship, Steve," Delano ordered. He let his body float up from the chair. "Confirm that Klegg got all that, and he knows the Ktarrans are coming. It's game time, people. Kosloff, you better get out of here. We don't know how long it will take the Ktarrans to send a shuttle."

"Yes, if only we could," Kosloff muttered. "Get out of here, I mean." He lingered for a moment, then extended his hand. "Major Delano, it's been a pleasure serving with you."

Delano took it and grinned. "I feel the same way, Colonel. You've been a big help. And we're not dead yet, Kosloff. Only two ships are moving out, so Earth has a chance."

"Yes, of course. For us, it will be a fair fight. One against one."

"Right." They both smiled. "Better get going," Delano said. "I'm sure Colonel Welsh needs your help." Kosloff swam away, heading for the Exercise compartment to join Peter and Welsh.

Time to move on to the next crisis, Delano thought. "Steve, where's Linda?"

"I'm here, Major," Linda said, pushing herself through the door frame and into the Control Room. A red medical kit hung around her neck. "Who's first?" She pulled a syringe injector from the kit.

"That would be me," Delano said moving toward her. "What bad drugs are you selling today?"

She shoved the nozzle against his arm and pulled the trigger. "For you, no charge. It's Linda's special secret recipe – a super dose of painkiller – you can lose an arm or a leg and barely notice. It also contains a slow release adrenaline boost, plus a little bit of my own concoction – a dose of glutamate to speed you up, with a little dopamine to improve your cognitive function. It's a formula the miners on Io use when they get injured or need a pick-me-up. If they use too much, sometimes it kills them."

"Sounds perfect," Delano said. "No wonder Peter loves you."

She laughed. "You're going to feel real good about yourself, believe you can do anything, even the impossible. Oh, by the way, you'll reach macho level in about three minutes, so try not to do anything stupid."

"Damn, that hurt." Delano rubbed his bicep until the sting faded away. A large dose, he guessed. He'd seen military stimulants used in the field, before and during a firefight or some other close encounter with the enemy. He'd used them himself a couple of times, but he'd never heard of anything like her concoction. No doubt it had some serious side effects, but right now that didn't concern him.

"How long will the dose last?" Delano realized he should have asked that question before Linda started.

"About ninety minutes, maybe two hours," Linda said. "After that, you'll crash pretty hard. You'll need to rest at least three hours."

Lian received the second injection. Shen, who had just returned to the Control Room, received the third, and Steve the fourth.

"Lian, better watch these guys," Linda said. "Their testosterone is going to spike and they'll probably start fighting with each other."

The Asian linguist nodded. "How will it affect me?"

"You'll feel pretty tough, too." Linda turned the gun on herself and pulled the trigger. "It may boost your pheromone production, so don't operate any heavy machinery or sign any important papers." Linda's light-hearted words broke the tension, at least a little.

Delano and Lian both laughed. "Better get down to Gunny Stecker and take care of the rest," he said. "Anything on the monitor yet, Steve?"

"No, nothing. Big ugly is still just sitting there."

Delano sat back down and donned the curved shooting glasses, secured by a thin, almost unnoticeable elastic band around the back of the head. The lightweight ballistic glass, primarily meant to protect the eyes from shell ejections, possessed a secondary capability. The glasses could be polarized to allow as much or as little light to pass through the lenses. He activated the glasses, then turned them down. The light level in the Control Room, already set to a much lower level than normal, dimmed considerably.

Sgt. Shen handed Delano a pair of shooters' ears. The plugs, a combination of hard and flexible material, would block sound waves up to a hundred and eighty-five decibels, except for those within a certain frequency range.

"Put one in each ear," Shen said, "push it all the way, and press the button. The material will configure itself to your ear canal and make a tight seal. Put the control in your pocket. I've already programmed each device. All it will let through is sound in our normal conversational range. Anything above or below will be blocked. Most of it."

Delano inserted the ear plug, shoved deep into the ear canal, then pushed the button with his pinky. He'd never seen anything like this before either, didn't even know this technology existed. It might be Chinese made, courtesy of Sgt. Shen. The foam-like material expanded in his ear canal, filling the chamber and pressing painfully on his eardrum. By the time he had the second inserted, Shen had passed out all of them. Gradually the pressure on Delano's ear drums eased off, as the flexible material conformed to his ear canal.

"How do we know if they're working?" Delano could hear his voice, though it sounded a bit odd to him.

"They're working." Shen's voice sounded a bit strange, too. He smacked his hand hard on the table.

To Delano, the noise sounded like a tap of a finger.

"The louder the sound, the more it is neutralized. The chip in each plug reacts almost instantly to the decibel level and compensates."

We're about to find out how fast "almost instantly" really is. Delano tried to settle himself in the chair. Nothing was happening and all the preparations in the Control Room were completed. His fingers drummed on the table and he couldn't seem to find a comfortable position. He wanted to get up and move around, burn off some adrenaline, but in zero gravity that didn't really work.

When his comm link went active, Delano jumped at the resonance.

"Major, I've given everyone their injections." Linda's voice sounded a bit breathless. Even if you knew what was in the drugs, didn't mean you wouldn't be affected by them.

"Major, Gunny here. We're all set."

"OK, and good hunting. Colonel Welsh, are you ready?"

"Yes, Major. Peter and Kosloff are suiting up. All our gear is ready."

"Then we'll open the Main Airlock outer door," Delano said. "Steve's already turned on the docking bay lights, so they'll know where to board. Good luck to everyone."

"Yeah, you, too, Major. See you on the flip side." Gunny signed off.

Fifteen minutes passed slowly, almost agonizingly, with nothing from the Ktarrans. How long did it take to put together a prize crew to take over a ship? Now Delano wondered whether Linda's shots would wear off before the fucking Ktarrans got around to sending the shuttle. Another Marine Corps basic training quote came to mind. *Assumptions lead to bad decisions which lead to fatal consequences.*

"Major, just got a message from Klegg's Headquarters," Steve said. "The Ktarran ships are attacking Earth. One started on Japan, and the other on the North American West Coast. Acapulco took the first hit, then they moved on to Mexico City. Damn, I can see the smoke from here."

Delano didn't realize he'd clenched his fists, not until his fingernails dug into his palms. The Ktarrans were killing millions of people, for no reason except the pleasure it gave them. A feeling of rage surged through his body. Lian saw his tight jaw and took his hand. He nodded, sighed, and slowed his thoughts.

"There's something happening on the ship!" Steve's voice sounded more high pitched than usual, as if he were back in puberty.

Delano turned to the monitor, grateful for anything that ended the inaction. A small shuttle craft, at least compared to the Ktarran mothership, crept out from the plasma field. Meter by meter it glided through the screens until it broke free. Then with a few puffs of some type of vapor it moved smoothly toward the Station.

He studied the approaching craft, longer and thicker than the Halkin shuttle, as it gradually drew closer. A single, wide viewport on its nose showed vague movement within. Delano guessed that someone with shuttle experience, like Peter Tasco, could probably make a good estimate of its crew size. If the Ktarrans sent a big contingent, the Station wouldn't have much of a chance. Everything now depended on the Ktarrans doing what they customarily did.

"What do you think?" Lian, seated beside him, had kept hold of his hand.

Her presence reassured him. One way or another, Lian would not end up in Ktarran clutches. He'd save one bullet for her, if it came to that. No doubt Shen would be thinking the same thoughts. "It can't carry too many aliens," Delano said. "Not if it needs to ferry ten of us back to the ship."

"Maybe they intend to kill a few of us," she said.

"That's likely, but not until they know who's who. They won't want to exterminate any leaders or engineers." He glanced at her. "Or linguists. They'll definitely want the two of us alive, so they can begin communicating with Earth."

Delano put his other hand atop hers. "Lian, just wanted to say . . . working with you . . . it's been good. Without you, we never would have learned the Tarlon language." That sounded lame. What the hell, they were probably going to be dead within the hour. "I really wish we'd had more time to get to know one another. I'd . . . uh, I'd like to . . ."

She moved her grip to his arm, pulling herself closer. "I know. I feel the same way. Perhaps we can . . ."

Another shout from Steve interrupted her words. "Jeez, the Ktarrans ships are still blasting Earth! The Japanese Islands are already torched, and they're moving on to Korea."

Delano blocked that thought. What happened on Earth didn't matter anymore. Right now, he couldn't help them, and they couldn't help him. "Good luck, Lian."

"To both of us," she said, releasing his arm and turning away.

Chapter 23

Airspace above Huairen Air Base, China

Day 9: 1529 Zulu

As luck would have it, Major Peng, still circling in his Strike Fighter, didn't have long to wait. The first message came from the Chengdu Base. "This is LION to all pilots. Hold your positions and standby. One enemy spacecraft has entered near-earth orbit and is attacking cities in Japan. South Korea will likely be next."

Peng decided that would keep the alien ship busy for some time. Japan was as densely packed as China, and Seoul in Korea was even more crowded. He eased his aircraft into a slight climb and turned the nose eastward. Peng immediately spotted the alien spacecraft on his radar, just over four hundred kilometers above sea level and about sixteen hundred kilometers away.

"*Go se*," he muttered. *Shit.* From the size of the blip, the fucker looked enormous, even at this distance.

He knew it would be Beijing's turn soon. Even if the spacecraft remained stationary, Earth's rotation would soon bring the Chinese capital or Shanghai within range.

Peng decided to top off his fuel tanks, despite still having almost sixty percent of his fuel. He dropped down six kilometers and located the tanker. The big aircraft waited alone, with no fighter escort. In ten minutes he topped off his tanks, pulled away, and climbed back to ten kilometers.

The next LION broadcast brought the bad news. "Enemy ship approaching Beijing. All pilots, hold your position." Peng checked his radar and saw the alien spacecraft had dropped down to three hundred fifty kilometers. He wondered what delayed the pilots' attack order. The missiles could reach that height.

However China's fleet of almost a hundred fighters held position at ten kilometers. Thirteen minutes passed before another LION message arrived. "Enemy spaceship attacking Beijing. First wave, commence attack."

The first wave of missile-carrying fighters started climbing. Almost sixty fighter jets ascended to sixteen kilometers. He knew from the briefing that these aircraft carried only conventional weapons, no nuclear warheads. That seemed like a stupid waste of a first counterstrike, but hopefully somebody in command knew what they were doing. Peng could track both planes and their missiles on his radar.

As he watched, he saw the planes race upward and launch their missiles. Then ships and missiles began to vanish from the screen, each disappearance marked by a visible explosion. A glance out of the cockpit showed wide beams of reddish light flashing down from the alien ship. A single touch of the beam made any plane or missile explode or burst into flames. In less than a minute, the initial wave of fighters was either destroyed or running for the deck. Most had launched their missiles, and Peng had noted several upper atmosphere blasts, but none anywhere near the alien ship.

He couldn't believe what he'd just witnessed in less than three minutes. The flickering beams, moving almost too fast for the eye to follow, had swept the sky and blasted every missile and half the aircraft from the sky. Flaming wreckage fell toward the ground, almost like a fireworks display. When the last plane had scrambled beyond the beams, no aircraft remained at the twelve kilometer level.

The alien ship's energy beams, which had widened to destroy the aircraft and missiles, narrowed again. The assault on Beijing resumed. Peng glanced down and saw huge swaths of China's capital and the adjacent military bases in flames. What looked like secondary explosions sparkled among the burning structures and enormous clouds of black smoke rose into the air. He watched one beam travel over the city's outskirts. Whatever it touched burst in flame.

The beams – he counted at least eight or ten – continued their destruction, but the second wave did not receive the attack order. For a moment he wondered if all the command centers, deep within their thick bunkers, had been destroyed.

The assault on Beijing continued. In fact, the alien vessel descended even lower, which Peng guessed would increase the devastation. Still no attack order was given, and the alien spaceship spiraled ever closer.

Peng worried about his wife, pregnant with his first child. She lived with his parents in Mancheng, only a hundred and eighty kilometers from Beijing. The small city, less than a million, might not attract the alien spaceship today. But if the aliens were not stopped, who knew how long it might take them to target Mancheng.

He pushed aside thoughts of his family. Peng checked his targeting computer and observed the alien vessel now holding position only two hundred and seventy kilometers above the city. If the attacks didn't cease, in thirty minutes Beijing would be a smoldering ruin. He wondered if Command had forgotten about him, if he should launch his missiles anyway. Perhaps he should break radio silence and ask if his orders had changed.

Get your emotions under control. Peng realized his hands were shaking. Watching the devastation of China's capital and the slaughter of his fellow pilots, had rattled his nerves. He remembered General Jang's words. *Do your duty. Follow your orders.*

Then a strange voice blared in his ears. Definitely an American speaking Chinese.

"FOX this is EAGLE. FOX this is EAGLE. Transmitting your target coordinates."

The message from the Americans was clear enough. As he received the data, Peng punched them into the fighter's computer.

"FOX, this is EAGLE. Repeat back the coordinates."

He did so, forcing himself to speak clearly.

"FOX, you are good to go. Launch at maximum altitude at once. Repeat, FOX, attack at once. Good hunting. EAGLE out."

Peng acknowledged the command even as he switched the strike fighter's fuel system to the external fuel tanks. Then he pulled back on the stick, and shoved the throttle to the max. In two minutes the tanks were nearly empty and he'd reached thirteen kilometers, still climbing at a steep angle. He dropped the externals, switched back to the internal tanks and kept climbing.

As his fighter clawed its way upward, Peng wondered if the LION Command Base still existed. Perhaps it had already been destroyed. But no, he heard LION transmit the attack orders for the second wave. The remaining fighters, less than forty, were to gain altitude and prepare to attack. Those fighters began to climb and move toward the alien ship.

Peng's trajectory took him far to the left of the massive

spaceship. For a moment, he asked himself if he had entered the wrong coordinates. But no, the American had confirmed them. Unless they both had made a mistake . . .

At sixteen kilometers, Peng had a clear view of the enemy spacecraft off to his right. Dark red beams of energy radiated downward from the craft, either wreaking havoc on the city below or perhaps now targeting the remaining fighters closing in. Then he had no more time for observations. He concentrated on his plane, rocketing upward, and traveling now at close to Mach 3.

Peng kept climbing. He crossed eighteen kilometers, or about sixty thousand feet, the theoretical maximum for this fighter, and felt the controls grow sluggish. At this altitude, the air thinned. Without sufficient air flow over the wings and despite the plane's speed, it handled poorly. The nose drifted. Peng needed all his expertise and a delicate touch to keep the Strike Fighter aimed at the target. Soon the plane would stall, and then he would be unable to launch. The time had arrived.

At twenty kilometers he fired the first missile. It dropped cleanly off the rail and accelerated away, accelerating to Mach 3.5, its long flaming tail clearly marking its passage. Ten seconds later Peng launched the second warhead and watched it shoot out from beneath the craft. Good. Two clean releases. Both weapons were on their way. Time to get back to base.

As he started to level out, Peng heard the attack and launch orders being issued to the second wave and knew those pilots would soon be racing toward the alien ship. They would try to avoid the beams for as long as they could, then release their missiles. Peng knew at least a dozen of these fighters carried nuclear missiles, and he hoped they reached the alien ship. He checked his coordinates. His target was to the west and north of the ship, and as far as he could see, simply empty space except for the Moon in the background.

Peng pushed down the stick of the Strike Fighter, but because of the thin air, the aircraft didn't respond. The nose stubbornly remained pointed upward, and now the back end of the fighter began to sag. He tried to correct but the controls refused to react. For a few seconds he fought the stick, but within moments he lost control. The engine flamed out, the fighter rolled over and began to fall, all aerodynamics lost.

In a moment the J-23 fighter started plummeting, turning itself into a falling brick. Inside the cockpit Peng struggled with the stick, trying to restore stability. The tumbling motion slung him from side to side, his helmet banging again and again against one side of the canopy or the other. He didn't dare try to restart the engine, as it would turn the craft into a roman candle, spinning completely out of pilot or computer control.

The altimeter spun down, the force of gravity accelerating the fighter's fall faster and faster. The onboard computer's voice announced "Propulsion System Failure, Navigation System Failure, Targeting System Failure, Atmospheric System Failure," until the monitoring system itself failed.

Outside the windscreen the sky alternated with the ground every three or four seconds. At six kilometers, Peng prepared to eject despite the risk, but even that last ditch effort needed the plane to be somewhat level.

Then for a few seconds the jet fell straight down. Instantly he switched on the manual fly-up selector and trimmed the wings. Peng pushed the engine restart button. The engine whined, but didn't restart. The ground grew closer and closer, the bird aimed like an arrow directly at the ground. Suddenly he knew he was going to die.

Desperate, Peng punched the restart again. This time the whine disappeared in a rush of power and the fighter shook. But he continued falling straight down. If he couldn't pull out soon, he'd corkscrew right into the ground. He wrestled with the stick for another ten seconds, before the nose began to lift.

When Peng finally leveled off, he was less than a kilometer above the ground. The J-23 shuddered and rumbled, but it held together despite the extreme stress. Peng managed to climb a little. His head pounded and one of his eyes wouldn't focus. He could taste metallic blood inside his mouth and feel it on his face.

Five minutes later he located the base at Huairen, lowered the wheels, and made a quick descent. His radio refused to work, so he just came in, hoping no one else would be in his way. Then the wheels banged down hard on the runway, hard enough to rattle his teeth. The fighter bounced back up into the air, before it finally thumped onto the concrete. The worst landing in his career. Peng managed to stop a few meters before the tarmac ended. When he tried to turn off the runway, the nose wheel collapsed, and with a grinding of metal the aircraft finally came to rest.

Exhaustion swept over him. His hands shook, his head throbbed in his helmet from the repeated banging against the canopy, and his entire body trembled from the physical and mental strain. He'd come so close to death. Another few seconds, and he wouldn't have had enough room to pull up.

Blood now dripped steadily down his chin. But at least he'd completed the mission, and brought the bird down in one piece. Peng's part of Earth's first space battle had ended. He had no idea what he'd accomplished, if anything, or what had happened to the second wave of fighters. He'd survived, and right now nothing else mattered.

Chapter 24

Aboard the Tarlon ship *Ningpo*

Day 9: 1536 Zulu

In the ship's control room, the Talmak stood beside Jarendo, who had not taken his usual seat at the navigation station. Instead Jarendo sat at the backup science console monitoring a probe the Tarlons launched earlier.

The Talmak's ship, along with the two Halkin vessels, nestled in a small crater on the far side of the Moon. The mini-fleet had completed its preparations, and now rested on the lunar surface sheltered by the crater's low walls. Meanwhile the Ktarrans paid a brief visit to Earth's lunar settlements, all on the nearside of the Moon, blasting everything above ground into rubble.

That bombardment did not concern the Talmak. Instead he prepared for the coming encounter, one that carried enormous risks and consequences the pleading humans could scarcely comprehend. But Delano and Lian made a persuasive argument to the Tarlons and an emotional one to the Halkins. And so now they would attack two or three Ktarran battle cruisers, any one of which had the advantage of power and weapons over the three of them.

Once again, the Talmak worried about his decision. The human Delano had proved clever, subtly baiting Horath until the Halkin's pride demanded that he stay and fight. Not that Horath didn't know what the human intended, but once the Talmak declared his intention to remain, the Halkin had no other choice but to join in. Horath's honor would not let him leave while his companions and allies went into battle against his enemy.

The Tarlon tracking probe, six thousand meters away, hovered just above the lunar surface, where it had line-of-sight to both the Station and Earth. It would monitor the Ktarran ships and relay their positions to Jarendo's console. As long as the Tarlons kept their ship in the crater, and their instruments and screens at low power, the three ships would likely remain undetected. The two Halkin vessels had grounded themselves next to the Talmak's. For this mission, Horath would take his lead from War Captain Kaneel and the Tarlon ship.

The remote device transmitted its observations to Jarendo's screen. Now everything depended on the Ktarrans following their usual procedures. Otherwise the Tarlons and Halkins would be in trouble. The commanders on Earth had already broadcast the Ktarran bombardment of the Moon. With the lunar bases blasted to rubble, the Ktarran fleet moved quickly to begin its assault on Earth. The three Ktarran ships had stopped at the Station. On board the *Ningpo*, Captain Kaneel waited patiently, at least outwardly, for the enemy's next move.

"The Ktarrans cruisers are moving into high orbit around the . . . Earth, heading for the Station." At least the navigator had learned the correct name for the alien planet and its confusing inhabitants. Not long afterward came the second report. "The first signal from Earth has arrived. Two ships have left the Station, descended into lower orbit and begun attacking the planet's cities."

The War Captain accepted what was for now good news. As long as the Ktarran captain of the third battle cruiser remained focused on the Station a little longer, Delano's plan had a chance of success.

"*Ningpo* and the Halkin ships are ready," Jarendo announced, proud that his crew completed its preparations faster than expected. The human Lian had translated the *Ningpo's* name as '*Wanderer.*'

The Talmak placed his hand on Jarendo's shoulder, then turned to War Leader and Captain Kaneel, who would lead the attack, and spoke the words that gave Kaneel complete command of the *Ningpo*. "Please initiate the mission."

"Please take your seat, Talmak," Kaneel said. Then, settling into his command chair, he turned to his crew. "Lift off the surface." He fastened the wide seat belt that would secure him. For most of this operation, the gravity generators would be off, along with every other nonessential system. Kaneel's words were broadcast to the two adjacent Halkin ships, but at such low power that anyone more than a few kilometers distant would be unable to detect the transmission. "Jarendo, position the ship to begin the attack."

"Yes, War Commander," Jarendo replied, shifting to his usual station.

The Talmak secured his own belt. Everything had now passed beyond his control. He wondered what it would be like to die. He had enjoyed an extended lifespan, and might live as long again in the future, if not for this horrible, ceaseless war with the Ktarrans.

Still, what mattered a few more deaths in an endless war that killed billions of sentients? The human Delano had enticed the Tarlons when he spoke words seldom used in reference to the Ktarrans – attack, not defend. Resist, not succumb. Victory, not survival. The humans indeed proved shrewd. Now the Talmak had to hope they would show themselves worthy.

The *Ningpo* rose from the Moon's surface and headed not toward the planet Earth, but away from it. The three ships would move two thousand kilometers from the Moon, always keeping the planet's single companion between themselves and the enemy ships now orbiting the planet. For this plan to be successful, surprise and speed were essential.

At two thousand kilometers, the three ships executed a turn, until their bows pointed back toward the lunar horizon. When the vessels confirmed their alignment, War Commander Kaneel glanced at the Talmak.

Your last chance to call this off, the Talmak understood. But the time has passed for that. He and the Halkins were committed. "You may begin, War Commander," the Talmak said, "as soon as you receive the signal from the humans."

The mini-fleet held its position. The Talmak had prepared himself for a long wait, but apparently the Ktarrans had wasted little time on the Station and its tiny crew. Another message arrived, broadcast from Earth. First, it confirmed what the probe monitored. Only two Ktarran ships had dropped down from the Station and started destroying cities. Second, it asked that the Tarlons stay their attack until receipt of a signal from the Alliance.

"So the Ktarrans have begun," the Talmak said. "The humans will learn a hard lesson."

"It is one we have all faced," Jarendo agreed.

The fateful waiting began. The Talmak wondered about Horath and his two ships, and if fear ever troubled the big Halkin. Meanwhile, time passed with maddening slowness and nothing happened. Perhaps the relay probe had failed. Out of his sight, Earth cities were being demolished. Or perhaps the humans, already crushed and defeated, had decided to surrender. It seemed as though enough time had elapsed to destroy half the planet. But then Jarendo announced the Alliance attack signal had been received. The moment for doubt had passed. The moment for action had arrived.

Even War Leader Kaneel appeared relieved to initiate the battle. "Begin attack run. Commence acceleration at half speed," he ordered. The *Ningpo* began to accelerate. It retraced its course, gaining velocity as it traveled back toward the Moon. Kaneel took a moment to verify that the Halkin ships maintained their proper positions. His commands were being broadcast to the Halkins. "Increase to designated maximum speed," the War Commander ordered. "Send the signal to the humans."

All three ships continued accelerating, and with each second the ships increased their velocity. The Tarlon vessel set the pace for the slightly slower Halkin ships, both now moving in on the *Ningpo*. They needed to be as close together as possible, almost touching, when they entered the hyperspace window. Only the *Ningpo* had sufficient energy to generate a plasma field large enough to encompass all three ships at one time. The two Halkin ships lacked the power to create a temporary hyperspace fissure. For each ship in the little fleet, this maneuver would be a first.

The risky tactic required close coordination, and the possibility of a collision remained high. Even momentary contact between ships or a brush with the wormhole walls might collapse the highly-unstable subspace opening. That would annihilate the Tarlons and Halkins in an instant.

"Humans report atomics detonated."

"Thermal bursts detected," Jarendo called out, his systems confirming the human message. The humans had launched their atomic missiles moments before Kaneel and his ships started their run. The weapons were targeted to explode above and to the side of the enemy cruisers. The resulting nuclear detonations, the human Delano assured the Tarlons, would emit a powerful electro-magnetic pulse, one strong enough to temporarily overload the Ktarran ships' sensors.

Most of the *Ningpo's* sensors had already been withdrawn into the plasma screen, to make certain that the ship's sensors remained unaffected. Now they could be once again extended into their proper positions.

The three ships raced ahead. On each vessel, secondary plasma fields were reduced to a minimum. Meanwhile, Kaneel ordered almost all generated power diverted to propulsion and maintaining hull integrity. He wanted his ships to travel at maximum velocity. At least each vessel in the mini-fleet had its energy compartments fully fueled, thanks to the humans' delivery of additional helium-3.

The three vessels hurled around the edge of the Moon and flung themselves toward the planet, continuing to accelerate at what the human Delano called Mach 4. The Talmak felt the heavy weight press upon his chest and found it difficult to breathe. The ship had never reached this velocity before.

At this acceleration, which the ships could sustain for only a brief time, the combined mass of the vessels, now traveling within a single plasma screen, would generate sufficient momentum. When the *Ningpo* activated her deep range plasma field, the ships would be traveling fast enough to open an artificial and narrow hyperspace window. Or so the theory claimed.

"Opening hyperspace wormhole," the propulsion officer called out. He had adjusted the screen generators with great care.

Staring through the forward monitor, the Talmak watched the dull golden glow of the conical opening appear.

"Enter hyperspace," Captain Kaneel ordered.

The *Ningpo*, flanked by the two Halkin ships, flung themselves through the artificial wormhole and disappeared into the hyperspace fissure. The little flotilla could exist inside that generated hyperspace for a very limited time, but within that span the mini-fleet would traverse almost nine tenths of the distance to the planet. An instant later, after an interval of time almost too small to be measured, the three ships burst out of hyperspace. If nothing had gone wrong, if the entry and exit calculations were precise, they would arrive above the planet Earth and almost within range of the unsuspecting Ktarrans.

At least the Talmak hoped they would be caught by surprise. If the Ktarrans detected the fleet's approach and were waiting . . .

Kaneel needed a moment to be certain his vessel had completed the exit to normal space. "Break formation," he ordered. Immediately the two Halkin ships moved apart, each vessel needing room to maneuver and to reestablish their screens. The image of the human planet, Earth, filled the forward monitors.

Jarendo sat at his console, assessing the situation. "Two Ktarran battle cruisers are attacking the planet. The third cruiser continues hovering near the human's Station. The attack signal is being broadcast. Humans have launched . . . missiles at both cruisers." His voice sounded deeper, a reaction to the high acceleration. The Tarlons' bodies, unlike the Halkins, could not endure such physical stresses for long.

"All screens to minimum power," Kaneel directed.

Jarendo glanced at the Talmak, both thinking the same thought. The human Delano had guessed right. Only two Ktarran ships had initiated the attack on the planet.

"Attack speed," Kaneel said. The effect of the command lowered the acceleration force. "All remaining power to the weapons. Horath, we see two Ktarran battleships. The *Ningpo* will attack the farther target." That last statement was for the Halkins, whose ships immediately began to diverge from the *Ningpo*. The Tarlon ship adjusted its course and headed for the slightly more distant Ktarran ship, which happened to be attacking the West Coast of the United States.

Aboard the Halkin ship, Horath scanned the monitors, his hands on the ship's main controls. For this maneuver, he trusted no one but himself to guide the craft. Horath had already closed most of the distance to the Ktarran cruiser. A little nearer and it would be in range. More important, Horath's ships, traveling at maximum speed, had not yet been detected.

Somehow the puny humans had succeeded. Their electromagnetic pulse must have temporarily blinded the Ktarran vessel. Its nonfunctional sensors would soon be replaced, but that would take time, and at this velocity, Horath didn't need much.

Horath saw that the nearest enemy ship was hovering nose down toward the planet. All of its energy weapons appeared fully engaged, as it attacked targets below or defended itself against any approaching missiles. Explosions blanketed the airspace far beneath the Ktarran vessel, as missiles and the atmosphere-only ships that launched them were blasted from existence.

Horath no longer cared about the humans or even the Tarlons. His blood called for revenge against the Ktarrans. No matter what happened to him or his ships, if he could help destroy this cruisier, he would avenge at least some of the murders of his people. "Continue at present speed. Set course for collision. All remaining power to the weapons. Commence firing as soon as we are in range. Target enemy propulsion system for as long as possible."

He intended to give his weapon controllers a dead-on target, and would turn away from a collision only at the last moment.

Five seconds later both Halkin ships activated their weapons. Four bright red beams of energy, two from each ship, lashed outward, each aimed at the rear of the unsuspecting Ktarran ship.

Aboard the Ktarran ship *Trigata*, Under-Captain Sudra sat in the massive control chair, raised up on a platform. This provided the Ktarran Captain with an unobstructed view of the entire compartment and every member of its crew complement. He had struggled for almost all his life to attain control of a Battle Cruiser. Despite vicious infighting with his rivals, Sudra had emerged victorious over the dead bodies of many of his kin.

Now he saw beneath him a planet filled with such riches of life, technology, and slaves that assured Sudra's and his clan's future. With this planet's conquest, he would advance to Full Captain. That promotion would ensure he would command both the *Trigata* and a second cruiser, with its Under-Captain groveling at his feet and eager to obey his every command.

Generations had passed since any Ktarran discovered such a world as this. The planet held many billions of life forms, and the ruling species had constructed vast numbers of cities and roads, easily visible from orbit. Truly a new race of semi-intelligent animals might be gleaned from the realm below. If the slaves proved half as valuable as Sudra expected, the wealth and prestige that would flow to his clan would be immense. Yes, he found much for a warrior to enjoy in this system.

Six primary system control stations formed a half-circle below Captain Sudra, but at a lower height so as not to obscure sight of his subordinates. These included Navigation, Plasma Screen Generation, Fuel Creation, Power Utilization, Sensor Array, and Weapons Control. All six stations were manned by a Ktarran and his Peltor assistant.

The Weapons Control station, located directly beneath the Captain's control chair, possessed two large display screens that could easily be monitored from Sudra's position. The Ktarran in charge of Weapons Control was the second in command of the *Trigata*.

Another half circle of nine stations, each manned by two Peltors, sat at the lowest level. These stations controlled the ship's individual weapons, each assigned a sector of space to defend or attack.

Sudra's ship struck the first blow at the new planet, pounding the population centers on the islands adjacent to a vast blue ocean. He left vast cities in flames, long smoking trails rising in the atmosphere. Secondary explosions contributed to the destruction. One target that Sudra attacked had been so massive that he slowed his ship until he felt satisfied that at least half the city lay in ruins.

He encountered no resistance. This planet possessed no defensive screens or beam weapons. Under-Captain Sudra took the ship down lower to increase the power of his nine energy weapons. By then the *Trigata* moved over a large land mass, blasting two cities on the coast before moving inland toward what had to be another major population center, this one surrounded by what looked like air fields and military bases.

The first resistance occurred as Captain Sudra commenced his assault on that city. A swarm of small aircraft rose up toward him, launching missiles which streaked upward toward his ship at an impressive speed, but still far too slow to present a threat. His Peltor weapon masters knew their business. The beams of high energy were widened, adjusted to maximum power, and they swept the thin atmosphere beneath them.

Anything touched by the directed energy flashed into incandescent dust. Some of the missiles exploded, but Sudra saw no atomic blasts, the only weapon that might present a minor threat to his ship. Of course he didn't expect that the animals of this world would have such weapons. Perhaps he should move the ship to an even lower orbit.

"Twenty-six missiles destroyed, Captain." The Ktarran Weapons Controller reported. "Attacking ships that survived are descending back to the surface. Should we return to striking the city?"

The animals inhabiting this place must have expended all their weapons, Sudra decided, and clearly they did not have even a rudimentary plasma shield to protect their missiles. "Yes, we will destroy this place as a lesson. Our new animals must learn that any attack on a Ktarran vessel will result in total destruction."

The energy weapons were refocused, narrowed for maximum power, and directed at the structures below, many already burning. Sudra would scorch this city to the ground as an example to the animals. But there were many targets, the beams were taking too long, and even these weapons could not function indefinitely. He gave another order. "Take the ship down to optimum attack distance."

The *Trigata* dropped closer to the surface. At this new lower altitude, the damage from his weapons would quickly devastate the city below.

One of the Peltor weapon controllers spoke up. "Single ship climbing toward us . . . no, not on attack vector. Heading away from us."

"Ignore it," Sudra ordered. "Continue attack."

"Ship has launched one . . . no, two missiles, but not directed at *Trigata*. Missiles are heading for open space. Should I destroy?"

The slave who commanded that weapon station knew his place. Ordered to destroy the city, he would not shift his beam weapons on his own authority except in an emergency.

Sudra glanced at his battle monitor. The planet's inhabitants obviously could not control a missile once launched, which confirmed how primitive their technology was. But better to be safe. Sudra was about to order the missiles destroyed . . .

"More air ships are on approach, Captain." The Ktarran Weapons Controller spoke up. His voice held more than a hint of surprise. "At least forty atmosphere ships climbing toward us.

"Destroy them," Sudra ordered. "Destroy them all."

The nine weapon stations switched back to defensive beam spread. Sudra watched on his monitor as the aircraft launched missiles that hurled themselves upward. But they remained far too slow compared to an energy beam that could blanket an area with high-energy particles moving at near the speed of light. One by one, the missiles were destroyed.

With the wave of missiles eliminated, the weapon controller returned to tracking the two mis-aimed projectiles, readjusting his weapons. Those two missiles continued far off course, still accelerating and heading for empty space.

"Ignore those," Sudra ordered. Even if they were atomic

devices, the distance separation would be far too great even to warm the ship's plasma screens or penetrate its photochromatic field, the main defensive layer against radiation and beam weapons.

"Yes, Captain," the Ktarran slave acknowledged, and once again swung his weapon down toward the planet, searching for any targets of opportunity.

Sudra returned to scanning the burning city below. A few moments later, the two off-course missiles exploded with a blaze of atomic energy, far more powerful than he'd expected. At that distance the blasts did nothing to his shields, but revealed that the animals of this planet did possess atomic weapons of considerable power.

"Sensors seven, eight, ten, eleven, and twelve damaged," announced the Ktarran tech monitoring the ship's sensors.

Sudra ignored that message. Those sensors were at the rear of the ship and projected out from the plasma fields. The strong nuclear explosions must have overloaded the instruments closest to the blast. For a moment he wondered why the animals hadn't tried to direct them toward his ship, but . . .

"Sensor nine reports incoming enemy ship! Two ships!"

Sudra's jaw gaped, and his tongue flickered in and out over his sharp teeth. No! There were no ships in this system. The animals had no ships, and the Halkins had departed long ago. *Or had they?*

"Two ships! Traveling at high speed! Halkin signature! Firing weapons!"

The words boomed through the control chamber. Sudra felt the *Trigata* shudder as the Halkin beams slammed into his screens. "All power to the shields!" He pounded his fist on the arm of his chair. "Now! Hurry!"

The crew obeyed with alacrity, but it required a few moments to rechannel the power to the photochromatic shield layer. Meanwhile, drained of power, the Ktarran beam weapons flickered and died.

"Ships still approaching at high speed . . . possible collision course!"

Sudra's ship trembled again, and this time an explosion rumbled through his vessel. He glimpsed the two ships, Halkins, flash by, passing so close and moving so fast that his weapon controllers had no time to aim their beams. Not that it mattered. With all the ship's power redirected to the plasma field, Sudra's weapons were useless.

Before Sudra's power utilization controllers could redirect power to the weapon stations, the Halkins had moved out of range. By the time the animals could slow their speed and return, Sudra would be ready to blast the Halkin creatures into atoms.

Then the damage reports began coming in.

"Aft compartments damaged. Main engine damaged. Power chamber two destroyed. Photochromatic shield down sixty percent, high energy shield down, laser shield at fifty percent." Almost every system was reporting serious malfunctions. The Halkin ships hadn't fired until they drew close, and their beams struck hard on his ship's stern.

"Bring secondary engine online," Sudra bellowed. The ship's orientation was drifting – the bow still pointed toward the city below – and he needed to regain control and climb higher. He bared his teeth in uncontrolled rage. At the very least Sudra would be chastised for this . . .

"Missiles on approach! Missiles closing!"

Sudra glared down at his view screen. Three missiles, faster than those launched earlier, were climbing, rising rapidly toward him. As he watched, the rockets powering two of them flamed out, then disappeared. But that did not stop their progress. "Move the ship. Move the ship!"

But the secondary engine had just switched over, and the *Trigata* responded sluggishly against the planet's gravity. The first animal missile, traveling at high speed, exploded its shaped charge ten meters from the ship. The non-atomic blast punched right through the weakened photochromatic shield and the nanotube layer. Almost the full force of the explosion lanced through the hull and into the ship. The detonation destroyed one of the plasma stanchions, and the nanotube defense layer disintegrated into individual, free flowing carbon atoms. Until repairs could be effected, the ship no longer possessed a defensive screen.

Sudra activated his communicator, transmitting his words to the other Ktarran cruiser attacking the planet. "We are under attack! Halkins. Need help . . ."

"Missiles closing in!" The Weapons Controller shouted to Captain Sudra.

His jaw gaped open again, but this time Sudra forgot the communicator. He could not tear his gaze from the view screen, and watched in horror as the remaining two missiles approached.

"Stop those missiles!" Sudra roared at his Weapons Commander. His ship had stopped drifting, the secondary engine finally beginning to move the big ship. But the beam weapons had not yet recharged, and Sudra had no way to destroy the missiles.

The magnetic fuses in the second missile locked onto the Ktarran mass, decided it was close enough, and detonated. Sudra never even saw the flash. The two-megaton atomic blast, which exploded less than a hundred meters away, demolished Under-Captain Sudra and his ship. Ten seconds later, the third missile arrived. Its nuclear explosion blasted what rubble remained of the *Trigata* into cosmic dust.

The Talmak's ship, still accelerating at Mach 4, flung itself toward the second Ktarran cruiser. Glancing around the *Ningpo's* control room, the Talmak observed the crew going about their duties. No one looked toward him, though he was the one who committed them to this battle, one they stood little likelihood of surviving.

"Commence attack as soon as in range," War Leader Kaneel ordered, a hint of satisfaction in his voice. "Target propulsion only."

"They have not detected us," Jarendo called out, excitement clear in his voice. "The humans' pulse weapon must have damaged their sensors."

The second Ktarran vessel was farther away from the EMP blast, but still close enough to overload some of its sensors. Then the commands and reports came in a rush.

"Humans are attacking with missiles."

"Opening fire at Ktarran. All three beam weapons at maximum and on target."

The *Ningpo* shuddered, and the lights and non-essential monitors within the control room dimmed and flickered from the abrupt power drain.

"Ktarran propulsion engines damaged, rear sensors damaged."

"Hold steady course," Kaneel ordered. "Get as close as possible without colliding."

"Ktarran attempting to gain altitude."

"Keep firing."

The *Ningpo's* attack run lasted less than fifteen seconds, from the firing of the first beam weapons to the moment the strike ended. The Talmak's ship flashed by the Ktarran vessel, clearing its plasma shields by less than thirty meters. The Tarlon gunners attempted to swing their beam weapons around. But by the time they managed that, the Ktarran ship was out of range and left far behind. The *Ningpo* continued its flight into empty space, traveling faster than its designers ever anticipated.

Kaneel had done his utmost. He'd damaged the Ktarran cruiser. Whether that would be enough for the humans to finish it off remained to be seen. Now he needed to save his ship, its crew, and especially the Talmak, before the enemy came after the *Ningpo*.

Aboard the second Ktarran battle cruiser on the other side of the great blue ocean, Full Captain Relnick also discovered a target-rich coastline. Sudra's ship had attacked against the planet's rotation, while Relnick drifted in the opposite direction. He'd followed the long coast line, starting above the equator and moving northward. Attracted by a large city nearly concealed beneath a layer of pollution, Relnick moved inward, blasting much of the city to ruins. Satisfied, he moved back toward the coast line. Cities and harbors burned beneath his passage, and with each advance to the north, the cities grew larger and larger.

A sprawling city with a vast complex of ships and docks burned ferociously before he ceased his attack and moved further north. Then he found an even larger city, this one spread out over a surface so extensive that Relnick could scarcely believe it. He turned his beams on the heavily populated city, starting with the harbor complex, then moving inland. The inhabitants lacked shields and offered no resistance.

Relnick didn't notice when Sudra's ship disappeared to the west, behind the curvature of the planet. With so much waiting to be destroyed and encountering no active defense from the planet, Captain Relnick ordered his ship lower into the atmosphere.

Leaving only smoking ruins behind, Relnick continued up the coast, striking at any target that seemed worthwhile. He reached another large city, this one encircling a wide, island-filled harbor, with several large bridges connecting the land masses. Relnick grunted in satisfaction as one of his beams sliced through the spans of the largest, sending the structure plunging into the blue water.

Suddenly a wave of aircraft approached from the east, and more than forty missiles were launched toward his ship. Some of the missiles came from high altitude, others from closer to the ground. His weapon stations responded efficiently, turning their weapons on this sudden menace of missiles and aircraft.

Most of these rockets were destroyed, but three reacted to the Ktarran beam weapons and exploded into blinding fireballs of atomic energy. Within seconds, three successive waves of radiation struck his ship.

The plasma screens, at close to full power, prevented any damage to the ship, but several forward sensors were burned out. Then a monitoring station reported a second group of aircraft were on approach. Damn these animals. Relnick had not expected them to have atomic weapons. He considered returning to a higher orbit.

"Sensors eight and ten and eleven damaged!"

Those sensors were near the rear of the ship, and shouldn't have been exposed to the nuclear shock wave from the missiles. Unless there was something above and behind him. "Defensive configuration," Relnick ordered, taking no chances. That directed sixty percent of the ship's available energy to the shields, thirty percent to the weapons, and ten percent to the ship's engines.

"Contact Under-Captain Sudra," Relnick ordered.

"Captain, a ship is approaching at a high rate of speed. Signature is that of the Tarlons."

Before Relnick could react, the Tarlon intruder fired its beam weapons at long range. Three beams of energy lashed out, all converging on his ship's power plant, and increasing in intensity as the Tarlon ship rapidly closed the gap. Fortunately for Relnick's ship, the plasma shields had just been strengthened, and the boosted fields absorbed most of the energy. But the Tarlon ship continued its high speed approach, and its weapons never ceased firing.

"Rear sensors damaged!"

"Enemy vessel closing! Possible collision!"

"Garbled response from Captain Sudra. Unable to establish contact."

Something was wrong with Sudra, but Relnick had his own problems to solve. He grasped the attack strategy. The Tarlon ship was making a single run, hoping to inflict enough damage to keep Relnick's ship from pursuing.

"Take the ship up," Relnick ordered. "Divert all power from weapons to engines. Engage backup engine.

"Still no response from Captain Sudra."

An explosion rumbled through Relnick's ship, and a moment later, the Tarlon vessel flashed by, still accelerating at high speed and definitely leaving the scene. But the Ktarran shields had mostly held, and hopefully any damage sustained would be minimal.

"Propulsion feeder system impaired. Operating at half-power."

Relnick swore again. That would delay moving power to and from the storage cells.

"Another wave of missiles approaching from the planet. Twenty-two missile trails detected."

If these were atomic, and Relnick had to assume some of them were, his ship might be in serious trouble. The Ktarran ship had started to climb, but slowly, too slowly. He would not be able to get out of range of the animals' incoming missiles.

"Defensive configuration," Relnick snapped. "Divert all power from engines to weapons." He wouldn't be able to maneuver, but he should still be able to blast the missiles before they could reach him.

"Sensors seven and twelve detect incoming missiles! Very high speed."

"How many?"

"Two, Captain! Wait! More missiles detected on same flight path, following the first two."

Fear surged through Relnick's thick body. Missiles were approaching from beneath his ship, while others, clearly launched from the other side of the planet, must have crossed the northern pole and were now streaking toward him far faster than the others.

By now Relnick recognized he faced a well-coordinated attack plan. If he were correct, these two incoming missiles would . . .

"Kill those missiles! Hurry! Kill them!"

Four weapons stations that could swivel their weapons toward the missiles did so. But before the beams could strike, the leading two missiles, launched thirty seconds before the others, exploded five seconds apart. A powerful EMP wave swept over his ship. Half the monitors in the control room went dark, their components temporarily overloaded or destroyed by the intense electromagnetic pulse.

"All rear sensors burned out! Believe two nuclear explosions."

Panic sounded in the voice of the Ktarran monitoring the ships sensors.

One rear sensor remained functional. "Sixteen missile trails coming through the blast cloud! Sixteen . . ."

For the first time in his life, Relnick felt death approaching. "All power to the shields!" He heard the dread in his voice.

The missiles began to explode, each nuclear blast sending a damaging wave of particles through the shields, and with each wave the shield weakened. More explosions from below struck the ship.

Relnick watched his plasma shields drop to thirty percent, nowhere near strong enough to . . .

Two more missiles from below, both carrying only conventional explosives and reaching their target only moments apart, slammed into his ship and exploded. The nanotube mesh, despite its strength, failed under the stress of the shaped explosives. A moment later one of the three shield generators collapsed, effectively eliminating the plasma shields.

Like Under-Captain Sudra, Captain Relnick never felt the nuclear explosion that blasted his ship, and tore it – and him – into fragments. By chance the detonation also released some of the anti-matter from its containment field, and that secondary discharge literally turned the Ktarran ship into individual molecules and atoms. The resulting explosion also released a blinding light high above San Francisco and visible across half the planet.

Aboard the fleeing *Ningpo*, updates continued to arrive. "Humans reporting that the first Ktarran cruiser, the one attacked by Horath, is destroyed by atomics."

"Sensors confirm report. First Ktarran cruiser destroyed."

Even the Talmak felt a surge of victory. One Ktarran battle cruiser destroyed! Even if the *Ningpo* didn't survive, the victory would be worth it.

"Human air ships and their missiles are attacking the second Ktarran vessel, the one we damaged."

"Wait! Humans reporting that second Ktarran cruiser damaged . . . no, destroyed by atomics! Both cruisers terminated!"

No one felt as much surprise, shock, as the Talmak. He turned to Kaneel, and saw the same emotion on his face. To eliminate one Ktarran vessel constituted a major victory. Two destroyed was unheard of. That left only the battle cruiser at the Station as an immediate threat to Earth, and the fourth ship at the Jupiter gate.

Delano had boasted that he and his team would at a minimum damage any Ktarran ship that tried to board his Station. The time for boastful human rhetoric had passed. If Delano wanted to save his planet, he had better deliver more than mere words.

Chapter 25

New International Space Station

Day 9: 1509 Zulu

In the Control Room, Delano watched the Ktarran transport as it leisurely moved toward the Station. At least the waiting had ended. He'd always struggled to control his nerves while he waited for the action to begin. As every soldier knew, the waiting sapped your strength and flooded your mind with doubts. Once the fighting began, a warrior could put aside his misgivings and fears, and concentrate on the only thing that mattered – staying alive and accomplishing the mission.

He pushed his feelings aside. The best thing he could do for Lian was kill these Ktarran sons of bitches, as many as possible. Whether it was thoughts of Lian, or Linda's drugs messing with his head, Delano clenched his jaw. The time had arrived to take care of business. "*Zabij bastardy*," he muttered.

Lian needed a moment to identify, then translate the Czech phrase. "Yes, kill the bastards," she said. "Before they destroy my country and yours. And our planet."

Delano nodded. His thoughts seemed clearer, his thinking sharp and quick. No doubts, no fear, only the urge to hurl himself into battle against these aliens. Now only the Ktarran battleship and its boarding party filled his mind. The aliens were coming to kill and torture and possibly feed on Delano's crew. Right now he wanted every one of them dead.

He glanced out the viewport. The enemy shuttle had crossed over toward the Station and decelerated as it aligned itself with the Station's Main Airlock. Peter and Kosloff had sealed the smaller one. The exterior lights would guide them in. Delano wondered how the Ktarrans would get onto the Station. The boarding party would need to cycle the airlock a few times, to get ten or twelve aliens aboard.

Delano studied the split-screen image on his tablet, fastened to the work table in front of him. Steve had mounted five miniature cameras throughout the Station to monitor the airlock and the main corridors. One covered the Primary airlock, the only entry point for the aliens, unless they wanted to blast through the hull. The second camera took in the loading dock, while three and four monitored the corridors leading to the Control Room. The fifth displayed the corridor from the airlock to the Engine Storage compartment, where Gunny and his team waited.

The same camera feeds Delano watched also went to Gunny Stecker's tablet.

Kosloff, Welsh, and Peter had made other preparations for the arriving guests. All other section integrity hatches and compartment doors were closed, sealed, and in two cases welded shut. Once the aliens entered the Station through the Main Airlock, they could turn right, toward the stern and what remained of the Engine Room. Or go left, toward the forward section of the Station. That route made two turns, but now led only to the Control Room.

In the Control Room, Kosloff had earlier removed the three consoles in the center of the compartment, leaving the middle area empty. He also repositioned the table Delano and Lian had used working with the Halkins, and secured it to the deck with extra bolts.

Nearly eight hours of frantic activity had ended. The Station was as well-prepared as Delano and his team could make it. Now he needed the Ktarrans to do their part and show up. Logically, they should enter the Station, move to the Control Room, and capture the human animals in charge. If they decided to examine the rear of the Station first, the odds against Delano and the Station increased.

Suddenly the interior hatch opened. For a moment Delano, watching all the cameras on his tablet's split screen display, thought the Station's integrity was breached, but no alarm sounded and no air burst outward into space. The Ktarrans must have extended a plasma screen. Twenty seconds later, an alien in some type of space suit, a non-Ktarran, stepped from the airlock and into the Station's A-corridor. It paused and glanced around. The alien held what looked like a weapon in one hand, while carrying some instrument in the other.

The creature studied his instrument for a good two minutes,

removed his helmet, then moved forward. With its first step, Delano realized it wore magnetic strips on its boots. By the third step, he observed something else, something important. The alien was not comfortable in zero gravity, its motions jerky and uneven. But it had entered the Station, and now more figures emerged from the airlock, following the first one. Delano took a quick count.

"They're coming in," he said. "Gunny, they do not seem very happy in zero gravity. That may slow them down. I count two Ktarrans and eight Dalvaks, all heading toward the Control Room. All the Dalvaks are carrying what looks like stun weapons. Everyone take your places. Good hunting. Steve, you're up first."

Delano glanced at his tablet. Behind the first visitor came two more of the same species, but not wearing suits. Apparently the first creature had tested the air and found it breathable. Two Ktarrans followed, both wearing gold-colored space suits that resembled armored fighting suits, stepping confidently into the corridor. They towered over the others by at least half a meter. Five more non-Ktarrans trailed them. In all, ten aliens had boarded the Station. The last one to enter closed the hatch and sealed it. So they understood about airlocks.

Thank you, Lord. "At least we won't be breathing vacuum if their shuttle breaks contact," Delano said, thinking aloud. He found himself breathing hard, mouth open, his chest rising and falling. His teeth were bared. He wanted the fight to start, wanted to fuck these Ktarran assholes bad. He took another breath, and this time forced himself to let it out slowly. *Stay calm, breathe deeply.* Don't let the drugs goad you into something stupid.

He felt no fear, only anger. Delano wiped his palms, suddenly damp, hard against his shorts. Definitely Linda's pharmaceutical cocktail had kicked in. Now he just hoped it would be strong enough and last long enough.

"Take your places," Delano said. "Steve, they're alongside the Pharma Lab. Close the panel. Get into position."

Steve activated the control, and the gray steel outer-panel slid over the Station's only viewport. Delano heard the thump as the protective metal panel closed over the thick glass and locked into place. Now no one aboard the Ktarran vessel could see into the Station's interior.

Delano rose and swung over to the other side of the table. He settled his back against the now-shuttered viewport. Looking across the table and its three empty chairs, he faced the entrance to the Control Room. He hooked a leg around the table. Just enough room remained between the hull and the table for Delano and his team to take this position.

They would be facing the aliens when they entered the Control Room. The removal of the center workstations left plenty of space in the compartment. Delano had time for a final glance around the Control Room. Sgt. Shen appeared calm, Steve kept licking his lips, and Lian seemed tense. For an instant Delano wondered how he looked to his team.

And then they arrived.

The first creature, still wearing its suit but without the helmet, reached the entrance to the Control Room. It stopped and looked around – it had to be a Dalvak – as if vigilant about what resistance it might find. Not that the aliens would be expecting a confrontation. Logically any opposition would have tried to contest the boarding.

Nevertheless, the Dalvak remained cautious. In one hand it carried what appeared to be a small, oddly-shaped carbine. It didn't have a barrel. Instead a bell-shaped nozzle extended forward from a bulbous mass.

From the Tarlon's description, Delano recognized the Ktarran stunner weapon. It could emit electrical and aural waves that would temporarily disrupt mental processes and physical motor function by inducing intense pain to the nervous and auditory systems. The two disruptive processes could also be used separately, to deliver specific and graduated stimulation levels that did not render the victim unconscious or helpless.

Delano faced the alien. To his left was Shen, two meters away and farthest from the portside entrance to the Control Room. Lian stood at Delano's right, but about one meter separated them. Steve, another two meters from Lian, completed the rough line. All four had their backs to the closed viewport and looked toward the hatch that allowed the Ktarran prize crew entry to the Control Room.

"We are unarmed," Delano announced in Ktarran, as the lead Dalvak edged its way inside. More aliens followed. "We wish only to be friends with the Ktarran people."

By now the Control Room held four Dalvaks and two Ktarrans – the only ones wearing full suits – who halted just inside the chamber. Despite Delano's peaceful words, the aliens knew better than to crowd together inside one compartment. They formed a loose line fronting Delano and the shuttered viewport. The remaining four Dalvaks held their position in the corridor, just outside the entrance.

Up close, Delano realized the Ktarran suits appeared far too bulky for mere space suits. They had to be armored fighting suits, something he hadn't expected. Nor had the Tarlons or Halkins mentioned such a possibility. *Damn, the fucking Glocks better be up to the job.*

The Ktarrans' faceplate didn't have a bubble shape like a human helmet but displayed what looked like an ten inch square of thick glass. Each Ktarran carried a slim weapon in its hand, and not the clumsy-looking stunner. Delano recognized the laser weapon from the Tarlon's records. A killing device, it projected a narrow laser beam capable of punching through flesh or slicing it off. It could switch from pulse to continuous. If used in that manner, the beam could penetrate the hull within a few seconds.

The lead Ktarran must have said something on its internal communications link. The lead Dalvak, still ensconced within his space suit, lifted his hand.

Delano felt the shock wave strike him, turning his knees to jelly and shooting pains through his head. Every nerve in his body seemed on fire. At the same time, the directed sound waves disoriented him, and he sagged back against the hull, banging his elbow, then lurched forward against the table, his body twitching. The sound reverberation lasted only a second or two. However the effect from the electrical jolt seemed to last much longer, and he struggled to recover from the pain. He fought the urge to vomit.

Clutching the table with both hands, Delano moaned loudly. He didn't need to fake it. The shock to his nervous system was real enough. Even his bowels felt loose. He heard Steve and Shen's sharp gasps of pain, while Lian let out a shriek. The electrical shock disoriented him but the pain faded away in a few seconds. The shooters' ears had absorbed most of the stunner's sound waves, weakening the combo punch the alien weapon normally delivered. Delano's head hurt, but he already had his mind and muscles under control, thanks to Linda's painkillers and Shen's earplugs.

Without those two helpers, Delano would have been a feeble

blob writhing and thrashing about, helpless in the zero gravity.

And that was exactly what he wanted the Ktarrans to believe. Moving as if he barely had command of his body, Delano remained hunched over the table. He lifted his eyes to the first Ktarran, who seemed in charge.

"We mean you . . . no harm. We want . . . to be your friends," Delano said, stumbling over the words, taking his time as if he had to force each syllable through the pain.

Lian then repeated almost the same words, at the same slow pace. They needed the Ktarrans to realize that she also spoke their language, in case they decided to start killing randomly.

The lead Ktarran seemed satisfied with the effect of the stun blast. He lowered his own weapon somewhat. "Where are the others?" The voice sounded cold and hollow, emanating from what had to be a small speaker mounted somewhere on the helmet. "We know there are ten animals on this ship. Where are the rest?"

Delano bobbed his head up and down in subservience, his shoulders hunched. He continued to clutch the table with both hands for support. "The others are afraid. They do not speak your language. They are hiding in the back of our . . . ship." No sense trying to explain the differences between a ship and a research station.

"Summon them, or I will kill you." However, the Ktarran didn't raise his weapon.

"I cannot. The communication link within the Station has been broken," Delano said, gushing the words out quickly. "They will not come, but I can guide you to them."

The Ktarran thought about that for a moment, then spoke to his companion. Neither Delano nor Lian could hear what was said, but the second Ktarran turned away.

"We will find them," the first Ktarran announced.

Delano watched as the second Ktarran plodded out of the Control Room and started back down the corridor toward the airlock, clumping along in his magnetic boots. The four Dalvaks waiting just outside moved aside to let the Ktarran pass, then followed.

Yes! Plan A! Delano breathed an inward sigh of relief, but made sure nothing but fear showed on his face. The aliens were dividing their force, the best possible scenario for Delano's team. If all the aliens stayed at the Control Room, Plan B called for Stecker to leave his prepared position in the Engine Storage compartment and attack the enemy rear. If, on entry, all the aliens headed toward Stecker's position, Plan C required Delano and Shen to attack the aliens from behind.

The first Ktarran – Delano decided this one was in command – moved a few steps deeper into the Control Room, taking his time and glancing around at the humans' primitive equipment. His men fanned out on either side. His weapon remained in his hand, while the four aliens kept their stunners pointed at the humans. The Ktarran leader was in complete control, safe in his armored suit, and with the newly-captured animals under the watchful eyes of his Dalvak slaves. Meanwhile the human's pitiful ship remained at the mercy of the Ktarran flagship. The stun weapons ensured there would be no resistance. The Ktarran stopped about five meters from the work table.

"What is it that you want from us?" Delano had to stall for a few minutes, to give the second Ktarran and his armed slaves time to reach the rear of the ship where the Gunny waited. "We have much we can offer you. Do not hurt us. We will do whatever you ask."

"What we want is no concern to you." The Ktarran's natural arrogance reinforced his sense of control, and he obviously felt secure in the presence of these cringing humans. "You will be taken aboard our ship for examination. One, perhaps two of you will be butchered, to provide food for us. Those who cooperate the most may be allowed to live."

"I beg forgiveness," Delano said, bowing again, "but I did not understand. Can you please repeat your words? A little more slowly?"

The Ktarran must have said something to one of the Dalvaks. Another burst from the stun weapon washed over Delano. His body twitched, his eyes burned, and his nerves felt on fire. This time it took a few more moments before he had himself under control. He raised his hands, letting them tremble, which didn't take much effort to fake. "Please don't hurt us!" He had to stall for time, even if that meant inviting another pain blast from the stunner.

"You must listen with care when your master speaks," the Ktarran said. But he did repeat his words.

Delano nodded his head in submission. "I understand. Only Lian and I," he pointed to her, "speak your language. Please do not hurt us anymore. The pain is too much. If you spare us, we can help you talk to our leaders."

"Ktarrans do whatever pleases . . ."

Steve, shaking and clutching the table all this time, had kept his eyes on his tablet, which displayed the same split-screen feeds from the five corridor cameras. Delano had instructed Steve to count to ten after the last alien disappeared around the corner of the Loading Dock. That would mean the aliens had entered A-corridor and were moving past the Main Airlock. More important, it positioned them almost halfway to the Engine Storage compartment, where Gunny Stecker, Petrov, and Linda waited. Now Steve touched a fingertip to a button on his tablet.

Instantly five two-hundred lumen lights, set to strobe function, flashed on. The powerful beams shined over the heads of Delano and Shen, and right into the faces of the aliens. The blaze of bright white lights froze the aliens into a tableau of slow motion, the kaleidoscope of brilliant illuminations momentarily overloading their visual organs. Even the Ktarran in his fighting suit must have felt the effect.

The polarized shooting glasses Delano and the others wore absorbed much of the intensity. But despite having the strobes at his back, he still felt the glare from the pulsating beams. The extra-bright lights, meant for repair work outside the Station, had been modified by Kosloff who had added the strobe function. The devices, boosted by additional batteries, lasted only five or six seconds. That gave Delano the time he needed. Gripping the table's edge with his left hand, left leg still wrapped around one of the table's support stanchions, he snatched up the Glock half-concealed by papers scattered on the tabletop in front of him.

The aliens, caught in the intense flickering beams, appeared to be frozen in place, rendered momentarily helpless by the unexpected assault on their eyes.

Well before Delano raised his weapon, Shen started shooting, his gun snatched from a speed-draw holster fastened behind his back. His targets were the Dalvaks with the stunners. Delano's initial target was the Ktarran, who still held a lethal weapon in his hand. Shen's assignment was to take care of the others. Delano needed an extra moment to aim the Glock. The holographic red dot sight quickly centered on the alien's helmet.

The Ktarran, his eyes protected somewhat by the helmet's glass, reacted faster than his slaves. Both Delano and the Ktarran fired at almost the same time. But the alien warrior was shooting half-blind, still trying to recover from the rapidly pulsating lights. The brilliant red flash of the Ktarran's laser passed harmlessly over Delano's shoulder, and hit six inches above the viewport.

Delano's first armor-piercing, nine millimeter bullet was well aimed, but even as he fired the weapon he knew he had jerked the trigger. The slug smashed into the Ktarran helmet, but missed the face plate by an inch. Whatever tough material constituted the helmet, the AP round failed to penetrate. But all that energy had to go somewhere. The force of the impact snapped the creature's head back, and before it could get off another laser burst, Delano used the extra moment of time to put his second round right through the center of the helmet's glass.

The Ktarran's transparent panel, glass or some other substance, might be strong. And was probably polarized to diffuse an enemy laser beam. But it didn't equal the tensile strength of the helmet. It also didn't stop Delano's bullet from smashing through and striking the flesh within.

A hole had appeared almost in the center of the Ktarran's face plate, and the alien rocked back on his heels, held upright and in place by its magnetic boots. It might not be dead, but only momentarily stunned. But the effect was what mattered. The creature made no effort to discharge his weapon.

Meanwhile Shen, shooting far faster, had already fired four times. Each of the rounds went dead-center into the head of a Dalvak. Caught by surprise, blinded by the bright light, and disoriented by the strobe effect, they became easy prey for a speed-shooter like Shen, who could get off four rounds in less than two seconds. One Dalvak managed to activate its stun weapon, but most of the nerve-punishing blast went over the heads of Delano's team and caused little pain. However Shen wasn't taking any chances. Bullets five through twelve were simply insurance.

Delano kept shooting as well, keeping the illuminated reticle in the Glock's sighting system fixed on the Ktarran's head. He fired round after round into the helmet. The face plate shattered after the third penetration, shards zinging through the air. Four more rounds went through the opening, and a spurt of purple fluid spewed from the hole, separating into small globules that floated toward the Station's bow.

By then, all the creatures in the Control Room were dead or neutralized. Held upright by their magnetic boots, the five aliens swayed grotesquely in the zero gravity, all oozing body fluids.

Satisfied, Delano put a few rounds into the Ktarran's center mass, just to be sure. Curiously, the armored suit didn't withstand the AP rounds like the creature's helmet. Perhaps the Ktarrans were unfamiliar with high powered projectiles, which might be a useful nugget of data. Delano kept shooting even after the Ktarran released its weapon, leaving it floating harmlessly in the air. The sound of the gunfire in the enclosed chamber, which would have deafened him without the ear plugs, finally ended with his fifteenth bullet.

The click of the Glock's slide mechanism locking open, caught Delano by surprise. He couldn't believe he'd emptied the fifteen round magazine. Traces of dust and gunpowder floated in the air, and he tasted the familiar battlefield smell, amplified by his heightened senses.

Shen had emptied his weapon as well and had already loaded a second magazine. Now he pointed the Glock at the corridor, ready for any intruders who might respond to the noise.

Steve, who hadn't managed to get off a shot, launched himself toward the swaying aliens. He caught one of the floating stun weapons and tossed it toward Delano. Then Steve swam over to the Ktarran and recovered its laser weapon.

Delano, still powered by Linda's stimulants, didn't try to reload. Instead he released the pistol, letting it hang in the air, and took a second Glock from Lian's outstretched hand. She'd ducked down beneath the table as soon as the shooting started and retrieved her Glock, carefully taped to the underside of the table. Then she waited, ready to hand it to Delano or if necessary, use it herself.

At the same time, Lian snatched Delano's empty Glock from the air, ejected the spent magazine, and loaded a fresh one, following the step-by-step procedure Sgt. Shen had carefully taught her.

Meanwhile Delano's quick look around the Control Room showed nothing but five dead aliens, and a glance at the tablet's screen revealed no creatures rushing back to the aid of their master. Delano heard Steve on his comm, his usually high-pitched voice now little more than a hoarse whisper, giving Welsh the go-ahead.

The sound of gunfire, coming from the Engine compartment, could still be heard in the Control Room. Shen, Glock in hand, had already pushed away from the table, grabbed a stun weapon in addition to his Glock, and headed for the Loading Dock, in case Stecker needed any help.

"Lian, Steve, get into your suits," Delano called out. His team had stashed their space suits in the Lounge. "We need to suit up." The Ktarrans might blow a hole in the Station at any time. Meanwhile, his squad remained alive, and they still had a chance.

For now, the fight for the Control Room had ended. But the real battle, for the Station and for Earth, hadn't even started.

Chapter 26

New International Space Station

Day 9 1532 Zulu

Five aliens, led by the second Ktarran, left the Control Room and retraced their steps toward the airlock. When they reached A-corridor, they turned left and passed the loading dock. They followed the passage, and headed toward the compartment at the far end, where Gunny Stecker, Linda and Petrov waited for them in the Engine Storage compartment.

Gunny watched their progress on his tablet. The aliens had split their force, always a possibly fatal mistake when dealing with an unknown enemy. The Ktarrans might be efficient in ship-to-ship battles, but he doubted if they had much experience in sweeping a building or an enemy bunker clean.

Stecker and his team had prepared their defenses, but like Delano in the Control Room, Stecker, Petrov, and Linda had nowhere to go if things went bad. The secondary access hatch to the Engine Room no longer provided a possible means of escape from the storage compartment. When the Ktarrans sheared off the back part of the Station, they opened the entire engine room to hard vacuum.

Win or go home, Stecker thought, only this time it had to be win. Once the shooting started, he had to kill every alien in the corridor. He had no doubt about his ability to take them down. Civilians and even most military had no idea how deadly a speed shooter could be. Stecker had two gold trophies on his wall at home, for First Place in Marine Corps run-and-gun competitions. But in competition shooting, the targets didn't shoot back.

From what Delano had told the team, the Ktarrans had learned how to use overwhelming force and firepower in space conflicts. How good their personal weapons might be remained to be seen. Stecker knew one thing for certain. These Ktarrans would slaughter all three of them for daring to resist. Or worse, the flesh-eating aliens might take them alive and put them on tonight's dinner menu.

Once again Stecker glanced at his tablet, taped to the deck plate beside him, and saw the approaching aliens on Steve's pinhole camera mounted on the corridor wall. All five of them had entered the long corridor, and the one on point had almost reached the airlock. A reasonable number to take out, he decided. Now he had to put them down before they could bring their weapons into play.

He thought about the mission Klegg had given him. Make sure the aliens do not capture the Station intact. Stecker and Shen still carried detonators attached to their belts, ready to blow the Station to bits. Now the mission had changed into destroying the Ktarran battleship. Welsh and Kosloff had worked out the plan, and Delano had approved. With that decision, Delano became expendable.

In the Control Room encounter, Stecker felt certain Shen would take out the aliens. Delano's only role was to keep the Ktarran busy until Shen could take over. Stecker suspected Sgt. Shen might be even more skillful with a pistol that he was. In competition, both men could fire six rounds in two seconds. Stecker would have preferred to be with Delano in the Control Room, but Shen clearly had no intention of leaving Lian's side.

Once Stecker and Shen dealt with the Ktarran boarding party, they, too, would be expendable. Only Peter and the transport would matter then. Stecker felt good about that, too. He'd seen and understood the look on Peter's face. The JovCo navigator knew what would happen to his wife if the Ktarrans captured her. That wasn't going to happen. Peter had killed for her before, and he'd do it again, even if it meant sacrificing his own life.

Stecker pushed those thoughts aside. In the brief time available, he and Shen had done their best. They'd set up a small target range in the Engine Room, using the bullet box they brought with them. Behind and around the box they packed a dozen mattresses and blankets, back-stopped with four steel door panels. Everyone fired forty rounds of hollow point, so at least the team's civilians and desk jockeys familiarized themselves with the weapon, including how to change the magazine.

In the hurried Glock familiarization session, Petrov had proved to be a fine shot, and he claimed to have combat experience fighting off bandits in the Ukraine wilds. In a rapid-fire situation, Stecker didn't expect too much from the Russian, but the support of a second accurate shooter would be welcome. At the least, it would distract the aliens and present them with another target. As for Linda, she had the determination, but her shooting eye and weapon control proved lousy. He told her to just fire at anything that moved in the corridor and hope for the best.

After everyone finished, Stecker and Shen spent time adjusting the triggers on their Glocks for maximum rate of fire, and then each shot a hundred rounds to get used to the weapon's movement in zero gravity. The private session increased their confidence in themselves and each other. Come what may, they were ready.

Stecker and Delano would be the only shooters using AP loads in the Glocks, though Shen carried two magazines loaded with that ammo on his belt, just in case. The hollow-point rounds, fired down the length of the corridor, didn't have the punch to penetrate the hull's nanocrystalline material, or so he, Delano, and Shen hoped. At the far end, the Physics lab would take some hits, but nobody worried about that.

Gunny Stecker took one last look at his team and their position. The air-tight hatch to the compartment remained wide open. It had a raised lip around it. He lay stretched out on the deck, anchored by his left hand and right leg to hold him steady against the recoil.

Petrov, a left hander, took his position on the opposite side of the hatch, also on the deck. The burly Russian had barely enough room to conceal himself. From this position, both men could shoot without exposing much of their bodies. Linda, more familiar with a zero gravity environment, had fastened herself to the overhead. None of them could be seen, at least until the aliens came within a few meters.

Stecker glanced up at the Med-Tech. To his eyes, Linda appeared to be hanging upside down. The aliens helped the gravity illusion, tramping down A-corridor, their magnetic boots making the deck a floor.

A final glance at his tablet showed Stecker that the Ktarran and his four companions had passed the Main Airlock and started down the thirty meter corridor that now led only to Stecker and his team. All other openings had been sealed off. A little closer and they would be well within range. Just a few more steps, he thought, readying himself. Then a burst of rapid gunfire echoed through the Station. The din from the Control Room, bouncing off the metal walls, alerted the aliens.

"Now!" Stecker spoke the single word, loud enough to be heard by Linda and Petrov.

He needn't have bothered. Linda knew what the gunfire meant. Holding on to the top of the hatch, she extended her left hand toward the corridor. She held three tactical flashlights, duct-taped together, wrapped with Velcro, and set to strobe function. While not as bright as the lights Kosloff rigged in the Control Room, the effect remained disorienting. Without exposing any part of her body, Linda shoved the flashlights around the door frame and actuated the beams.

The Velcro-wrapped lights clung firmly to another strip of Velcro secured to the edge of the hatch. That allowed her to send the bright light down the corridor and into the faces of the aliens without having to hold on to the flashlights. Hopefully the strobe would distract enemy reflexes. Looking toward the lights would also make spotting the shooters difficult.

Stecker didn't hesitate. At the first sound of gunfire he leaned to his right, exposing only his right eye and right hand with the Glock. Like Delano's, the Gunny's weapon contained only armor piercing ammo. Unlike Delano, the Gunny had complete faith in the long-barreled pistol and its hot-loaded ammunition. Stecker trusted himself to not risk putting a round through the Station's hull. But to be on the safe side, he'd given Linda and Petrov only the standard hollow-point loads.

He needed only an instant to lock onto his target. The Ktarran, in the center of the file of five, towered over the others. Stecker saw the helmet of the armored suit, which meant he had to hit a ten inch square faceplate at twenty-plus meters.

Surprised by the noise emanating from the Control Room, the Ktarran stopped and shifted his body to look behind him. The remaining aliens slowed their pace. Two turned their heads back toward the airlock. That meant an angled and tougher shot for Stecker. But unlike the wider Control Room, here the aliens had stumbled into a kill box, with no place to hide. The Ktarran might be surrounded by his soldier-slaves, but his helmeted head stood out above the others. When Linda activated the strobes, the Ktarran made the mistake of turning his head back toward the lights, giving Stecker an almost perfect aim point.

The Gunny lay in a prone position, with his body and left arm braced, and the Ktarran's face plate showed clearly in the holographic sight. The creature raised its weapon, but before it could activate the laser, Stecker put the first AP round right through the center of the alien's viewport. He put two more in the same location by the time Petrov got off his first shot. Linda, after securing the lights, had started shooting, too, contributing to the deafening noise issuing from the storage compartment.

Petrov's second or third shot scored a hit on the lead Dalvak carrying a stun weapon. But the bullet didn't kill the creature, and it managed to activate its stunner.

Instantly a wave of pain flowed down the passageway and passed through the defenders' nervous systems. For a few moments Stecker lost trigger control as his muscles went into spasm. The auditory overload seemed almost as bad, as the corridor channeled the sound waves toward the Engine Storage compartment. But Shen's magical sound deadeners proved equal to the task, filtering out almost all the disorienting sound waves before the effect could increase to paralysis.

Despite Linda's drug cocktail, Stecker's nerves felt on fire, his eyes wouldn't focus, and he had to grit his teeth to regain control, ignoring the pain that continued to lance through his body from the electrical jolt. Somehow Petrov recovered first and scored another hit on the wounded alien operating the stun weapon. Even with magnetic boots, the alien lost his balance. By now badly injured from at least two rounds, it lowered the stunner. The directed energy went down toward the deck.

The slight respite let Stecker recover. He took two quick shots, this time into the second alien in the line, before that Dalvak could get its weapon into play. One more blast from a stun weapon might paralyze the defenders. Either the wounds distracted the alien's efforts to activate its weapon, or its companion blocked the shot. In any case, the Dalvak never got a chance to use his stunner.

Linda had lost her Glock, releasing it when the stun weapon pain struck. Her hand must have struck the lights, because the Velcro holding the lights came loose. However she managed to catch the flashlights before they floated away. Even as she redirected the lights, Stecker kept shooting.

"Take out the stun weapon!" Stecker shouted, but the words

came out of his mouth as little more than a horse whisper. Petrov understood, however, and began targeting his bullets.

Stecker tightened his hand on the compartment hatch, squeezing the metal as hard as he could. He used that self-inflicted pain to distract him from the stun weapon's effect on his nerves. A moment later, he refocused on the big Ktarran, just as the first blood-red laser beam streamed toward the defenders. But the Ktarran couldn't see clearly through the shattered helmet plate while staring into the flickering strobes. He waved the laser around, but Stecker resumed shooting at the helmet's shattered glass.

Meanwhile Petrov's fourth bullet again hit the lead alien, the one still clutching the stunner, this time right in the head. It released the stun weapon, which tumbled randomly in the zero gravity.

Under fire, the Ktarran struggled to regain its footing. Stecker's first bullet had penetrated its helmet, but was deflected enough by the thick glass so that the bullet only injured him. Now he twisted helplessly in the zero gravity, his magnetic boots pulled from the corridor deck by the force of the bullet and his attempt to move and fire his weapon at the same time. The Ktarran's laser weapon continued operating, sending laser burst after burst down the corridor. However every move the creature made just caused it to rotate and flail even more. That, and the confusion caused by the strobe, prevented it from accurately aiming its weapon.

All the same, Stecker heard Petrov cry out, as the laser bore right through the flesh of his left forearm. But the tough Russian, boosted by Linda's drugs, didn't release his Glock, and he continued carefully and calmly firing his rounds down the corridor.

So did Stecker. The Gunny sent bullet after bullet into the helmet, taking his time and putting every slug into the armored helmet of the floating target. The laser weapon ceased firing, but Stecker kept shooting, stopping only when the Ktarran floated head down in the corridor, its green blood mixed with some dark fluid pumped out of its suit and into the air. Petrov added his rounds to the slaughter, still taking the time to properly aim each round before squeezing the trigger.

The fifth Dalvak, wounded by Petrov or Linda, miraculously regained its feet and tried to return the way it came, but that target was almost too easy. Stecker and Petrov each put three rounds into its back. Still not satisfied, Stecker reloaded in less than three seconds, then placed a well-aimed round through the floating body of each of the remaining three Dalvaks.

The firefight lasted less than twenty seconds, but felt like hours had passed. All five aliens were down, filling the corridor with drifting bodies surrounded by swirling droplets of black, purple, and green blood, all churning by the softly sighing air from the ventilation system. The surprise ambush, aided by unfamiliar zero gravity environment and strobe lights, had caught the aliens off-guard. Linda's pain-killers and Shen's ear plugs kept Stecker going just long enough.

Linda probably never hit a target, but the sound of her few gunshots merged with Stecker's and Petrov's, deafening in the corridor, which added to the aliens' confusion. For the three humans, however, the ear plugs filtered almost all of the tumult.

"Cease fire!" The Gunny directed the words at Petrov, but the Russian didn't stop shooting until he emptied the magazine.

Stecker checked his tablet, but saw no aliens emerging from the Control Room. Shen and Delano must have taken out the aliens there. He shifted his gaze to another camera, and saw Shen moving toward A-corridor, Glock in one hand and stun weapon in the other, to assist Stecker. The Gunny found his voice had returned, and he shouted out the all clear, so that Shen could return to the Control Room.

The five aliens facing Stecker appeared lifeless. Three remained upright, their dead bodies held in place by their magnetic boots. The Ktarran and the last Dalvak's body tumbled randomly in the corridor, until one of the Ktarran's magnetic boots caught against a ventilation grill, leaving it twisting grotesquely in the air.

"Linda, get Petrov to Med Lab. Take your suits with you." Stecker pushed himself off the deck and started down the corridor to check the bodies. Despite the zero gravity, he automatically ejected the second magazine and loaded a full one as he moved. He intended to make certain the aliens, especially the Ktarran, were dead. Two bullets in the head of each at close range should finish the job. Then he'd climb into his own suit, and rejoin the others in the Control Room.

In the Exercise compartment, and at the first sound of gunfire, Peter, Kosloff, and Colonel Welsh, all wearing their suits, unlatched the door that faced C-corridor and pushed it open. Immediately the air inside the chamber decompressed, flinging the door outward. The three swam out, turned right, passed through what remained of the Engine Room, and out into space. Fortunately, the Ktarrans had inadvertently created a new point of egress for Welsh's team when they blasted off the rear of the Station.

The original plan had called for them to exit the Station via a service access hatch in the Engine Room. But with the rear of the Station open to space, the three-man raiding party saved at least thirty or forty seconds.

Delano and Welsh gambled that, with the addition of the Ktarran boarding party's life signs to those of the Station, the aliens aboard the mothership wouldn't notice the three life forms now outside. Suspicious activity like that would immediately be questioned.

Kosloff and Welsh wore their regular suits, suitable for EVA repairs and modifications to the Station. Peter had donned the command suit he'd arrived in, the one he'd managed to claim for his own before departing the JovCo lunar base.

That suit provided the main reason Peter now took the lead. He might not be good with a firearm, but he had the most maneuverable suit and he could move about in space faster and with more control than Welsh or Kosloff. Delano and the others agreed that the quicker someone got on board the Ktarran shuttle, the better.

Besides, Welsh, although an Air Force pilot, hadn't fired a pistol in nineteen years, so he didn't have much better weapons skills than Peter. The second reason Peter led the way was more recent. He had killed a man with his hands not long ago aboard the freighter *Lady Drake*, and later outfought in space the ship's vicious captain and left him to die. Delano decided that experience made Peter more qualified than Welsh, who agreed.

Peter had to jet his way at least sixty meters from the back of the Station, around the portside cargo boom, and over to where the Ktarran transport had parked adjacent to the Main Airlock. For the last part of the journey, he had to stay beneath the Station, so as not to be seen from the shuttle's viewport.

In his right hand Peter carried a Glock with its trigger guard removed so that his gloved finger could work the trigger. Gunny Stecker had also removed the weapon's grips and replaced them with wrapping from a heat pack. No one knew how well or how long any firearm would work in the cold of outer space, so Stecker decided to keep the Glock as warm as possible.

To prevent the gun's lubricant from freezing up and jamming the weapon, Stecker and Shen had soaked the disassembled components in alcohol borrowed from the Med Lab to remove every trace of oil and moisture. The firearms experts then treated Peter, Welsh, and Kosloff's weapons with Metal Slick, another specialty item from their bottomless bag of goodies. Shen had removed the original front sight and replaced it with a much larger version, bright green in color. Both florescent and luminescent, the new sight should help Peter line up his target against the black background of space. Last, Shen fastened the weapon to Peter's suit with a cord, so he couldn't lose it. Now he just had to remember how to aim and fire it.

At least the pistol would be more efficient than the hammer Peter had used to smash engineer Carl Brock's head into mush. Thinking of that incident recalled the image of Brock's shattered skull, with the purple and pinkish brain matter floating weightless amid the bright red blood globules. If it weren't for Linda's stimulants racing through his veins, Peter would have shivered at the gruesome memory. But Linda's survival might depend on him, and to that end he would kill any number of Ktarrans or other aliens who threatened her safety.

The visual stayed in Peter's mind until he reached the alien hatch. Only a meter or so separated the transport from the Station. Taking a firm grip on the Glock, he passed through the flickering plasma screen that extended between the vessels without a qualm – Delano had explained in detail how it would feel – and found himself inside the Ktarran shuttle. The dim lighting, obviously not meant for human eyes, forced Peter to take a moment until his eyes adjusted.

The Ktarran airlock was amidships. Peter glanced to his right and saw nothing aft. But when he turned toward the bow, he identified a Ktarran sitting at the controls and a second alien of a different species seated beside him. Neither had reacted, so the shuttle's two inhabitants hadn't noticed him passing through the plasma screen. Nor had the aliens aboard the Station broadcast a warning.

Peter hit the suit's motion kill switch, and the suit's computer fired jets of air until the suit stabilized. At the whooshing sound of the jets, the alien glanced over his shoulder, then stared in disbelief at the apparition that appeared inside his craft. Neither the big Ktarran at the controls or the second alien wore a spacesuit, armored or otherwise. But the Ktarran did have what appeared to be a weapon belted around his waist.

That surprise didn't last long. The Ktarran shuttle pilot twisted around and lunged for his weapon. By then Peter had stabilized himself and started shooting, his targets only about seven meters away. Caught up in the moment, Peter forgot everything Gunny Stecker and Shen had taught him during his training session on the Station. Despite the forty practice rounds he'd fired, Peter's first two shots somehow missed the Ktarran, notwithstanding its bulk. But the third one caught the alien in the shoulder, as he brought up his weapon. The shock of the bullet, a hollow point load, spun the weightless Ktarran against the console, slowing him down. Peter, adjusting his suit's jets with one hand to compensate for the recoil, kept firing and delivered more rounds into the wounded pilot.

However Peter's first two shots hadn't gone to waste. One of the soft-nosed slugs had slammed into the transport's only viewport, creating a concentric web of cracks in the transparent material. The second bullet either weakened the glass to failure, or punched a hole through it. The air inside the shuttle rushed through the fist-sized opening, doubling the breach in an instant, as Peter's fourth and fifth bullets tore through the Ktarran's center mass. Either the shock of each round or the immediate drop in air pressure slowed the Ktarran's effort to use his weapon. His body, caught by the air exiting the transport, jerked backward, against the remains of the viewport.

The wounded alien didn't completely block the ever-widening opening, and air continued to rush out. Peter kept shooting and in his excitement forgot about the second alien. By his seventh shot, however, Colonel Welsh had arrived. He gripped the door frame, took careful aim and opened fire on the other alien.

This one apparently did not have a weapon, but had turned around to face aft, then froze in place, either too surprised or too slow to react. Without any means of defense, the creature panicked when the atmosphere started streaming out into space through the shattered viewport.

Whether it was alive or dead, Welsh's first three shots struck the

Peltor – his suit's recorder later confirmed the alien's species – punching one hole in its arm and two more in its chest area. With most of the air already out of the shuttle, Welsh had time to take careful aim. He put three rounds into the Ktarran's head, just to be sure, as he later explained. By then Peter had emptied his Glock, fifteen rounds, into the Ktarran pilot's body.

The Ktarrans might be tough, but a few hot-loaded slugs to the head and multiple hits to the body, combined with exposure to hard vacuum, killed anything that lived, no matter how strong. Peter and Welsh had captured the Ktarran shuttle.

Now they had to get to work.

Ignoring the dead aliens and forgetting Delano's order not to use the radio except in an emergency, Peter pushed his comm button. "Linda, are you OK? We've got the shuttle." For a long, anxious moment, he heard nothing. Finally Linda's excited voice came over the speaker.

"Yes, Peter, we're all good here. Delano says the Control Room is secure. Hurry."

"We're on it." Peter glanced behind him, but Welsh, satisfied by the copious amounts of blood droplets floating inside the shuttle, had already left. The vessel's air had disappeared as well. Comfortable in hard vacuum, Peter moved forward, letting go of the Glock. He grabbed the Ktarran body and shoved it toward the rear of the shuttle. Positioning himself behind the pilot's controls, Peter let his magnetic boots hold him against the deck.

He removed a small tablet from his pocket and pulled up the images Delano had taken aboard the Halkin shuttle. As Peter expected, the controls didn't match, but he had captained cargo freighters, ore loaders, and various shuttles before. Now Peter needed to figure out how to fly the strange craft before the Ktarrans aboard the battleship became suspicious.

Forty seconds later, Peter thought he'd figured out the basic controls. Through the suit he heard a clang against the hull and knew Welsh and Kosloff had started attaching the booster rockets. Both NASA specialists had plenty of EVA activities logged while on the Station, and they were better at moving cargo and repairing scientific instruments than Peter. Besides, the ungainly booster rockets required only two men to guide them. A third would just get in the way.

In another ninety seconds Peter grasped how to power the shuttle – so he hoped. He felt a second thump against the bottom of the hull. A few moments later Welsh appeared inside, his helmet touching Peter's so they could speak without using their suits' radios. The less they broadcast the better. "Kosloff's attaching the detonators. Time to get moving. Are you ready?"

"Almost. Need another minute or so, then I'll take her out," Peter said. "You've set the fuses?"

"Not yet, but Kosloff will do that first. No matter what, the boosters will go in seven minutes. Hurry."

"Got it. Go help Kosloff."

"Will do," Welsh said. He disappeared through the transport's entrance. A few moments later, Welsh's radio broadcast a single word – "Armed." The seven minute countdown had begun.

Peter didn't wait for Welsh or Kosloff to maneuver away from the alien shuttle before he started the craft moving. Time was racing by, and they needed every second they could get. Using as light a touch on the controls as possible, Peter edged the transport away from the Station, dropped it below the Ktarran cruiser's line of sight and started the ship on its way. As soon as he cleared the Station and lined up the shuttle, he flipped what he decided – hoped – was the auto recall switch.

Nothing happened. The shuttle just floated in space, drifting slowly away from the Station. Panicked, Peter almost started punching buttons at random. Then he realized there might be a delay, to allow the pilot to exit the craft. He decided to give it one more full minute. He glanced at the chronometer inside his helmet. Sixty seconds that felt like sixty hours slowly ticked by. Peter swore, sweat dripping from his chin. He jerked his head to shake off the drops. Another thirty seconds passed. Still nothing.

"Dammit," Peter muttered. He reached for the throttle, but before he touched anything, the shuttle's jets fired, and the transport began moving.

"About fucking time," he muttered.

First it oriented itself, and then, pushed by a gentle burst from its thruster, it headed toward the mothership. Peter remained at the controls until he decided the craft did indeed know where to go. He checked the heading, ready to take over manually if the shuttle started drifting.

Peter had already decided that, if necessary, he would fly it inside the mothership himself, or at least up against its plasma screen. Listening to Delano and Lian's description of alien tactics, he'd figured out what would happen to Linda if the Ktarrans captured the crew. The aliens wouldn't eat or cut open a linguist, but the only other woman would go right under an exploratory surgical knife.

The shuttle maintained its line of flight and jetted slowly back toward the battleship. Once Peter felt certain of its course, he left the controls and dove through the airlock.

When he cleared the shuttle, Peter used the command suit's jets to propel him back toward the Station. He took a moment to glance behind him at the leisurely moving shuttle. He had to strain to see the two spare booster rockets, carried to the Station by the spaceplane and now attached to the belly of the vessel. Unless the aliens had better eyesight, they likely wouldn't notice them either.

Four inch-wide magnetic strips held the two rockets against the underside of the shuttle's hull. Each booster had three detonators attached, one at the front, one in the middle, and one directly above the rocket's exhaust port. A thin copper wire, stripped bare of insulation and less than a meter in length, hung from each of the rear detonators. Despite knowing they were there, Peter couldn't see them against the blackness of space.

The wires would act as antennae to receive the detonation signal. The multiple fuses, Stecker assured Peter, were cross-connected as well. As long as one worked, it would simultaneously trigger the others. That would ensure maximum explosion as all the fuel ignited at the exact same millisecond.

Peter joined Welsh, floating just outside the hatch, a backup detonator in his hand. They shifted position, to move their helmets above the Station so they could see the Ktarran mothership. Peter and Welsh watched as the shuttle crept along toward the battleship.

Anything could still go wrong. Someone aboard the mothership might spot the boosters, or decide to contact the original crew. Or had spotted Peter leave the shuttle. There could even be some code needed before the shuttle could reenter the mothership. Or the alien crew might have noticed something threatening and ordered its beam weapons to blast the transport and the Station into harmless fragments.

The journey seemed to take forever, but finally the nose of the shuttle sparkled as it touched the outer screen. Welsh, his hands encased in the thick gloves, fumbled with the detonator but managed to push and hold the oversized red button for a good ten seconds before the Ktarran shuttle disappeared behind the flickering screens.

If Welsh's radio signal worked the way Sgt. Shen claimed, it would have deactivated the initial seven minute setting and activated a new, one hundred and twenty seconds timer. Peter had estimated it would take that long for the shuttle's auto pilot to guide itself through the plasma screens and into the interior docking bay of the Ktarran vessel. Even if the shuttle didn't get all the way inside, it should still be in close enough proximity to the hull to cause plenty of damage.

"Let's get inside," Welsh said. "Delano, the detonator is active!"

Peter and Welsh entered the Station's main airlock. Waiting for them, Kosloff closed the large outer door as soon as they were inside. The moment the airlock cycled, the three men opened the inner door and swam toward the Control Room. No one removed his helmet or wasted more than a glance at the dead aliens and droplets they saw floating aimlessly in the corridor. Each corpse displayed, among other wounds, at least one bullet hole to the head. Peter swallowed hard and decided that Gunny Stecker must be a very, very cautious man.

At the Station's viewport, its shutter once again opened, Delano watched the Ktarran shuttle disappear through the mothership's plasma screen. He and the others had donned their flight suits, except for their helmets. He held a second backup detonator in his hand. If the Ktarrans had detected anything as their shuttle approached, Delano would have detonated the rockets immediately in the hope of causing some destruction to the battleship, maybe even enough to keep it out of action for a while.

Once the Ktarran shuttle disappeared from sight, Delano moved his hand away from the detonator's button. He'd heard Welsh's radio signal that he'd activated the two-minute timer as soon as the shuttle started its entry.

"Peter, Kosloff, and Welsh are back inside the Station and on the way to the Control Room," Steve called out.

"Time to say goodbye," Delano said. "Steve, do we still have our comm link to the Ktarran ship?"

"Oh, yes, Joe. Already up. Don't know if they'll answer, though."

Delano grinned, though anyone watching wouldn't have detected any mirth. "Hell, give it a try. I want to say a few words to the good captain. Make sure you turn up the volume all the way."

Linda, Gunny Stecker, and Petrov crowded behind Delano, Lian, and Shen, all watching the monitor.

Steve reactivated the comm link between the Station and the Ktarran vessel, which the Ktarrans hadn't fully disconnected on their side. At first nothing happened, but then some Ktarran tech must have become curious and opened the link. Once again Delano gazed into the alien control room and at the captain of the battleship, still seated on his enormous throne. Steve increased the magnification until the Ktarran seemed only a few meters away.

By then Peter, Kosloff, and Welsh arrived, joining the rest of the team.

"Hello, Turhan!" Delano yelled, determined to make sure he was heard over the normal background noise. "Turhan! TURHAN! Just wanted to say goodbye."

Startled faces on the Ktarran bridge turned to see the speaker. Turhan glanced about, then his head shifted until he once again faced Delano on his monitor. The Ktarran leader leaned forward and bared his teeth, no doubt in surprise or annoyance. "I thought . . . why are you still there? The transport . . . where is Merrer?"

Whoever the hell he was. "Dead. They're all dead, Turhan, and so are you. What we humans call Catastrophic Failure, End of Mission. You should have remembered that terror is a two-edged sword, asshole!" Delano lost control and sent spittle flying through the air. He'd shouted his hatred into the mic, but he practically screamed the last word. Then he pulled on his helmet and glanced at the timer. One hundred and fifteen seconds had passed since Welsh pushed the button.

The Ktarran captain stared at Delano in what had to be disbelief. Then Turhan understood. He roared something, but before anyone aboard the bridge could react, the timer reached zero.

Six digital detonators embedded in double blocks of C-4, all wired together to explode at the exact same instant, went off. Sixteen hundred pounds of solid booster rocket fuel ignited. The combination of powdered aluminum instantly reacted with the plentiful oxygen in the chemical ammonium perchlorate mixture. That amount of fuel, powerful enough to lift the spaceplane from the New Mexico base into the atmosphere, proved more than sufficient to do the job. Delano couldn't see the explosion but felt certain the blast would produce more than enough force.

The comm link to Turhan's control room flared, then went dark. But Delano and his entire team watched the alien battleship die through the viewport. First a brilliant flash of light shone through its plasma screens. He raised his hand to shield his eyes as the explosion blasted through the Ktarran's hull. The exterior plasma screens vanished, their generators destroyed by the blast. However, for a few milliseconds, the screens attempted to contain the shock wave. Plasma shields, Delano now realized, worked both ways.

Those few thousandths of a second concentrated the entire force of the explosion inside the battleship's interior. The blast split the big ship almost in half. Though Delano couldn't know it, the initial shock wave blew apart the antimatter containment fields, which triggered an even more massive secondary explosion as matter annihilated antimatter and transformed into pure energy.

Catastrophic failure! In two seconds, the Ktarran battleship was reduced to burning shards, tiny fragments, and large molecules, all blasted outward in an expanding sphere, preceded by a visible thermal shock wave.

Everyone in the Control Room roared their approval, cheering like maniacs and filling the compartment with pandemonium.

"Here it comes." Delano had to shout to be heard. He snapped the seals on his helmet shut and put his arm around Lian. The Station, only a kilometer away, had already been struck by the first wave of debris, smaller pieces of hull or ship contents blasted apart and sent flying at high speed into space. There was nothing they could do about that. Except hope that enough of the Station's hull held together to give them some protection. And pray that no massive pieces of metallic wreckage came their way.

Dozens, maybe hundreds of fragments struck the Station but nothing large enough to crack the hull. Most were small, and the old freighter's nanocrystalline casing, despite its age, absorbed nearly all of them without fatal damage. Delano watched as remnants of the Ktarran ship flamed outward like fireworks. He stared in fascination as slabs of metal, heated to such a degree that they burned even in the vacuum of space, spun away in every direction, like a pyrotechnics display.

While Delano and Lian enjoyed the spectacle, Kosloff got back to work. The first thing the Russian engineer did was test the integrity of the Station. After a few moments, Kosloff took off his helmet. "The Control Room is still airtight, but some of the other chambers are damaged. Basically we're stuck in here, the Lounge, and what's left of 'A' Section. Everything else is vacuum."

Delano shrugged. Right now he didn't really care. "How long do we have?" He kept his eyes on the viewport as he unsnapped his helmet. Gradually the blazing metal shards dissipated into glowing embers that the coldness of space soon extinguished.

"Plenty of food and water," Kosloff answered, "but the oxygen supply won't last more than eighteen, maybe twenty hours. And there's no way to generate any more. We lost the oxygen concentrator when the Ktarrans opened up the rear of the Station. The batteries will last much longer, so we'll stay warm, but that's not going to help us breathe. Communications with Earth are down, but maybe Steve and I can fix that." Despite delivering all that bad news, Kosloff sounded pretty gleeful.

"Anyway, I'm sure Klegg can see that the Ktarran is gone," Delano said. "Maybe it's time for us to phone home and ask for help." Delano knew he should be worried about the lack of air. Instead he heard himself laughing excitedly and knew Linda's drugs continued coursing through his bloodstream. He didn't realize he'd shed tears of joy until Lian reached out and tenderly wiped them away from his eyes.

Well, why not feel a little macho? Delano and his makeshift space marines had blown the bastard Turhan and his ugly flagship out of existence. No matter what happened to the Station or Earth, at least that arrogant asshole wouldn't see any of it. *Eat that, motherfucker.*

Of course the Station's crew remained trapped and floating helplessly in space, with no propulsion system or attitude control, and with no way to return to Earth. Any surviving Ktarran ships could finish them off with ease. All they could do now was hope for a rescue. With luck, Klegg had something that could reach the Station in time.

"Anybody got any ideas?" Welsh, a huge smile on his face, made his words upbeat despite the dismal situation.

Delano thought about options but at first couldn't come up with anything. Then he remembered the Talmak. "Here's a long shot. If the Tarlons and Halkins can't fight their way through the gate, maybe they can get back here before we run out of air. After all, they'll have no place else to go for help. Let's send him an SOS, too."

"OK, Major, as soon as Steve can contact Earth," Kosloff said, "I'll reopen the comm link we setup for the Tarlons. Maybe they will get the message. Give me five minutes."

"Good work, Steve, Kosloff." Delano made his words lighthearted, though he doubted the Talmak would be back. "I'll tell him about the fighting here. He'll be glad to learn about the destruction of Turhan's ship. Who knows, we may get lucky again."

Lian moved beside him, a big smile on her face. Before she realized what was happening, Delano took her in his arms and gave her a long kiss that ended only when he realized the others were cheering them on.

Lian made no move to pull away. Instead she put one arm around his neck and held on with the other, so that they didn't float apart. Delano wondered if Linda's cocktail had affected Lian's responses as well. She looked up at him, then closed her eyes. *OK, maybe it wasn't the drugs.* He kissed her again and forgot all about their impending doom or the shouts of encouragement from the others.

Only after the third kiss ended did Delano wonder how the battle for Earth was coming along.

Chapter 27

Aboard the Tarlon ship *Ningpo*

Day 9: 1542 Zulu

For the Tarlons and the Halkins the fight hadn't ended yet. All three ships gradually reduced their velocity to safe levels. In so doing, they merged again into a mini-fleet. They curved their path and navigated toward the gas giant the humans called Jupiter. The fourth Ktarran battle cruiser waited there, blocking their escape path.

Even so, the Halkins and Tarlons remained desperate to depart this system. The three ships rushed ahead, determined to fight their way past the Ktarran rear guard. With luck, at least one would get through the gate to report what had happened above the planet the humans called Earth.

They hadn't gone far before the communications console aboard the *Ningpo* relayed a transmission from the Station. "Receiving message from humans on Station. Ktarran command vessel destroyed. Station has sustained serious damage, life support failing. We are short on air supply, but intact for present. Request immediate assistance if possible. Will continue sending battle results. Delano out."

Despite the incredible news, War Leader Kaneel ignored the message. He had his own problem to deal with, namely the Ktarran cruiser guarding the wormhole. "Maintain course."

The *Ningpo* and the two Halkin ships continued their high speed voyage to Jupiter's gate. Reports from Earth and the Station continued arriving.

"Humans on the Station report that first Ktarran cruiser, the one attacked by Halkins, is destroyed by atomics."

"Sensors verify destruction of target." Jarendo confirmed the human intel. "Large detonation above atmosphere where Halkins attacked."

Moments later, another report from the Station was received. "Earth now reporting that second Ktarran cruiser damaged . . . no, also destroyed by atomics!"

Kaneel couldn't believe the news. Within the span of a few moments, two Ktarran battle cruisers and their flagship obliterated? Astonishing. He kept his voice calm. At least now he did not have to worry about a possible enemy behind him. Instead he could prepare for the coming conflict.

"Continue course for Jupiter. Reduce speed. Optimum power spread. Confirm that Horath has received the reports."

War Leader Kaneel turned toward Jarendo and the Talmak, each still registering surprise at the news. Three Ktarran cruisers had been destroyed! As far back as any Tarlon could remember, no force had ever destroyed so many enemy battle cruisers without the loss of a single ship.

"Perhaps these humans have value after all," Kaneel said. "They certainly fight bravely."

"Yes, I think they have some value," the Talmak agreed. "Perhaps quite a lot."

"Now if we can only escape this system to spread the news," Kaneel said. "There is still the battle cruiser waiting for us at the gate, and it will be ready for us. This time we will have no surprises for them."

Even at their reduced velocity, Kaneel expected to close with the Ktarran gatekeeper in less than eight hours. But just over two hours into their voyage, the long range sensors reported the remaining Ktarran vessel had disappeared through the wormhole. The enemy had abandoned, at least for now, the human solar system.

An excited Jarendo brought the news to the Talmak, alone in his quarters. "The last Ktarran is gone. Departed the system."

The Talmak rose from his relaxation couch. The stress of the battle and the hard acceleration had nearly exhausted him. But this news swept away all weariness. "Gone! You mean they ran away before confronting us?"

"Yes, Talmak," Jarendo laughed. "Kaneel believes they are afraid of us. Perhaps they think we have some new weapon. They watched their other ships disappear in atomic blasts, and must have decided we are armed with a new and powerful weapon. After all, we are heading straight for them, as if eager to offer battle."

"So rather than risk a fight with us, they fled," The Talmak said. "Inconceivable. I cannot . . . cannot believe it. Perhaps our descendants will yet see the Ktarrans checked in their advances, or even defeated."

"Perhaps. But that goal is a long way in our future," Jarendo said. "For now we must return home and let our people and allies know what has happened. We, too, will now face the Ktarrans' wrath."

The departing Ktarran ship would have identified the energy signatures of Halkin and Tarlon vessels. But the Talmak had something else on his mind. "I must speak with Horath," he said. "This development is too important to ignore. Ask him if he will come aboard."

This time the Talmak sat in his usual chair in the conference room, at the head of the table. War Leader Kaneel, Jarendo, and Celeck occupied one side. Horath and Ahvin took seats facing the Tarlons, in the places previously occupied by Delano and Lian. As the Halkins settled in, a messenger delivered to Jarendo another communication from the Station, transmitted in the Tarlon language. Jarendo examined it, then turned to the Talmak.

"It's another signal from the humans," Jarendo announced. "The Station continues to report severe damage. Their air supply is almost gone and they are being pulled down by the planet's gravity. The Alliance suffered major damage and is unable to rescue them in time."

The Talmak looked at Kaneel. "Is there nothing we can do for Delano and Lian?"

"If we return, we will not have sufficient fuel to get back to the wormhole," Kaneel said. "We expended most of our supply during the attack. Even if we had adequate fuel, there might not be enough time to return to the wormhole before it becomes unstable. Besides, we must get news of this battle to home world, so that they can prepare for an increase in Ktarran operations against us."

"We could use the Sentinel to report," Jarendo suggested.

The Talmak considered that. The humans remained unaware of the existence and power of the Sentinel, still in orbit around the innermost planet. It had the capability to broadcast the news to the home worlds of the Tarlons and Halkins, but the Ktarrans would also hear the messages. Once alerted to its existence in this system, the enemy might even be able to use the Sentinel's sensors to monitor Earth's activity.

"No, I would prefer not to use the Sentinel," the Talmak said. "It would be better to deliver the news ourselves." He lowered his eyes to the table, immersed in thought.

"Then Delano and Lian will die," Celeck said, after a suitable interval. "The next time we come, we will have to begin again with strange humans."

"It is unfortunate, but they have transmitted our language to their leaders," Jarendo said. "With their devices and the data downloaded to Earth, it will be less difficult to establish communications on our next encounter."

No one spoke. The Tarlons had accepted the impending deaths of the humans.

Horath broke the silence.

"The humans destroyed a Ktarran cruiser," Horath began, "without our support or even a beam weapon. That has never happened before. Warriors who can do such deeds need to be saved. What they did once, they may yet do again."

The Talmak lifted his eyes. "What do you suggest, Horath?"

"We, too, must return to our home world," Horath said, "both for repairs and to report on the fighting in this system. We must tell our people to ready themselves for more conflict. A great battle will be fought in this place when next the wormhole opens. However I do not need to send both ships home to Halkin to convey the message. Commander Morad's ship has suffered damage and must return for repairs. But he can deliver the report to the Halkin Council. And Morad's ship has room enough so that I can send most of my crew with him. Then I will take my ship back to Earth and rescue the humans on the Station. The humans Delano and Lian will need a new base in orbit over their home world, at least for a time. After this victory, I am certain many of my crew will volunteer to remain in this system and work with the humans."

The Talmak appeared surprised. The Halkins had never offered such services before to another species, not even to the Tarlons. "That would be desirable, Horath. But whoever remained behind would be dealing with the humans for many cycles, transferring technology and planning for the next Ktarran assault. Remember, even Tarlons have never committed ourselves to such a battle as the one that will come. Earth and any that remain to help it may be overwhelmed. Are you certain you want to do this?"

Horath bristled at the question. Before he could respond, Jarendo leaned forward.

"Talmak, I am willing to remain behind with Horath, to assist him. With my help, the learning and training of the humans could proceed much faster."

"I will also join Horath," Celeck said, "if he will have me. There is much more we need to learn about these humans, their history, their leaders, their people. Most important, they possess technology that we do not have. In the long run that knowledge might prove more valuable than this defeat of the Ktarrans."

"Horath, you will have to negotiate with the leaders of the planet," the Talmak said, "what they call the Alliance. That may be difficult, dealing with so many."

"With Ahvin's help, I can manage it," Horath said. "And if we rescue Delano and Lian, they will assist me."

"Horath," the Talmak began, "will you accept Jarendo and Celeck aboard your ship?"

"Yes, their presence would be most welcome," Horath said, "and I will have plenty of room after I transfer most of my crew to Morad's ship. I am sure the humans will soon be able to supply us with food, water, helium, and whatever other materials we need."

Everyone turned toward the Talmak, who appeared lost in thought for a few moments. "I believe, Horath, that you speak wisely. But I think you will need another aboard your ship, to assist you in your communications. If you approve, I would also like to stay with you and help negotiate with the humans. That is, if you will accept my services."

Now Horath registered surprise. To host the Talmak, one of the most illustrious Tarlon leaders and deeply respected by his people, would be a great honor. The Talmak explained his reasons, detailing them one by one. When he finished, even War Leader Kaneel had accepted the Talmak's decision.

"Then it is decided," Kaneel said. "Horath will off-load most of his crew, and we will transfer you three to his ship, along with whatever supplies and equipment you require."

"We must move at once," Jarendo said. "Or Horath may not get back to the human Station in time."

Horath nodded. "It will be instructive to see Delano again. I wonder what he will say if we save his life? For the second time."

Even the Talmak smiled at the prospect. "Truly it is a new day, perhaps for all of us. The humans may prove invaluable to our own survival. They will be in our debt. Without our help they would have lost their world. Without our assistance in the future, they will surely fall to the Ktarrans when they return. At least now there is hope for us, and hope may be all that we can ask for."

Chapter 28

New International Space Station

Day 9: 1551 Zulu

Fifteen minutes after the fighting ended, Kosloff and Steve finally reestablished reliable communications with Earth. But when Delano explained the situation aboard the Station, Klegg had no good news for them.

"Sorry, Major, but no one in the Alliance has anything that can fly, no ships that can reach you in less than thirty-six hours, if we're lucky. We were already searching for one. The birds in Japan and San Diego went up in smoke. One of the private space corporations had a ship at the ready, but it developed an engine problem and won't be repaired for another fourteen hours, minimum. Then there's the flight time to reach you. Everyone knows what's at stake and will do what they can, but you'll have to hang on for at least twenty-eight hours."

Delano glanced around the Control Room as the crew heard the news. "We might have lasted that long, General, but we discovered another leak. Before we could seal it up, we lost some more air. Colonel Kosloff says we have enough air remaining for about sixteen hours, more or less."

"Try and do what you can," Klegg said. "Maybe you can stretch it out. NASA and everyone in the Alliance understands the problem and wants to bring you back."

Kosloff leaned closer to the microphone. "There's another problem, General. The Station sustained damage from the blast that destroyed the Ktarran ship. The debris has knocked us out of orbit, and without stabilizing jets, we've started to spiral down toward the atmosphere. We've lost most of our instruments, so I can't calculate the drift. I'd guess less than twenty-four hours. Can you have NASA calculate when and where the Station will re-enter?"

Maintaining the Station's high earth orbit required daily adjustments from the guidance system. Without those minute corrections, gravity tugged at what remained of the Station and they were dropping lower with no way to compensate.

"We'll get back to you, Major Delano," Klegg said, "as soon as we have some data."

So do we prefer asphyxiation or burning up in reentry? Let me think about that. "OK, General, we'll hang on as long as we can," Delano said. What else could he say?

"You've done a great job," Klegg said. "If we come up with anything sooner, we'll give you the word. Meanwhile, the damage to the planet and the Alliance is severe. Millions are dead or injured, and the EMP pulses have damaged a lot of equipment. Every government is pitching in to halt the fires and tend to the victims. I don't think we could have taken out a third Ktarran ship. Any one of them could have destroyed every major city on the planet within a few days. And we've still got the alien hanging out by Jupiter. We're hoping the bastard doesn't decide to come in and take a shot at us. We don't have much left to resist."

No one had anything else to say, and at a nod from Delano, Kosloff ended the call.

Welsh broke the grim silence. "You know, I didn't expect to survive the fight, so I said some prayers, hoping against hope for some kind of miracle. Maybe it's time to say a few more. If anyone wants to join me, I'll be in the Lounge." Taking his time, Welsh pushed off and headed for the door.

"I'll join you," Petrov said. "Maybe we'll get lucky twice."

Without a word, Shen followed, heading for the Lounge.

Delano hadn't thought much about their victory, but it was a miracle of sorts. Maybe Welsh had the right idea. Delano exchanged looks with Lian, who seemed as surprised as he was.

"Perhaps I should go check on the oxygen supply." Kosloff pushed himself away from the console. "We can use whatever air is left in the suit tanks."

"I've got some drugs that might help," Linda offered. "They can slow down your metabolism. If anyone wants them . . ."

"Good idea, Linda," Delano said. "Thanks." No matter what anyone came up with, even he could do the math. There was just not enough air to stretch sixteen hours into twenty-eight.

With the threat of eminent destruction by the aliens gone, and without any good news for the Station, communications with ground control dropped off. Nobody on Earth wanted to talk to the doomed survivors. Besides, they had their own problems to deal with. For the ten people aboard the Station, not much remained to be done.

Linda produced a bottle of what she called happy pills, a mild tranquilizer with a euphoric additive that she claimed would slow everyone down and improve the conservation of oxygen.

For all Delano knew they could be placebos, but he took one along with everyone else. No one had any booze. Petrov kept a flask in his quarters, but that part of the Station was open vacuum, and it wasn't worth the effort or the loss of air to suit up and try and find it.

Perter and Linda drifted out of the Control Room and into one of the two crew quarters still intact, closing the door behind them. Well, they deserved whatever privacy they could get. Delano, suddenly feeling useless, stared out the viewport, until Lian took his hand.

"Nothing you can do," she said. "Funny how we expected to die trying to blow up the Ktarran ship, but we may still end up dead."

He nodded. "Lian, I couldn't have done any of this without you. I just wish there was some way to make up for all you've done. I'm sorry we're trapped up here. Maybe if I kept the escape vessel . . ."

She shook her head. "Don't think that way. You accomplished more than anyone could have done." Lian took his hand and held it firmly. "Come with me. I'd like your arms around me when the time comes." She led him into the one remaining cabin and closed the door.

"Good for them," Kosloff said after they left. He and Steve stayed in the Control Room, trying to figure out ways to maximize what little air and power remained.

The rest took their ease in the Lounge. Gunny Stecker produced a deck of cards and started a poker game. To everyone's surprise, Sergeant Shen proved all too familiar with the pastime, and he continued to rake in pot after pot. Muttering under his breath at Shen's luck, Stecker managed to stay even, but Welsh and Petrov were losing big.

No one noticed the single Halkin ship returning toward Earth space. Most Earth-based and lunar telescopes were focused on Jupiter.

Fourteen hours after the space battle, one of the comm links blared to life. Steve, shocked by the sudden burst of sound, forgot his zero gravity muscles and would have bounced off the ceiling if Kosloff hadn't caught his arm.

"Jeez, it's the Talmak calling," Steve blurted. "Big fucking signal. What's he saying?"

"Who knows? Get Delano," Kosloff said, already turning to his instruments.

Lian and Delano lay stretched out on one of the bunks, held in place by a single strip of webbing that looped over them. The bed really didn't have room for two people, so they were forced lay on their sides and hold each other close, their bodies pressed against one another.

Though it didn't really matter, Delano told her about how he grew up in Brooklyn, the death of his parents, and his determination to join the Marine Corps. Lian described a simple childhood, one suddenly complicated by her uncle's ascension to political power and eventually to the Premier of China.

Now they took comfort in each other's arms. With the end looming, they could speak without reservation, without worrying about misunderstanding. For the last few days, they had worked together so closely that they seemed to have bonded into a single person, thinking as one, and with the same goals and determination. So they nestled together, kissed often, and held tight to one another.

Delano decided it was as good a way to go as you could choose.

"I'm just sorry I never got to see much of France," he said. "Only a month in Paris, and I hadn't really seen the sights."

"I was there for seven months, at the Sorbonne," Lian said. "I spent weeks traveling around the country. The south of France is beautiful."

"Well, I have some leave time coming," he said. "Maybe you could show me around the city."

"I'd like that, Joe. I'd like it very much."

It might be foolish, but they would keep pretending until the end.

Lian's last statement required another long kiss, to explain how serious she was. But before the kiss ended, Steve pounded on the door.

"Joe, we just made contact with the Halkins! One of their ships is on the way back. Get up here and figure out what he's saying."

Before Steve finished, Delano and Lian were on the move,

squirming and twisting to unfasten the strap and get out of the bed. A few moments later, they swam their way into the Control Room.

It took a few minutes before the video link restarted, but then Delano and Lian stared into the camera. To their surprise, they didn't see Horath, but Jarendo and Celeck, both sitting side by side.

Delano finally got his mind working. "What happened to your ship? Did the Ktarran cruiser stop you from getting through the gate?"

"No, the Ktarran cruiser left the system," Jarendo said. "Apparently they were afraid of our ships. The *Ningpo* is on its way back to the Tarlon home world, and the other Halkin ship is heading back to their own planet with most of the Halkins."

Delano needed a moment to recall that the *Ningpo* was the Talmak's ship. "So you are with Horath?"

"Yes, Horath commands, but most of his crew went aboard the second Halkin ship. It was his idea to come rescue you."

Lian translated for the others, all standing behind an astonished Delano.

"How long before you can reach us?" He prayed they weren't too far away to help. "We're running low on air, and the Station is full of holes and falling toward the planet."

"Soon," Celeck said. "Jarendo says in less than one of your hours. We are already decelerating as quickly as we can. When we arrive, we will be almost out of fuel, so we will require help from your planet."

Cheers erupted behind Delano as Lian told everyone they were saved.

"Tell Horath that I will . . ." Delano realized that the phrase 'kiss his furry butt' wouldn't translate. "I will thank him properly when I see him."

Sixty-six minutes later, the Halkin shuttle was alongside. It took Horath two trips to ferry everyone and their personal gear from the Station to the Halkin ship. When Delano paused in the airlock, ready to abandon the Station, its stuffy atmosphere already smelled like a lifeless tomb. Less than an hour of air remained.

He and Lian floated hand-in-hand through the screen into the Halkin shuttle, the last to leave the Station. A few minutes later, they welcomed the feel of gravity aboard Horath's ship. The knowledge that they would both survive made it all the sweeter. He held her hand, both anticipating more opportunities to get to know one another.

Life, they agreed, might not be so bad after all. Delano leaned over to whisper in her ear. For what he wanted to say, there was only one language.

"J'taime."

Epilog

Aboard the Halkin ship *Meseka*

Day 30

Three weeks later, the Talmak took his hard seat in the cramped chamber aboard the Halkin vessel. Not a dedicated conference room, since the Halkins rarely wasted more than a few moments to discuss tactics or make plans. But with Jarendo and Celeck at the table, and Delano and Lian participating by the comm link, the tiny room served as a communications center. At least once per planetary rotation, often two or three times, the Talmak found himself in this room. The amount of communication with the humans far exceeded what he'd expected or wanted.

Plenty of contact, the Talmak mused, but little progress.

For this gathering, no humans attended via the communication link. Only Horath, Jarendo, and Celeck faced the Talmak for what the humans would call a situation report. The participants immediately noticed the Talmak's body language as he faced his audience. Today's meeting would be different.

"Let me begin by saying the negotiations process with the human leaders is not functional," the Talmak began. "In fact, their entire species is so confusing and disorganized that it may not be possible for us to act in conjunction with them."

Those abrupt and unexpected words led to a long moment of silence.

At last Jarendo spoke. "Talmak, with Delano and Lian's assistance, I have been working with the human scientist named Maks. He seems quite helpful. Technically, they have many mechanisms that could improve the performance of our ships. Their use of computing devices for almost everything they do is remarkable. One of their beliefs is that anything a human can do, a computer can do it faster and more efficiently. To me, working with only a few humans at a time seems functional and productive."

Every eye turned to Celeck. "Since we arrived in Earth orbit, I have spent my time learning two of their major languages, English and Chinese. I have begun studying a third, one they call Russian. With this knowledge, I have read several of their histories, and attempted to understand what is now happening on their world. They are as the Talmak says, very chaotic. One history contradicts another, and often little is agreed upon. The same historical event is frequently depicted in opposite ways."

Celeck hesitated, then continued. "Their planet has over two hundred principalities, what they call countries, each with its own ruler and differing laws and customs. The number of languages is even greater, as some countries have multiple languages. This adds to the confusion and complicates our exchange of information."

"Then there is no single leader we can deal with?" Horath had not participated in most of the interactions with the humans, other than Delano and Lian, who often spoke with him. "Is not their Alliance the ruler of the planet?"

"Yes and no," Celeck said. "The Alliance represents the three strongest principalities, militarily speaking, and together they possess the most advanced weaponry. But unless another country threatens their control or attempts to weaken their influence, the Alliance is content to ignore them. In response, many countries choose to ignore the Alliance, and act as if it didn't exist. It is true that the Alliance worked together to repel the Ktarrans, but that is not their normal custom. Even within the Alliance, each country has its own sphere of influence and guards that rigidly. They agree to work together only when something confronts their combined safety or economic development."

"So far I have spoken with twelve of their leaders." The Talmak's face looked serious. "Each believed he was the equal of the others. Each demanded certain benefits before his country would begin cooperation. All preferred to ignore my suggestions. Today Delano informed me that there are at least seven more leaders I am expected to meet before any real progress can be made."

"How can the humans have accomplished so much in spite of such confusion?" Jarendo asked.

"Their history, what little I have been able to translate," Celeck said, "is a long list of wars of aggression and defense. Principalities come and go, strong ones grow weak, and the weak frequently grow strong. They thrive amid constant struggle, and they have rebuilt their cities many times after each war. The planet, it seems to me, consists of disorder and population growth, interrupted on occasion by ever more serious conflict. Several times in their recent past the human world nearly destroyed itself."

"Then you concur with me that it may not be possible to utilize the resources of these humans to help us fight the Ktarrans," the Talmak declared. "Before these humans agree on a common plan of defense, let alone build any weapons, the Ktarrans will be here and in power. We have never encountered a species as tumultuous. Almost all other worlds eventually form a single council, or establish an individual leader who rules for the good of the entire planet. That Earth has survived without destroying its own civilization is astonishing to me, especially given their history of atomics."

"Yet they have survived," Jarendo argued. "We must find a way to cooperate with the humans. With their help, we can fight against the Ktarrans. We did work with them to achieve this victory."

"And how will you accomplish this cooperation?" The Talmak's tone conveyed his discouragement.

Jarendo and Celeck glanced at each other, but no one spoke. Planetary negotiations was a new concept for them. Both realized that the Talmak had made up his mind that the situation had deteriorated almost beyond repair. The unruly humans not only refused the Talmak's guidance and wisdom, but they failed to show the proper respect. Some had even demanded favors from him, in return for cooperation.

Another uncomfortable silence settled over the participants.

"We must find a way," Jarendo said. "If Earth can mobilize its resources, we may have a real chance to defeat the Ktarrans, blunt their expansions, even drive them back from their latest conquests. In the last four generations, we have never encountered a world such as Earth. It may be as long before we find another, assuming Tarlon and Halkin can survive that long. We cannot just leave this opportunity behind."

"Talmak, the humans offer much advanced technology," Celeck said. "I have read of their machines, what they call computers, that provide them with such benefits as Tarlon has never even considered. They already have ships that fly themselves, robots that can work alongside a human, devices that can be implanted within their bodies to store knowledge or monitor health. Even if we cannot work with them, we should remain as long as possible and obtain as much technology as we can. Such devices and knowledge will only help us in the Great War."

Jarendo leaned forward. "What Celeck says is true. So is the opposite. If the Ktarrans captured this world, they will be the ones who benefit from these new technologies. Even if only a portion of Earth survives, the advantage in knowledge the Ktarrans will gain over time would be enormous."

Horath rapped the table with his fist. "We must not abandon them. These puny humans wiped out three Ktarran warships. We helped destroy two of those, but Delano and nine others of his kind eliminated a third, the most powerful of the three. They did this without any real weapons. As Celeck has explained to me, human history is little more than a journal of constant conflicts and wars. These humans understand the science of warfare. It is part of their genetics. We need that skill to defeat the Ktarrans."

"What you all say is true," the Talmak said. "But I believe they will never unite in time to withstand the Ktarrans. Perhaps we should just learn as much as we can of their technology before we depart."

"I do not want to depart!" Horath raised his fist, ready to pound on the table, but deference to the Talmak stayed his hand. "I want to win! I want to crush the Ktarrans, annihilate their nests of evil once and for all time."

"What do you suggest, Captain Horath?" The Talmak's voice soothed the Halkin.

"We should work with Delano and Lian, just as we did before," Horath answered. "If the leaders of Earth are incapable of uniting their planet under a single leader, then we should select one for them. Delano and Lian shared decision making during our first encounter. Let them lead the Alliance."

"As I understand the Alliance power structure," Celeck said, "Delano and Lian take their guidance from many intermediaries placed above them. How can they speak for Earth, or even the Alliance? Remember, they were only chosen because of their skills in learning new languages."

Horath looked at the Talmak. "Earth is weak. The Ktarrans

destroyed many of Earth's airships. We possess the only real warship in this system and we have already replenished our supplies of helium, water, and food protein. Without the combined fleets of Tarlon and Halkin, the humans will not be able to withstand the Ktarrans when they return. No time must be lost because of these foolish demands. An invasion of this solar system is coming and Earth needs to prepare, starting now. So we tell the humans that we expect all decision making to be placed in the hands of Delano and Lian. Otherwise we will leave this system to the Ktarrans."

"The Alliance leaders will not accept that," Celeck said. "They will not give up their authority, especially to ones they have not chosen."

"Tell them it is only a temporary measure," Horath said, "until the Ktarrans are defeated. Then they can restore whatever leaders they want."

"It might work," Celeck said. "In one of their histories, many cycles ago, there was a country that faced and solved this problem. Whenever outside danger threatened, the political rulers invested all power in the hands of a single person, who ruled only until the danger passed. Then he relinquished power."

"There you have it!" This time Horath couldn't restrain himself and thumped his fist on the table. "We tell the humans that this is what they must do, and that we trust only Delano and Lian to speak for Earth. Give them a simple choice. Either they allow Delano and Lian to speak and decide for this world, or we abandon them."

"What if the humans refuse?" The Talmak glanced around the table. "We have already handed over the plans to our power and antigravity systems. And the beam weapons."

"Plans can only take them so far," Jarendo said. "Horath is correct. We are the only real ship in this system. Without our help, Earth will not be able to build and test new ships before the Ktarran fleet arrives. Remember there is still much their scientists do not know, and much more we can offer them. Meanwhile, we will be studying these humans and learning all their technologies."

"I agree," Celeck said. "Even with my limited knowledge of Earth's history and culture, I can see they need a significant reason to unite. Let us give them one, even if it is one they do not like. Humans will blame us, but all that matters is the defeat of the Ktarrans. Even if Earth is destroyed in the war, the Ktarrans may lose many ships, enough to delay their expansion into our home worlds."

The Talmak studied each impassioned face, and saw only determination. He resigned himself. "It might work. If you are all willing, We will attempt to deal with the humans one last time. We will have to be firm and resolute. Anything less will fail."

One by one they nodded acceptance.

"Then we are agreed," the Talmak said. "Now let us find the best way to bring this about."

The next morning's communication session with the Talmak began innocently enough. As usual, Ahvin initiated the link from the Halkin ship. In the Pentagon, Delano – recently promoted to Lieutenant Colonel – sat beside General Klegg, NSA Director Dr. Vivian Spencer, and the Chancellor of Germany. On the conference call were General Secretary Liu, Lian, and General Zeng. For Russia, the new president and former General, Anatoly Demidov, faced the camera. Delano smiled and nodded at Demidov, one recent promotion to another.

Once again the American president, Mathew Clark, would not attend. Ten days ago he decided that his first priority was to work with the survivors in California. Clark needed those West Coast voters. As before, Clark turned everything relating to the aliens over to Dr. Spencer. If anything went wrong with the negotiations, she could take the blame.

To be fair, Mexico and California were a true disaster. Most of the fires had burned themselves out after two or three days. But the devastation remained. The multiple EM pulses from the nuclear missiles had damaged plenty of electronic equipment. Many millions had died, and others faced starvation. Estimates of casualties, still being revised, remained horrific. Before the attack, San Diego, Los Angeles, and San Francisco alone had more than twenty million inhabitants. At least half that number had died or would succumb shortly.

More people had perished along the coast, as the Ktarran ship traveled from San Diego to San Francisco. With many hospitals, power stations, police and fire units destroyed, the death toll continued climbing. The old, the sick, and the very young faced the greatest peril, as did anyone on special medications. The destruction of the California ports, railroads, and highways meant intolerable delays and difficulty moving food, supplies, and personnel to the affected areas.

The even grimmer situation, repeated in Japan, China, and Korea, overshadowed everything. Loss of life there would likely surpass twenty-five million. At least that number had lost their homes and possessions. The infrastructure damage would linger for years. Damage to plant and animal life would keep much of those lands barren for even longer.

Meanwhile many in Europe, South America, and Africa gave the impression that the crisis had ended. Some openly rejoiced that the devastation had confined itself to Alliance powers. Most of the European countries pledged to send aid, but their contributions to rebuilding would be small.

To give the devil his due, President Clark did have his hands full economically and politically. But his absence made Delano's job easier. He didn't have to waste time explaining the same ideas over and over.

Delano fingered his warm cup of fresh coffee. He expected this meeting to be as boring and unproductive as the ones before. Since his return from the Halkin ship nearly three weeks ago, he had attended meetings such as this almost daily. Given that he and Lian remained the most experienced translators, at least one of them had to be present at every communication session. The Tarlons felt that way as well.

Nothing much had happened so far, despite the near-endless days of talk that droned on with no sense of urgency. He wondered when the Alliance would get off its collective ass and start preparing for war with the Ktarrans.

Delano had tried to take some leave, but Klegg denied his request. The General insisted that Delano's debrief would take weeks, and meanwhile his translator skills were required. Once again Delano had his own team of FBI agents guarding him, and they wouldn't even allow him take a car to work. After all, he might be killed in an accident. Instead he was assigned temporary quarters in the Pentagon. Military logic was, of course, an oxymoron.

In the meantime, bored out of his mind, Delano debriefed and translated. About the only benefit he found occurred after each session ended. Delano and Lian kept the link open to talk.

Since leaving Horath's ship, they had not spent much time together. When their spaceplane landed back at Spaceport, New Mexico, a contingent of Chinese officials and military staff, as well as Lian's mother, awaited her arrival. They had practically whisked her away, loading her aboard her uncle's jet and taking off for Beijing.

For the first few days after their return to Earth, Delano and Lian had been hailed as heroes. Together they had established communications with three alien species and devised the plan that had destroyed all three Ktarran cruisers. But before a week passed, they had faded from the news, replaced in part by the reality of widespread destruction of the West Coast of the United States and the major cities of Japan and China. Already more than a few voices blamed Delano and Lian for failing to negotiate with the Ktarrans.

Delano had received his latest promotion at the Pentagon with little fanfare, while Lian had received the Peoples' Medal of Honor, given to her by her uncle in a private ceremony. At least her award was broadcast over every channel in China.

So Delano and Lian had no opportunity to be together since the return to Earth. The thirty-six hours aboard the Halkin ship before they boarded the spaceplane hadn't provided any privacy. The Halkin species, it seemed, didn't waste time or effort on that concept. Still, they had talked and laughed and relaxed, and the feeling of trust and affection between them continued to grow.

Now today brought yet another meeting, probably more time wasted. Delano understood that Hell and Damnation would be arriving in seventeen months. However everyone on Earth not directly affected thought and acted as if the danger had passed. As usual, humans tended to forget every disaster once it ended. Meanwhile those impacted remained too busy trying to recover from the destruction inflicted by the Ktarrans.

Delano suppressed a yawn. He looked forward to the end of the conference call, when he and Lian would talk privately.

In Earth orbit, Ahvin made some final adjustments to the Halkin comm link, then stepped aside. Delano saw only Celeck and Jarendo facing the cameras, an empty seat between them. Delano assumed the Talmak hadn't arrived yet, but a moment later, Horath entered the chamber and took the vacant seat, his broad shoulders brushing against the two Tarlons.

Uh-oh. Something is up. Delano glanced at the Chinese monitor, and saw that Lian had noticed it as well.

"We are ready to speak," Celeck announced. "We have much to say."

"Will the Talmak be joining us?" Delano repeated the question in English for the benefit of General Klegg, though a translator device rested on the table before the group. Despite Delano's endorsement of its accuracy, not everyone trusted the apparatus.

"No, he will not attend. There has been a change," Celeck said. "Captain Horath has taken charge of the negotiations with Earth. The Talmak and Captain Horath feel that insufficient progress is being made, and so the Talmak has decided to take no further part in these discussions."

Delano noted the German Chancellor sit back in his chair at the obvious slight to his presence. He'd expected to deal with the Talmak, not some obviously unimportant Halkin ship captain.

Horath? In charge? Jeez, what the hell was this all about. The Halkin hadn't attended many of the sessions since Delano and his team left Horath's ship.

"Horath insists on knowing when the preparations for the coming Ktarran invasion will begin." Celeck's tone sounded harsh, almost accusatory. Twenty-two of your rotations . . . days have passed, and he does not see any progress. The Alliance has not . . . **organized/marshaled/militarized** its forces. Captain Horath does not intend to remain in this system if no effective resistance will be prepared."

Oh, shit. Obviously the Talmak's patience had run out. Delano's mouth went dry and he saw Klegg stiffen in his chair. Demidov had a surprised look on his face, and Lian's eyes had gone wide. "These things take time," Delano said. "The Alliance is already reaching out to the other countries, all those who will need . . ."

"Captain Horath demands to know who speaks for your planet," Celeck said. "Captain Horath allied himself with Delano and Lian, and wants them to continue to represent Earth. Let me make Captain Horath's position clear. He wants Delano and Lian to take charge of the planet's defenses. He has agreed to wait seven days. If no significant progress is made, if Lian and Delano are not given the authority, Captain Horath intends to leave this system. Earth will stand alone."

General Klegg swore under his breath. "What the hell is happening, Delano? Why is this Halkin . . ."

"Celeck, may we speak with the Talmak?" Delano tried to sound positive.

"The Talmak no longer believes Earth can withstand the Ktarrans," Celeck replied. "He has asked several times to speak with the single leader of your planet. That has not happened. In consequence, the Talmak now agrees with Captain Horath, who commands this ship."

"Celeck," Lian broke in, "the Alliance represents the major powers on Earth. The Alliance can guide, can lead the other countries."

Celeck glanced at Horath, who leaned forward, making his face appear larger in the camera. "No, Lian. No more dealings with Alliance." Horath's words growled through the speaker. "I will communicate only with you and Delano, and only when you both speak for the planet Earth, just as you did when we destroyed the Ktarran ships. You and Delano will give the orders for your planet, and see that they are carried out. If your planet does not agree to this, I will depart. I will waste no more time in useless meetings."

Horath rose and glided smoothly out of the picture.

"Celeck, what is going on?" Delano asked.

"It is as Captain Horath says. He will only stay if Delano and Lian take charge of Earth's defense," Celeck replied. "By that he means that you and Lian will be the absolute leaders of the planet, with full and complete authority over all military and economic decisions. It is Horath's ship after all."

Delano tried to reply, but Celeck didn't give him an opportunity.

"Did you not lead the fight against the Ktarrans?" Celeck sounded as harsh and angry as Horath. "Did you and Lian not destroy the Ktarran battleship? Who on your Earth is better suited to lead the fight? If your planet expects to fight the Ktarrans, it must be united under a single authority. Since Captain Horath and the Talmak have seen no leader taking charge of the planet Earth, to speak for your world, they think . . . they know that no strong defense can be mounted. Your planet will be defeated and destroyed. That is why they intend to leave this system. We will face a long and difficult voyage, but Captain Horath is determined."

"Without your help," Delano said, "we won't be able to survive the Ktarran attack."

"Delano and Lian, I have tried to argue your position, despite the fact that I agree with the Talmak," Celeck said. "But I cannot withstand Captain Horath, who wants only immediate action from the people of Earth, or the Talmak, who will work only with a planetary leader."

"Celeck, we cannot do as you ask," Delano said. "There is no single voice that speaks for Earth."

"Then your situation is unfortunate. At least you understand the problem," Celeck said. "I read in one of your histories a time of similar challenge. When those you call the Ancient Romans consisted of many bickering tribes, did they not hand over complete authority to a single individual to rule over all of them until the danger had passed? The situation is no different now. Did not the Romans accept all his decisions? As they once did, you must now do also. The Alliance and the other countries must accede to Delano and Lian's authority. Once the Ktarran threat has passed, Earth can do as she chooses."

Oh, God, Delano prayed, please don't say the word "Dictator," the term the Romans had used for that person given supreme command. But either Celeck understood the negative connotations or he had forgotten the word.

Celeck rose. "The time for talking is past. Now the hour of deciding has arrived. If your planet truly accepts Delano and Lian as their leader, we can begin our planning for the Ktarran invasion. Do not contact us until you have agreed. Otherwise in seven days we will depart."

He gestured to Ahvin, and the feed from the Halkin ship went dark.

Delano sagged back in his chair, his mouth agape. He'd expected a routine session, and now the Tarlons and Halkins had dumped all the problems of Earth on him. And Lian. He looked at the China feed, and saw the same shocked expression on her face. She also understood fully what this meant. If Horath had decided to take control of the negotiations, things were really bad. The blunt Halkin had little patience or sympathy with anyone, let alone those on Earth.

But her uncle's hard eyes stared straight at the camera, glaring at Delano as if this were all his fault. A quick glance around showed the astonishment on Dr. Vance's face, anger on the German Chancellor's, and cold fury on General Klegg. Only Demidov had the hint of a smile. The Alliance, let alone the rest of the planet, would never accept the Halkin ultimatum.

Now everyone would blame Delano and Lian for the collapse of the talks.

"So, Colonel Delano," Klegg bit off the words and leaned back in his chair. "It looks like you've got yourself another promotion. What are your orders?"

The words dripped with sarcasm. Delano clenched his jaw. His heart pounded in his chest, but only one thought raced through his mind – the brig at Camp Pendleton beckoned once again, and this time it might be his best option. A single word jumped into his head.

Merde!

The End

Acknowledgments

I am indebted more than usual to my writing critique group (Joe, Gretchen, and Toni), and to advance readers (Bill, John, Jack, and Scott), who all provided much valuable feedback and suggestions.

But as always, my first debt is to my wife, Linda, best friend and life partner, and also a superb editor and patient sounding board. Without her help and suggestions, this book could not have been written.

Lest I forget, there was the help of our three cats, Minga, Norton, and Varney, whose incessant assistance probably delayed the book by months.

Printed in Great Britain
by Amazon